The Bastonnais
Tale Of The American Invasion Of Canada In 1775-76

by

John Lesperance

The Bastonnais
Tale Of The American Invasion
Of Canada In 1775-76
by John Lesperance

ISBN: 978-93-60467-42-5

Published by

DOUBLE 9 BOOKS
2/13-B, Ansari Road
Daryaganj, New Delhi – 110002
info@double9books.com
www.double9books.com
Tel. 011-40042856

ABOUT THE AUTHOR

John Lesperance literary masterpiece, "The Bastonnais," stands as a testomony to his brilliance as a writer. Known for his incredible potential to forge connections via literary fiction, Lesperance paintings serves as a bridge that brings human beings together, fostering understanding. His writing is a rich tapestry of creativity and ardour, immersing readers in numerous landscapes and a spectrum of feelings. Lesperance narratives are a harmonious mixture of elegance and accessibility, inviting readers from all walks of life to enjoy his outstanding tales. In "The Bastonnais," he weaves a charming story that resonates with each depth and relatability, showcasing his dedication to the craft of storytelling. John Lesperance contributions to literature make bigger beyond mere words on a web page; they encompass a profound exploration of the human enjoy, leaving an indelible mark on the hearts and minds of folks that engage along with his work.

CONTENTS

BOOK II

THE THICKENING OF THE CLOUDS

BOOK III
THE BURSTING OF THE TEMPEST

BOOK IV
AFTER THE STORM

BOOK I
THE GATHERING OF THE STORM

I
BLUE LIGHTS

He stood leaning heavily on his carbine. High on his lonely perch, he slowly promenaded his eye over the dusk landscape spread out before him. It was the hour of midnight and a faint star-light barely outlined the salient features of the scenery. Behind him wound the valley of the St. Charles black with the shadows of pine and tamarac. Before him rose the crags of Levis, and beyond were the level stretches of the Beauce. To his left the waterfall of Montmorenci boomed and glistened. To his right lay silent and deserted the Plains of Abraham, over which a vapor of sanguine glory seemed to hover. Directly under him slept the ancient city of Champlain. A few lights were visible in the Chateau of St Louis where the Civil Governor resided, and in the guard-rooms of the Jesuit barracks on Cathedral-square, but the rest of the capital was wrapped in the solitude of gloom. Not a sound was heard in the narrow streets and tortuous defiles of Lower Town. A solitary lamp swung from the bows of the war-sloop in the river.

He stood leaning heavily on his carbine. To have judged merely from his attitude, one would have said that he was doing soldier's duty with only a mechanical vigilance. But such was not the case. Never was sentry set upon watch of heavier responsibility, and never was watch kept with keener observation. Eye, ear, brain—the whole being was absorbed in duty. Not a sight escaped him—from the changes of cloud in the lowering sky over the offing, to the deepening of shadows in the alley of Wolfe's Cove. Not a sound passed unheard—from the fluttering wing of the sparrow that had built its winter nest in the guns of the battery, to the swift dash of the chipmunk over the brown glacis of the fortifications. Standing there on the loftiest point of the loftiest citadel in America, his martial form detached from its bleak surroundings, and clearly defined, like a block of sculptured marble, against the dark horizon—silent, alone and watchful—he was the representative and custodian of British power in Canada in the hour of a dread crisis. He felt the position and bore himself accordingly.

Roderick Hardinge was a high-spirited young fellow. He belonged to the handful of militia which guarded the city of Quebec, and he resented the imputations which had been continually cast, during the preceding two months, on the efficiency of that body. He knew that the Americans had carried everything before them in the upper part of the Colony. Schuyler had occupied Isle-aux-Noix without striking a blow. Five hundred regulars and one hundred volunteers had surrendered at St. Johns. Bedell, of New Hampshire, had captured Chambly, with immense stores of provisions and war material. Montgomery was marching with his whole army against Montreal. The garrison of that city was too feeble to sustain an attack and must yield to the enemy. Then would come the turn of Quebec. Indeed, it was well known that Quebec was the objective point of the American expedition. As the fall of Quebec had secured the conquest of New France by the British in 1759, so the capture of Quebec was expected to secure the conquest of Canada by the Americans in the winter of 1775-76. This was perfectly understood by the Continental Congress at Philadelphia. The plan of campaign was traced out with this view for General Schuyler, and when that officer resigned the command, owing to illness, after his success at St. Johns, Montgomery took up the same idea and determined to carry it out. From Montreal he addressed a letter to Congress in which he said pithily: "till Quebec is taken, Canada is unconquered."

Roderick Hardinge was painfully aware that the authorities of Quebec had little or no confidence in the ability of the militia for the purposes of defence. It was necessary in the interest of that body, as well as in the interest of the city, that this prejudice should be exploded. Hardinge undertook to do it. No time was to be lost. In a fortnight Quebec might be invested. He set to work with the assistance of only one tried companion. Their project was kept a profound secret even from the commander of the corps.

It was the night of the 6th November, 1775. Hardinge left headquarters unnoticed and unattended, and proceeded at once to the furthest outpost of the citadel. He was hailed by the sentinel and gave the countersign. Then, addressing the soldier by name—the man belonged to his regiment— he ordered him to hand over his musket. No questions were asked and no explanations were given. Hardinge was an officer, and the simple militiaman saw no other course than obedience. If he had any curiosity or suspicion, both were relieved by the further order to keep out of sight, but within hailing distance, until his services should be required. The signal was to be a whistle.

Roderick Hardinge remained on guard from ten till twelve. As we have seen, he was sharply observant of everything that lay before him. But there was one point of the horizon to which his eye more assiduously turned. It was the high road leading from Levis over the table-land of the Beauce back to the forests. It was evidently from this direction that the object of his watch was to appear. And he was not disappointed.

Just as the first stroke of twelve sounded from the turret of Notre-Dame Cathedral, a blue light shot into the air from a point on this road, not more than a hundred yards from the river bank.

Roused by the sight, Roderick straightened himself up, snatched his carbine from his left side, threw it up on his right shoulder and presented arms.

The sixth stroke of midnight was just heard, when a second blue light darted skyward, but this time fully fifty yards nearer. The man who fired it was evidently running toward the river.

Roderick made a step forward and uttered a low cry.

The last stroke of the twelve had hardly been heard, when a third light whizzed up from the very brink of the river.

Roderick turned briskly round and gave a shrill whistle. The faithful soldier, whose watch he had assumed, immediately rushed forward, had his musket thrust back into his hands, with an injunction from Hardinge to keep silence. The latter had barely time to recede into the darkness when the relief-guard, consisting of a corporal and two privates, came to the spot and the usual formality of changing sentries was gone through.

II
BEYOND THE RIVER

With a throbbing heart, Roderick Hardinge walked rapidly over the brow of the citadel into Upper Town. He glanced up at the Chateau as he passed, but the lights which were visible there two hours before, were now extinguished, and the Governor was sleeping without a dream of the mischief that was riding out upon the city that night. He passed through the Square and overhead the wassail of the officers over their wine and cards. He answered the challenge of the sentinel at the gate which guarded the heights of Mountain Hill, and doubled his pace down that winding declivity. The old hill has been the scene of many an historic incident, but surely of none more momentous than this midnight walk of Roderick Hardinge. Along the dark, narrow streets of Lower Town, stumbling over stones and sinking into cavities. Not a soul on the way. Not a sign of life in the square, black warehouses, with their barricades of sheet-iron doors and windows.

In twenty minutes, the young officer had reached the river at the point where now stands the Grand Trunk wharf. A boat with two oars lay at his feet. Without a moment's hesitation he stepped into it, unfastened the chain that held it to the bank, threw the oars into their locks, and, with a vigorous stroke, turned the boat's nose to the south shore. As he did this, his eye glanced upward at the city. There it stood above him, silent and unconscious. The gigantic rock of Cape Diamond towered over him as if exultant in its own strength, and in mockery of his forebodings. He rowed under the stern of the war-sloop. A solitary lantern hung from her bows, but no watchman hailed him from her quarter.

"The Horse Jockey is evidently a myth for them all," he murmured. "But he will soon be found a terrible reality, and it's Roddy Hardinge will tell them so."

The St. Lawrence is not so wide above Quebec as it is at other places along its course, and in a quarter of an hour, the oarsman had reached his destination. As the keel of his boat grated on the sands, a man stepped forward to meet him. The officer sprang out and slapped him on the shoulder.

"Good old boy, Donald."

"Thanks to you, maister."

"Punctual to a minute, as usual, Donald."

"Aye, sir, but 'twas a close scratch. The horse, I fear, feels it mair than I do."

"No doubt, no doubt. Rode much?"

"Nigh on ten hours, sir, and nae slackened rein."

"Oh, but my heart leaped, Donald, when I saw your first rocket. I could hardly believe my eyes."

"Just saved my distance, maister. If I had broken a gairth, I would have been too late. But it's dune, sir."

"Yes, old friend, and well done."

The two men then entered upon a long and earnest conference, speaking in low tones. From the animated manner of the old man and the frequent exclamations of the younger, it was evident that important information was being communicated by the one to the other. During a pause in the conversation, Donald produced a small paper parcel which he handed to Roderick Hardinge.

"'Twas stuckit in the seat o' my saddle, maister," said he, "an I wadna hae lost it for the warld."

Roderick wrapped the parcel in his bandanna, and carefully placed it in his breast pocket, after which he buttoned his coat to the chin.

At the end of half an hour, the two men prepared to separate.

"I will now hurry across," said Roderick. "And you, Donald, return to the inn. You must need rest terribly."

"Twa hours or sae will set me to richts, sir."

"And your horse?"

"He's knockit up for gude, sir."

"Then get another and the best you can find. Here are fifty sovereigns. Use them freely in His Majesty's name."

Donald bowed loyally and low.

"I will be awake and awa' a gude hour before dawn, maister Roddy. The sunrise will see me weel oot o' the settlements."

"And we meet here again at midnight."

"Depend upon it, sir, unless the rapscallion rebels should catch and hang me up to one of the tall aiks o' the Chaudière."

"Never fear, Donald; a traitor's death was never meant for an old soldier of the King, like you."

The young officer entered his boat and immediately bent to the oars. The old servant walked up the hill leading to Levis, and was soon lost in the darkness.

III
AT THE CHATEAU

Roderick reached the north shore in safety. He fastened his boat to the same green, water-worn bulwark from which he had loosened it not more than an hour before. He walked up to the city along the same route which he had previously followed. Nothing had changed. Everything was profoundly quiescent. Every body was still asleep. If he courted secrecy, he must have been content, for it was evident that no one had been a witness of his strange proceedings.

When he got within the gates of Upper Town, his pace slackened perceptibly. It was not hesitation, but deliberation. He paused a moment in front of the barracks. The lights in the officers' quarters were out and no sound came from the mess-room. This circumstance seemed to deter him from entering, and he continued on his way direct to the Chateau St. Louis. Having passed the guard satisfactorily, he rapped loudly at the main portal. An orderly who was sleeping in his clothes, on a lounge in the vestibule, sprang to his feet at once snatching up his dark lantern from behind the door, and opened. Throwing the light upon the face of his visitor, he exclaimed—

"Halloa, Hardinge, what the deuce brings you here at this disreputable hour? Come in; it's blasted cold."

"I want to see His Excellency."

"Surely not just now? He was ailing last evening and retired early. I don't think he would fancy being drummed up before daylight."

"Very sorry, but I must see him."

"Some little scrape, eh? Want the old gentleman to get you out of it before the town has wind of it," said the orderly, who by this time was thoroughly awake and disposed to be in good humor.

"Something far more serious, Simpson, I am concerned to say. You know I would not call here at such an hour without the most urgent cause. I really must see the Governor and at once."

This was said without any signs of impatience, but in so earnest a way, that the orderly, who knew his friend well, felt that the summons could not be denied. He, therefore, proceeded at once to have the Governor awakened. With more celerity than either of the young men had looked for, that official rose, dressed and stepped into his ante-chamber where he sent for Hardinge to meet him. After a few words of apology, the latter unfolded to His Excellency the object of his visit. He stated that while every body in the city was busying himself about the invasion of the Colony from the west, by the Continental army under Montgomery, the other invading column from the east, under Arnold, was almost completely lost sight of. For his part, he declared that he considered it the more dangerous of the twain. It was composed of some very choice troops, had been organized under the eye of Washington himself, and was commanded by a dashing fellow. In addition to his other qualities, Arnold had the incalculable advantage of a personal knowledge of the city from several visits which he had quite lately paid it for commercial purposes. The people of Quebec seemed completely to ignore Arnold's expedition. They had a notion that it was or would be submerged somewhere among the cascades of the Kennebec, or, at least, that it would never succeed in penetrating so far as the frontier at Sertigan.

The Governor wrapped his dressing gown more closely about him, threw his head back on the pillow of his arm-chair, and gave vent to a little yawn or two, as if in gentle wonder whether it were worth while to rouse him from his slumbers for the sake of all this information with which he was quite familiar already. But the Governor was a patient, courteous gentleman, and could not believe that even a militia officer would presume so far on his good nature as to come to him at such an hour, unless he had really something of definite importance to communicate. He, therefore, did not interrupt his visitor. Roderick Hardinge continued to say that, fearing lest Arnold should pounce like a vulture upon the city while most of the troops of the Colony were with General Carleton, near Montreal, and in the Richelieu peninsula, and while, consequently, it was in an almost defenceless condition, he had determined to find out for himself all the facts connected with his approach. It might be presumption, on his part, but he had not full confidence in the few reports on this head which had reached the city, and wished to satisfy himself from more personal sources.

Here His Excellency smiled a little at the ingenuous confession of the subaltern, but a moment later, he opened his eyes very wide, when Roderick told him in minute detail all the circumstances which we have narrated in the preceding chapters.

"Your man, Donald, is thoroughly reliable?" queried the Lieutenant-Governor.

"I answer for him as I would for myself. He was an old servant of my father's all through his campaigns."

"He says that Arnold has crossed the line?"

"Yes, Your Excellency."

"And that he is actually marching on Quebec?"

"Yes, Your Excellency."

"And that he is within — —?"

"Sixty miles of the city."

The Lieutenant-Governor plucked his velvet bonnet from his head and flung it on the table.

"Did you say sixty miles?"

"Sixty miles, sir."

His Excellency quietly took up his cap, set it on his head, threw himself back in his seat, placed his elbows on the elbows of the chair, closed his palms together perpendicularly, moved them up and down before his lips, and with his eyes cast to the ceiling, entered upon this little calculation.

"Sixty miles. At the rate of fifteen miles a day, it will take Mr. Arnold four days to reach Levis. This is the seventh, is it not? Then, on the eleventh, we may expect that gentleman's visit."

"Arnold will make two forced marches of thirty miles each, Your Excellency, and arrive opposite this city in two days. This is the seventh; on the ninth, we shall see his vanguard on the heights of Levis."

"Ho! Ho! And is that the way the jolly rebel is carrying on? He must have had a wonderful run of luck all at once. The last we heard from him, his men had mutinied and were about to disband."

"That was because they were starving."

"And have they been filled, forsooth?"

"They have, sir."

"By whom?"

"By our own people at Sertigan and further along the Chaudière."

"But horses? They are known to have lost them all in the wilderness."

"They have been replaced."

"Not by our own people, surely."

"Yes, sir, by our own people."

"Impossible. Our poor farmers have been robbed and plundered by these rascals."

"Excuse me, Your Excellency, but these rascals pay and pay largely for whatever they require."

"In coin?"

"No, sir, in paper."

"Their Continental paper?"

"The same."

"Rags, vile rags."

"That may be. But our farmers accept them all the same and freely."

Roderick here produced the small parcel which he had deposited in his breast pocket, and having unfolded it, drew forth several slips which he handed to His Excellency. They were specimens of American currency, and receipts signed by Arnold and others of his officers for cattle and provisions obtained from Canadian farmers.

"Indeed," continued the young officer, "Your Excellency will excuse me for saying that, from all the information in my possession—information upon which I insist that you can implicitly rely—it is beyond question that the population, through which the invading column has passed and is passing, is favourable to their cause. A trumpery proclamation written by General Washington himself, and translated into French, has been distributed among them, and they have been carried away by its fine sentences about liberty and independence. These facts account for all the misleading and false reports which we have hitherto received concerning the expedition. We have been purposely and systematically kept in the dark in regard to it. Left to itself, Arnold's army would have disbanded through insubordination, or perished of starvation and hardship in the wilderness. Comforted and replenished by His Majesty's own subjects, it is now marching with threatening front toward Quebec."

"Traitors to the King in the outlying districts cannot unfortunately be so easily reached as those who lie more immediately under our eyes. But their time will come yet. Meanwhile, we have to keep a sharp watch over disaffection and treason within the walls of this very city," said the Lieutenant-Governor with great earnestness and very perceptible warmth.

"This parcel may probably assist Your Excellency in doing so," replied Hardinge, at the same time delivering the remainder of the package which he had received from Donald.

"What have we here?" questioned the Governor, while unfastening the strings which bound the parcel.

"Letters from Colonel Arnold to General Schuyler, the original commander of the army of invasion. Arnold will be surprised, if not chagrined, to learn that Schuyler has been succeeded by Montgomery."

"Ah! I see. Well, as these letters are not addressed to General Montgomery, and as Gen. Schuyler has left the country, it will be no breach of etiquette on our part if we open them. No doubt they will furnish very interesting reading. And these?"

"They are letters from Arnold to several prominent citizens of Quebec."

"Impossible."

"Your Excellency will please read the addresses."

The Governor examined the superscriptions one by one, and in silence, while he made his comments in an undertone.

"Mr. L.—It does not surprise me."

"Mr. F.—I shall inquire into it."

"Mr. O.—As likely as not."

"Mr. R.—Must be some mistake. He is too big a fool to take sides one way or the other."

"Mr. G.—His wife will have to decide that matter for him."

"Mr. X.—I'll give him a commission, and he'll be all right."

"Mr. N.—I don't believe a word of it."

"Mr. H.—Loose fish. He was false to France under Montcalm. He may be false to England under Carleton."

And so on through a dozen more. At length he came upon the twentieth address, when he exclaimed:

"Mr. B.—Impossible! My best friend! But what if it were true? Who knows what these dark days may bring about? B—! B—! I will see to it at once."

Saying which, he flung all the letters on the table, and striving to master his excitement, turned towards Roderick Hardinge, and asked:

"Have you anything else to say to me, my young friend?"

"Nothing more, sir, unless it be to apologize for having occupied so much of your time, and especially at this hour."

"Never mind that. If what you have told me is all true, the information is incalculable in importance. I shall lose no time in acting, and shall not forget you, nor your old servant. I will send out scouts at once, and proceed myself to the examination of these letters which you have placed in my hands. The situation is grave, young man. You have done well, and to show you how much I appreciate your conduct, I intend employing you on a further mission. You have not slept this night?"

"No, Your Excellency."

"It is now half-past five. Go and rest till noon. At that hour come to me with the best saddle horse in your regiment. I will give you your instructions then."

Roderick Hardinge gave the salute and took his departure just as the first streaks of dawn lighted the sky.

No one accosted him in the vestibule. The sentinel at the entrance did not even notice him. He walked straight to the barracks. As he crossed the Cathedral-square, a graceful hooded figure glided past him and entered into the old church. It was pretty Pauline Belmont. Roderick recognized her, and turned to speak to her, but she had disappeared under the arcade. Alas! if either of them had known.

IV
IN CATHEDRAL SQUARE

There was a notable stir in Quebec on the morning of the 7th November, 1775. The inhabitants who had retired to their houses, the evening before, in the security of ignorance, rose the next day with the vague certainty of an impending portent. There was electricity in the air. The atmosphere was charged with moral as well as material clouds. People opened their windows and looked out anxiously. They stood on their doorsteps as if timorous to go forward. They gathered in knots on the street corners and conferred in low tones. There was nothing definite known. Nobody had seen anything. Nobody had heard anything. Yet all manner of wild stories circulated through the crowds. Strange fires were said to have burned in the sky during the night. A phantom sentinel had kept watch on the citadel, a spectral waterman had crossed the river with muffled oars, a shadowy horseman from the forest had dashed through Levis, and his foaming steed had fallen dead on the water's edge. Those who disbelieved might see the corse of the animal in a sand-quarry not a hundred yards from where he fell. And there was more. A mysterious visitor had called upon the Governor in the small hours. A long conference had taken place between them. The Governor was in a towering rage, and the stranger had departed upon another errand as singular as that which had brought him to the Chateau. These and other more fantastic rumors flew from mouth to mouth and from one end of the city to the other. It is wonderful how near the truth of things above them the ignorant crowd can come, and how powerful is the instinct of great events in vulgar minds. By ten o'clock Quebec was in an uproar, and Cathedral-square was full of people.

Facing the Square from the east was the barracks. But no signs of commotion were visible there. Two sentries walked up and down their long beats as quietly as if on parade. Privates who were off duty stood leaning against the wall or the door-frames of the building, with their hands in their pockets and one leg resting over the other. Some even smoked their pipes with that half-blank, half-truculent expression which people find so provoking in public officials at times of popular excitement. Still a close inspection showed that the military were busier than usual. Patrol guards issued from the courtyard at more frequent intervals, and the knowing ones observed that they were doubled. It was noticed also that more parts of the city were being guarded than the day before. For instance, fully one hundred men were detached for service along the line of the river where previously there were few or none. Officers, too, were constantly riding to and from the barracks, evidently carrying orders. Passing through the Square, they moved slowly, but in the side streets accelerated their pace.

The forenoon thus wore away. The sky kept on thickening and lowering until it broke into a snow-storm. A light east wind arose, and the white flakes tossed and whirled, blotting out the lines of the horizon. The heights of Levis melted in the distance, the bed of the river was surmounted by a wall of vapor, and the tall rock of the citadel wavered like a curtain of gauze. What a delicious sense of isolation is produced by an abundant snowfall. It hems you in from all the world. You extend your hand feeling for your neighbor, and you touch nothing but a palpable mist. You raise your face to the heavens, and the soft touch of the flossy drops makes you close your eyes as in a dream. The great crowd in the Square was thus broken into indistinct groups, and its mighty rumor dwindled to a murmur in the heavy atmosphere. But all the same the expectant and anxious multitude was there, and its numbers were continually increasing. Women, wrapped in scarfs or muffled in hoods, now added to its volume. Priests from the neighboring Seminary, in shovel hats, Roman collars, and long black cloaks, quietly edged their way through the masses. And the irrepressible small boy, the very same a hundred years ago as he is to-day, dashed in and out, from the centre of the crowd to its circumference, intent upon seeing and hearing everything, yet blissfully incurious of the dread secret of all this gathering.

Suddenly there was a movement in the centre of the Square. The concentric circles of people felt it successively till it rippled to the very outskirts of the assemblage. Everybody inquired of his neighbor what had happened.

"Two men are fighting," said one.

"A woman has fallen into a fit," said another.

"Old Boniface is glancing a jig," said a third.

Whereupon there was a laugh, for Boniface was a mountebank of La Canardiere, famous in the city and all the country side.

"A Bastonnais prisoner has just been brought in," said a fourth.

At this a serious interest was manifested. A Bastonnais prisoner meant an American prisoner. The expedition of Arnold was known to have started from Boston. Hence its members were called Bostonese. Bastonnais is a rustic corruption for the French Bostonnais, and the corruption has extended to our day. The whole American invasion is still known among French Canadians as *la guerre des Bastonnais*. There is always a certain interest attached to national solecisms, and we have retained this one.

"It is none of any of these things," said a grave old gentleman, who was working his way out of the crowd with a scared look.

"What is it?" asked several voices at once.

"One of our own citizens has been arrested."

"Arrested! arrested!"

"Well, if he is not arrested, he is at least summoned to the Chateau."

"Who is it?"

"M. Belmont."

"What! the father of our nationality, the first citizen of Quebec? It cannot be."

"Ah, my friends! let us disperse to our homes. This is a day of ill-omen. Things look as if the sad times of the Conquest were returning. '59 and '75! It seems that we have not suffered enough in these sixteen years."

And the old gentleman disappeared from the throng.

What happened was simply this. A tall young man, dressed in a long military coat, had for a time mingled in the crowd, looking at nearly every one as he moved along. When at length he was well in the midst, he seemed suddenly to recognize the object of his search, for he stepped deliberately up to a middle-aged gentleman, and handed him a paper. With a movement of surprise, the gentleman received the missive and looked sharply at the messenger. He glanced at the address, while a perceptible thrill shot over his features. He then hurriedly broke the seal and ran his eye over the brief contents of the letter, after which he crumpled it into his pocket.

"How long since this paper was despatched?" he asked rather testily of the young messenger.

"Over an hour ago, sir."

"And why was it not delivered at once?"

"Because I could not find you at your residence, and had to seek you in this dense multitude," was the firm, yet respectful reply.

"Are you an aide de camp of His Excellency?"

"I have that honor, sir."

"There is then no time to be lost. Let us go immediately."

The two men turned and a way was immediately opened for them by the crowd, while a suppressed murmur greeted them as they passed. A frail girl, with azure veil drawn closely over her face, hung heavily on the arm of the elder. When they reached the corner of Fabrique-street, which debouches into the Square at the north-west angle of the Cathedral, these two separated.

"What does it mean, father?" asked the girl in a timid voice.

"Nothing, my child. Go home directly and await my return. I will be with you within an hour."

The girl went up the narrow street, and the two men wended their way in silence to the Chateau St. Louis.

After this incident the Square gradually emptied until only a few idlers were left.

V
RECEIVING DESPATCHES

A little before noon Roderick Hardinge stepped down from his quarters into the courtyard of the barracks, booted and spurred. A full-blooded iron-grey charger, instinct with speed and strength in every limb, stood saddled and bridled for him. The man who held him by the head happened to be the soldier whose watch Hardinge had kept the night before.

"Is that you, Charles?" said the young officer tightening his girth by two buckle holes.

"Yes, sir," replied the soldier, showing the white of his teeth.

"And all right this morning?"

"Yes, thank you, sir."

Hardinge vaulted into the saddle at one spring. Then lacing the reins in his left hand, he continued:

"Not been blabbing, Charles?"

"Oh, no, sir. Mum's my word."

"That's right. But did you see everything?"

"I saw the three rockets, sir, if that's what you mean, and knew they were meant for you. But what they were fired for I didn't know till this morning, when I heard the talk in the Square. Folks are pretty wild altogether this morning, sir."

"So they are, but they will be wilder when they know all. In the meantime keep everything to yourself, Charles, till you hear from me again. Good-bye."

The soldier touched his cap, and the officer trotted through the archway.

A moment later he dismounted at the portal of the Chateau, threw the bridle into the hands of a groom in waiting, and entered. The Lieutenant-Governor was in his office, and evidently expected him, for he immediately rose and congratulated him on his punctuality. He then proceeded to business without delay.

"You are well mounted?"

"I think I have the fleetest and best-winded horse in the army."

"You will need him. Three Rivers is eighty miles from Quebec."

"As the crow flies, Your Excellency. By the road it is something more."

"You must be there by ten o'clock to-night."

"I will be there."

"Here are despatches for the Commandant of Three Rivers."

And he handed the officer a sealed package which the latter at once secured in his waistcoat pocket.

"These despatches," the Governor continued, "contain all the information of military movements in this vicinity which I have been able to procure up to the last moment. But as no written statement can ever be so full as a verbal communication, I authorize you to repeat to the authorities of Three Rivers all the details which you gave me during the night. There was considerable exaggeration in the story of your man Donald"—here the Governor smiled a little—"but I have reason to believe that the substance of it is true, and I am going to act upon it. Arnold's column is marching on Quebec. That is the great point. Its arrival is only a question of time. It may be in ten days, eight days, six days, four days—"

"Or two days," Hardinge could not help suggesting in a jovial way.

"Yes, perhaps even two days," continued the Governor quite seriously. "Hence the necessity of your speed to Three Rivers. When you spoke to me this morning, I was so impressed that I resolved then to communicate with the military posts up the river, but before actually sending you, I thought it best to make further inquiries. The information I have now received justifies me in despatching you at once. The letter of Arnold to Schuyler and some of those he addressed to residents of this city, especially one, yes, one"— and here, for a moment, the Governor got very excited—"have revealed his whole plans to me. To horse then and away for King and country."

Hardinge bowed and walked to the door. On reaching the threshold, he paused and said:

"Pardon me, Your Excellency, but there is one thing I forgot to tell you before, and which, perhaps, I ought to tell you now?"

"What is it?"

"I promised to meet Donald again to-night."

"When?"

"At twelve."

"Where?"

"On the other side of the river, just above the Point."

"Will he have important news?"

"It may or may not be important, but it will be fresh, inasmuch as he will have been all day reconnoitering the enemy on a very fast horse."

"Can he not cross to this side?"

"He has no instructions to that effect. Besides, he will arrive at the rendezvous at the last moment."

"Then I will meet him myself. Good morning."

Noon was just striking when Roderick cleared the gates and took the high road to Three Rivers.

VI
PAULINE'S TEARS

When Pauline Belmont reached her home, after separating from her father at the Square, she was considerably troubled. She could not define her fears, if, indeed, she had any, but mere perplexity was enough to weigh down her timid, shrinking little heart. She went up into her room, put off her furs, and, as she removed her azure veil, there was the gleam of tears in her beautiful brown eyes. She seated herself in her low rocking chair, and placing her feet on the edge of the fender, looked sadly into the flames. Little did Pauline know of the great world outside. Her home was all the universe to her, and that home centred in her father. Mother she had none. Sisters and brothers had died when she was a child. She had spent her youth in the convent of the gentle Ursulines, and now that she had finished her education, she had come to dedicate her life to the solace of her father. M. Belmont was still in the prime of life, being barely turned of fifty, but he had known many sorrows, domestic, social and political, and the only joy of his life was his darling daughter. An ardent Frenchman, he had lived through the terrible days of the Conquest which had seared his brow like fire and left only ashes in his heart. He had buried his wife on the memorable day that Murray made his triumphal entry into Quebec, and within three years after that event, he laid three babes beside their mother. Had Pauline died, he too should have died, but as that lovely flower continued to blossom in the gloom of his isolation, he consented to live, and at times even to hope a little for her sake. Fortunately large remnants of his fortune remained to him. Indeed, he was accounted one of the wealthiest men of Quebec. As his daughter grew to womanhood, he used these riches to beautify his home and make existence more enjoyable to her. He was also a generous friend to the poor, especially those French families whom the war of 1759 and 1760, had reduced to destitution. Those who could not abide the altered forms of British rule and who desired to emigrate to France, he assisted by every means in his power, while those whom circumstances forced to remain in the vanquished province always found in him a patron and supporter. As time wore on, his friends induced him occasionally to withdraw from his solitude and take a feeble part in public affairs. But this interest was purely civic or municipal, never political. He persistently kept aloof from legislative councils and his loyalty to England was strictly passive. The ultra-British did not like him, always putting him down in their books as a malcontent.

When the news of the revolt of the Thirteen Colonies reached Quebec, it had at first no perceptible effect upon him. It was only a quarrel of Englishmen with Englishmen. The casting of tea chests into the waters of Boston Bay he scoffed at as a vulgar masquerade. The musketry of Concord and Lexington found no echo in his heart. But when one day he read in his favorite *Gazette de France* that *la patrie* had designs of favoring the rebels, a flash of the old fire rose to his eyes, and he tossed his head with a show of defiance. Then came the thunders of Bunker Hill, and he listened complacently to their music. Then came rumors of the rebel army marching into Canada with a view of fraternizing with the conquered settlers of its soil. There was something after all then in this revolution. It was not mere petulant resistance to fancied oppression, but underlying and leavening it, there was a germinating principle of freedom, a parent idea of autonomy and nationality. He read the proceedings of the Congress at Philadelphia with ever-increasing admiration, and for once he admitted the wisdom of such British statesmanship as that of Pitt Burke and Barre, the immortal friends of the American Colonies.

All these things little Pauline remembered and pondered as she sat in her low chair looking into the fire. She did not do so in the consecutive form or the big words which we have just employed, but her remembrance was none the less vivid and her perplexity none the less keen, for all the phases of her father's mental life were well known to her in those simple intuitive ways which are peculiar to women. She concluded by asking herself these questions:

"Has my father said or done anything to compromise himself within the last few hours? Why did M. de Cramahé send for him in such haste? The Governor is a friend of the family and must surely have cause for what he has done. And why was my poor father so agitated, why the young officer so grave, why the people so deeply impressed at the scene?"

She looked up at the clock over the mantel and found that an hour had been spent in these musings. Her father had promised to be back within that hour, and yet there were no signs of him. She went to the window and looked out, but she failed to see his familiar form advancing through the snow-storm.

We have said that Pauline's life was wholly wrapped up in her father. That was strictly true in one sense, but in another sense, we must make note of an exception. There were new feelings just awakening in her heart. She was entering that delicious period of existence which is the threshold of the paradise of love.

"Oh! if he were only to come," she murmured, "or if I could go to him. He would relieve my anxiety at once. I will write him a note."

She went to her table and was preparing paper and pen, when the maid entered the room and delivered her a letter.

"It is from himself, I declare," she exclaimed, and all the sorrow was dispelled from her eyes. She opened the letter and read.

Dear Pauline:—

I saw you going into the church this morning and wanted to speak to you, but you were too quick for me. I should very much have liked to run up in the course of the forenoon, but that too was impossible. So I send a line to say that I am off at noon on military duty. I don't know yet where I am going, nor how long I shall be away. But I trust the journey will be neither far nor long. I shall see you immediately on my return. I suppose you and your father saw the crowd in the Square this morning. It was great fun. Give my respects to M. Belmont and believe me,

Ever yours, devotedly,

Roddy.

Pauline was still holding this note in her hand, thinking over it, when her father surprised her by walking into the room. He was very pale, but otherwise bore no marks of agitation. Setting his fur cap on the table and throwing open his great coat, he took a seat near the hearth. Before his daughter had time to say anything, he asked her quietly what she had in her hand.

"It's a letter, papa?"

"From whom?"

"From Roddy."

"Roderick Hardinge? Burn it, my dear."

"But, papa—"

"Burn it at once."

"But he sends you his love."

"He has just sent me his hate. Burn it, my daughter."

Poor Pauline was overwhelmed with surprise and sorrow, but, without a word further, she dropped the paper into the fire. Then throwing her arms around her father's neck, she burst into a tempest of tears.

VII
BEAUTIFUL REBEL

Hardinge had not been gone more than half an hour when the skies lifted and the snow-storm ceased. The wind then shifted to the north, driving the drifts in banks against the fences and low stone walls, and leaving the road comparatively clear. He thus had splendid riding in the open spaces. He was in exultant spirits, of course, for he had everything in his favor—a magnificent horse upon whose speed and endurance he could rely, the opportunity of exploring a long stretch of country previously unknown to him, and, above all, the sense of being employed on a military expedition of the greatest importance. He had played for high stakes and had won them. At one stroke, he had rehabilitated the militia and brought his own name into prominence. The way was now open to him in the career which he loved and which his father had honored. If all went well with him he would win advancement and glory in this war. And he had no misgivings. What young soldier has with the bright sky over his head, the solid earth under his feet, the wide world before him, and the whiff of coming battle in his nostrils?

He imparted his own animation to his steed. The noble grey fairly flew over the ground, and Roderick saw from the first that he would have to restrain rather than impel him. His first stoppage was at Pointe-aux-Trembles, a beautiful village, which became historic during the war of invasion and with which will be associated several of the incidents of this story. He passed the inn of the place so as to avoid the queries and comments of the loungers who might be congregated there, and pulled up at a neat farm house on the outskirts. Without dismounting, he asked that his horse might be watered, while he requested for himself a bowl of milk and a few drops of that good old Jamaica which all Canadian families had the good sense to keep in their houses at this period. As he was thus comforting himself, he noticed a pair of sparkling blue eyes laughing at him through the narrow panes of the road window. He did not try to be very inquisitive, but he could not help observing, in addition, that the roguish blue eyes belonged to a face of rare beauty, and that the form of the lady— for she was a lady, every inch of her—so far as it could be defined by the diminutive aperture, was of an exquisitely graceful mould. One observation led to another, and he very naturally associated this lady with the purple pinion that sat on the back of a little bay mare which was hitched near the door.

His own horse had drained his bucket, and was champing his bit, as if anxious to be off once more; he himself had emptied his bowl and he was vainly endeavoring to force a few pieces of coin upon the denying farmer, when the door of the dwelling opened and the lady walked forth. She arranged the bridle herself, and placing her foot on the lowest step of the porch, seated herself snugly in the saddle without assistance. Then wishing the farmer and the farmer's jolly wife and the farmer's multitudinous children a sweet *bonjour*, she gently cantered away, not without a parting shaft from those murderous blue eyes at the handsome cavalier. Venus and Adonis! but she was going in his direction. So, bowing politely to the household, he immediately followed, and to his unspeakable delight—for this was an adventure he certainly had not looked for—he caught up with her at the first turn of the road. When he came alongside, he pulled in his reins, took off his cap and bowed. The salute was returned with a superb yet easy grace. His ardent glance took a full view of her with lightning speed and precision. He felt that he was in the presence of a grand woman.

"As we seem to be travelling in the same direction, will mademoiselle allow me to accompany her to her destination?"

"Thank you, sir; a military escort is always welcome, especially to a lady, in these troublous times, but I really do not live very far—only ten miles."

"Ten miles!" exclaimed Hardinge.

The lady broke out into a merry laugh, and said:

"You wonder. This little beast is like the wind. You are well mounted, but I doubt you can follow me. Will you try?"

So saying, she snapped her white fingers, and the little Canadian pony, making a leap into the air, was away like an arrow. Hardinge dashed off in pursuit, and for a time held his own bravely, the horses keeping neck to neck, but presently he fell behind and the lady disappeared out of sight. When at length he came up with her, she was waiting at the gate of her father's house, a mansion of fine colonial dimensions, standing in a bower of maples. She was laughing heartily and enjoying her triumph. Hardinge, touching his cap gracefully, acknowledged his defeat.

"This will be a lesson for you, sir," she said.

"A lesson, mademoiselle?"

"It will teach you to chase rebels again."

"Beautiful rebel," murmured Roderick, bowing profoundly and wholly unable to conceal his admiration.

"You don't choose to understand me," she said, half seriously and half jestingly, "but later, perhaps, you will do so. I believe I am speaking to Lieutenant Hardinge?"

"That is my name, at your service, mademoiselle, and am I mistaken in presuming that I address a member of the Sarpy family, for this is the mansion of Sieur Sarpy, well known to me."

"I am his daughter. I have only lately returned from France where I spent many years."

"Not the Zulma of whom I have heard your brother speak so often?"

"The same."

And the wild frolic of her spirits broke out into a silvery peal, as she seemingly recollected some idea connected with the name. She invited Roderick to dismount and enter, but he was obliged to excuse himself as having tarried already too long, and thus this adventure terminated. Its romantic sequel will be related in subsequent chapters.

Hardinge pursued his journey without further episodes of interest. The road between Quebec and Three Rivers was not what it is at present. There were no corduroys across the swamps, no bridges over the streams and the way was blocked for miles upon miles by the unpruned forest, through which a bridle path was the only route. Notwithstanding all these drawbacks, however, our horseman had reached Three Rivers, stabled his grey, and delivered his despatches before ten o'clock that night. He was very tired, indeed, when he retired to rest, but this did not prevent the youthful brain from dreaming, and the youthful lips from murmuring:

"Beautiful rebel!"

VIII
THE HERMIT OF MONTMORENCI

His name was Baptiste, but he went by the more familiar appellation of Batoche. His residence was a hut near the Falls of Montmorenci, and there he led the life of a hermit. His only companions were a little girl called Blanche, and a large black cat which bore the appropriate title of Velours, for though the brute was ugly and its eyes,

> "Had all the seeming
> Of a demon's that is dreaming,"

its coat was soft and glossy as silken velvet. The interior of the hut denoted poverty, but not indigence. There was a larder in one corner; a small oven wrought into the chimney to the right of the fire-place; faggots and logs of wood were piled up near the hearth, and diverse kitchen utensils and other comforts hung brightly on the wall. In the angle of the solitary room furthest from the door, and always lying in shadow, was a curtained alcove, and in this a low bedstead over which a magnificent bear-skin was thrown, with the head of the animal lying on the pillow, and its eyes, bulging out in red flannel, turned to the rafters above. Directly behind the door stood a wooden sofa which could sit two or three persons during the day, but which, at night, served as the couch of little Blanche. A shallow circular cavity in the large blue flag of the hearth was the resting place of Velours. On two hooks within easy reach of his hand, rested a long heavy carbine, well worn, but still in good order and with which, so long as he could carry it, Batoche needed never pass a day without a meal, for the game was abundant almost to his very door. From the beams were suspended an array of little bags of seeds, paper cornets of dried wild flowers and bunches of medicinal herbs, the acrid, pungent odor of which pervaded the whole room and was the first thing which struck a stranger upon entering the hut.

The habitation of Batoche was fully a mile from any other dwelling. Indeed, at that period, the country in the immediate vicinity of the Falls of Montmorenci was very sparsely settled. The nearest village, in the direction of Quebec, was Beauport, and even there the inhabitants were comparatively few. The hut of the hermit was also removed from the high road, standing about midway between it and the St. Lawrence, on the right side of the Falls as one went toward the river, and just in a line with the spot where they plunge their full tide of waters into the rocky basin below. From his solitary little window Batoche could see these Falls at all times, and under all circumstances—in day time, and in night time; glistening like diamonds in the sunlight, flashing like silver in the moonbeams, and breaking through the shadow of the deepest darkness with the corruscations of their foam. Their music, too, was ever in his ears, forming a part of his being. It ran like a web through his work and his thoughts during the day; it lulled him to sleep at night with the last ember on the hearth, and it always awoke him at the first peep of dawn. The seasons for him were marked by the variation of these sounds—the thunderous roar when the spring freshets or the autumn rain-falls came, the gentle purling when the summer droughts parched the stream to a narrow thread, and the plaintive moan, as of electric wires, when the ice-bound cascade was touched upon by certain winter winds.

Batoche's devotion to this cataract may have been exaggerated, although only in keeping, as we shall see, with his whole character, but really the Falls of Montmorenci are among the most beautiful works of Nature on this continent. We all make it a point to visit Niagara once in our lives, but except in the breadth of its fall, Niagara has no advantage over Montmorenci. In altitude it is far inferior, Montmorenci being nearly one hundred feet higher. The greater volume of Niagara increases the roar of the descent and the quantity of mist from below, but the thunder of Montmorenci is also heard from a great distance, and its column of vapor is a fine spectacle in a strong sunlight or in a storm of thunder and lightning. Its accessories of scenery are certainly superior to those of Niagara in that they are much wilder. The country around is rough, rocky and woody. In front is the broad expanse of the St. Lawrence, and beyond lies the beautiful Isle of Orleans which is nothing less than a picturesque garden. But it is particularly in winter that the Falls of Montmorenci are worthy of being seen. They present a spectacle unique in the world. Canadian winters are proverbial for their severity, and nearly every year, for a few days at least, the mercury touches twenty-five and thirty degrees below zero. When this happens the headlong waters of Montmorenci are arrested in their course, and their ice-bound appearance is that of a white lace veil thrown over the brow of the cliff, and hanging there immoveably. Before the freezing process is completed, however, another singular phenomenon is produced. At the foot of the Falls, where the water seethes and mounts, both in the form of vapor and liquid globules, an eminence is gradually formed, rising constantly in tapering shape, until it reaches a considerable altitude, sometimes one-fourth or one-third the height of the Fall itself. This is known as the Cone. The French people call it more poetically *Le Pain de Sucre*, or sugar-loaf. On a bright day in January, when the white light of the sun plays caressingly on this pyramid of crystal, illuminating its veins of emerald and sending a refracted ray into its circular air-holes, the prismatic effect is enchanting. Thousands of persons visit Montmorenci every winter for no other object than that of enjoying this sight. It is needless to add that the youthful generation visit the Cone for the more prosaic purpose of toboganning or sledding from its summit away down to the middle of the St. Lawrence.

IX
THE WOLF'S CRY

It was an hour after sunset, and the evening was already very dark. Batoche had stirred the fire and prepared the little table, setting two pewter plates upon it, with knife and fork. He produced a huge jack-knife from his pocket, opened it, and laid that too on the table. He then went to the cupboard and brought from it a loaf of brown bread which he laid beside one of the plates. Having seemingly completed his preparations for supper, he stood still in the middle of the floor, as if listening:

"'Tis strange," he muttered, "she never is so late."

He walked to the door, which was flung open into his face by the force of the wind, and looked long and intently to the right and to the left.

"The snow is deep," he said, "the path to the high road is blocked up. Perhaps she has lost her way. But, no. She has never lost her way yet."

He closed the door, walked absently over the room, and after gazing up and around for a second or two, threw himself into a low, leather-strapped chair before the fire. As he sits there, let us take the opportunity of sketching the singular being. His face was an impressive one. The chin was long and pointed, the jaw firm. The lips were set as those of a taciturn man, but not grimly, and their corners bore two lines as of old smiles that had buried their joys there forever. A long and rather heavy nose, sensitive at the nostrils. High cheek bones. A good forehead, but rather too flattened at the temples. Long, thin meshes of white hair escaping through the border of the high fox-skin cap. The complexion was bronze and the face beardless. This last feature is said to be characteristic of low vitality, but it is also frequently distinctive of eccentricity, and Batoche was clearly eccentric, as the expression of his eyes showed. They were cold grey eyes, but filled with wild intermittent illuminations. The reflection of the fire-light gave them a weird appearance.

Batoche sat for fully half an hour in front of the fire, his long thin hands thrust into his pockets, his fox-skin cap dashed to one side of his head and his eyes steadily fixed upon the flames. Although immoveable, he was evidently a prey to profound emotions, for the lurid light, playing upon his face, revealed the going and coming of painful thoughts. Now and then he muttered something in a half articulate voice which the black cat seemed to understand, for it purred awhile in its circular nest, then rising, rounded its back, and looked up at its master with tender inquiry in its green eyes. But Batoche had no thought for Velours to-night. His mind was entirely occupied with little Blanche who, having gone into Quebec upon some errands, as was her wont, had not yet returned.

The wind moaned dismally around the little hut, at times giving it a wrench as if it would topple it from its foundations. The spruces and firs in the neighborhood creaked and tossed in the breath of the tempest, and there was a dull, heavy roar from the head of the Falls. Suddenly, amid all these sounds, the solitary old man's quick ear caught a peculiar cry coming from the direction of the road. It was a sharp, shrill bark, followed by a low whine. He sat up, bent his head and listened again. Velour's fur stood on end, and its whisker bristled like wire. The sound was heard again, made clearer and more striking by a sudden rush of wind.

"A wolf, a wolf!" exclaimed Batoche, as he sprang from his seat, seized his gun from its hooks and rushed out of the house. He did not hesitate one moment as to the direction which he should take, but bent his steps to the main road.

"Never. Oh, it can never be," he gasped, as he hurried along. "God would never throw her into the wolf's embrace." —

He reached the road at last, and paused on its border to listen. He was not disappointed, for within one hundred or two hundred yards of him, he heard for the third time the ominous yelp of the wolf. Then all the hunter showed itself in Batoche. He became, at once, a new man. The bent form straightened, the languid limbs became nerved, the sinister eyes shot fire, as if lighting the way before them, and the blank melancholy features were turned and hardened into one single expression—watching. In a moment he had determined the exact direction of the sound. Cautiously he advanced from tree to tree, with inaudible footfall and bated breath, until he reached the outskirts of a thicket. There he expected to bring the wolf to bay. He peered long and attentively through the branches.

"It is a den of wolves," he whispered to himself. "Not one pair of eyes, but four or five pairs are glancing through the dark. I must make quick work of the vermin. They must not be allowed to take their residences for the winter so near my cabin."

Saying which he raised his carbine to his shoulder and pointed. His finger was upon the trigger and was about to let go, when he felt the barrel of his gun bent from its position and quietly but firmly deflected towards the ground.

"Don't be a fool, Batoche. Keep your ammunition for other wolves than these. You will soon need it all," said a voice in a low tone.

The hunter immediately recognized Barbin, a farmer of Beauport.

"What are you doing here?"

"No time for questions to-night. You will know later."

"And who are those in the thicket yonder?"

"My friends and yours."

Batoche shook his head dubiously, and muttered something about going forward to satisfy himself by personal inspection. He was an enemy of prowlers of all sorts, and must know with whom he had to deal before abandoning the search.

A low whistle was heard and the thicket was instantaneously cleared.

Barbin tried to retain him, but the old man's temper rose, and he snatched himself away.

"Don't be a fool, I say to you again, Batoche. You know who I am and you must understand that I would not be out in such a place and on such a night without necessary cause. These are my friends. For sufficient reasons, they must not be known at present. Believe me, and don't advance further. Besides they are now invisible."

"But why these strange cries?"

"The bark of the wolf is our rallying cry."

"The wolf!"

"Do you understand now?"

The old man passed his hand rapidly over his forehead and his eyes, then grounding his musket, and seizing Barbin by the collar, he exclaimed:

"You don't mean it. I knew it would come, but did not expect it so soon. The wolf, you said? Ah! sixteen years are a long time, but it passes, Barbin. We are old now, yet not broken—"

He would have continued in this strain, but his interlocutor suddenly stopped him.

"Yes, yes, Batoche, it is thus. Make yourself ready, as we are doing. But I must go. My companions are waiting for me. We have important work to do to-night."

"And I?" asked the old man reproachfully.

"Your work, Batoche, is not now, but later, not here, but elsewhere. Be quiet; you have not been forgotten."

Barbin then disappeared in the wood, while Batoche slowly returned toward the road, shaking his head, and saying to himself:

"The wolf! I knew it would come, but who would have thought it? Will my violin sing the old song to me to-night? Will Clara glide under the waterfall?"

X
THE CASKET

Little Blanche had not been forgotten all this time. The old man when he reached the road, looked in the direction of Quebec for a moment, as if hesitating whether to turn his steps in that direction. But he apparently changed his mind, for he deliberately walked across the road, and plunged into the narrow path leading to his cabin. When he arrived there, he saw a horse and sleigh standing a little away from it under the trees. He paid no attention to them, however, and walked up to the door, which was opened for him by little Blanche. Bending down, he kissed her on the forehead, laid his hand upon her hair, and said:

"It is well, child, but why so late?"

"I could not return earlier, grandpapa."

"Who detained you?"

She pointed to a muffled figure seated in a shaded angle of the room. Still trailing his carbine in his left hand, Batoche walked up to it. The figure rose, extended its hand and smiled sadly.

"You don't know me, Batoche?"

The old man looked into the face of the stranger for a long time, then the light of recognition came and he exclaimed:

"I must be mistaken. It cannot be."

"Yes, it is I—"

"M. Belmont!"

"Yes, Batoche, we remember each other, though we have not met for some years. You live the life of an anchorite here, never coming to the city, and I remain in retirement, scarcely ever going from the city. We are almost strangers, and yet we are friends. We *must* be friends now, even if we were not before."

The old man did not reply, but asked his visitor to sit down, while he, having hung up his weapon, and drawn a chair to the fire-place, took a seat beside him. The fire had burned low and both were seated in the deep shadow. Blanche had offered to light a candle, but the men having refused by a sign, the child sat down on the other side of the hearth with the black cat circled on her lap.

"I brought back the child to you," said M. Belmont, by way of opening the conversation. "She was in good hands with Pauline, her godmother, but we knew that she never spent a night out of your hermitage, and that you would be anxious if she did not return."

"Oh, Blanche is like her old grandfather. She knows every path in the forest, every sign of the heavens, and no weather could prevent her from finding her home. I have no fear that man or beast would hurt the little creature. Indeed, she has the mark of Providence upon her and no harm will come to her so long as my life is spared. There is a spirit in the waterfall yonder, M. Belmont, which watches over her and the protection is inviolable. But I thank you, sir, and your daughter for having taken care of her."

"I kept her for another reason, Batoche," and M. Belmont looked furtively at his companion, who returned his glance in the same dubious fashion.

"It gave me the opportunity of paying you a visit which, for special reasons, is of the greatest importance to me."

Batoche seemed to divine the secret thought of his guest, and put him immediately at his ease by saying:

"I am a poor solitary being, M. Belmont, severed from all the world, cut off from the present, living only in the past, and hoping for nothing in the future except the welfare of this little orphan girl. Nobody cares for me, and I have cared for nobody, but I am ready to do you any service in my power. I have learned a secret to-night, and—who knows?—perhaps life has changed for me during the last hour."

M. Belmont listened attentively to these words. He knew in the presence of what strange being he was, and that the language which he heard had perhaps a deeper meaning than appeared upon the surface. But the manner of Batoche was quiet in its earnestness, his eye had none of its strange fire, and there was no wild incoherent gesture of his to indicate that he was speaking outside of his most rational mood. M. Belmont therefore contented himself with thanking the hermit for his good will. A lull then ensued in the conversation, when suddenly a low howl was heard in the forest beyond the high road. By a simultaneous impulse, both men sprang to their feet and glared at each other. Little Blanche's head had fallen on her shoulder and she was sweetly sleeping unconscious of all harm, while Velours, though, she stirred once or twice, would not abandon her warm bed on her mistress' knees.

"Wolf!" muttered Batoche.

"Wolf!" replied M. Belmont

And the two men fell into each other's embrace.

"We are brothers once more," said M. Belmont, pressing the hand of the old man, while the tears flowed down his cheeks.

"Yes, and in the holiest of causes," responded Batoche.

"There is no more mystery between us now," resumed M. Belmont. "That call was for me. I must be away at once. I have delayed too long already. What I came to you particularly for, Batoche, was this."

And he produced, from the interior of his huge wild-cat overcoat, a small casket bound with clasps of silver.

"In this small casket, Batoche, are all my family relics and treasures. For my money I care nothing; for this I care so much that I would give my life rather than that it should perish. You are the man to hide it for me. You know of secret places which no mortal can penetrate. I confide it to you. This has been a dark day for me; what to-morrow has in store I almost fear to guess. The times will probably go hard with all of us, including you, Batoche. For ourselves the loss will be nothing. We are old and useless. But Pauline and little Blanche! They must survive the ruin. Should I perish, this casket is to go to my daughter, and should you too come to grief, entrust the secret of its hiding place to Blanche that she may deliver it. Take it, and good night. I must go."

Without waiting for a word of reply, M. Belmont embraced the old man on the cheek, stooped to imprint a kiss on the forehead of the sleeping child, rushed out of the cabin, threw himself into his cariole and drove away.

As he disappeared, the same low cry of the wolf was borne plaintively from the forest.

XI
THE SPIRIT OF THE WATERFALL

Batoche gave a single moment to deliberation. He stood silently holding the latch of the closed door. Then he walked slowly across the room and entered behind the chintz curtains of the little alcove. What he did there is unknown, but when he issued forth his face was hard set, every lineament bearing the stamp of resolution. He took up the silver casket which had been left in his charge and balanced it in his hands. It was heavy, but heavier still appeared to him the responsibility which it entailed, if one might judge from the deep sigh which escaped him. He glanced at little Blanche, but she still slumbered quietly, with her head resting on the wall and bent over her shoulder. Velours was more wakeful, looking furtively at her master from the corners of her eyes but, knowing his habits well, she did not deem it prudent to stir from her nest or make any noise.

"There is a place of all others," murmured Batoche, "where I may hide this beyond all fear of detection. There neither the birds of the air, nor the beasts of the forests, nor the eye of man will ever discover it. Blanche only will know, but I will not tell her now. She sleeps and it is well."

He then placed the casket under his arm and stole out of the house. He took a footpath leading from his cabin to the Falls, and having reached their summit, turned to the right, descending from one rock to another, until he reached the depths of the basin. There he paused a moment, looking up, as if to ascertain his bearings. An instant later, he had disappeared under the Fall itself. Grasping the casket more tightly under his right arm, he used his left to grope his way along the cold, wet wall of granite. The rocks underneath his feet, some round, some angular, some flat, were slippery with the ooze of the earth fissures above and the refluent foam of the cascade. Beside these dangers, there was the additional peril of darkness, the immense volume of descending waters effectually curtaining out the light of heaven. When he had attained about the middle of the distance between the two banks of the river, Batoche paused and stooped at the mouth of an aperture which would admit only his bent body. Without faltering, and as if sure of his locality, he thus entered into the subterranean cavity. He was gone for fully half an hour, but when he issued forth, he straightened himself up with ease, and by the assistance of his two hands, rapidly retraced his steps to the foot of the Falls. There he stopped, looking above and around him, to assure himself that he was really alone with his secret.

But no, he was not alone. Upon the brow of the waterfall, along the perilous ridge, where the torrent plunges sheer into the chasm below, a fragile figure in white glided slowly with face turned towards him. Her yellow hair, bound with a fillet about her forehead, fell loose upon her shoulders; there was the light of love in her eyes and a sweet smile irradiated her lips. Her white hands hung at her sides, and from under the hem of her flowing garb, a tiny, snowy foot appeared barely touching the surface of the water.

What was it—a phantom or a reality? A mockery of the vapor and the night, or a spirit of God truly walking over the waters? We cannot say, or rather we shall not stop to inquire. Enough that the poor old hermit saw it, and seeing, was transported into ecstacy. His whole being appeared transfused into the ethereal vision which shone before him. The gross outlines of old age and shabby costume were melted into the beautiful forms of exultation and reverence. Under the misty moon, under the faint light of the stars, he fell upon his knees, stretched out his arms, and his face turned eagerly upwards in the absorption of prayer.

"Once more, O Clara! Once more, O my daughter! It is long since I have seen you, and my days have passed sadly in the lonesomeness of solitude. You come once more to smile upon your old father, and bring a blessing upon your orphan child. She sleeps sweetly yonder near the hearth. Protect her from the harm which I know must be impending and of which your visitation is the warning. You are the guardian angel of my cabin, shielding it from all the dangers which have threatened it these many years. Give me a sign of your assistance and I shall be content."

These were the words the old man uttered as he knelt upon the wet rocks. Let no one smile as he reads them, for even the ravings of a diseased brain are beautiful when they have a spiritual significance.

Batoche rose and advanced nearer, with arms still outstretched, as if he would clasp the Spirit of the Waterfall, and seize the token which he implored. But in this he was disappointed.

> Not a word her lips did utter, and without a start or flutter,
> She crossed her hands upon her bosom in the attitude of prayer;
> And his stricken soul beguiling with the sweetness of her smiling,
> Raised her bright eyes up to heaven, and slowly melted into air.

A thick bank of cloud floated in the sky, veiling the moon. The stars paled, and it was very dark. The great Falls thundered with a sullen roar. The wind beat against the forest trees with a moan. The hermit knelt once more and engaged for a long time in silent prayer; then rising, returned directly to his hut. He found little Blanche standing in the middle of the room and in the full light of the hearth, with a scared look in her brilliant, black eyes. He stooped to kiss her, and noticing the supper still untasted on the table, said:

"You have eaten nothing, my dear."

"I cannot eat, grandpapa."

"Then go to sleep. It is late."

"I cannot sleep."

The old man understood. The white wings of the mother's spirit had hovered over the child.

"Then pray," he said.

And dropping on her knees, little Blanche repeated all the prayers which her godmother, Pauline Belmont, had taught her.

XII
THREE RIVERS

Roderick Hardinge's mission to Three Rivers was completely successful. He found that town and the surrounding country in a state of alarm and excitement consequent on the march of events in the upper part of the province. The whole Richelieu peninsula was overrun with Continental troops and the Montreal district was virtually in their power. The only chance was that the British army might make a stand at Sorel, which commanded the Richelieu and the St. Lawrence, at the confluence of these two rivers, and accordingly around that point concentrated the interest of the war in the first week of November. It was only natural, therefore, that the people of Three Rivers should be in a turmoil of excitement, for if the British were unable to hold their own at Sorel, the whole of the St. Lawrence would be swept by the Americans, and Three Rivers would be the very next place which they would occupy.

The arrival of Hardinge was not calculated to allay the excitement, and the tidings which he brought were spread through the town that very night notwithstanding all attempts at official secrecy. The Commandant of the town was considerably alarmed.

"The news from above was bad enough," he said to his principal secretary, after reading Hardinge's despatches, "but the intelligence from below is not more reassuring. Three Rivers thus finds itself between two fires. Montgomery from the west, and now Arnold from the east. I am very much afraid that we shall have to succumb. And the worst of all is that being masters of the intervening country, with emissaries in all the villages along their route, they improve their opportunity by tampering with our simple-minded farmers. Here in Three Rivers the disaffection among our own people is already quite marked, and I very much fear that this new source of danger will only increase it."

The secretary was a very old man who listened attentively to his superior, biting the feathers of his pen and giving other signs of nervous excitement.

"I am certain, sir, that you do not exaggerate the situation," he said, speaking slowly, but with emphasis. "We are on the eve of a crisis, and I suspect that this time next week the town of Three Rivers will be in the hands of the Bastonnais. We have no means of resistance, and even if we had, there is too much dissension in our midst to attempt it with any hope of success. The next question which arises is whether it were best for you to provide for your own safety as well as that of the archives and registers of the town."

"I will do neither," replied the Commandant with dignity. "As for myself, the duty of my office is to remain in charge until I am dispossessed by force. Personal violence I do not fear, but should I be subjected to such, I will endure it. Remember that you and I know what war is. We both passed through the terrible years of the Conquest. With respect to the archives, you will see that they are properly guarded, but they must not be removed. The enemy are not barbarians. On the contrary it is their policy to conciliate as much as possible. Besides, they will only pass through Three Rivers."

"They will do more than that, sir. As they intend to march upon Quebec, around whose walls they will more than probably spend the winter, it will be a matter of military necessity for them to occupy all the little towns and villages on their route between Quebec and Montreal, both for the sake of their commissariat and as recruiting stations."

"Recruiting stations! Don't use those hateful words."

"They are hateful words, sir. But they express a fact which we must face. Unless we are very careful, this war will be aggravated by the circumstance of many of our countrymen turning their arms against us."

This conversation which we have briefly introduced in order to afford the reader glimpses of the situation, relieved as much as possible from the dryness of mere historical detail, was interrupted by the arrival of a messenger who delivered a letter to the Governor.

"This is from Sorel," exclaimed the official. "It comes just in time to throw light upon our affairs and will enable Lieutenant Hardinge, who returns to-morrow, to bring the latest news to Quebec."

Saying which, he read the despatch.

XIII
A SUCCESSFUL MISSION

At ten o'clock, on the morning of the 8th November, the day after his arrival, Roderick Hardinge presented himself at the residence of the Commandant of Three Rivers. It was the hour agreed upon between them for a conference, which circumstance did not prevent the Commandant from manifesting some surprise on seeing the young officer.

"You surely are not ready to start for Quebec already?" he asked.

"If possible, sir, I should very much like to do so. My horse is not as fresh as he was yesterday, and he will delay me longer, and besides I think my presence will be required in Quebec before midnight."

"Very well. Time is pressing, I know. I have jotted down a few lines giving Lieutenant-Governor Cramahé all the information in my possession. Here is the letter. But you have doubtless wandered about the town a little this morning, and thus learned many details which have escaped me."

"I have heard much more than I am willing to believe," said Hardinge, with a laugh.

"Tell me briefly what you have heard, and I will correct or confirm it."

"I have heard that Montreal has fallen."

"Not yet. Montgomery is still on the plateau between St. Johns, which he captured about a week ago, and Montreal, which is his next point of attack. But there are two obstacles which retard him. The first of these is the skirmishing of the British troops on his flank, and the second, the discontent among his own soldiers. Many men from Vermont and New York have returned home. Montreal is, however, really defenceless, and cannot hold out more than a few days, especially as Montgomery is anxious to get there in order to house and clothe his naked, suffering men. What else have you heard?"

"That the French of Montreal are secretly working for the enemy."

"It is false. Those who told you so are treacherous friends, and we have several here in Three Rivers. Next?"

"That the Indians under LaCorne have dug up the hatchet which they buried in the Recollets church, one month ago, and declared against us."

"That would be terrible news if true, but it is not true. My last courier from the west, who arrived not an hour ago, has particular information from the Indians about Montreal. They still maintain the neutrality pledged in the Recollets church. I admit, however, that it would not take much to turn them into foes, and I know that Montgomery has already his emissaries among them. But LaCorne is a true Frenchman, and so long as our own people retain their allegiance, he will maintain his."

After a pause, Hardinge said:

"I have heard, sir, in addition, that Colonel McLean, at the head of his Highlanders, has not been able to form a junction with Governor Carleton, at Longueuil, so as to intercept Montgomery between St. Johns and Montreal."

"It is true."

"That, owing to the defeat of Governor Carleton at Longueuil by a Vermont detachment, and the spread of Continental troops through the Richelieu peninsula, Colonel McLean was forced to fall back precipitately to Sorel."

"That is unfortunately too true. Do you know more?"

"That is all."

"Then, I will tell you more. McLean will have to retreat from Sorel. My *coureurs des bois* and Indian messengers have been arriving in succession all last night and this morning. They inform me that while Montgomery is marching on Montreal, a considerable body, under one of his best officers, is moving towards Sorel, with a view of occupying it, and thus commanding the river. McLean is in no condition to withstand this attack. What will hasten his retreat is the news he has by this time received from Quebec. Last night, so soon as I had read the despatches which you brought me, I sent him one of my fleetest messengers with the intelligence. The messenger must have reached Sorel early this morning. The special messenger to Governor Carleton, with the same news, will arrive in Montreal about noon to-day."

During the whole of this conversation, Hardinge's face had been grave and almost downcast. But at the last words of his interlocutor, it suddenly flushed with an expression of enthusiasm.

"If Colonel McLean and Governor Carleton know exactly how we stand at Quebec, I am content," he exclaimed.

"Then you may be content. I have stated all this briefly to Lieutenant-Governor Cramahé, but you may repeat it to him with emphasis."

"I will not fail."

And after a few parting words, he respectfully took his leave.

When he had cleared the streets of Three Rivers, and was alone upon the road, he could not restrain a long, loud whoop of exultation.

"The game is up," he cried. "The war is in full blaze. In twenty-four hours, my name has gone from one end of the province to the other. My mission has indeed succeeded. How proud little Pauline will be of her cavalier."

With such thoughts uppermost in his mind, he forgot his bodily fatigue, and rode back to Quebec with more eagerness than he had gone from it.

XIV
CROSSING THE BOATS

Notwithstanding the late hour at which he arrived in Quebec—it was considerably after midnight—Hardinge repaired directly to the Chateau St. Louis. There was no bustle in the Castle, but his eye noticed signs of unusual vigilance. The guard about the entry was a double one, and many of the lower windows were lighted. It was evident also that his coming was expected, for, immediately on his dismounting, his horse was taken charge of by a soldier, and he was at once ushered into the presence of the Lieutenant-Governor. Cramahé was in the Council chamber, and several members of the Council were seated around the centre table, on which was spread a number of papers.

"Welcome back, Lieutenant," said the Governor, with a weary smile and extending both his hands.

Hardinge bowed and at once delivered his despatches. Cramahé having rapidly glanced over them, handed them to his colleagues, then turning to the young officer, said:

"It is clear that the storm which has been gathering over this province must break upon Quebec. This is the old city of destiny. And we shall accept our destiny, Lieutenant," said the Governor, rising from the table, and advancing toward Roderick. "We have not been idle during your absence. Much can be done in a day and a half, and we have done it. We have done so much that we can await the arrival of Arnold with some assurance. I see, however, from the despatches you bring me, that Colonel McLean is in some danger at Sorel. I had calculated on his arrival and that of Governor Carleton who knows our exact position by this time. Should they have come to harm, it will go hard with us, but we will do our best all the same."

Hardinge replied that he was exceedingly glad to hear this, because the people of the upper country, through which he had ridden, looked to Quebec for the ultimate salvation of the province. It was pretty well understood that the rest of the country was lost.

"Your despatches make that painfully clear," replied the Governor, "and increase our responsibility. I rely upon you particularly, Lieutenant. I appreciate so much all that you have done, that I look to you, for something more. This is our last day, remember."

"Our last day?"

"Yes, Arnold will be at Point Levis to-morrow."

Hardinge could not help smiling.

"You may well smile. Your prediction was correct. I saw Donald last night. He had been hovering around the enemy all day and informed me that by direct and forced marches they would surely be at Levis to-morrow. This being the case, I have a duty for you to perform. But first, you must take some rest."

"I will be ready for orders at daylight, Your Excellency."

"Ten o'clock will be quite early enough. If we worked during the dark we should excite too much curiosity. The city is really ignorant of what is impending, though there are many rumors. The excitement of yesterday has entirely subsided, and it would be very unwise to renew it. At ten o'clock therefore, you will quietly cross to the other side of the river, with two or three of your men, and under pretence of wanting them for some service or other—I leave you to imagine a plausible pretext—you will cause every species of embarkation, canoe, skiff, flat-boat or punt, to be taken over to this side. Not a floating plank must be left at Levis. If Arnold wants to get over, he will have to hew his boats out of the trees of the forest. Donald will be there to assist you, and may possibly be in possession of fresh news."

Roderick thanked His Excellency for entrusting to him this task which he regarded as the crowning act of the services which he had been rendering the cause of his country in the past two days. After giving expression to his obligation, he added:

"The removal of the boats, sir, will give us three or four days of respite, for I suppose Donald repeated to you that Arnold has no artillery and must procure boats if he really intends to attack the city. In the interval, we may look for Colonel McLean and Governor Carleton."

The Lieutenant-Governor nodded assent, and ordering the subaltern to report to him when his work was done, he dismissed him to his quarters.

When the appointed hour came, Hardinge set about his business which he conducted very quietly and judiciously. In those days everybody living on or near the river owned a boat which was almost the only conveyance whereby to reach the markets of Quebec. And the inhabitants had learned from the Indians how to use their craft with skill, so that women were as expert at the oars as men. Those who resided on the banks of the St. Lawrence usually kept their boats chained near a little house on the water's edge, where the women did their washing. The practice is maintained to this day along many parts of the river which are distant from large cities and where there are no ferries. Those who lived a short distance in the interior were in the habit of drawing their boats a little way into the woods, after they had used them, and leaving them there in some marked spot till they were required again. It thus happened that, at the time of which we write, there were perhaps no less than a thousand boats within a radius of three miles up and down from Quebec and on both sides of the St. Lawrence. Directly opposite the city there were probably about a hundred, not belonging only to Point Levis, for that was then an insignificant village, but mostly to farmers of the neighboring parishes. The number was important if Arnold had been able to lay hold of the craft, but it gave Hardinge little or no difficulty to dispose of. Some thirty or forty of them that were leaky, or otherwise disabled, he quietly broke up, sending the fragments afloat down the river. The remainder he despatched over to the other side, at intervals and from different points, with the aid of a dozen men whom he had joined to his party. Operating thus from ten in the forenoon till five in the afternoon, he succeeded in clearing the south shore of all its boats, without exciting undue attention in the city.

He himself came over with the last canoe, about twenty minutes after the sun had gone down and just as the twilight was creeping over the waters. As he neared the landing, he distinguished a female figure walking very slowly along the bank. He could not be mistaken. It was she. A few vigorous strokes of the paddle having brought the boat to its destination, he leaped ashore and approached.

Yes, it was Pauline.

XV
THE MEETING OF THE LOVERS

Swift as the lightning's flash are the instincts of love. Before a word had been spoken and without being able to read her face in the dusk, Roderick felt in his heart that Pauline's presence there was an omen of ill. But, like a true man, he smothered the suspicion and spoke out bravely.

"Why, Pauline, what an agreeable surprise. How did you know that I had returned? I should have sent you word this morning, but I was so occupied that it was impossible.... You probably heard it from others.... But I am so glad to see you.... How is your father?... And you, darling, I hope you are well...."

To these words of the young officer, broken by breathing spaces so as to admit of replies, not an answer was returned. But when he had finished, all that Pauline did was to stretch out her arms and lay her two ungloved hands in the hands of Hardinge, while her face looked imploringly into his and she murmured:

"O, Roddy, Roddy!"

They were then standing alone near the water, the two companions of Roderick having ascended to the city. Gently and silently, he drew the yielding form toward him until he could scan her features and learn in those eyes, which he knew so well, the secret of her sorrow. But the light of the eyes was totally quenched in tears, and the usually mobile face was veiled by a blank expression of misery. Hardinge was thunderstruck. All sorts of wild conjectures leaped through his brain.

"Speak to me, Pauline, and tell me what this means," he said imploringly. "Has anything befallen you? Has any one injured you? Or am I the cause of this grief?"

Still holding her extended hands clasped in his, and casting her eyes upon the ground, she replied:

"O, Roddy, you cannot tell, and you will never know how wretched I am, but it is some comfort that I can speak to you at least once more."

"At least once more!" These words quivered through him, chilling him from head to foot.

"Pauline, I entreat you, explain the meaning of all this," he exclaimed.

"It means, Roddy, that I who have never disobeyed my father, in my life, have had the weakness to disobey him this evening. I did not mean to do it. I did it unconsciously."

"Disobeyed your father?"

"Yes, in seeing you again."

"Surely, you do not mean—?"

"Alas! dearest, I mean that my father has forbidden me ever to meet you."

Roderick was so astonished that he staggered, and the power of utterance for a moment was denied him. At last he whispered falteringly:

"Really, there must be some mistake, Pauline."

She shook her head, and looking up at him with a sad smile, replied:

"Ah! I also thought it was a mistake, but, Roddy, it is only too true. These two days I have brooded over it, and these two nights. To-day, hearing that you had returned, I could endure the burden no longer. I thought of writing to you, but I had not the heart to put the terrible injunction on paper. I have wandered the whole afternoon in the hope of meeting you. I walked as in a dream, feeling indeed that I was doing wrong, but with this faint excuse for my disobedience, that, by telling you of it myself, I would spare you the terrible disgrace of being driven from my father's door, if you presented yourself there without knowing his determination. For myself such a misfortune would have been a death blow."

Every word went burning to Roderick's heart, but he had to master his own agony a moment, in the effort to support Pauline who had utterly broken down. When she had recovered sufficiently, he protested tenderly that there was a mystery in all this which he was unable to fathom, and entreated her to help him discover it by telling him minutely all that had happened since they had last met. She gradually summoned strength and composure enough to do so, relating in detail the scene in Cathedral square; the arrival of the Lieutenant-Governor's aide-de-camp; his delivering of a letter to her father; the conversation that took place between the latter and the officer; her father's visit to the Chateau; his return therefrom; and, relapsing into tears, she narrated how her father had found her reading a note from Roderick, and how he had ordered her to cast it into the fire.

The young officer did not lose the significance of a word. At first the mystery remained as impenetrable as ever, but after a while a thread of suspicion wove itself into his brain. He tried to brush it away, however, by rubbing his hand violently over his brow and eyes. It was too painful. It was too odious. Finally, he asked:

"Did your father give any reason why you should burn my note?"

"Ah! Roddy, why do you force me to say it? When I told him that you had sent him your regards, he replied '*he has just sent me his hate!*'"

These words solved the mystery. Hardinge saw through it all, distinctly, sharply, unmistakeably. He drew a long breath, and his broad chest swelled with the fresh air from the river.

"Pauline, my dear," he said with that tender authority with which a strong man can miraculously revive a weak, drooping woman, "Pauline, take heart. It is all a terrible mistake and it will be explained. Your father has suspected me of a dreadful thing, but I am innocent and will convince him of it. I will see him this very night and make him and you happy."

She raised her hands imploringly.

"Fear nothing, darling, I am as certain as that we are standing here together, that it is all a fearful misunderstanding, and that I will make it clear to your father, in a quarter of an hour's conversation."

"But why not tell me, and I will tell him?"

"Because there are several points connected with the matter with which you are not familiar, and because he might misconstrue both your motives and mine. No. It is a matter to be settled between man and man. Besides, it is late and your absence must not be prolonged. I, too, have a military report to make to the authorities without delay."

Pauline suffered herself to be convinced, and the two, after a few mutual words of love, which wonderfully recuperated them, bent their way up Mountain Hill. At the gate they separated.

"I will be with you within two hours," said Hardinge, as he took the direction of the Chateau.

Pauline stepped into the old church on her way, and in its consecrated gloom poured out a prayer at the feet of Her whom she worshipped as the Comforter of the Afflicted. *Consolatrix Afflictorum.*

XVI
THE ROUND TABLE

There was high festival at the Chateau St. Louis. Sieur Hector Théophile Cramahé, Lieutenant-Governor of the Province of Quebec, and Commander of the Forces in the capital, during the absence of Guy Carleton, Captain General and Governor Chief, was a man of convivial spirit. He had for years presided over a choice circle of friends, men of wealth and standing in the ancient city. They were known as the Barons of the Round Table. An invariable rule with them was to dine together once a week, when they would rehearse the memories of old times, and conduct revels worthy of the famous Intendant Bigot himself. They numbered twenty-four, and it so happened that in five years not one of them had missed the hebdomadal banquet—a remarkable circumstance well worthy the attention of those who study the mathematical curiosities of the chapter of accidents.

The ninth of November was dinner night. The Lieutenant-Governor had a moment's hesitation about the propriety of holding it, but all objections were at once drowned in a flood of valid reasons in favor of the repast. In the first place, His Excellency had been particularly burdened with the cares of office during the past two days. That young fellow Hardinge had kept him as busy as he could be. In the next place, though the citizens of Quebec really knew nothing of the true state of affairs, they were making all kinds of conjecture, and if the dinner did not take place, the gossips would hear of it immediately, and interpret it as the worst possible sign of impending trouble. In the third place, if the banquet were postponed for a day or two, that villain Arnold might turn up and prevent it altogether. Cramahé paced up and down in his drawing room, rubbing his hands and smiling as these fancies flitted through his brain. If he had been serious, which he was not, his doubts would all have been dissipated by the arrival of the Barons almost in a body. Up they came through the spacious entrance and illuminated hall, in claret-colored coats, lace bosom-frills and cuffs, velvet breeches, silken hose, silver-buckled shoes, and powdered wigs, holding their gold-knobbed canes aslant in their left hand, and waving salutations to their host with their feathered tricorns. A lordlier band never ascended the marble stairs of Versailles. Handsome for the most part, exquisite in manners, worldly in the elevated sense of the term, they represented a race which had transplanted the courtly refinement of the old world into the wilds of the new—a race the more interesting that it did not survive beyond the second generation after the Conquest, and is at present only seen at glimpses amid the wreck of the ancient seigniorial families about Quebec.

It was not long before the company was ushered into the banquet hall, brilliantly lighted with waxen candles. A round table stood in the centre of the floor charged with a treasure of plate and crystal. There were twenty-four seats and a guest for every seat. We need not enter into the details of the entertainment. It is enough to state that it was literally festive with its succulent viands, its inspiriting wines and its dazzling cross-fire of wit and anecdote. The present was forgotten, as it should always be at well-regulated dinners; the future was not thought of, for the diners were old men; the past was the only thing which occupied them. They talked of their early loves, they laughed at their youthful escapades, they sang snatches of old songs, while now and again the memory of a common sorrow would circulate around the table, suddenly deadening its uproar into silence, or the remembrance of a mutual joy would flash merrily before their eyes like the glinting bubbles of their wine cups.

It was five o'clock when the Barons sat down to their first course. It was nine when they reached the *gloria*. Just at that supreme moment, a waiter handed a paper to the Lieutenant-Governor. He opened it, and having read it, exclaimed:

"Another glass, gentlemen. The rebel Jockey will have to swim the St. Lawrence on horseback, if he wishes to pay us a visit."

The allusion was readily understood and hailed with a bumper.

The note was from Hardinge who, on arriving at the Chateau and finding the Lieutenant-Governor engaged with his guests, wrote a line to inform him that he had safely crossed all the boats. As the matter was not particularly pressing, he had requested the orderly not to have the note delivered before nine o'clock.

Scarcely had the noise of the toast subsided, when another waiter advanced with another note.

"This news will not be as good as the other," whispered one of the Barons to his neighbor, while the host was reading the despatch.

"And why, pray?"

"Because alternation is the law of life."

The old Baron was not mistaken. M. Cramahé perused the paper with a very grave face, and folding it slowly, said:

"My friends, I regret that I must leave you for to-night. But first, let us sip our cognac with the hope that nothing will prevent us from meeting again next week."

A few moments later the guests had retired.

The message which the Lieutenant-Governor had received was from the faithful Donald who informed him that the enemy had arrived within five miles of Point Levis and encamped for the night.

XVII
A NOBLE REPARATION

After leaving the Chateau, Roderick Hardinge repaired to his quarters, where he refreshed himself with a copious supper and then arrayed himself in civilian evening dress for his visit to M. Belmont. His mind was intensely occupied with the details of Pauline's conversation at the waterside, but his love for her was so ardent, and he felt so strong in the consciousness of duty accomplished, that he experienced no serious misgivings as to the result of the interview which he was about to hold. His feeling, however was the reverse of enthusiastic. The more he reflected on the incident, the more he appreciated both the extent of M. Belmont's mistake and the profundity of the wound that must rankle in his proud spirit. He, therefore, resolved to hold himself purely on the defensive and to enter upon explanations to the simple extent of direct replies to direct charges. The stake was Pauline herself. On her account he was prepared to push prudence to the limit of his own humiliation, and to make every concession that would not directly clash with his loyalty as a soldier.

Having fully made up his mind on these points, he threw his long military cloak over his shoulders and issued from the barracks. In less than ten minutes, he found himself at the door of M. Belmont's residence. In spite of all his resolution, he paused before the lower step and looked about him with that vague feeling of relief which a moment's delay always afford on the threshold of disagreeable circumstance. The lower portion of the house was silent and dark, but above, a faint light appeared in the window of Pauline's room. In other days, that light had been his beacon and guiding star, beckoning him from every part of the city and attracting him away from the society of all other friends. In other days, when he approached, that light would suddenly rise to the ceiling, flash along the stairway and hall, and meet him glistening at the open door, held high over Pauline's raven hair. But to-night, he knew that he could expect no such welcome. He summoned all his courage, however, and struck the hammer. The door was opened by the maid, but as the vestibule remained in darkness, she did not recognize him.

"Is M. Belmont at home?" he asked in a low voice.

"Yes, sir, he is."

"Is he visible?"

The maid hesitated a moment, then said falteringly, "I will see, sir," and left him standing in the obscure passage.

Without loss of time, M. Belmont himself stepped forward. Bowing stiffly and looking up in the vain attempt to distinguish the features of his visitor, he said:

"To whom am I indebted for this call?"

There was a tone of sarcasm in the query which almost threw Roderick off his guard. He saw that M. Belmont was racked by suspicions and must be approached with caution. He, therefore, extended his right hand and said:

"M. Belmont, do you not know me?"

That gentleman did not accept the proferred hand, but stepping backward and drawing himself up to his full height, exclaimed:

"Lieutenant Hardinge!"

Roderick made a slight inclination, but said nothing. M. Belmont continued:

"Do you come here, sir, in your military capacity?"

For all answer, Hardinge threw open his long cloak.

"Ah! you are in citizen's dress. Then I cannot understand the object of your visit. If you came as an officer of the King, the house would be yours and you could do as you liked. But if you come as a private citizen, I would remind you that this house is mine and that I will do as I like. To-night, I would particularly like not to be disturbed."

This was said with a polite sneer which cut the young officer to the quick, but he contained himself, and began quietly:

"M. Belmont...."

"Sir," was the sharp interruption, "I have given no explanations and require none. You will oblige me by...," and he finished the sentence with a wave of his hand toward the door.

Roderick did not stir, but made another attempt to be heard.

"Really, M. Belmont...."

"Sir, do you mean to force yourself upon me? I know that there is a sort of martial law in the city. You are an officer. You may search my house from cellar to garret. You may quarter yourself in it. You may detain me as a prisoner. In fact, you may do whatever you please. If such is your intention, say so, and I will not resist. But if such is not your intention, I stand by my right of inviolability. Your boast is that every British subject's house is his own castle. My desire is to maintain this privilege in the present instance."

At this third summons of ejection, Hardinge's equanimity was completely shaken, and he was about to turn on his heel when, on looking up, his eye caught the hem of a white dress fluttering at the head of the stair. The sight suddenly altered his determination. Pauline was there listening to the interview upon which the future of both depended, and her presence was omnipotent to nerve his courage, as well as to inspire him with the means of successfully extricating himself from his difficult position. Roderick at once resolved to change his tactics. Drawing his cloak tightly across his chest and flinging the border of the cape over his right shoulder, in the manner of a man who has come to a decision, he said calmly:

"M. Belmont, I cannot be treated thus. I *must* be heard."

These words were slightly emphasized, but without bluster or defiance, and they had a visible effect on the listener, for he immediately folded his arms as if to listen. Hardinge continued:

"It is true, sir, that I came to your house as a private citizen and as a presumed old friend of your family."

M. Belmont uttered a moan and made a gesture of deprecation.

"But since it is plain that my presence in that capacity is distasteful, I will add now that I am also here in my quality as a soldier. The object of my visit is really a military one, and as such I beg you to hear me."

"Why did you not say so at first?" exclaimed M. Belmont with a bitter laugh. "Mr. Hardinge I do not know. Lieutenant Hardinge I cannot choose but hear. Lieutenant, please step into my parlor."

Lights were immediately brought into that apartment and the two took their stand before the fire place, Hardinge having declined a seat. Glancing at M. Belmont, Roderick was shocked at the change that had come upon him within three days. He seemed like another man, his features being pinched, his eyes sunken, and his manner quick and nervous. The normal calm of his demeanor was gone, and his stately courtesy was replaced by a restless petulance of hands. He stood uneasily near the mantel waiting for the young officer to speak. Hardinge at length said:

"M. Belmont, this interview shall be brief, because it is painful to both of us. Indeed, so far as I am concerned, there is only one word to say, and it is this—that, although I have had some important military duties to perform in the last few days, not one of these was or could be directed against you."

M. Belmont looked dubiously at Hardinge and shook his head, but answered nothing. Roderick bit his lip and resumed:

"The statement that I make, sir, though brief, covers the whole ground of your suspicions and accusations. I know what these are and hence my statement is very deliberate. I ask you to accept it as my complete defence."

M. Belmont looked into the fire and still kept silent.

"Must I construe your silence as incredulity, sir? If so, I will instantly leave your house, nevermore to enter it. But before taking what to me will be a fatal step, I must observe that I had never believed that a perfect French gentleman like you, M. Belmont, would doubt the faith of a British officer like me, and my distress will be intensified by the reflection that your daughter, who formerly favored me with her esteem, will hereafter see in me only the brand of dishonor stamped upon my character by her own father. For her sake I will say no more, but take my departure at once."

At these words there were heard the rustling of a dress and suppressed sobs outside the parlor door. Both the men noticed the sounds and instinctively looked at each other. The eyes of Hardinge were suffused with tears, while those of M. Belmont mellowed with an expression of solemn pity.

"Stay, Lieutenant," he said in a low voice. "It strikes me all at once that my silence may possibly be unjust. If I thought your statement embraced all the circumstances of the case, I should not hesitate to accept it, but I fear that you do not know how far my grievances extend."

"I am certain that I know all," said Hardinge in a significant tone, which was not lost upon his interlocutor, who immediately subjoined:

"This can be easily ascertained if you will answer me a few questions. You called upon Lieutenant-Governor Cramahé early on the morning of the seventh?"

"I did so."

"You delivered to him a parcel of letters purporting to have come from Colonel Arnold, the commander of the Bastonnais?"

"Yes, sir."

"Some of those letters were addressed to citizens of Quebec?"

"They were."

"You know the names of those citizens?"

"I do not."

"Did not the Lieutenant-Governor open the letters before you."

"He did."

"And read them?"

"Yes, and read them."

M. Belmont's lip curled in scorn and his eyes darted fire at Hardinge, who responded with a smile:

"The Lieutenant-Governor opened and read the letters in my presence and, after reading, made his comments aloud, but in no instance did he reveal the name of the persons to whom the letters were addressed, so that I am, to this moment, in profound ignorance of them. Except by inference from what has occurred between us, I should not know that one of those letters was addressed to you, and, indeed, as yet I have no positive proof that such was the case."

"Such is the case," cried M. Belmont in a voice of thunder. "I received such a letter and it has brought me into trouble. I was summoned to the Chateau in the face of the whole city. I have been suspected and threatened, and the consequence is that I have been driven to...."

"Stop, M. Belmont," said Hardinge quietly, and interposing his hand. "Tell me nothing of your plans. I do not want to know them. I will do my duty to my King and Country. I believe you will do yours, but should your principles lead you to another course, I prefer to ignore the fact, and thus avoid becoming your enemy."

"You are not and will not be my enemy," exclaimed M. Belmont, clasping the extended hand of Hardinge in both of his, and then embracing him on the cheek. "I owe you a full apology. My suspicions were cruelly unjust, but you have dispelled them. My treatment of you this evening was outrageous, and I beg you to pardon me. Your explanations are thoroughly satisfactory. You did your duty as a soldier in delivering those letters to the Lieutenant-Governor, and even if you had known to whom they were addressed, your obligation would have been no less."

"I did not need to be told my duty," said Hardinge with just a shade of haughtiness, which he immediately qualified by adding, "but I am flattered to know that I have the approval of one who has always appeared to me a model of honor."

"You have my unqualified approval, Lieutenant. Although you were the indirect instrument of the crisis through which I am passing, I am satisfied that you are clear of the imputation of traitor and spy to me which

I had charged upon you in my indignation and despair. We are on the eve of important events. Within a few days war with all its anxieties and horrors will be upon us. You have high duties to perform both as a citizen and a soldier. Perform them with all the energy of your nature. It is your sacred duty. I will watch your course with the deepest interest. Your successes will be a source of personal pleasure to me, and I sincerely trust that no harm will befall you."

Roderick was quite overcome by this cordial speech, which was to him more than a reparation for all he had endured during the interview. He rejoiced, too, at his own perspicacity in having so accurately divined the real cause of M. Belmont's misunderstanding. It was lamentable, indeed, that Arnold's letters which he had delivered to the Lieutenant-Governor should have implicated M. Belmont—if they did implicate him, a fact of which he had yet no proof, and which he still refused to credit—but they had been the means of awakening the authorities to a sense of the peril with which Quebec was threatened, and that was some compensation for what he had suffered. But there was, however, another compensation for which he longed, notwithstanding that the hour was considerably advanced and he had to return to his quarters. Approaching closer to M. Belmont, with a pleasantly malicious smile on his lips, he said:

"I have to thank you, sir, for the kind words which you have spoken. I regard them in the light of the reparation which I knew you would not withhold so soon as you became acquainted with the facts, but you will excuse me for saying that there is just one little thing wanting to make the reparation complete."

M. Belmont looked up in some surprise, but when he saw the expression on Roderick's face, he comprehended the allusion at once, and replied with genuine French good-humor and vivacity:

"Oh, of course, there is a woman in the case. You want to be rehabilitated in the eyes of Pauline as well. It is only just, and it shall be done. I told her all my suspicions against you, and repeated all my charges to her. And, by the way, that reminds me that I never told anybody else about the matter. How, then, pray, did it come to your ears? You must have known of it before you came here to-night."

"I did, sir, and came expressly on that account."

"Who in the world could have told you?"

Hardinge broke out into a hearty laugh. The laugh was re-echoed by a silvery voice in the passage.

"Treason is indeed rampant," roared out M. Belmont, cheerily. "A man's worst enemies are those of his own household." Saying which, he advanced rapidly to the door and opened it wide. Pauline stood before him, her eyes swimming in tears, but with a smile of ineffable joy playing on her white lips.

"Don't embrace me, don't speak to me," said M. Belmont, with mock gravity. "I will hear no explanations. Settle the matter with this gentleman here. If he forgives you, as he has forgiven your father, then I will see what I can do for you."

He went out of the room, leaving Pauline and Roderick together for a full quarter of an hour. There is no need to say that the twain laughed and wept in turns over their victory.

When M. Belmont returned from his cellar, with a choice bottle of old Burgundy, the reconciliation was complete, and that night the happiest hearts in Quebec were those of Roderick Hardinge and Pauline Belmont. M. Belmont was content at having done a good deed, but he was not really happy. Why, the sequel will tell.

XVIII
RODERICK HARDINGE

It was a little before nine o'clock when Hardinge entered his quarters at the barracks. He had passed through an eventful day, and he felt weary. The interview which he had just held with M. Belmont was, however, so absolutely the object of his pre-occupation, that he appeared in nowise disposed to seek the rest required by his exhausted physical powers. Mechanically divesting himself of his civilian costume and assuming the undress uniform of his rank, he moved absently about his little room, muttering to himself, humming fragments of song, and occasionally breaking out into low laughter. Arnold and his rebel crew were clean forgotten, the military events through which he had passed, during the preceding few days, were blotted from his mind, and the coming and going of the troops in the courtyard below completely escaped his attention. It has been said, and with easily assignable cause, that the soldier on the eve of battle is more sensitive to the softer passions of the heart and the oblivion of all else which these passions induce, than any other mortal. Such was the case with Roderick on this evening. He keenly appreciated the extent of the dangers which he had experienced, and the importance of the victory which he had won within the last hour. What to him would have been the glory of arms, the fame of patriotic service, if he had lost Pauline? And—if the whole truth must be told—would the country itself have been worth saving without her?

Roderick Hardinge was seven and twenty years of age. He was a Scotchman by birth, but the best part of his life had been spent in Canada. His father was an officer in Fraser's famous Highland regiment, whose history is so intimately associated with the conquest of New France. After the battle of the Plains of Abraham, in which it took a leading part, his regiment was quartered in the city of Quebec for some time, and when it finally disbanded, most of its members, officers as well as men, settled in the country, having obtained from the Imperial Government large tracts of land in the Gulf region. This colony has made its mark in the history of Canada, and to the present day the Scotch families of Murray Bay rank among the most distinguished in the public annals of the Province. While retaining many of the best characteristics of their origin, they have thoroughly identified themselves with their new home, and by intermarriage with the French natives, have almost completely lost the use of the English language.

Roderick's father imitated the example of many of his brother officers, and in the autumn of 1760, a few weeks after the capitulation of Vaudreuil at Montreal, and the definitive establishment of British power in Canada, he resigned his position in the army, and settled on a fine domain in Montmagny, a short distance from Quebec, on the south shore of the St. Lawrence. Thither he summoned his family from Scotland. Roderick, his only son, was twelve years of age when he landed in Canada, and thus grew up as a child of the soil. He never left the country afterwards, and, on the death of his parents, he succeeded to the paternal estates which he greatly improved, and cultivated with considerable success. Much of his leisure time was spent in the city of Quebec where his position, wealth and accomplishments procured him admission into the most select circles of the small but exclusive capital. From the circumstances of the times, the French language was almost more familiar to him than the English, and the reader will have readily understood that most of the conversations, which we have represented him as holding, were carried on in that language. This was more particularly the case in his intercourse with Pauline and her father, neither of whom spoke a word of English.

When the first news of the invasion of Canada by the Continentals reached his ears, he immediately abandoned his estates to the care of his old friend Donald, and buckling on his father's sword, rode in haste to Quebec, and enrolled himself in the service. The remnants of Fraser's Highlanders, with other recruits, were formed into a regiment, called the Royal Emigrants, under Colonel Allan McLean, and we should naturally have expected that Roderick would have joined it, but for some reason or other, he did not do so. He took a regular commission in a regiment of Quebec militia, commanded by Colonel Caldwell. It was in this capacity that he performed the notable services which we have recorded in the preceding chapters.

Roderick Hardinge was tall, robust, athletic and active. He was very fond of field sports. He had made many a tramp on snow-shoes with the *coureurs des bois* far into the heart of the wilderness. He had often wandered for months with some of the young Hurons of Lorette in quest of the deer and the bison. He was a magnificent horseman, as his ride to Three Rivers has proven.

His education had not been neglected, and his good native parts were well cultivated by the instruction of his father and the best tuition which the learned French ecclesiastics of Quebec could impart. He was very fair complexioned, with flossy hair and flaxen beard. As man is usually ruled by contrast, this was probably the reason why he loved the dark-tressed, brown-eyed Pauline. He was ten years her senior, and had known her from her childhood, but his florid air and perfect health made him look much younger, and, as the two walked together, there appeared no undue disparity of age.

Roderick had just fastened the last button of his fatigue jacket when there was a call at the door, and Donald entered the room. After a few words of hearty greeting, he informed his master that his reconnoitering of the rebels was over, and that they would speak for themselves the next day. He stated that he had just come from the Chateau, where he had conveyed that intelligence to the Lieutenant-Governor. Hardinge thanked him for his diligence and fidelity, and as a recompense, in answer to an inquiry of Donald, ordered him not to return to the farm, but remain in the city to take part in its defence. While the country was in danger the Montmagny estate might take care of itself.

XIX
THE FRIGHTENED DOVES

Pauline had few or no misgivings. Her little being was all heart, and her mind could not grasp the significance of the political events which passed before her eyes, and on which her future more or less depended. For her, loyalty to France consisted simply in reverence and obedience towards her father. For her, fealty to the King did not extend much beyond love for his handsome, manly representative, Roderick Hardinge. Happy woman that need not walk beyond the beautiful round of the affections. Noble woman whose heroism is purely of the heart, not of the head. There are many species of martyrdom, but that of mere love is the grandest in the concentration of its own singleness.

After Roderick's departure, Pauline felt the need of being alone for a brief period in order to go over quietly in her own conscience all the varied pathetic scenes of that evening. It was not a process of analysis. Her mind was incapable of that. It was merely a quiet rehearsal of all the facts, that their vividness might be made more vivid, and their effect brought home more tenderly to her heart. For a long hour she sat on the foot of her bed, now weeping, now smiling, now tossing her lovely head backwards, then burying her sweet face in her hands. At times a shadow would flit over the delicate features, but it would soon be replaced by a glamor of serenity, until finally her whole demeanor settled into an air of prayerful content. Her hands joined upon her knee, her brow was bent, and her lips murmured words of gratitude. Beautiful Pauline! Sitting there with inclined body, and her whole being divided between her love on the earth and her duty to heaven, she was the true type of the loveable woman.

It was eleven o'clock at the small ivory clock over the mantel, when a scratch was heard at the door. What was Pauline's surprise, on answering the call, to see little Blanche step into the room.

"Why, my little wood-flower, what could have brought you here to-night?" she exclaimed.

The child sidled up to her godmother and did not answer at first, but there was that in her eye which at once led to suspicion that everything was not right. Her very presence there at such an hour was the indication of an unusual event, for Pauline knew that Blanche had never passed a night out of Batoche's cabin.

"Are you alone, my dear?" she asked.

"Oh no, godmother, grandfather is with me."

"Where?"

"Down stairs."

"And is any one with him?"

"Yes, M. Belmont is with him. He came to see M. Belmont."

These words somewhat reassured Pauline. She knew that Batoche seldom, if ever, came to the city, but probably the circumstances of the time forced him to do so this night, and he had carried his granddaughter with him in case he should have to tarry too long. She, therefore, proceeded to unfasten the child's hood and cloak.

"Come to the fire," she said, "and warm yourself, while I get you some cakes and sweets from the cup-board."

As she said this, she noticed the same peculiar look in the eyes of the little girl.

"Tell me, Blanche, what is the matter?" she asked.

"I don't know, godmother, except that I must spend the night with you."

"Spend the night with me? Well, that is right. I will take good care of you, my dear. But are you sure of what you say? Who told you so?"

"M. Belmont himself."

"My father sent you up to me."

"Yes, and he said I must remain with you until he and grandfather called for me."

"And they are both downstairs?"

The child's face put on that strange look again, as she answered:

"They were there just now, but—"

A great fear fell on the heart of poor Pauline. She knew instinctively that something was amiss.

"Come down with me, Blanche," she whispered, taking the child by the hand and leading her, on tip-toe, to the lower rooms. There was silence in the

passage. The lights in the parlor were extinguished. The sitting apartment behind was deserted. Her father's cap and great coat were gone from their hooks in the hall. She went to the maid's room and found the girl fast asleep, in consequence of which there was no information to be obtained from that quarter. She went to the front door and looked out upon the street. She could easily distinguish the footprints of men in the snow on the steps, and the trace of a carriole's runners describing a sharp curve from the edge of the sidewalk.

"They are gone," she murmured.

And folding Blanche in her embrace, she returned to her chamber.

"Don't cry, little godmother," said Blanche, throwing her arms around Pauline's neck. "Grandfather told me he would come for me before morning."

Just then the muffled tread of soldiers was heard along the street, and low words of command reached the listening ears of Pauline. She understood that something momentous was going on. She closed her shutters tight, drew down the heavy curtains of her windows, mended the fire on the hearth, and crouching there, on low seats, like two frightened doves, she and Blanche awaited the coming of the dawn.

XX
THE SPECTRAL ARMY

After leaving the banquet hall, the Lieutenant-Governor immediately set about acting upon the important intelligence which he had received from Donald. Now that the long suspense was over, and that the threatened invasion of the Bastonnais had become a reality, he felt himself imbued with the energy demanded by the occasion. Some of the ancient chroniclers, Sanguinet more particularly, have accused Mr. Cramahé of remissness in preparing for the defence of Quebec, but the researches we have made, in the composition of the present work, convince us that the charge is only partially true. He acted slowly in the earlier stages of the campaign because he shared the general disbelief in the seriousness of the Continental attack. Montgomery's movement from the west he had no pressing reasons to dread, inasmuch as that officer was confronted in the Montreal district by the Governor-General and Commander-in-Chief, Guy Carleton himself. Carleton had nearly emptied Quebec of regular troops for his army, and as long as he employed them in keeping back Montgomery, Cramahé had really little or no responsibility to bear. Arnold's march from the east, through the forests of Maine, was known to be aimed directly at Quebec, but the Canadians of that day, who understood all the hardships and perils of winter in the primeval woods, had no idea that Arnold's column would ever reach its destination. And, as we shall see, in the next book, when describing the principal episodes of this heroic march, there was every good reason for the scepticism.

But when at length, after many contradictory rumors and much false information which would have bewildered any commander, Cramahé learned from the intercepted letters of Arnold, and from the volunteer reconnoitering of such faithful men as Donald, that the Continental army was really approaching Quebec, it is due to the memory of a worthy officer, even in these pages of romance, to say that he acted with judgment and activity in making all the preliminary preparations necessary to protect Quebec, until the arrival of Governor Carleton, and reinforcements of regular troops.

After leaving the banquet hall, he put on his uniform, and wrapping himself closely in his military cloak, he resolved upon making a personal inspection of all the defensive posts of the city. He first repaired to the barracks in Cathedral-square, where he had a brief conference with the principal officers. He next visited every gate and the approaches to the citadel, where he was pleased to find that the sentries were unusually alert, and quite alive to the exigencies of the situation, without precisely knowing what they were. The Lieutenant-Governor then walked down into the darkness of Lower Town and wandered a long time in silence along the dusky bank of the St. Lawrence.

About three o'clock in the morning a sleigh drew up at the door of a large square house in a retired street. Two men issued from it, one middle-aged, erect and dressed in rather costly furs; the other old, thin and arrayed like an Indian hunter, with a large fox-skin cap on his head. As they stepped across the footpath from the sleigh to the front steps of the mansion, a tall muffled figure stalked slowly on the other side of the street.

"It is the Governor," whispered the younger man to his companion. "I know his stature and carriage! Let us enter."

"I wonder what Belmont is doing out at this unseasonable hour," muttered the tall man in the folds of his cloak. And he walked on, while the door of the mansion closed with a thud upon the two sleighmen.

It was five o'clock on the morning of the 10th November, 1775. The first faint light of the morning was touching the tops of the far mountains. The air was frosty, with indications of snow.

Two men stood at an angle of the ramparts, on the highest point of the citadel of Quebec. They were looking eastward.

"See, Lieutenant," said one pointing his gloved hand across the river.

"Ay, there they are, Your Excellency, issuing from the woods and ascending the hill," replied the other.

"They are *on* the hill, swarming up in hundreds," rejoined the Governor.

Cramahé pressed the hand of Hardinge, and the two descended rapidly but silently into the city. On their way, they heard the confused mutter of the streets:

"The Bastonnais have come!"

Yes, there they were. Arnold's men stood like a spectral army on the Heights of Levis.

BOOK II
THE THICKENING OF THE CLOUDS

I
ZULMA SARPY

It was a damp bleak morning, and the snow was falling fast. Zulma Sarpy sat in her bedroom, indolently stretched upon a rocking chair before a glowing fire. She was attired in a white morning dress, or *peignoir*, slightly unbuttoned at the collar, and revealing the glories of a snowy columnar neck, while the hem, negligently raised, displayed two beautiful slippered feet half buried in the plush of a scarlet cushion. Her abundant yellow hair, thrown back in banks of gold over the forehead and behind the rosy ears, was gathered in immense careless coils behind her head and kept in position by a towering comb of pearl. Her two arms were raised to the level of her head, and the two hands held on languidly to the ivory knobs at the top of the chair. On the second finger of the left hand was a diamond ring that flashed like a star. The whole position of the lovely lounger brought out her grand bust into full relief.

Beside her stood a little round table supported on three carven feet of exquisite workmanship, and covered by a beautiful netting of crimson lace. On the table was an open book and several trinkets of female toilet. The table gave the key to the rest of the furniture of the apartment, which was massive, highly wrought and of deep rich colors. The tapestries of the wall were umber and gold; the hangings of the bed and windows were a modulated purple. The room had evidently been arranged with artistic design, and just such a one would be employed to exhibit a statue of white marble to the best effect. Zulma Sarpy was this living, breathing model, fair as a filament of summer gorse, and statuesque in all her poses.

She had been educated in France, according to the custom of many of the wealthy families of the Colony. Although confined for five years—from the age of fourteen to that of nineteen—in the rigid and aristocratic convent of Picpus, she had been enabled to see much of Paris life, during the waning

epoch of Louis XVI's reign and the times of morbid fashionable excitement immediately preceding the great Revolution. Her natural disposition, and the curiosity incident to her previous Colonial training, led her to mingle with keen interest in all the forms of French existence, and her character was so deeply impressed by it that when she returned to her Canadian home, a few months before our introduction to her, she was looked upon very much in the light of an exotic. Yet was the heart of Zulma really unspoiled. Her instincts and principles were true. She by no means regarded herself as out of place in her native country, but, on the contrary, felt that she had a mission to fill in it, and, having had more than one opportunity of honorable alliance in France, preferred returning to Canada and spending her days among her own people.

But she had to be taken as she was. If the good simple people around her did not understand her ways, she could afford to leave them in their wonderment without apology or explanation. The standing of her family was so high, and her own spirit so independent, that she felt that she could trace out her own course, without yielding to the narrow and antiquated notions of those whose horizon for generations had never extended beyond the blue line of the St. Lawrence.

Was she thinking of these very things this morning, as she lounged before the fire? Perhaps so. But if she did, the thoughts had no palpable effect upon her. Rather, we fancy, were her thoughts straying upon the incident of three days before, when she had that rattling ride with the handsome British Lieutenant and distanced him out of sight. That glance in her great blue eyes was a reflection of the one which she cast upon the youthful horseman through the little window squares of the farmer's house. That tap of the slippered foot, on the edge of the shining fender, was the gentle stimulant she administered to her pony's flank as he leaped forward to win the race. That smothered, saucy laugh which bubbled on her red, ripe lips was an echo of the peal which greeted Hardinge when he pronounced the name of "Zulma," at the road gate. And as she rolled her fine head slowly to and fro on the velvet bosses of the back of her chair, was she not meditating some further design on the heart of the loyal soldier? Conspiracies deeper than that, designs of love that have rocked kingdoms to their foundation have been formed by languid beauties, recumbent in the soft recesses of their easy chairs.

Zulma had reached the culminating point of her revery and was gradually gliding down the quiet declivities of reaction, when she was aroused by a great uproar in the lower part of the house. She did not at first pay much attention to it, but as the sound grew louder and she recognized the voice of her father, speaking in loud tones of alarm, she sat up in her chair and listened with concern. Presently some one rushed up the stair and precipitated himself into the apartment, without so much as rapping at the door. It was her brother, a youth of about her age, who was at school at the Seminary of Quebec. He evidently had just arrived, being still wrapped up in a blue flannel coat, trimmed with red cloth, hood of the same material, buckskin leggings and rough hide boots. He gave himself a vigorous shake, like a Newfoundland just emerged from the water, and stamped upon the floor to throw off the particles of snow adhering to his feet.

"What means all this disturbance, Eugene?" asked Zulma, holding out one hand, and turning her head over the side of the chair, till her face looked up to the ceiling.

"Oh, nothing, except that the rebels have come!" was the rejoinder, as the youth walked up to his sister, and dropped globules of snow from his gloves into her eyes.

"The what have come?"

"Why, the rebels."

"You mean the Americans."

"Americans or rebels,—what is the difference?"

"A world of difference. The Americans are not rebels. They are freemen, battling for their rights."

"We have been taught at the Seminary to call them rebels."

"Then you have been taught wrong."

Zulma had risen out of her chair, and stood up in front of the fire, with a glow of enthusiasm on her cheek. She would doubtless have continued to deliver her ideas on the subject, but her young brother evidently took no particular interest in it, and this circumstance, which did not escape her quick eye, suddenly brought her back to more practical questions.

"Where have the Americans arrived?"

"At Point Levis."

"When did they arrive?"

"This morning, early."

"Have you seen them?"

"They are quite visible on the heights, moving to and fro, and making all kinds of signs toward the city. The whole of Quebec turned out to look at them, the scholars of the Seminary along with the rest. After I had seen the fellows, the Superior of the Seminary called me aside, and directed me to take a sleigh, and come at once to notify you."

"Notify me?" said Zulma, arching her brows. "M. Le Superieur is very amiable."

"Well, not you exactly," said Eugene, laughing, "but the family."

"Oh!" exclaimed she. "That is different. I never saw your Superior in my life, and I do not know that he is aware of my humble existence."

"There you are mistaken. Our Superior knows all about you, your tricks, your oddities, your French notions; and he often speaks to me of you. He is especially aware that you are a rebel, and is much grieved thereat."

"Rebel! There is that hateful word again."

"I thought you liked it, when applied to yourself. You told me as much the last time."

Zulma laughed and seemed propitiated, but she said no more. Her brother then told her that their father was considerably agitated at the news. He was particularly alarmed lest his son should be exposed by remaining in the city, and thought of withdrawing him from the Seminary during the impending siege. What did Zulma think of it?

"When do you return to Quebec?" was the abrupt query.

"I will return at once, and father is going with me."

"I will go too. I want to see these Americans for myself, and then I will tell you what I think of your staying at the Seminary, or the reverse. Go down stairs, while I make ready."

When Zulma was alone, it did not take her long to prepare herself for the journey. All her languor had departed. The idle fooling in which she had indulged during the previous hours was replaced by an earnest activity in moving about her room. Her fingers were skilful and rapid in the arrangement of her dress. In less than a quarter of an hour, she walked up to the mirror for the last indispensable feminine glance. And what a magnificent picture she was. In her sky-blue robe of velvet, with pelisse of immaculate ermine, and hood of the same material, quilted with azure silk, her beautiful face and queenly proportions were brought out with ravishing effect. Encasing her hands in gauntlets, she went down to meet her father and brother, and a moment later, the three rode away at a brisk pace in the direction of Quebec.

II
FAST AND LOOSE

Pointe-aux-Trembles, or Aspen Point, in the vicinity of which stood the mansion and the estates of the Sarpy family, is a little more than twenty miles above Quebec, on the north shore of the St. Lawrence. The road which connects it with the city follows pretty regularly the sinuous line of the river. Over this route the sleigh bearing Sieur Sarpy, with his daughter Zulma and his son Eugene, had travelled rapidly and without interruption till it reached an elevated point, two or three miles outside of Quebec, overlooking Wolfe's Cove and commanding a full view of the Heights of Levis. Here Sieur Sarpy reined in his horse.

"Do you see them?" exclaimed Eugene, standing up in the sleigh, and pointing across the river.

"I see nothing," responded his father. "The snow is blowing in our faces, and my old eyes are very feeble."

Zulma remained buried in her buffalo robes and said nothing, but her eyes were fixed intently at the distant summits, and her face bore an expression of the most earnest interest.

"They are moving up and down," resumed Eugene, "as if busy storing their provisions and ammunition. But they are very indistinct. I wonder if they see us better than we see them?"

"They do," said his father. "The wind is behind them and they are not incommoded by the drift."

After a pause, Eugene added:

"They seem to have no general uniform. They must belong to different corps. Some have no uniform at all. Their appearance is not much that of soldiers, and there are a good many small, young fellows among them."

"It must be the effect of refraction," said Zulma, in a low voice and with a sneer. "But to me they seem like giants, towering on the heights and stretching great arms toward us."

"In menace?" queried the Sieur with a strange affectionate look at his daughter.

"That depends," she whispered smiling, but immediately subjoined:

"Let us drive on, papa."

A few minutes afterwards they reached the city. For some reason or other Zulma declined accompanying her father and brother to the Seminary. The pretext which she gave was that she had a few purchases to make in the shops. But probably her real object was to visit some of her friends and ascertain the real condition of things. Whether she did so or not we need not stop to inquire, but an hour later she met Sieur Sarpy and Eugene at the place agreed upon between them, to learn the decision that they had come to.

"My fate is in your hands," said the youth opening the conversation in high good humor. "You promised to give me your advice after you had set your eyes on those gentlemen yonder, and now I have come to receive it."

"Yes," said the father, "we have determined to submit the matter to your arbitration. Shall Eugene remain at the Seminary, or shall he return with us?"

"What does M. Le Superieur say?" asked Zulma.

"He thoroughly appreciates the gravity of the situation. He believes there will be a siege, perhaps a bloody one, certainly a long one. He has strong opinions about the duty of every able-bodied man assisting in the defence of the city. The young children he will send back to their parents, but, at eighteen, Eugene ought to be accounted a man. He would remain at the Seminary, one of the safest asylums in the city, always under the eye of his tutors, and his studies would not be interrupted. But he might do some minor military service all the same, and in the event of a great emergency could help to swell the ranks of the troops. The Superior thinks that practically he would be more secure within the city than out of it. At home, he might be harassed by solicitations from the enemy, and draw down upon us a great deal of annoyance."

At this Zulma smiled.

"And," added her father, "you know that, at my age, and with my infirmities, I must have peace and quiet. From the beginning of these hostilities, I have vowed neutrality, and I would not like to see it disturbed."

Zulma's manner changed at these words. She looked at her father with a mingled air of tenderness and determination, and said:

"What does Eugene think about it? Surely if he is old enough to fight, he ought to be old enough to know his own mind and to be consulted."

The boy's answer was not very distinct. He did not seem to have any opinions. His ideas were decidedly hazy about the King's right to his allegiance, or the claims of the rebels to his sympathy. But there was good blood in the fellow, and his uppermost thought evidently was that it would be a grand thing for him to do a little fighting. Quebec was his native city; everybody in it knew him, and he knew everybody. Perhaps it would be as well if he joined in its defence.

"Then stay here," exclaimed Zulma peremptorily.

She added that she would take proper care of her father, and that Eugene need have no solicitude on that score. In the meantime, things had not come to the worse; perhaps, it would take even weeks before the siege commenced, and they would have ample time to communicate with each other again.

After this conference, Eugene accompanied his father and sister to the street where their sleigh awaited them. The three were engaged in a few parting words, when a young British officer passed hurriedly along. He would certainly have gone on without noticing them, had not one of Zulma's gauntlets fallen on the side-path at his feet. Was it accidental or was it a challenge? Who shall tell? But whatever it was, the officer stooped immediately for the glove, and handed it to the owner with a profound salutation. Roderick Hardinge then recognized the beautiful amazon.

There was time for the interchange of only a few words between them.

"Lieutenant," said Zulma, with that bright laugh which had so enchanted Roderick the first time he heard it, "I have the honor of presenting to you a loyal soldier in the person of my brother, who has just decided upon entering the service in defence of the city."

"I am proud to hear that. Eugene and I are old friends, and I am glad to know that we shall now be brothers in arms."

"But, Lieutenant," continued Zulma, "you will perhaps be surprised to learn that he has acted thus at my recommendation."

"Indeed! That is certainly an agreeable surprise. I may then be justified in hoping that you too, mademoiselle, will take part in our cause."

"That is quite a different matter. Before I take, I must be taken, you know," with another merry laugh.

"You mean that before we take you — —."

"You must catch me."

"I own that is hard to do, considering my first experience, but it will be done all the same."

"Never!" exclaimed Zulma, with a flush on her cheek.

"I repeat it—and mark me—it *shall* be done."

And after a little more pleasantry, the party separated.

On their way homeward, Sieur Sarpy lightly questioned his daughter. He knew the strength of her character, the high metal of her temper. Her words with Hardinge, all playful as they appeared on the surface, had, he was certain, a deeper significance. But this wonderful girl was dearly affectionate, in the midst of all her follies, and she would not grieve her father by telling him the secret of the thoughts which had moved her bosom since the morning. He had pleaded for quietude during the unquiet days that were coming. She was resolved he should have it in so far as it depended upon her. At least it was much too early in the day to vex his mind with forebodings. She therefore comforted and calmed him by words of assurance, and, when he crossed his threshold, that evening, the lonely old man felt that he was indeed secure under the protection of his daughter.

III
THE SHEET-IRON MEN

The next morning the snowfall had ceased, and although the sky remained lowering, there was no sign of a storm. Indeed, it was still too early in the season for frequent or abundant snow. The climate of Canada has this peculiarity which meteorologists have failed to explain—that whereas, in other parts of the continent, such as the north-west, and even so far down the Mississippi Valley as St. Louis, the winter temperature has moderated with the clearing of the forests and the cultivation of the soil, in Canada it remains precisely the same as it was two and three hundred years since. A comparison of the daily registers kept at present with those diurnally consigned in the Relations of the Jesuits, shows—as the historian Ferland tells us—that, day for day and month for month, the indications of the thermometer in 1876, for instance, tally with those of 1776. At the present time, in Canada, although the cold really begins to be felt in the beginning of November, the winter is not regarded as having finally set in till the 25th of the month. That is known as St. Catharine's day, and its peculiar celebration will be described further on, being connected with one of the episodes of our story. The last month of the autumn of 1775 may therefore be supposed to have followed the general rule. Indeed, we know from the records that it was, if any thing, milder than usual, and that the winter was uncommonly tardy, a vessel having sailed from Quebec for Europe as late as the 31st December.

As we have said, the weather, on the particular morning on which we write, was cold but calm. The snow lay crisp and hard upon the level places; in the hollows and gorges it was piled in light fleecy banks. The atmosphere was of that quality that, although it had a sting when first it was faced, so soon as the ears, hands, cheeks, and other exposed parts got used to it, the whole system felt a pleasureable glow of buoyancy. It was capital weather to work in, and so a number of sturdy farmer's wives, residing on the north bank, a little above Quebec, gathered at the river to do their washing. They had on immense quilted mob-caps, with large outstanding ears, petticoats of thick blue or purple woollen, the work of their own hands, heavy stockings to match, and pattens lined with flannel. A great double handkerchief, of flowery design, was set upon their broad shoulders, covering their necks and crossed over their voluminous bosoms; but there was free play left to the arms, which flushed with rosy color under the influence of work and weather. A broad board fastened to the bank, jutted out five or six feet into the water, and was supported there at a proper level by a solid trestle. A boat was attached to this primitive jetty, and there was besides a small building of rude timber, which served for the women to boil their clothes in, or hang them up to dry.

Four women were working together along one plank, and of course there was continuous talk among them. But whenever the conversation became more than usually animated, or they would fall to disagreeing among themselves, they would call out to their companions who were similarly working and talking some yards away to the right and left.

One lively old girl, who was striking her pallet so hard on a bombed bundle of yellowish clothes, that meshes of brown hair broke from under her cap and fluttered on her forehead, seemed to be the oracle of the party.

"Perhaps this will be the last time we shall wash clothes here. Those are terrible fellows who have come. They call them Bastonnais. They come from very far, and are very bad men. They will burn our houses and barns. They will empty our cellars and granaries. I saw M. le Curé yesterday, and he told me that we will have to shut ourselves up, and not show our faces, because ... you know."

"Pshaw, Josephine," said another, "it will not be so bad as that. My old man says that they are like other men. I'm not afraid. I will talk to them. I am sure there are some pretty fellows among them."

"Marguerite is always a coquette," continued a third. "But she will have no chance. These strangers are poor, lean, broken-down, and badly dressed. They are not soldiers at all, like the men at the citadel. No lace, no gold tape, no epaulettes, no feathers in their hats. The officers have no swords, and many of the soldiers are without muskets. Men like that I would not allow to approach me, and if they come to our house, I will dance them out with this paddle."

Saying which, the speaker fell to, beating her clothes with renewed vigor.

The youngest and prettiest of the four women having listened to all this, straightened herself up from her tub, and placing her arms akimbo, said:

"Pierriche" — meaning her husband — "was in the city all yesterday afternoon. You know Pierriche is a great talker, and likes to know all the news. Every time he goes to the city he has enough to talk about for a week afterwards. Well, do you know what he says? He is such a hoaxer, such a *blagueur*, that I did not believe him, and hardly believe him now, but he swore to me that it was true."

"What was it?" asked her three companions simultaneously.

"Well, he said that after he had been in the city a little while, and sold what was in his sleigh, he thought he would take a stroll into Lower Town. There he met a lot of his friends, and one of his cousins from Levis. And they told him...."

"What did they tell him?" asked the three women, who had now abandoned their work and gathered around the speaker.

"Well, you know all the boats were taken away from the other side of the river, but these men were so frightened that they ran down the bank till they came opposite the Isle of Orleans. Then making a kind of raft with a few logs they got over to the Island. There they found boats which took them to the city. And they immediately spread the news of what they had seen."

"What had they seen?" queried the excited women. "You are provoking, Matilde, with your long story."

"You will not believe me."

"I'll believe everything," said one.

"I'll believe nothing," said another.

"Never mind what we will believe. Only tell us what it is," said the third.

"Well, they told Pierriche that these Bastonnais are terrible men, tall and strong. They suffer neither cold nor heat. Nothing can hurt them, neither powder, nor ball."

"And why not?"

"Because...."

Here the pretty housewife paused suddenly, and with a look of mingled fear and surprise, pointed to the river. Her companions turned and saw a light birch-bark canoe, shooting out from the opposite shore and directed for mid-stream. Three men were in it.

"There!" said the first speaker. "Just what Pierriche said. Look at them. Look especially at that tall man sitting in the stern. The boat is approaching very quick. See, he raises his cap and salutes us."

"What a handsome fellow," said Marguerite.

"Yes, but look at his dress and that of his companions," exclaimed the others.

"Just what Perriche said," repeated the first.

"They are devils, not men," cried out a second.

"Just what Pierriche said. They are clad in sheet-iron."

"Yes, that is true. Sheet-iron men!"

And the frightened women, leaving the clothes on the jetty, fled precipitately up the bank.

The boat described a wide semi-circle in the river, and the young man sitting at the stern swept the north shore with a field glass. It was Cary Singleton, an officer of Morgan's riflemen, one of the chief corps of Arnold's army. He had been sent to reconnoitre.

Morgan's riflemen were all tall, stalwart men from Virginia and Maryland, and they were dressed in tunics of grey unbleached linen. The French would say *vêtus de toile*. But the panic of their sudden arrival, at Levis, changed *toile* into *tôle*, and the whole country side rang with the cry of "sheet-iron men." The amusing incident is historic.

IV
BIRCH AND MAPLE

Arnold's men stood like a spectral army on the Heights of Levis, but unlike spectres they did not vanish in the full glare of the light. After gazing their fill upon the renowned city which they had come so far to see—its beetling citadel, its winding walls, its massive gates, the peaked roofs of its houses, the tall steeples of its churches, the graceful campaniles of its numerous convents—they set actively to the work of attack which remained as the culmination of their heroic march through the wilderness. The enchantment of distance had now vanished, and the reality of vision was before them. Arnold had the quick insight of the born commander. He understood that he could accomplish nothing from Levis. The broad St. Lawrence rushed by him with a sullen moan of warning, isolating him effectually from Quebec. He had no artillery. There were no boats. An ice-bridge was out of the question for at least two months to come. And yet he saw his way clear. He must cross to the north shore. He must attack Quebec. The prize was worth even a desperate attempt. If he took Quebec before Montgomery joined him, his name would be immortalized. He would rank with Wolfe; indeed, considering the exiguity of his means, his feat would surpass that of Wolfe. The capture of Montreal would be glory enough for Montgomery. That of Quebec belonged of right to Benedict Arnold. If there were risks, there were also chances. The regulars were away. The walls were manned only by raw militia. Lieutenant-Governor Cramahé was no soldier. The French inhabitants of the city were at least apathetic Many of the English residents were positively the friends of the Continental cause.

Yes, Arnold must cross the river, and that speedily. On the very afternoon of his arrival, he ordered Morgan, the commander of the rifle corps, to prepare a number of canoes without delay. With the assistance of some Indians who were hanging around the camp in quest of fire-water and other booty, a squad of Morgan's men, under the command of Cary Singleton, repaired to the neighboring woods skirting the river, and there proceeded to strip the oldest and girthiest birch trees. Autumn is not so favorable a time as spring for the stripping and preparing of birch bark, but the result is satisfactory enough provided the frost has not penetrated too deep into the heart of the tree.

The maple and the birch are the kings of the Canadian forest. Two strong, tall, unbending trees, they stand as fit pillars to the entrance of a boreal climate. For fuel they rank first on the market of hard woods, and each has its special advantage. The maple is rather more appreciated for its heating properties; the birch is decidedly more valuable for its ash. The ash of the birch is a fair thing to see, white as snow and soft under the touch as flour. The leaf of the maple and bark of the birch are national emblems in Canada, and it is well that they should be, for they are both associated with the history of the country, and enter largely into its domestic comforts. The annals of New France may be compared to an album of maple leaves bound in a scroll of birchen bark, and a contemporary writer in Quebec has adopted the idea for the title of one of his works. The solid beams of the Canadian house are hewn out of columns of birch, as sound if not so fragrant as the cedar of Lebanon, and the furniture of the Canadian home is wrought of bird-eye maple, susceptible of the velvetest polish, and more beautiful, because more variagated, than walnut or mahogany.

Every season of the year has its peculiar amusements, and among a people of primitive habits, these amusements are gone through with a kind of religious observance. There is the hay-time in summer when, under the sultry sky, and amid the strong scents of the hardier field-flowers, the huge wain is driven from the stubble field into the shadows of the impending woods, and around it the workers sing and make merry in token of joy for the abundant yield of sweet grass that shall fatten the kine in the drear barren months of snow. The young men rest on their scythes, that glisten like Turkish sabres, and, from under their broad-brimmed hats of straw, the town girls smile, as they tress garlands of garish flowers to bind the last and the largest of the sheaves.

In autumn, there is the season of the harvest with its traditional ceremonies of a religious or convivial nature. The granary is decorated up to the roof in hangings of odorous verdure, and the barn floor is cleared for the dance of the weary feet that have long toiled in the five acre. Under the crescent moon, in those mild September evenings, the old superstitions of the Saxon Druids are repeated, while many a beautiful Norma, crowned with vervain and mistletoe, a gleaming sickle in her hand, and her eyes filled with the prophetic light of love, reigns a queen over the honest loving hearts of swains who lay at her feet the brightest wisps of the upland. And the humble Ruth is there, too, with her sweet patient face, and her timid look fixed on the generous Boaz who allowed her to pick the gleanings of his golden corn.

Winter also has its feasts and its holidays. No where better than in arctic climates are these celebrated by persons of every age and sex. There are innumerable games and pastimes around the fire, where the wildest merriment drives away the tedium of the long wintry night. Stories are told, songs are sung, tricks are played. There is dancing in the lighted hall; there is love making in the dark corners; and to crown the festival there is a sleigh-ride under the cold moon, when the music of the bells, the tramping of the hoofs, the shouts of the drivers, and the shrill whistle of the Northern blast, are to the buoyant spirits of the young promenaders like draughts of exhilarating wine.

In Canada, all these pleasant rural ceremonies of the old countries are well preserved. And it is the only portion of this continent where they are to be met with.

The American who has read of them, but has never witnessed them in Europe, can find them faithfully reproduced in Canada.

But in spring, Canadians have a pastime peculiar to themselves, furnished by their own climate. It is the season of sugar-making. At the period in which the events of our story occurred, the cultivation of the maple was much more extensive than now, but even at present it is sufficiently well maintained to enable a traveller to study all its picturesqueness and charm. In Vermont, New Hampshire, Michigan and Wisconsin, the maple is cultivated, but in such a matter-of-fact, mercantile fashion, that there is no rural poetry in the process.

The maples stand in an area of half an acre. Each one is notched at the height of about a foot or a foot and a half from the ground. A piece of shingle is fastened in the lips of the wound, at an angle of forty-five, and down this trickle the sweet waters in a trough set at the foot of each tree. There stand the forest wives distilling their milk, while the white sunlight rests on their silver trunks and the soft winds of March dally with their leafless branches. The sugarman has his eye fixed on each of them, and as fast as the urns are filled, he empties them into a large vessel preparatory to boiling. In an open space, towards the centre of the area, is a huge cauldron dangling from a hob, and under it crackles a fire of pine and tamarac. At a little distance from this stands the cabin of the proprietor, where are stowed away all the utensils necessary for sugar-making. There too his hammock swings, for during the whole period when the maple bleeds, he lives like an Indian in the forest.

Presently the sound of voices is heard coming up the slopes, and in a short time the whole party that has been invited to the sugar-festival finds itself collected under the maples. They bring with them baskets of provisions, hams and shoulders, eggs, and the indispensable allowance of strong waters.

"The first thing to be done, my friends," cries the host to his guests, "is to drink the health of the forest wives in a draught of maple water."

And immediately tin cups are applied to the notches. When they are filled, the toast is drunk with all the honors.

"Now," resumes the host, "come up to the cauldron and get your share of the syrup."

One by one, the guests approach the huge vessel where the maple water is boiling and bubbling. Each one holds in his hand a wooden basin filled with fresh clean snow, and into that the hospitable host ladles out the golden stream. With the accompaniment of new bread, this dish is delicious, for it is peculiar to the maple sugar and syrup that they do not satiate, much less nauseate, as other saccharine compositions do.

After this preliminary repast, the guests indulge in various amusements. The older folks sit together at the cabin door, chatting of their youthful frolics in former sugar-making days, while the young people sing, flirt, promenade and enjoy themselves as only the young know how. Some of the more active go about gathering dry branches and wood to keep up the fire, and others saunter a little out of sight on a visit to the demijohns which they have hidden behind the rocks.

After a time, the host gives the signal for taffy-making. This part of the fun is reserved for the girls. They throw aside their mantles, push back their hoods, tuck up their sleeves and plunge their white fingers into the rapidly cooling masses of syrup. The mechanical process of drawing the arms backwards and forwards is in itself an uninteresting occupation, but somehow under these Canadian maples, in that bracing mountain atmosphere, and amid all the accessories of this peculiar vernal pic-nic, taffy-making is an exhilarating, picturesque amusement. The girls get ruddy with the exertion; they pant, they strain, they duck their heads when their lovers creep behind to steal a kiss, or they run after the shameless robber and slap his naughty cheeks with their sticky palms. Under the rapid kneading the dark syrup becomes glossier, then it reddens, next it grows a golden hue, till finally it gets whiter and whiter, thinner and thinner, and the taffy is finished.

Towards the middle of the afternoon, the principal repast takes place. All the provisions which the guests have brought are produced and spread on a long table prepared for the purpose. Maple water and maple sugar are the accompaniments of every dish. When all the meats have been discussed, the feast winds up by the celebrated maple omelet. Whatever Soyer or Brillat Savarin might say, it is a pleasant dish, though too rich to be partaken of copiously, and according to every hygienic principle, very apt to be difficult of digestion. It consists of eggs pretty well boiled and broken into maple syrup, slightly diluted and piping hot. After a meal of this kind, exercise is indispensable, and it is the custom to get up a series of dances until the hour of breaking up.

"Friends," exclaims the host, when they are about to retire from the table, "I am glad to find that you have done justice to my syrup and sugar. It is the best sign that they were good. It keeps up the reputation of my sugary. Try to retain the taste of them till next year, when I hope we shall all meet again under these same trees."

A round of applause follows these words, and the whole company breaks out into hunting songs in honor of the host.

"Now," resumes he, "we must by all means have a dance. I never let my friends go without at least one, and I intend to join in the first myself. Come, hurry up, one and all. I see a suspicious cloud or two in the sky yonder, and we may possibly have a storm before the day is over."

A fiddler is soon found and the dance is organized. He leans his left cheek lovingly on his instrument, and has just run his bow across the discordant strings, when suddenly a loud crash is heard in the gorges of the mountain. It is the roar of the storm. The maple tops writhe and twist in the sweep of the winds that come up in eddies from the river far beneath. The sky is suddenly darkened. The snow falls thick and fast. These portents are sufficiently significant to startle the whole party. The dance is broken up and every one prepares to depart as fast as he can.

Cary Singleton and his men had a sterner duty to perform by the maple trees. They cut them down and of the trunks constructed a number of rafts wherewith to transport the baggage and provisions of the army across the St. Lawrence.

At the same time, the Indians of the party were detailed to build birch-bark canoes. With their long knives they swept around the slender trunks, making an incision as regular and precise as any surgeon might have done on a human limb destined to amputation. The first circle was made about one foot from the ground, the other about three feet from the branches where the tree began to taper. This was to secure slips of about equal length. They then ran down their knives longitudinally from the edge of one circle to the edge of the other circle, making four or five sections according to the size of the tree. This was to obtain slips of about equal breadth. They next inserted the point of their knives under the layer of bark, and with rapid action of the arm pulled off slip after slip. As these slips fell upon the ground they rolled up in scrolls, but other Indians as quickly unrolled them, stitched them together with light thongs of moose or buckskin, and sharpened them at the two extremities. In this way, three men could build a good sized canoe, within two hours. There remained only the process of drying which was not indispensable indeed, but contributed to the lightness and safety of the craft.

So soon as the first canoe was made, Cary Singleton launched it, and, accompanied by two men, made the reconnoissance which so much frightened the gossipping laundresses. He did not approach the north shore as near as he had intended, for fear that the women might give the alarm and betray his design, but he saw enough through his glass to enable him to report that the secluded basin, sheltered by dense trees, and known as Wolfe's Cove, would be a favorable place for the landing of the invading army. Accordingly, after three days devoted to the repose of his troops, and the replenishing of his stores from the neighboring farm houses, Arnold, on the night of the 13th November, undertook to cross the St. Lawrence. He was favored by darkness and a storm, and from ten in the evening till four in the morning, by the aid of thirty birch-bark canoes and a few rafts, he was engaged in the hazardous work. Backwards and forwards the fragile vessels plied silently over the broad bosom of the river, bearing a freight of taciturn armed men, on the point of whose muskets literally trembled the fate of Canada. As the morning dawned the whole of the Continental army, with the exception of 160 men who were left at Levis, was safe in the recess of Wolfe's Cove, and Arnold had won another stake in the lottery of war.

V
ON THE RAMPARTS

Very early that same morning, Zulma Sarpy drove into Quebec, accompanied by a single servant. As she neared the city, she caught a glimpse of the rebel troops surging up the gorge of Wolfe's Cove and forming in groups on the fringe of the skirting wood. They could not as yet be seen from the city, although the authorities had, an hour or two previously, been apprised of their landing. The sight wonderfully exhilarated the girl. She was not astonished, much less intimidated by the warlike view. Rather did she feel a thrill of enthusiasm, and a wild fancy shot through her mind that she too would like to join in the martial display. She stopped her horse for a moment to make sure that her eyes were not betraying her, and when she was satisfied that the men in the distance were really Continentals, she snapped her whip and drove rapidly into Quebec, in order to enjoy the malicious pleasure of being the first to communicate the fact to her friends.

In that anticipation she was not disappointed. Her story at first was not credited, because a glance at the Heights of Levis, across the river, revealed the presence of troops there. But when she insisted and detailed all the circumstances, the news spread with rapidity. From one street it passed into another; from Upper Town it flew into Lower Town, and according as the news was confirmed by other persons coming into the city, the people grew wild with excitement and crowded to the ramparts to satisfy themselves.

Pauline Belmont had not been as intimate as she might have been with Zulma Sarpy, both because they had been separated for many years during the school period, and because their characters did not exactly match. The timid, retiring, essentially domestic disposition of the one could not move on the same planes with the dashing, fearless, showy mood of the other. Intellectually they were not equals either. Pauline's mind was almost purely receptive and her range of inquiry limited indeed. Zulma's mind was buoyant with spontaneity, and there was a quality of aggressive origination in it which scattered all conventionalities as splinters before it. Pauline was likely to lean upon Zulma, listen with admiration to her brilliant talk, ask her advice and then smile, fearing to act upon it. Zulma, on the other hand, was not inclined to claim or exercise patronage. She was actually too independent for that, and in regard to Pauline, more particularly, she rather preferred bending as much as she could to her level. In the few months after Zulma's return from France, however, the girls had frequently met, and they would have liked to see more of each other, had they not both been retained a great deal at home by the seclusion of M. Belmont and the infirmities of Sieur Sarpy respectively.

On the present occasion Pauline was one of the friends upon whom Zulma called, and naturally her first business was to acquaint her with the landing of the Continentals. She was surprised to find that the intelligence caused a deathly pallor to spread over the features of her companion.

"The siege will begin in earnest, and we shall be cut off from all the world," murmured Pauline. "And my father has not yet returned."

"Is he outside of the city?" asked Zulma.

"Yes. He went away yesterday, promising to return early this morning. His delay did not alarm me, but now from what you tell me, I fear he may get into trouble."

"Do not fret, my dear. It will take several days before the city is invested, and your father's return will not be interfered with. Besides, he is not a militant, I believe."

Pauline drew a sigh, but said nothing. Zulma resumed:

"I am sure he is neutral like my father, and such will not be annoyed."

"I wish I could be sure of that, but— —," and Pauline suddenly checked herself as if fearful of giving expression to her suspicions.

"You must remember, my dear, that these Americans are not so black as they are painted. They are men like others, and true soldiers are always merciful," added Zulma.

"Indeed! Do you think so? I hardly know what to say about them. Father says very little of late, but there is a friend of ours who speaks of them in terms of hostility."

"He must be an ultra loyalist."

"He is a British officer."

"A British officer? Why, Pauline, I thought your father kept aloof from British officials."

"Oh, but this one is really a Canadian and speaks French like ourselves," said Pauline, blushing.

"That makes all the difference," replied Zulma, with a pleasant laugh that was slightly tinged with sarcasm. "I declare I should like to know this specimen."

"You know him, dear."

"Impossible!"

"He has spoken to me of you."

"Indeed!"

"And is a great admirer of yours."

"You mock me!"

"You can't guess who it is?"

And little Pauline brightened up with childish glee at having gained this slight advantage over her companion.

"You puzzle and excite me, darling. I can't guess. Tell me who it is."

"Lieutenant Hardinge!"

"Lieutenant Hardinge?"

Why was the cheek of Zulma suddenly touched with flame? Why did her blue eyes darken as in a lurid shadow? And her lips—why did they contract into marble whiteness, without the power of articulation? There was a pause of deep solemnity. To Pauline it was perplexing. She feared that she had said too much, both for her own sake and that of her friend. But she was soon relieved of her misgivings by the touch of Zulma's hand laid upon hers, and a deep, penetrating look, which showed, better than any words, that the latter understood all, and generously sympathized with her friend.

"Of course," she said with a laugh, "if you borrow your ideas from Lieutenant Hardinge, you cannot have much of an opinion of the Americans, and I suppose it would be loss of time for me to controvert that opinion."

"Fortunately the result of the war does not depend on the notions of two girls like ourselves," retorted Pauline, with an argumentative spirit which was quite foreign to her, and which made her companion laugh again.

"Never mind," said Zulma. "Let us do something more womanly. Let us go and look at these new soldiers."

"Very well, and I may hear something of my father on the way."

They stepped out of the house and joined a crowd of men, women and children bending their steps to the ramparts. When they reached the walls, they found them already lined with people talking and gesticulating in the most excited manner. Some spoke aloud, some shouted at the top of their lungs, some waved their hats, some fluttered their handkerchiefs attached to the end of their walking sticks, like flags, and some openly beckoned a welcome to the rebel host. There stood Arnold's army spread out before them, deployed into a loose double column on the Plains of Abraham. They had brushed their clothes, furbished their arms, and put on the best possible appearance. They were not more than seven hundred in number, but by a judicious evolution of the wings were made to appear more numerous. Some of the officers looked very smart, having donned the full-dress uniforms which had not been used since the expedition left Cambridge two months previously.

Pauline and Zulma occupied a favorable position in the midst of a large group where they could see everything and hear all the commentaries of the crowd.

"Why don't the Bastonnais come on?" said an old Frenchman, dashing his blue woollen bonnet to one side of his forehead. "They are imbeciles. They don't understand their chance."

"You are right," answered another old man near him. "If the rebel General only knew it, the gates are not properly manned, and the stockades only half made up. He could rush in and carry the city by a *coup de main*."

This conversation was striking, and later in life Zulma used to say that it expressed what was true. If Arnold had made a dash upon Quebec that November morning, it is asserted by Sanguinet and others, that he would have carried it. Thus would he have been immortalized, and the world would have been spared the most dastardly traitor of modern times.

The foregoing dialogue took place to the right of Zulma and Pauline. The following was held on their left, between two Englishmen—a tavern-keeper and a sailor.

"If our commander made an attack on these ragamuffins he would sweep them into the St. Lawrence," said the sailor.

"Or capture the most of them," said the tavern-keeper.

Here was a contrary opinion to the foregoing, and yet it too has been expressed by subsequent historians. The Quebec garrison was fifteen hundred strong, and well supplied with arms and ammunition. The American army was only half that number, ill accoutred and poorly armed. The British had a base of operations and a place of retreat in Quebec. The Continentals had no line of escape but the broad St. Lawrence and a few birch-bark canoes which a dozen torches could have destroyed. Who knows? A great opportunity of fame was perhaps lost that day.

"I wish they would sally forth against the Americans," said Zulma to Pauline. "But the shadow of Montcalm is upon them. Had the Marquis remained behind his intrenchments, we should never have been conquered by the English. If the English would now only follow his bad example." And she laughed heartily.

VI
THE FLAG OF TRUCE

Suddenly a singular movement was observed among the American troops, and silence fell upon the eager multitudes who lined the ramparts. The principal rebel officers were seen grouped together in consultation. From their gestures it was evident that a matter of grave importance was argued, and that there was far from being a harmonious counsel. In the centre of the party stood a short, stout man, of florid complexion and apparently about thirty-five years of age. He was advocating his views with vigor, sometimes with a persuasive smile, sometimes with angry words. This was Arnold. A few of the officers listened in silence; others walked away with a scowl of derision and contempt on their faces. Finally, the interview closed, the troops fell back a little along the whole line, and all seemed intent upon watching the important event which was about to follow.

A trumpeter stepped forward, followed by a tall young officer dressed in the uniform of a rifleman. Both gave the salute to Arnold and received their instructions from him in a low voice. The young officer took from his commander a sealed despatch, and, drawing his sword, attached to it a white handkerchief.

The sight of this handkerchief explained the whole movement.

"A summons to surrender!" was the word that passed along the Continental ranks, and nearly everybody laughed. The officers could scarcely conceal their disgust, and some of them loudly protested against being compelled to witness the humiliation which they were certain was about to ensue.

"A flag of truce!" exclaimed the crowds on the ramparts of the city, and their curiosity was excited as to the purport of the contemplated parley. It is safe to say that no one suspected a demand for capitulation, as nothing could appear more ridiculous under the circumstances.

The officer with the trumpeter advanced rapidly over the vacant ground which lay between their line of battle and the walls of Quebec. At stated intervals, according to the rules of the service, the trumpet was sounded, but no response came from the city. Finally the two envoys stopped and stood in full view of the two camps.

"What a handsome fellow it is," said Zulma to Pauline.

The girls were in an excellent position for observing all that took place, and were so interested that even the timid Pauline forgot her anxieties about her father.

"Do you mean the trumpeter?"

"Oh, he is well enough. But I mean the officer who bears the flag."

The two friends were discussing this point when their attention was arrested by a movement at the gate almost beneath them. A British officer walked out alone and went direct to the flag-bearer.

"It cannot be," exclaimed Pauline.

"Yes, it is no other," replied Zulma with a laugh.

"Roderick!"

"Yes, and no better choice could have been made. A handsome loyalist against a handsome rebel. But there is a disparity of age."

"Hardly."

"I beg your pardon. Our tall, beautiful rebel is hardly twenty-one, I am sure, while your Lieutenant, Pauline, is more mature."

It was indeed Roderick Hardinge who had been commissioned to go forward and meet the American messenger. As he neared him, the two young officers bowed politely to each other and exchanged the military salute. Then the following brief conversation took place, as learned afterwards from the lips of the participants themselves.

"I presume, sir, that you have been detailed to meet me here," said the Continental.

"I have that honor, sir," responded Roderick.

"And to receive my message."

"I beg your pardon, sir, but I regret to say that I have instructions *not* to receive any message whatever."

"But Colonel Arnold demands a parley according to the usages of war."

"I am sorry, sir, that I cannot argue the point. My orders are to inform you that the commandant of the garrison of Quebec does not desire to have any communication with the commander of the Continental force.

"But, sir, this — —"

"Excuse me, we are both soldiers. We have done our duty and I beg to salute you."

Lieutenant Hardinge bowed and retreated a step or two. The flag-bearer looked perplexed for a moment at this turn of affairs, but recovering his self-possession, returned the bow, wheeled about, and, followed by the trumpeter, started at long strides over the plain.

An universal tumult arose. Both parties were aroused to the highest pitch of excitement. The Americans, seeing the insult which had been offered to their messenger, could scarcely contain themselves within the ranks. The citizens on the wall sent up cheer after cheer, and the ladies fluttered their handkerchiefs. Zulma was an exception. She had no pleasure to manifest, but the contrary. She resented the affront made to the handsome young rebel, and had immediate occasion to show her feeling. As Roderick Hardinge turned to retrace his steps toward the gate, he glanced upward at the dense line of spectators on the ramparts, and caught sight of Pauline and Zulma. He gave them both a smiling look of recognition. Pauline returned it with ardent eye and an animated face that betokened the joy and pride she felt in the service which her friend was called upon to perform. Zulma affected not to see Hardinge and looked away over to the American side with an ostentatious air of offence.

Presently there was the report of a fire-arm, and a puff of pale blue smoke floated over the edge of the wall. If there was excitement before, there was uproar and consternation now. An outrage had been committed. Some one in Quebec had fired on the flag of truce. Pauline uttered a shrill cry and hid her face in her hands.

"What has happened?" she asked. "Is the battle going to begin? Let us hasten away. And Roderick—where is he?"

"Safe within the gate," exclaimed Zulma, bending forward, with a keen nervous movement, and pointing in front of her. "But the American is not so safe. He has been fired at. The laws of war have been violated. See, he is the only one who is calm. He walks proudly along, without even turning his head. There is the hero. He is shot at as if he were a dog, in violation of all civilized usages. Yet he is nobler than any of those who pretend to regard the Americans as unworthy of human treatment."

The Americans could hardly maintain their discipline. If the troops had been allowed their way, they would have rushed headlong against the walls to avenge the insult. But fortunately the officers succeeded in calming them. The shot had not been repeated. It was perhaps an accident, or it had been fired by some militiamen without orders. The flag-bearer was not injured, neither was the trumpeter.

The army contented itself with a last yell of defiance, and fell back, partially deploying to the left so as to occupy the main road leading from the country to the city. Arnold was bitterly disappointed. His summons for surrender was a characteristic bit of impudence, as we have seen, not so much on account of the summons itself, as of the threats and other terms of rhodomontade in which it was couched. Still it might have succeeded as a mere ruse of war. That it did not succeed was matter for profound chagrin, and the circumstances of insult and humiliation by which the refusal was accompanied added poignancy to the pain.

On the other hand, the citizens of Quebec were jubilant. It was a first trial of strength and the garrison had not failed. It was the first time the terrible Bastonnais were seen by the inhabitants, and they did not inspire any terror. Roderick Hardinge pretty well interpreted the general feeling in a conversation which he held that same afternoon with Pauline and Zulma. The latter had argued that the flag of truce should have been received. Roderick replied that he had, of course, no explanations to give in regard to the order of his superiors, but judging for himself he would say that any other commander except Arnold might perhaps have deserved more consideration. But Arnold was well known in the city. He had often come to Quebec from New England to buy horses for the West Indies trade in which he was engaged. Indeed he was nothing better than a Horse Jockey, with all the swagger, vulgarity and bounce appertaining to stablemen. He had been appointed to head this expedition, chiefly because of his local knowledge of the country. He boasted that he had friends in Quebec who could help him. It was well therefore to treat him with merited contempt from the first, and prove to him that he had no allies among them.

VII
THE COVERED BRIDGE

After this interview the two girls separated. Pauline was anxious to reach home in order to get information about her father. Zulma proposed driving back to Pointe-aux-Trembles. Her friend did her best to dissuade her. She pleaded that the day was too far advanced for safe travel, and entreated Zulma to postpone her departure till the following morning.

"And my old father?" objected the latter.

"He will have no apprehensions. The news of the enemy's arrival will not reach him to-day."

"Oh, but it will. Such news travels fast."

"But he can have no fear, knowing you to be safe with your friends in the city."

"My father has no fears about me, Pauline. He knows that I can take care of myself; but it is for himself that I am desirous of returning. He is feeble and infirm, and requires my presence."

"But, my dear, consider the risk you run. The roads will be infested with these horrid soldiers, and what protection have you against them?"

For all answer the cheek of Zulma flushed, and her blue eyes gleamed with a strange light that was not defiance, but rather betokened the expectation of pleasurable excitement.

"Wait till to-morrow morning," continued Pauline, "and you can go under the shelter of some military passport. I am sure Roderick would be delighted to get you such a paper."

Zulma's lips curled with scorn, but she made no direct reply. She simply repeated her determination to go, tenderly reassuring her friend, and embracing her with effusion.

It was about four o'clock in the afternoon, and the day had already considerably lowered, when Zulma's sleigh reached the outer gate of the city. The officer in charge would fain have prevented her from going further, but she stated her case so plainly, and argued with such an air of authority, that he was obliged to yield to her wishes.

"Well," said she to herself, with a smile, "I have broken through one circle of steel. It remains to see how I will pass through the other."

She did not have long to wait. About two miles from the city, the road which she was following went down a steep hill at the foot of which flowed a little stream much swollen at this season with snow and cakes of ice. Over this stream there was a covered bridge whose entrance was very dark. As she began the descent, the gloom and solitude of the gorge rather agitated the nerves of Zulma, and she stimulated her horse in order to pass through the bridge as rapidly as possible. Her eyes glanced over every point of the ravine, and it was with a sigh of relief that she approached the bridge without seeing any human being. But suddenly, as the horse's hoofs touched the edge of the planked floor, the animal grew restive, tossed up his head, balanced right and left in the traces, and gave other unmistakeable signs of danger ahead. Zulma attempted to urge him forward, but this only increased his terror. Her servant, a green young rustic, with more strength than courage, turned to her with consternation stamped upon his blank face, and muttered something about obeying the animal's instinct and not venturing to proceed farther.

"Jump out and see what is the matter," she exclaimed. "If you are afraid, I will do it."

The fellow slowly stepped from the vehicle, and feeling his way along the shaft, reached the horse's head where he paused and peered into the dark cavity of the bridge. He then seized the bridle and tried to lead the beast along. But the latter wrenched the bit from the driver's hand, raised his forelegs high in air, shaking the sleigh and imperilling the seat of Zulma. She, too, was about to leap forth, when her servant ran back precipitately, exclaiming:

"The Bastonnais!"

At the same moment the gleam of bayonets was seen under the arch of the bridge, two soldiers advanced into the light, and the sharp, stern summons of halt resounded through the hollow.

The servant stood trembling behind the sleigh. Zulma quietly signalled the two soldiers to approach her. They did so. She said a word to them in French, but they shook their heads. They then spoke in English, but she in turn shook her head. They smiled and she smiled. By this time, the horse, as if he appreciated the situation, having turned his head to look at the soldiers, became tranquil in his place. The servant had not half the same sense, and stood trembling behind the sleigh.

The soldiers consulted together a moment, then the elder signified to Zulma that she would have to return to the city. She replied in the same language that she must go on. They insisted with some seriousness. She insisted with a show of rising temper. The position was becoming embarrassing, when a tall figure appeared at the edge of the bridge, and a loud word of command caused the soldiers to fall back. Zulma looked forward and an expression of mingled surprise and pleasure was discernible upon her countenance. The new comer advanced to the side of the sleigh, touched his cap and bowed respectfully to its fair inmate:

"Excuse my men, mademoiselle," said he, in excellent French. "They have detained you, I perceive, but we are patrolling the roads and their orders are strict. You desire to pass out into the country?"

"If you please, sir."

"With this man?"

"Yes; he is not a soldier, but a family servant. We entered Quebec this morning before the investment, and it is absolutely necessary for me to reach my home to-night."

Zulma's tone was not that of a suppliant. Her manner showed that, as she had not feared the commands of the soldiers, so she had no favor to ask of the officer. The latter, doubtless, observed this, and was not displeased thereat, for instead of giving the permission to proceed, he seemed to linger and hesitate, as if he fain would prolong the interview. Finally, he managed to introduce a link into the conversation by asking Zulma whether she did not fear to pursue her journey at that late hour, declaring that, if she did, he would be happy to furnish her with an escort. She answered laughingly that perhaps the escort itself would be the greatest danger she would be likely to encounter on the way.

"Then I will escort you myself," said the young officer with a profound bow.

Zulma thanked him, adding the assurance that she needed no protection, as she anticipated no annoyance. She then called her servant to his seat beside her, and was about driving off when the loud report of a gun was heard in the direction of the city. She and the officer looked at each other.

"A stray shot," said the latter, after listening a moment. "It is nothing. You are not afraid, mademoiselle?"

"Excuse me, sir," Zulma replied, "but this is the second shot I have heard to-day. This one may mean nothing, but the first was terrible, and I shall never forget it."

The officer looked at Zulma, but said nothing.

"Is it possible that you do not remember it too?"

"We are so used to it, mademoiselle, that—"

"The man who fired that shot is a scoundrel, and the man at whom it was fired," exclaimed Zulma, sitting upright and fixing a glowing eye upon the officer, "is a hero. Good evening, sir."

And, as if impelled by the spirit with which his mistress pronounced these words, the horse dashed forward, and the sleigh plunged into the gloomy cavern of the bridge.

VIII
CARY SINGLETON

It was Cary Singleton. He stood a moment looking in the direction of the bridge, then walked slowly away buried in thought. He was perplexed to understand the meaning of the words which the beautiful Canadian had spoken. Which was the shot that she referred to, and who was the fortunate man whom she proclaimed a hero? At last, the suspicion flashed upon him that perhaps the young lady had witnessed the scene of that afternoon under the walls of Quebec. It was very probable, indeed, that she was one of the hundreds who had lined the ramparts at the time that the flag of truce advanced toward the gate. In that case, she may have meant the treacherous firing on the flag, and if she did, her hero must be the bearer of that flag. But this was almost too good to be true. The girl was doubtless a loyalist, and to speak as she did, if she meant as he thought, would argue either that she was a rebel at heart, or that she was actuated by higher principles of humanity than he had a right to look for in exciting and demoralizing times of war. And then could she possibly have recognized him?—for it was no other than he that had borne the ill-starred flag.

This last question gave a new zest to his excitement, and he stopped short on the brow of the hill to nerve himself for a sudden resolution. A second rapid analysis convinced him that he had indeed been recognized by the lovely stranger. Her whole demeanor, her animated glance, her inflamed cheek, her gesture of agitation and her last passionate word, as he now vividly remembered them, pointed to no other conclusion. Yes, she remembered him, she knew him, and, in a moment of unguarded enthusiasm, she had expressed her admiration of him. And to be admired by such a woman! He came from a land proverbial as much for female beauty as for manly chivalry, but never had his eyes been blessed with a vision of such transcendent perfection. Every rare feature came out in full relief on his memory—the great blue eye, the broad entablature of forehead, the seductive curl of lip, the splendid carriage of head, and, above all, the magnificence of queenly form.

Cary Singleton was transported. He stormed against himself for having been a fool. Why had he not understood these things ten minutes ago as he understood them now? But he would make up for it. He would run over to his encampment, a few rods behind the wood which skirted the road, procure a horse, and start off in pursuit of the beautiful girl. He would learn her name, he would discover where she lived and then ... and then....

But a bugle-blast startled him from his dream, and shattered his resolve. It was a call to quarters for special duty. He looked up and saw great clouds of darkness roll into the valley. Alas! the day was indeed done, and it was all too late. He walked grimly to camp bewailing his lost opportunity, and devising all kinds of schemes to recover it. As he tossed upon his cold pallet of straw that night, his dreams were of the lonely gorge, the covered bridge, the fairy apparition, and when he awoke the following morning, it was with the hope that such an adventure would not remain without a sequel. He felt that it would be a mockery of fate that he should have travelled so far through the forests of Maine and over the desert plains of the Chaudière, suffering hunger, thirst and fatigue, and facing death in every shape, to see what he had seen, to hear what he had heard, the night before, and then be denied the fruition of eye and ear forever.

It must be remembered that Cary Singleton was barely one-and-twenty years of age, and that in him the enthusiasm of youth was intensified by an exuberant vigor of health. Your wildest lovers are not the sickly sentimentalists of tepid drawing-rooms, but the rollicking giants of the open air, and the adventures of a Werther are baby trifles compared to the infinite love-scrapes which are recounted of a Hercules.

Cary Singleton came of a good stock, Maryland on the side of his father, Virginian on that of his mother. The Cary and Singleton families survive to our day, through successive generations of honor, but they need not be ashamed of their representative who figures in these humble pages. He had spent his early life on his father's estate, mingling in every manly exercise, and his latter days were passed at old Princeton, where he attained all the accomplishments suited to his station. He was particularly proficient in polite literature and the modern languages, having mastered the French tongue from many years of intercourse with the governess of his sisters. Cary had prepared himself for the law and was about entering on its practice, when the war of the Revolution broke out. He then enlisted in the corps of Virginia riflemen formed by the celebrated Captain Morgan, and proceeded to Boston to join the army of Washington, in the summer of 1775. He had not been there many weeks before the expedition to Canada was planned. Washington, who agreed with Congress as to the importance of this campaign, gave much personal attention to organization of the invading army, and it was by his personal direction that Morgan's battalion was included in it. When the force took its final departure in September, Cary received the honor of a hearty clasp of hand and a few words of counsel from the Father of his Country, and this circumstance cheered him to those deeds of endurance and valor which distinguished his career in Canada.

IX
THE SONG OF THE VIOLIN

It was the hour of midnight, and all was still in the solitary cabin of Batoche. Little Blanche was fast asleep in her sofa-crib, and Velours was rolled in a torpid circle on the hearth. The fire burned low, casting a faint and fitful gleam through the room. The hermit occupied his usual seat in the leather chair at one corner of the chimney. Whether he had been napping or musing it were difficult to say, but it was with a quiet, almost stealthy movement that he walked to the door which he opened, and looked out into the night. Returning, he placed a large log on the fire, stirring it with his foot till its reflection lighted one half of the apartment. He then proceeded to the alcove, and drew forth from it his violin. The strings were thrummed to make sure of their accord, the heel was set in the hollow of the shoulder, and the bow executed a rapid prelude. The old man smiled as if satisfied with the cunning of his hand, and well he might, for these simple touches revealed the artist.

"What will you sing me to-night?" said Batoche looking lovingly at his old brown instrument. "There has been strange thunder in the voice of the Falls all the day, and I have felt very singular this evening. I do not know what is abroad, but perhaps you will tell me."

So saying, he raised his violin to his shoulder again, and began to play. At first there were slow broad notes drawn out with a long bow, then a succession of rapid sounds rippling over one another. The alternation was natural and pleasing, but as he warmed to his work, the old musician indulged in a revelry of sounds—the crash of the tempest, the murmur of the breeze, the sparkling clatter of rain drops, the monotone of lapsing water. The left hand would lie immoveable on the neck, and a grand unison issued from the strings like a solemn warning; then the fingers would dance backwards and forwards to the bridge, and the chords vibrated in a series of short, sharp echoes like the petulant cries of children. A number of ravishing melodies glided and wove into each other like the flowers of a nosegay, producing a harmonious whole of charming effect, and sweetening the very atmosphere in which they palpitated. Then the perverse old man would shatter them all by one fell sweep of his arm, causing a terrific discord that almost made his cabin lurch from its seat. For one full hour, standing there in the middle of the room, with the flickering light of the fire falling upon his face, Batoche played on without any notable interval of rest. At the end of that time he stopped, tightened his keys, swung his bow-arm in a circle two or three times as if to distend his muscles, and then attacked the single E string. It was there that he expected the secret which he sought. He rounded his shoulders, bent his ear close to the board, peered with his grey eyes into the serpentine fissures of the instrument, pressed his left-hand fingers nervously up and down, while his bow caressed the string in an infinite series of mysterious evolutions. The music produced was weird and preternatural. The demon that lay crouched in the body of the instrument was speaking to Batoche. Now loud as an explosion, then soft as a whisper; now shrill as the scream of a night bird, then sweet as the breath of an infant, the violin uttered its varied and magical language, responsive to the touch of the wizard. There were moments when the air throbbed and the room rocked with the sound, and other moments when the music was all absorbed in the soul of the performer. Finally the old man drew himself up, threw his head backward, ran his fingers raspingly up towards the bridge and made a desperate plunge with his bow. A loud snap was heard like the report of a pistol. The string had broken. Batoche quietly lowered the instrument and looked around him. Little Blanche was sitting up in the bed gazing about with wide vacant eyes. The black cat stood glaring on the hearth with bristling fur and back rounded into a semi-circle.

"Good!" muttered Batoche, as he walked to the alcove and laid by his violin. Then going as quietly to the door, he opened it wide. Barbin and two other men, closely wrapped in hoods, stood before him.

"Come in," said Batoche, "I expected you."

There was no agitation or eccentricity in his manner, but his features were pinched, and his grey eyes shed a sombre light upon the deep shadows of their cavities.

"We have come for you, Batoche," said Barbin.

"I knew it."

"Are you ready?"

"I am ready."

And he stepped forward to take his old carbine from its hooks.

"No gun," said Barbin, laying his hand upon the old man's arm. "You are not to attack, nor will you be attacked."

"Ah! I see," muttered Batoche, throwing his wild-cat great coat over his shoulders.

"You know the news?"

"I know there is some news."

"The day of deliverance has come."

"At last!" exclaimed the hermit, raising his eyes to the ceiling.

"The Bastonnais have surrounded the city."

"And will the Wolves be trapped?" asked Batoche in a voice of thunder. "Ha! ha! I heard it all in the song of my old violin. I heard the roar of their march through the forest; their shout of triumph when they reached the Heights of Levis, and first saw the rock of the citadel; the splash of their oars in crossing the river; the deep murmur of their columns forming on the Plains of Abraham. Thus far have they come, have they not?"

"Yes, thus far," responded the three men together, amazed at the accuracy of the information which they knew that Batoche had not obtained that day from any human lip.

"But they will go farther," resumed the hermit, "because I have heard more. I have heard the boom of cannon, the rattle of musketry, the hiss of rockets, the wail of the wounded, the shriek of the dying, the malediction over the dead. Then a long interval, and after it, I have heard the crackling of flames, the cry of the hungry, the moan of those who suffered, the lamentation of the sick, and the loud, terrible voice of insurrection. And all this in the camp of our friends, while within the city, where the Wolves are gathered, I have heard the clink of glasses, the song of revelry, the shout of defiance, the threat against treason,—mark the word, my friends. Are we traitors, you and I, because we love our old motherland too well, and hate the Wolves that have devoured our inheritance? Yes, I repeat, I have heard to-night the shout of defiance, the threat against treason, the mocking laugh against weakness, and the deep growl of inebriate repletion. Another interval and then the catastrophe. I heard the soft voice of the night, the fall of the snow, the muffled tread of advancing regiments, the low word of command,—then all at once a thunderous explosion of cannon,—and, finally, silence, defeat and death."

Barbin and his two companions stood listening to the old man in rapt wonder. To them he appeared like a prophet, as he unfolded before their eyes the vision of war and desolation which the genius of music had evoked for him. And when he had concluded, they looked at each other, as doubtful of what to say. Batoche added:

"I fear that things will not turn out as favorably as we could wish. We may hurt, but shall not succeed in destroying the pack of wolves. However, we must do our best."

The men did not reply, but abruptly changed the current of the old hermit's thoughts by walking towards the door, and urging him to follow them.

"It is late," said Barbin. "We have work to do and must hurry."

The four then walked out of the house, leaving little Blanche and Velours to the calm slumbers which they had resumed, so soon as the voice of the violin was hushed.

X
BLOOD THICKER THAN WATER

Batoche and his companions plunged into the forest. On the way, the object of the expedition was fully explained to the old man. He was expected to have an interview that night with some officer of the Continental army for the purpose of organizing a system of action between them and the malcontents of the environs of Quebec. These malcontents were of various degrees of earnestness, courage and activity. Some had boasted a great deal of what they would do when the Americans came, but when the Americans did come, and the loyalist troops showed a determined front of opposition, they quietly slunk into the background or even betrayed their former professions. Others of these malcontents confined themselves to secret action, such as furnishing information of what was going on within the city, harboring those who were tracked for treason, or affording supplies of food and ammunition to such of their friends as needed them for use. Finally, there were a determined few, chiefly old soldiers or the sons of old soldiers of Montcalm and Lévis, who, having never become reconciled to their English masters, in the sixteen years which had elapsed since the Conquest, hailed the appearance of the Americans as the prelude of deliverance, and openly raised the standard of revolt. Of these there were again two classes. One formed into a duly equipped battalion which joined the army of Arnold and took part in all the subsequent events of the siege. The second class consisted of farmers around Quebec, who, not being able to quit their families and perform regular military service, engaged in a species of guerilla warfare which was both effective and romantic. Among these were ranged Barbin and his companions. Among them Batoche was called to take a position. His well-known skill with the carbine, his rare knowledge of all the woods for miles in circumference, his remarkable powers of endurance, his reckless bravery and fertility of expedient in the midst of most critical danger, all fitted him for the trying events which circumstances thrust upon him and his friends. But the oddities of his mode of life, the eccentricities of his character, his generally accredited relations with the spirits of the departed, and the gift of divination which all the country-side accorded him, spite of occasional and deriding criticism, went still further to point him out as a foremost man in the secret insurrection of the farmers. He himself, in his own way, favored the movement with enthusiasm. He was not a Canadian, but a Frenchman born. His youth had been spent in the wars of his country. When the great Marquis de Montcalm was ordered to New France, he followed him as a member of the famous Roussillon regiment In that capacity, he fought at Carillon, and shared the glory of the campaign of 1758. In the same capacity, he shared the stupendous defeat of Sept. 13th, 1759, on the Plains of Abraham. He had the sad consolation of having been one of those who bore the wounded Marquis from the field, and accompanied him to the Hospice of the Ursulines where he died, and where his glorious remains still rest. This circumstance saved him from the ignominy of capture. Before Murray, the successor of Wolfe, entered the vanquished city in triumph, he effected his escape by creeping along the valley of the St. Charles during the darkness, and making his way into the country. After wandering some miles, he paused near the Falls of Montmorenci, and built himself a kind of rustic tent on the very spot where he afterwards erected his lonely cabin. He chose this place not only on account of the beauty of its scenery, and the shelter from hostile intrusion which it afforded, but also because it was in the immediate neighborhood of the fortifications—visible even to this day—which his beloved commander had constructed there, and from which he repulsed Wolfe with great loss, only two months before the disastrous battle of the Plains of Abraham.

"Alas!" Batoche would often exclaim, standing over those earthworks, "if the great Marquis had relied upon the walls of Quebec, as he did upon these fortifications, we should still be masters of the country. Wolfe owed his success solely to the imprudence of Montcalm."

In the spring of the following year, Batoche joined the army of the Chevalier de Lévis, and was present at the great victory of Ste. Foye. But the successful retreat of the British army, under Murray, behind the walls of Quebec; the inability of Lévis to press the siege of the city; the gradual disbanding of the French forces throughout the Province, and the final surrender of Vaudreuil, at Montreal, whereby the whole French possessions in America, were ceded to Britain—one of the most momentous events of modern times in its gradual results—forced Batoche to return to his Montmorenci solitude.

He might have gone back to France, if he had been so minded, but after lingering some time in indecision, a circumstance occurred which determined him to fix his abode definitively in the new world. This was the receipt of a letter from his family, informing him of the death of his wife and the utter poverty in which his daughter, a girl of seventeen, was left. The girl herself appended a note stating that she intended to sail by the first occasion to join her father in Canada. The old soldier wrote at once to dissuade her from taking the step, giving the characteristic reason that he did not want her to become a servant of the detested English, but before his letter reached France, the girl landed in Quebec, and thus the course of Batoche's destiny was changed. His daughter was bright, intelligent and good looking, and received at once advantageous offers of situations in several of the best families of the capital, but the old man would not listen to any proposition of the kind.

"Come with me, into the woods," he said to her. "We will live there happily together. I don't want an Englishman to set his eyes upon you. I am still able to work. You will help me. We shall want for nothing."

And he took her into his lonely habitation beside the Falls of Montmorenci, where in effect the two spent a tranquil, easy existence. At the end of three years, the son of a farmer of Charlesbourg fell in love with the girl, and spite of his attachment, Batoche consented to a marriage between them. It was a rude blow when the bride went forth from his cabin to take up her residence in her husband's house, about twelve miles away, but the sacrifice was generously made, and when ten or eleven months later, a grandchild was born to him, Batoche felt that he had received sufficient compensation for his loss.

"Little Blanche will live with me," he said, "and replace her mother."

He did not know how sad was the prophecy that he uttered.

XI
DEATH IN THE FALLS

It was a beautiful summer evening. The young mother, having recovered from her illness, decided that her first visit should be to the cabin of her old father, and, of course, the baby went with her. After resting awhile, and receiving the caresses of the hermit, the daughter, with the child in her arms, wandered about the familiar environs to enjoy once more all the pleasures attached to her old home. It was a beautiful summer evening. The forest was charged with perfume; a thousand birds fluttered from branch to branch; the earth was spangled with an endless variety of wild flowers; brilliant insects flashed and buzzed in the slanting beams of the sunset; the whole air gently undulated in a rhythmic wave that disposed the soul to revery and prayer. The young woman felt this influence, without, of course, being able to define it, and yielding to its sway, she wandered farther than she had intended, or than her bodily strength justified, from the hut of her father. It was so delightful to revisit all these scenes which she had learned to love so much, and to see them again under such different circumstances. Even the inanimate world is not the same to the wife as it is to the girl. Marriage for woman seems to alter the form, color, scent and effect of material things, giving them a character of pathos, if not of sadness, which they never wore in the pleasant days when the body owed no service to a master, and the mind was, in very literalness, fancy-free.

With her child in her arms — the flesh-and-blood pledge of her altered life — the young woman strayed away along the avenues of the forest, and out into the open spaces, until she reached the skirt of the high road, fully half a mile from Batoche's hut. The white dusty stretch of the road brought her to a pause, being as it were a dividing line between the expanses of greenery over which she was wandering. Feeling now the fatigue which she had not experienced before, she sat down upon the warm tufted grass to rest, and, like all mothers, became oblivious of self in attention to the wants of her babe. She had been nursing it at her breast about ten minutes, while her eyes were fixed on its rosy limbs, and her mind revelled in the half-sensuous, half-spiritual delights of maternity, when all at once a mighty clatter of hoofs was heard along the road, followed immediately after by loud shouts of men, the flash of red coats and the clang of sabre-sheaths on the flanks of rushing horses. What ensued was never fully known, but the young mother, with disordered dress, hair streaming behind, and babe convulsively pressed against her bosom, fled like a deer through the wood in the direction of the Falls. Behind her went two pursuers, fleet as fate, but indistinct as spectres in the twilight. Unfortunately the poor woman was on the side of the Falls opposite her father's cabin. When she reached the top of the headland, the cataract roared on her right, and the broad St. Lawrence flowed at her feet. There was no outlet of escape. Disgrace and death behind her; death and oblivion before her. There was not a moment to waste. In the highest access of her despair, she heard a voice across the Falls. It was that of her father, who, with hand and word, directed her to go down the steep side of the promontory to the foot of the cascade. He himself immediately disappeared under the overhanging rock and curtain of water, and joined her just as she had attained the desired spot. No time was lost in explanations. Seizing the babe in his right arm, and encircling his left around the waist of his daughter, the valiant old man turned and disappeared again under the Fall. Overhead a yell of baffled rage was heard above the thunder of the torrent, but it was not repeated.

Batoche had not advanced many steps when he noticed that the burden on his left arm was growing heavier and heavier—and, on looking down, he observed with terror that his daughter had swooned. The grand flower of love was broken on its stem. This circumstance added tenfold to the old man's peril. The slightest slip of his foot, the slightest jolt from the perpendicular, the slightest deviation from the protecting line of the granite wall, would hurl him and his precious freight into destruction. If he could only reach the subterranean cavity which opened about midway on his path, he might stop there to rest and all would be well. He dragged along slowly in this hope; his eyes strained till they saw the welcome haven approaching. A few more steps and he would reach it. He *did* reach it. As he bent down, on his right, to place the babe on a ledge of rock within the cave, he felt a sudden wrench on his left arm, then a sense of looseness, and to his horror he found that the circle made by his arm upon his hip was empty. His daughter had glided like a broken lily into the seething basin, at the point where the waters of the cataract fall sheer like lead, and where they at once battered the life out of her bare white breast.

"Great God of earth and heaven! What is this?" cried the old man, with eyes starting from their sockets.

Then, with a gesture of despair, he took up the child, held it aloft on his arm, and would have jumped into the gulf with it to complete the sacrifice of misery. But his fierce eye turned and caught that of the babe which was mellow with laughing light. There was also a smile upon its lip, and its chubby little hand flourished a wisp of grass plucked from a fissure in the ledge. That look, that smile, were like a flash of Paradise. The old man lowered the child to his breast, folded both arms over it, and rapidly passed out under the Fall. From that moment little Blanche never left him.

Such was the story gathered from Batoche himself, and which is still repeated as one of the traditions of Montmorenci. The hermit always insisted that his daughter's death was caused by two drunken British cavalry men. The version was never proven, but it was impossible to dissuade the old man of its truth. Hence his abiding, ineradicable hatred for the English, which, added to his aversion as a French soldier, rendered him the most bitter of foes during the war of 1775-76. Hence, also, the eccentricity of his character and subsequent mode of life, which have been described in preceding chapters.

XII
ADVICE AND WARNING

The rallying cry of the band of malcontent farmers was the yelp of a wolf. This was adopted out of hatred of the very name of Wolfe, the conqueror of Quebec. "Loup" was the title applied by them to every English resident, and more especially to the British soldier. We have seen how the sound was used to gather the conspirators in the forest at night, and how Batoche recognized it. Although the Americans had been only forty-eight hours in the environs of Quebec, they had already learned the meaning of the signal. This was apparent when the hermit with his three companions reached the bridge which spanned the little river St. Charles, on the high road leading directly to the town. There a squad of New Jersey militiamen were posted as sentry. As the Canadians approached they were challenged, and on uttering the cry of the wolf, were immediately admitted within the lines. The officer in command understood French, and Batoche was the spokesman of his party. The following colloquy took place:

"What is your desire?"

"We have come to offer you our services."

"In what capacity?"

"As scouts."

"Do you live in the town?"

"No, at Beauport."

"You are farmers?"

"Yes."

"Have you arms?"

"Yes, for we are also hunters."

"You know the country then?"

"For ten leagues around."

"And the town?"

"We know all our countrymen in it."

"Can you communicate with them?"

"We have many means of doing so."

"That is well. We shall need your services."

We have said that the object of Barbin and his companions was to enter into direct communication with some of the Continental officers, make known their plans of operation and devise some mode of systematising their services. This they partially accomplished in the course of a further conversation, and were told to return in a few days to receive direct commissions from headquarters. But they had a second duty to perform, or rather Batoche had, as he informed his companions on their way to the rendezvous, after hearing full particulars of everything that had taken place in the two days since the Americans had invested Quebec. Batoche delivered his ideas somewhat as follows. Addressing the officer, he said:

"You are aware that my countrymen within the town are divided in sentiment?"

"So we have heard."

"One party espouses the cause of England and has formed a regiment to fight for it."

"That we know."

"That party is now particularly incensed against you."

"Ah!"

"Another party favors the cause of liberty and liberation."

"Yes, they are our friends."

"Well, they are very much discouraged at what has recently happened."

"Indeed? How so?"

"May I speak freely?"

"As soldier to soldier."

"And will you believe my words?"

The officer fixed his eyes on the quaint energetic face of the old hermit and answered emphatically:

"I will."

"And you will report my words to your commander?"

"Yes."

"Then, listen to me. The day before yesterday, after landing on the north shore, you deployed your forces on the Plains of Abraham?"

Batoche went into this and the following other particulars, which he had learned from Barbin, in order to have them confirmed by the American officers, so that there be no mistake about the conclusion which he drew from them.

"We did," was the reply.

"And you sent forward a flag of truce?"

"Yes."

"That was for a parley."

"It was a summons to surrender."

"That makes matters worse. In the town it was supposed to be for a mere parley. When the truth is known, the effect will be still more disagreeable."

"What do you mean?" exclaimed the officer.

"Excuse me a moment. Your messenger was dismissed?"

"He was," replied the officer with impatience.

"And the flag fired upon?"

"Yes," was the answer accompanied by an oath.

"Then, this is what I mean. Your friends within the town are indignant and disheartened because you did not resent this double insult. They cannot explain it to themselves. They reason thus: either the Bastonnais were strong enough to avenge and punish this outrage, or they were not. If they were strong enough, why did they not sweep to the assault? If they were not strong enough, why expose themselves and us to this terrible humiliation? In the first instance, their inaction was cowardice. In the second supposition, their drawing up in line and sending a flag to demand surrender was a painful fanfaronade."

Batoche had warmed up to his old weird manner, as he spoke these words. He did not gesticulate, neither did he elevate his voice, but the light of the camp fire flickering upon his face revealed an expression of earnestness and conscious strength. Advancing a step or two towards the officer he said in a lower voice:

"Have I spoken too much?"

"You have spoken the truth!" roared the officer, stamping his foot violently, and then muttered in English:

"Just what I said at the time. This old Frenchman has told the truth in all its naked harshness."

The officer was Major Meigs, one of those who had most strenuously disapproved of the despatch of the flag of truce, and whose opinion of the event is recorded in history.

He thanked Batoche for his valuable information and assured him that he would repeat all he had said to Colonel Arnold.

"Perhaps you would allow an old soldier to add another word," continued the hermit, as they were about to separate.

The officer was so impressed with what he had heard, and with the peculiar manner of the strange being who addressed him, that he granted an eager permission.

"As a lover of liberty, as an enemy of the English, as a friend of the Bastonnais, I think, after what has happened, it would be better for your troops to withdraw for a time from within sight of the walls of Quebec."

The officer looked up dubiously.

"They might retire to some village a little up the river. There they could revictual at leisure."

No answer.

"And wait for reinforcements."

The officer smiled approvingly.

"And give their friends in and around the town time to organize and complete their arrangements. As yet we have done little or nothing. But in a week or ten days we could do a great deal."

"The idea is an excellent one, and will be considered," said the officer, shaking the hand of Batoche, after which the interview terminated.

Whether the old man's advice had any weight or not, the very course which he suggested was adopted a couple of days later. Feeling his inability to press the siege unaided, and learning that Colonel McLean, with his Royal Emigrants, had succeeded in reaching Quebec from Sorel, on the very day that he himself had crossed from Point Levis, thus strengthening the garrison of the town with a few regulars, Arnold, on the 18th November, broke up his camp and retired to Pointe-aux-Trembles, to await the arrival of Montgomery from Montreal.

XIII
A WOMAN'S TACTICS

When Zulma Sarpy reached home on the evening of her eventful journey to Quebec, her aged father observed that she was under the influence of strong emotions. She would have preferred keeping to herself all that she had seen or heard, but he questioned her closely and she could not well evade replies. It was quite natural, as she fully understood, that he should be anxious to obtain information about the state of affairs, especially as he had heard several rumors from his servants and neighbors during the day. When, therefore, she had composed herself somewhat, after the abundant and deliberate meal of a healthy, sensible woman, she narrated to him in detail all the events which she had witnessed. Sieur Sarpy frequently interrupted her with passionate exclamations which surprised her considerably, as they showed that he took a deeper interest in the impending war than he had intended or she had expected. The incident of the bridge particularly moved him.

"And you are certain," he asked, "that the young officer was the same who was fired at from the walls?"

"I am positive I cannot be mistaken," she replied. "His stature, his noble carriage, his handsome face would distinguish him among a thousand."

"But you do not know his name?"

"Alas! no."

"You should have inquired. The man who treated my daughter with such high courtesy should not be a stranger to me."

"Ah! never mind, papa, I shall find out his name yet," said Zulma with a laugh.

"Perhaps not. Who can tell what will happen? War is a whirlwind. It may blow him out of sight and remembrance before we know it."

"Never fear," interrupted Zulma with a magnificent wave of her white arm. "I have a presentiment that we shall meet again. I have my eye on him and — —"

"He has his eye on you," added Sieur Sarpy, breaking out into a little merriment which was unusual with him.

His daughter did not answer, but an ineffable light passed like an illumination over her beautiful face, and words which she would have uttered, but did not, died away in a delicious smile at the corners of her rich, sanguine lips. She rose from her chair, and stood immoveable for a moment, gazing at a vase of red and white flowers that stood on the mantel before her eyes. Her snowy night dress fell negligently about her person, but its loose folds could not conceal the outline of her bosom which rose and fell under the touch of some strong mastering feeling. Sieur Sarpy, as he looked up at her, could not dissimulate his admiration of the lovely creature who was the comfort and glory of his life, nor restrain his tears at the thought, vague and improbable though it was, that perhaps this war might, in some unaccountable way, carry with it the destiny of his daughter, and change for ever the current of their mutual existence. As she stood there before him, knowing her as he did, or perhaps because he did not know her so well as he might have done, he felt that she was about to make an important communication to him, ask him something or pledge him to some course which would affect him and her, and bring on precisely that mysterious result of which the shadow was already in his mind. But before he had the time to say a word either to quiet his fear or dissipate his conjecture, Zulma moved slowly from her place and dropped softly before his knees. All the color of her face, as she upturned it to his, was gone, but there was a melting pathos in those blue eyes which fascinated the old man.

"Papa," she said, "will you allow me to ask you a favor?"

Sieur Sarpy felt a twinge in his heart, and his lips contracted. Zulma noticed his emotion and immediately added:—

"I know that you are feeble, papa, and must not bear excitement, but what I have to ask you is simple and easy of accomplishment. Besides, I will leave you to judge and abide unreservedly by your decision."

Sieur Sarpy took his daughter's hand in his and replied:

"Speak, my dear, you know that I can refuse you nothing."

"You have resolved to be neutral in this war."

"That was my intention."

"Did you come to this resolution solely for your own sake?"

"For your sake and mine, dear. I am old and infirm, and cannot take part in the struggles of strong men. You are young and I must guard your future."

Zulma remained silent for a few moments, as if she could find no further words to say. Her father, observing her embarrassment, brought back the conversation to its original drift, by inquiring into the nature of the demand which she had intended to make.

"I had intended to ask you my liberty of action," she said, with suddenly recovered energy. "But I will not do so now. Circumstances will perhaps occur to modify the situation for both of us before hostilities have progressed very far. All I shall ask of you now is that you will allow me to see that young officer again."

The old man, on hearing this innocent request, breathed more freely, as he exclaimed:

"Why, is that all, my darling? You certainly may see him again. I would like to see him myself and make his acquaintance. As I told you before, I have great admiration for his bravery and gallantry towards you. And, Zulma, the next time you see him, don't fail to learn his name."

"That is precisely what I want to obtain," said the girl with a smile.

"Then we are quite agreed," rejoined her father, tapping her on the cheek and rising to close the interview.

He was now in great good humor, and she also affected to be gay, but there was a flush on her cheek which told of an interior flame that glowed, and when her father had departed, she walked up and down the floor of her bedchamber with the slow measured step of deep, anxious reflection.

XIV
THE ROMANCE OF LOVE

Four days later, the village of Pointe-aux-Trembles was startled by the approach of Arnold's men. Their appearance was so sudden and unexpected that the people did not know how to explain it, and the most of them barricaded their houses. But the American advance was very orderly. The vanguard wheeled to the left from the village and took up its quarters on the extreme edge of the St. Lawrence. The main body stacked arms in front of the church, and billets were at once secured in all the houses of the village. Arnold himself took up his residence with the curé who treated him well, and frequently during their short stay invited the principal officers to his table. This clergyman was opposed to the American invasion, in obedience to the mandate of the Bishop of Quebec, but for the sake of his people he judged it advisable to use the Continentals with as much respect as possible. And his courtesy was properly rewarded, as during their whole sojourn at Pointe-aux-Trembles, the Americans treated the inhabitants with unusual consideration. The rear guard passed through the village and echelonned along the road for a distance of fifteen or twenty miles. This division was mainly composed of cavalry and riflemen whose duty it was to scour the country in search of provisions, and to keep up communication with the upper country whence the reinforcements from Montgomery's army were daily expected.

All Arnold's officers approved of his temporary retreat, for the precise reasons which had been laid down by old Batoche appeared to every one of them urgent under the circumstances. But if there was any one of them more pleased than another it was Cary Singleton. He had other than military reasons for applauding this measure. The opportunity was afforded him— at least so he fancied—of recovering the treasure which he had lost under the dark covered bridge, of seeing once more the vision which, since that eventful night, had always floated before his memory. Glorious illusion of youth! At that favored period of existence so little appreciated while it lasts, and which, when it is gone, is the object of bitter lamentation for the rest of life, even hardship gives zest to enjoyment when the heart is buoyed— as what youthful heart is not?—by the sweet potency of woman's love.

Fatigue, hunger, thirst, disease, and poverty are only trifles that are laughed at, so long as there is seen in the background of it all the lambent light of tender eyes speaking, as nothing else can, the language of the devoted heart. For many of his brother officers, men with families, or already, advanced in years, this American invasion was a dreary reality, made up of a dismal succession of marches and counter-marches, parades and bivouackings, attacks and repulses, privations of every description, with the prospective of defeat at the last. But to Cary Singleton the war had been, up to the present, a constant scene of pleasurable excitement, as he will have occasion to testify himself in a subsequent chapter, while from this point to its close it rose with him to the proportions of a romance.

His single clue was that the beautiful girl whom he sought lived in the neighborhood of his present encampment. Whether it was above or below, on the line of the river, or somewhere in the interior, he could not of course tell, but he was determined to find out. He knew that the present quarters of the army were only temporary, that within eight or ten days, at the furthest, they would be on the forward march again, when the hurry of battle would ensue and his fate might be a bloody grave under the walls of the old capital. Hence the necessity for diligence. He thought he should be willing to die if his eyes were blessed only once more with the sight of the object of his worship.

These thoughts were passing through his brain, as he slowly rode along the road one quiet afternoon while the sun lay white on the frozen ground, tinging the leafless branches of the beeches and birches with a silver light. He little knew what was in store for him as he mechanically pulled in the reins, and looked up an avenue of maple leading to a mansion on his right.

XV
ON THE HIGH ROAD

The house attracted Cary's attention by the beauty of its site and its appearance of wealth and comfort. He at once concluded that it belonged to some old French seigneur who, after the conquest of the Province by the British, had retired to the seclusion of his estates, and there spent the evening of his life in the philosophic calm of solitude. He had no further curiosity about it, however, and would probably have passed on, had he not casually caught sight of a couple of figures coming down the stairs to the open space in front. The distance was considerable, and the intervening trees broke the line of vision somewhat, but he thought he could distinguish the forms of a young woman and an elderly man. He tarried a moment longer to look on. Presently he saw a horse led to the foot of the stairs, and the young lady assisted to her seat in the saddle. The site stirred him considerably. A suspicion—but it was only a suspicion—crossed his mind. What if it were she? He dismissed the thought, however, as altogether too good to be true. It was impossible that she should thus throw herself into his arms. Half the romance of all this adventure would be lost if it had so simple and easy a conclusion. No! He had to seek for her, he had to toil, to wait, to suffer still more before he could expect to attain the object of his desire. Thus do we add to our pain in the intensity of our love's longings, and Cary took grim pleasure in magnifying his own wretchedness. But somehow he kept his eye sharply fastened on the distant rider. After conferring with the elderly man for some moments, she drew herself up, settled herself in her saddle, and moved away from the front of the house. The avenue of maples, at the foot of which stood the young officer, lay directly in her path, and for a moment Cary thought she would take it. She halted her horse at the head of it and looked down toward the gate. She sat full in his sight. He sat full in hers. She must have seen him, as he certainly saw her. Did they recognize each other? O Love, that is so sharp-eyed ever, how perversely blind it is sometimes. Cary should have pulled up his horse's reins, cleared the fence and ridden like mad up the avenue. The lady should have waved her kerchief in token of a tryst and cantered down the path to meet her cavalier. Instead of which he sat dazed in his saddle, and she quietly walked her pony away from the opening of the avenue, and slowly passed along a narrow road through her father's grounds.

There is often a revelation in disappearance, as there is a light in darkness. Scarcely had he lost sight of the lady rider than Cary felt an irresistible impulse to meet her and discover who she was. Now that she was gone, the suspicion arose again that perhaps she was the loved one whom he sought. Had he frightened her? That was not probable from the ease and deliberation of her manner. Would he catch another glimpse of her? He felt that that depended entirely on himself, and he determined that if he did see her again, the sight would be a decisive one. He paused a moment longer before making up his mind what to do. He thought of opening the gate, sauntering up the avenue and turning down the path which she had taken. But the trespass on private property, and the fear of being stopped at the mansion to make explanations, deterred him from taking the step. He judged it wiser to spur up the main road and trust to luck. Perhaps he might find an outlet for that bridal path whence she would issue. In this surmise he was not mistaken. After riding about half a mile he came to the mouth of a rugged, unfrequented country road, the bed of which was moist from the ooze of rills on one of its banks. Here he stopped and reconnoitred with the keen eye of the soldier. To his surprise and delight he observed the fresh prints of pony's hoofs leading outward. He was satisfied that she had gone along this route, and pursued her journey further up the highway. The course was therefore clear for him. All he had to do was to follow, and he did so without delay.

Meantime the afternoon had worn on, and the sun was slowly sinking to the rim of the sky. There was the promise of a full hour of daylight yet, but the air was getting chilly and banks of pinkish clouds spreading fan-like in the western heavens gave portent of wind and storm. For a whole hour did Cary Singleton ride along that solitary road, watching the line of forest on his right and the steep embankment of the river on his left. But he heard nothing save the low lapsing sound of the water, and the monotonous simmer of the trees. He saw nothing that could divert his attention from the one object of his search. A fear came over him that his pursuit would be in vain. He was already far away from quarters and, without special cause, could not well prolong his absence much further. He therefore with a heavy heart resolved to turn his horse's head in the direction of the camp. As he advanced on a few steps slowly, deliberating sadly on this, he came to a sharp bend in the road, and a few hundred yards before him, observed the blue smoke of a little farm-house that stood in the clearing of the wood. Before the house there was a group of men, women and children standing around a saddled horse. To say that Cary was surprised would be using a very mild term indeed. He was so astounded that he did not venture to proceed another step. His presence excited a tumult among the people. The children ran into the house, the women retreated to the door, but a lady in riding-habit pacified them with a laughing gesture, and immediately mounted her horse. Addressing them a few words of farewell, she turned into the road and, a moment later, stood at the side of the young officer.

"Is it possible, mademoiselle?" was all that Cary could whisper, his agitation being so great that he had to hold on to his pommel for support. It would be falsehood to say that the lady was not similarly agitated, but she had that magnificent secret of disguise which places women far above men in many of the most critical passes of life.

Her answer was a delicious smile of recognition, and the offer of her gauntleted right hand.

"I never expected to meet you on this lonely road," said Cary, after recovering a little, in saying which he uttered a most palpable but unconscious falsehood. Else why had he ridden so far? Why had he suffered the torments of doubt and expectation the live-long afternoon? The lady was more direct and simple. The frankness of her reply almost startled Cary from his saddle.

"I expected to meet you, sir," she said, and broke out in one of her merriest laughs.

Explanations followed fast. The lady avowed that she had recognized Cary from the head of the avenue, had purposely avoided going down to meet him at the gate, had taken the bridle-path through her father's grounds instead, with the certainty that he would follow her. She only half intimated the reasons why she acted thus, but her partial reticence was the most charming portion of her revelations, and as he listened Cary was in a very ecstacy of delight. She knew that he would follow her! What adorable feminine ingenuousness in the confession! What consciousness of superiority and power!

The conversation, started from this point, did not flag. The young officer recovered full possession of his senses and the two rode briskly homeward in the roseate twilight which to them seemed the harbinger of a happy dawn flushed with the glories of an Eastern sunrise.

XVI
AN EPIC MARCH

The next day Cary Singleton sat with Zulma and her father in a room of the Sarpy mansion. A great fire glowed in front of them, and at their side was a little table bearing cakes and wine. Cary sat at one angle of the chimney, Sieur Sarpy at the other, and Zulma occupied a low chair in the apex of the semi-circle. After many topics of conversation had been exhausted, and the young officer had been made to feel quite at home, Sieur Sarpy demanded an account of Cary's march with Arnold through the forests of Maine.

"I have heard something about the hardships of that expedition," said he, "and I know enough about the nature of our woods and prairies to understand that yours must have been a particularly trying fate."

"We have a great deal of wood country in Maryland," replied Cary, "but nothing like this in your Northern climates. I am strong and healthy, but there were many times when I almost despaired of reaching Quebec in safety."

"Where did your army organize?"

"In Cambridge, at the headquarters of General Washington."

"When?"

"In the middle of August."

"What was your definite object?"

"Well, when war against Great Britain became inevitable, we had to prepare ourselves for the worse. The battles of Lexington, Concord and Breed's Hill threw us on the defensive. But we could not be satisfied with that. We must act on the offensive. Congress then resolved to attack the English in Canada."

"The English?" exclaimed Sieur Sarpy.

"Yes, the English," said Zulma, turning towards her father with animation of look and gesture. "The English, not the French."

"Precisely, mademoiselle," resumed Cary, with a smile and a profound bow. "The French in Canada are our brothers and have as much reason as we to detest the British yoke."

"Alas!" murmured Sieur Sarpy, raising his eyes to the ceiling and striking the arm of his chair with his palm.

A look from Zulma caused Cary to pass rapidly over this part of his narrative. He continued to say in general terms that Congress, having determined to invade Canada by way of the Northern lakes, judged it expedient to send a second expedition by way of the South, along the Kennebec river.

"It was a beautiful morning in September," he said, "when we marched out of Cambridge, under the eye of General Washington. Our first stopping place was at Newburyport. There we took to the water. Eleven transports conveyed us to the mouth of the Kennebec. Two hundred boats were awaiting us there, constructed by carpenters who had been sent ahead of us for that purpose. This place was the verge of civilization. Beyond it, for hundreds of miles in the interior, was the primeval forest. An advance party having been thrown forward for the purpose of reconnoitering and exploration, the main body proceeded in four divisions, of which our corps of riflemen held the van. After a pleasant march of six days, we came to Norridgewock Falls."

"Norridgewock?" said Sieur Sarpy, as if speaking to himself. "I think I remember that name."

"No doubt, you do, sir. It is a consecrated name. It recalls a great and good man, Father Ralle."

"Ah, I remember. It was about forty years ago, and I was very young, but I recollect with what horror the Superior of the Missions at Quebec heard of the massacre of the saintly apostle of the Abnakis."

"Who murdered him?" enquired Zulma.

"The English settlers in Massachusetts," replied her father with emphasis. "A party of them fell on the settlement and killed and scalped the missionary and thirty of his Indians."

The eyes of Zulma flashed fire, but she said nothing.

"Yes," said Cary, "the foundation of the church and altar of the Norridgewocks are still visible, but the Indians have disappeared and desolation reigns over the scene of blood. At these Falls we had our first portage."

"I know," said Sieur Sarpy, smiling.

"For a mile and a half we had to drag our boats over the rocks, through the eddies, and at times even along the woods. The boats were leaky, the provisions spoiled. We had to call oxen to our aid. Seven days were spent in this fatiguing work. When we arrived at the junction of Dead River with the Kennebec, one hundred and fifty men were off the rolls through sickness and desertion."

"Was the weather cold?"

"Not in the first part of our journey. The sky was balmy, the sun shone nearly every day, the watercourses were filled with salmon-trout, the trees were magnificent in their autumn foliage, and the tranquil atmosphere of the landscape was soothing to our wearied limbs. But in the middle of October, the scene suddenly changed. All the leaves of the forest had fallen, the wind blew chill through the openings, and suddenly there appeared before us a mountain of snow. Our commander pitched his tent and unfurled the Continental flag. One of our officers ran up to its summit, in the hope of seeing the spires of Quebec."

Sieur Sarpy smiled again and shook his head.

"That officer should have given his name to the mountain," said Zulma, laughing.

"So he did. We named it Mount Bigelow."

"And what did he see from the top of it?"

"Nothing but a wintry waste, and desolate woods. From this point, our sufferings and dangers increased until they became almost unbearable. Wading fords, trudging through the snow, hauling boats—it seemed that we should never cross the distance which separated us from the headwaters of the Chaudière. A council of war was held, the sick and disabled were ordered back to the rear, and, to add to our discouragement, Colonel Enos, the second in command, gave up the expedition and returned to Cambridge with his whole division."

"Traitor!" exclaimed Zulma, with characteristic enthusiasm.

"But the rest of us pressed on, spurred by the energy of despair. Seventeen falls were passed, and on a terrible October day, amid a blinding snow-storm, we reached the height of land which separates New England from Canada. A portage of four miles brought us to a small stream upon which we launched our boats and floated into Lake Megantic, the principal source of the Chaudière. We encamped here, and the next day, our commander with a party of fifty-five men on shore, and thirteen men with himself, proceeded down the Chaudière to the first French settlements, there to obtain provisions and send them back to us. They experienced unprecedented hardship. As soon as they entered the river, the current ran with great rapidity, boiling and foaming over a rocky bottom. They had no guide. Taking their baggage and stores to the boats, they allowed themselves to drift with the stream. After a time the roar of cascades and cataracts sounded upon their ears, and before they could help themselves, they were drifting among rapids. Three of the boats were dashed to pieces, and their contents lost. Six men were thrown into the water, but were fortunately rescued. For seventy miles falls and rapids succeeded each other, until at length, by a providential escape, the party reached Sertigan, the first French outpost."

"Saved!" exclaimed Zulma.

"And how were they treated there?" asked Sieur Sarpy with much curiosity.

"As friends. I am thankful to say that our wearied men received shelter and provisions from the French inhabitants who freely accepted our Continental scrip which they regarded as good money. But for their aid we should all have perished."

"The rest of the army did not follow at once?"

"It could not. We had to wait for provisions from our commander, else we should all have perished. We ate roots raw which we had to dig out of the sand on the river bank. We killed all our dogs for food. We washed our moose-skin moccasins, scraped away the dirt and sand, boiled them in the kettle and drank the mucilage which they produced. When the first flour and cattle reached us from Sertigan, the most of us had been forty-eight hours without eating. Refreshed in this way, encouraged by the friendship of the French inhabitants, and reinforced by a band of forty Norridgewocks, under their chiefs Natanis and Sabatis, to serve as guides for the remainder of the journey, we took up our march again and reached Levis two months after our departure from Cambridge."

"It was an epic march!" cried Zulma rising from her seat and pouring out wine into the glasses on the table. Sieur Sarpy pledged his guest in a bumper of Burgundy. And the compliment was deserved. That march of the Continental army was one of the most remarkable and heroic on record.

· XVII
O GIOVENTU PRIMAVERA DELLA VITA

In the fortnight that followed, Zulma and Cary met nearly every day, sometimes more than once a day. It was impossible that it should be otherwise. There is no power on this earth that can restrain two youthful hearts thrilling and surging with the first impulses of love. When the imagination is all aglow with the purple pictures of destiny; when the soul throbs with the unspeakably delicious sentiments of an affection that is requited; when the nerves are in tension and quiver like the strings of a harp; when the hot blood runs wild through the veins, suffusing lip and cheek and brow; and the eyes look out upon the roseate world through a mist of tears that are pleasureable pain and painful pleasure inexplicably blended, then there is no force of cold conventionality to check the outcomes of the spirit, no bolts or bars or chains to fetter the bounding limbs that go forth rejoicing through the enchanted landscape which the good God has opened to all of us, at least once in life, as an exquisite foretaste of Paradise.

What mattered it to Zulma and Cary that the autumn skies were low, that the winds moaned dismally through the leafless woods, that the snow clouded the face of the sun and charged the atmosphere with inclement moisture? They sat together before the blazing fire-place, and conversed for hours, quite forgetful of the dreary winter that was setting in. Or they stood together at the window, and as they conversed, unconsciously contrasted the light and warmth that reigned in their hearts with the cold and gloom of the waning year outside. Or they lingered on the portico, loath to part for the day, and never minded the bleakness of the weather, in the hope of meeting again. What mattered it that Singleton had military duties to perform which retained him in camp for many hours of each day, or sent him at the head of scouting parties, over the country in search of provisions or to watch the movements of the enemy? He managed his time so well that while never, in a single instance, neglecting his business as a soldier, he found the means of satisfying the claims of the lover. These very difficulties only gave zest to the excitement in which he lived, and he was happy to know, although she never said it, that they added to Zulma's sense of appreciation.

Another circumstance deserving of mention is that the young rifleman's visits to the Sarpy mansion were so conducted as to be a secret to his companions-in-arms. There was a purpose in this, although neither Cary, nor Zulma, nor M. Sarpy ever exchanged a word about it together. The stay of the Continental army at Pointe-aux-Trembles was only temporary. Its stay around Quebec, after it returned there, would be at least rather precarious. It was, therefore, hardly desirable that one of its officers should be known to have contracted other than military engagements which might bind his good name among the vicissitudes of a most hazardous war. Thus there was a dash of calculation in the romance of Cary's love, a reserve of good sense amid all the impetuousness which buoyed his heart. It is ever thus with men. They are rarely whole lovers. Their ingrained selfishness always pierces, however slightly, to mar the completeness of their sacrifice.

It was not so with the Canadian girl. She had that glorious independence—the gift of superior women—which cares not for the prying eyes of all the world. She did not mind who knew of the American soldier's visit to her father's home. She would not have concealed a single one of his interviews with herself. She liked him; she was delighted to think that he liked her; they were happy in each other's company—what more did she need for present happiness, and what harm if others knew that she was happy?

Neither had her father any of the misgivings so common and so hateful in meticulous old men. He was a loyal, frank character. He had unbounded confidence in his daughter, and his absorbing love for her made him rejoice in the present little episode as a bright spot amid the gathering gloom of war. He had taken a fancy to Cary from the first. He relished his conversation. He appreciated his attentions to Zulma with the proud consciousness that she fully deserved them. Apart altogether from political consideration, into which he never entered, and which the young officer had the delicacy never to approach, he was pleased to judge for himself of the men who came to invade his country in the sacred name of liberty, and of extending the hospitality of his house to a representative among them, as proof that he too was a friend of humanity and chose to regard the impending war only from the standpoint of right.

Fortunately, however, for all concerned, it so happened that the visits of Cary were known to very few of those who habitually went to the Sarpy mansion. The daily beggar hobbled up as usual, with his basket under his arm, or meal bag slung across his shoulder, to gather the abundant crumbs of the table, but he never penetrated beyond the kitchen. The poor widow of the neighborhood appeared regularly for the broken victuals that were almost the sole sustenance of her brood of little orphans, but she was a model woman of her class, not given to gossip and so devoted to her benefactors that she would repeat nothing likely to satisfy the vulgar curiosity of outsiders. The farmers and villagers, of Pointe-aux-Trembles were kept so busy providing food and lodgings for the army, or were so deterred from moving about by the sight of the patrols along the roads, that almost none of them called at the mansion during the whole period of occupation.

And so passed the fortnight away. It was all too short considered by the number of days. The mornings rose and the twilights came with a calm remorseless rapidity that had no regard for the calculations of the heart, but when the recapitulation was made, it was found that a mighty distance had been travelled, and that the vague impressions of each succeeding interview had verged at last into a blazing focus, whence the illumination of two youthful lives burst upon the view.

XVIII
BRAIDING ST.CATHERINE'S TRESSES

One incident of this eventful period must not be passed over in silence. The reader himself will judge of its importance. It was the 25th November, St. Catherine's Day. In Italy and the South of Europe, the Virgin-Martyr is venerated as the patron of philosophical students, and the collegiate bodies celebrate her festival with public disputations on logical and metaphysical subjects. But in Belgium and France, the day is kept as one of social rejoicing by the young, and in Canada, from the earliest times, probably because it marks the closing day of the navigation of the St. Lawrence and the beginning of the long dreary winter, it is observed with song, dance, games, and other tokens of revelry. One special feature is the making of taffy which the young girls engage in during the evening, and with which they regale their friends and lovers.

The day itself had been melancholy enough. Snow had fallen continually until it had piled a foot high on the level roads. The wind howled dismally around the gables, and the branches of a maple beat doleful music against the window of Zulma's room. She felt the influence of the inhospitable weather. A feeling of weariness weighed upon her from the early hours of the morning. Nothing that she attempted to do could distract her mind or dispel her loneliness. The book which she had taken up over and over again lay with its face down upon the table. The harpsichord was open, but the music on its rack was tossed and tumbled. Zulma was a good musician and passionately fond of her instrument, but could not abide it when her spirits were depressed. She used to declare that, even in her best moods, the simplest melody had for her a tinge of sadness, which, when she herself was sorrowful, became a positive pain.

She scarcely left her room during the whole day. The house was silent and could afford her no relief. There was nobody stirring in the courtyard or around the kitchen. Even the great watch dog had retired to sleep in his kennel. The snow fell noiselessly, curtaining out all the world; the line of the sky was low and leaden, and nothing was heard to break the death-like stillness of the air, save occasional gusts of wind sullenly booming in the hollows.

If Zulma could have slept! More than once she threw herself wearily upon her couch, but the eyelids which she would have closed remained rigidly open, and she surprised herself gazing with intense stare upon the arabesques of the window shades or the flowered patterns of her bed curtains, while all sorts of wild, incongruous fancies trooped through her brain, causing her brow to ache. She would then spring with impatience to her feet, stretch out her white arms, clasp her hands behind her neck, roll up the coils of golden hair that had fallen on her shoulders, and then walk up to the window, where she gazed vacantly out upon the bleak prospect.

"If he would only come," she murmured, as she stood there. "But it is impossible. There is no riding on horseback through such snow, or I should have gone out myself."

At length the weary afternoon had worn away. Five o'clock rang through the house from the old French clock at the head of the stair. Zulma had just finished counting the strokes with a feeling of relief when the tinkling of sleigh bells fell upon her ear. She rushed to the window, shot a glance upon the court, uttered an exclamation of joy and ran out of her room.

"No, it cannot be, my darling, and in such weather!"

But it was Pauline nevertheless. The two friends fell into each other's arms, kissed each other over and over again, and repaired together to Zulma's room, where, amid the work of unwrapping, and warming feet, and sipping a glass of wine, the congratulations and expostulations went briskly on. Pauline had come with Eugene Sarpy, as that young gentleman himself testified when he entered the house in noisy boyish fashion, after having put up the horse. It was a holiday at the Seminary where the youth was immured, and he had the opportunity to drive out to the old home once more. He had asked Pauline to accompany him, and she declared herself only too glad of the occasion to see Zulma again.

"It may be our last chance, you know," she said, half laughing, but with a slight shadow on her sweet face.

"And those horrid rebels," rejoined Zulma very merrily. "How did you make up you mind to encounter them?"

"We did not encounter them."

Zulma's face suddenly turned white.

"What? Are they gone?"

The fear flashed upon her mind that perhaps the Americans had left the neighborhood, which would account for the absence of Cary during the day, but she was reassured by Pauline, who informed her that Eugene had avoided the American camp by taking a roundabout way through the concessions.

"That must have increased your distance."

"It did at least by four leagues, but I didn't mind that so long as we were free from danger."

"You do not like these soldiers?"

"I dislike them all, except, perhaps, one."

Zulma looked up in surprise.

"And pray who may that one be?"

"Don't you remember the bearer of the flag?"

"Oh!" was the only exclamation that Zulma uttered, while cheeks were fit to burst with the rush of conscious blood.

"Roderick has spoken to me of him in the highest terms of admiration," continued Pauline quietly.

"He will doubtless be flattered to hear of this," said Zulma, with just a touch of sarcasm in her tone.

But it was lost upon the gentle, unsuspicious Pauline, and Zulma, regretting the remark, immediately said:

"If you had met him on your passage, he would have treated you kindly, depend upon it," and she proceeded to relate the incident of the covered bridge. One detail brought on another, and the two friends, sat for two hours talking together, and much of the conversation turned on the American officer. What two young women can tell each other in the course of two hours is something stupendous, and he would be presumptuous, indeed, who would venture upon the enumeration of even the topics of converse. One thing, however, may be taken for granted—that when they were called to supper, they kissed each other with a smack and trotted down stairs in jolly good humor.

After supper the table was cleared, a large basin of maple syrup was produced, and after it was sufficiently boiled, the two friends began drawing the coils of taffy, with the assistance of Eugene, and under the eyes of Sieur Sarpy, who sat at the table sipping his wine and enjoying the amusement of the young people. Zulma's spirits had completely revived; and she was in high feather, enlivening the occasion by songs, and anecdote and banter, while she bustled around the table playing tricks upon her brother, and teasing the gentle Pauline. Now and then she would stop suddenly as if to listen, and her face would assume an expression of disappointed expectancy, but the shadow would disappear as rapidly as it came. Pauline was less boisterous and talkative. She was, however, in the pleasantest state of mind, as if for this one evening, at least, she had unburdened herself of the cares which had weighed her down during the past eventful days. Eugene, like all schoolboys escaped from the master's eye, was perfectly ridiculous in his wild gambols and inconsequential talk, but his nonsense gave zest to the merriment precisely because it was suggestive of that freedom with which the horrid front of war and the constant spectacle of armed men in the neighborhood afforded so sad a contrast.

An hour had been spent in this pastime, when Zulma again checked herself in the conversation, and as she turned her eyes to the window, they flashed with a ray of exultation. Her long waiting had not been in vain. The weary day would still have an agreeable ending. She was certain that she heard the music of sleigh bells, and she knew who it was that had come. A moment later, there was a rap at the door of the dining-room, and Cary Singleton stood on the threshold. Zulma went rapidly forward to meet him, receiving him with a cordiality and enthusiasm which she had never previously manifested. After the formal introduction was made, Cary excused himself for calling so late in the evening.

"Better late than never," exclaimed Zulma with an earnest indiscretion which she tried to turn off by a laugh, but which the rapid wandering of her great blue eyes showed that she was ashamed of.

Singleton bowed low, but there was no responsive smile upon his lip.

"Thank you, mademoiselle," said he, "but a little more and I should perhaps *never* have returned here."

There was a general expression of surprise.

The young officer explained that a forward movement of the American army was about to take place, and that he had received orders that very afternoon to abandon his quarters.

"The order was peremptory," he added, "and I should have had to obey it without delay, but fortunately the snow-storm came on with such violence towards evening that our departure was postponed till to-morrow morning. The opportunity I regarded as providential and seized it to make what may be my last visit."

The light went out of Zulma's eyes and she bowed her head. Her father broke the perplexing silence by saying cheerily:

"I trust that this will not be your last visit, sir. Indeed, I feel certain that we shall meet each other again. If in the varying fortunes of war, you should ever need my help, only let me know and you shall have it."

Zulma looked up and there was that imploring tenderness in her eyes which gave Cary to understand that she too, in the hour of need, would fly to his assistance.

While this conversation was going on, Pauline sat a little in the background. She said not a word, but her eyes were full of tears. Cary, as he glanced around, to relieve himself of the melancholy of the moment, noticed her emotion and was strangely touched by it. He knew well who she was, as Zulma had often mentioned her name to him, explaining the embarrassing situation which the war had created for herself and family, and the relations in which she stood towards Roderick Hardinge. These marks of silent sympathy from one of the besieged in Quebec, and one who was tenderly attached to a leading British officer, moved him profoundly, and, from that moment, he took steps to enlarge his acquaintance with Pauline. By degrees the conversation turned into a more cheerful channel, and the anxiety of the morrow being temporarily forgotten, as young hearts will forget and are blest in forgetting, the evening passed agreeably on, and Cary had abundant opportunity of enjoying the society of Pauline. His manner and his words proved how much he was impressed with the charms of her person, and the beauty of her character, and the admiration which he expressed was reciprocated by Pauline in those half advances and still more eloquent reticences which are the delicious secret of loving women. Zulma was so little disconcerted by this mutual good understanding, that she openly favored it, being unable to conceal her delight that her own two best friends should be friends together. Far seeing girl as she was, she was rejoiced that, on the eve of separation and the consequent resumption of hostilities, the young Continental officer should have made the acquaintance of one who might perhaps be his saviour if the storm of war whirled him torn and bleeding within the walls of the beleaguered city. Divine instinct of women! How often it stands in good stead the headlong rashness of man amid the wildering strokes of fate!

Genuine gaiety resumed its sway, and the work of taffy-making was taken up again. Cary was fed with choice titbits until he was fairly satisfied and had to beg for quarter. Then, taking up a large roll of the *tire*, Zulma twisted it into a series of elegant and intricate plaits. The long coil flashed like a beautiful brazen serpent, as she held it up to the light, and set it beside her own golden hair.

"These are Saint Catherine's tresses!" she cried. "Who will wear them, you or I, Pauline?"

And the sally was greeted by the loud laughter of all the company, except Cary who did not understand its significance. When it was explained to him that she would wear the mystical tresses who was destined to remain an old maid, he smiled as he murmured to himself:

"I will see to that!"

XIX
PAR NOBILE

The evening had come to an end. Midnight had sounded and Cary Singleton had to take his departure. The whole family accompanied him to the outer door, where his sleigh was in waiting. The last words of farewell still lingered on the faltering lips of the two young women, as they stood in the embrasure of the entrance, when, through the darkness and the pelting of the storm, Zulma noticed a shadow leaning against the house, at a few feet from her. She at once, in a loud voice, challenged it to come forward. It did so. By the feeble light of the passage she saw before her a strange, uncouth figure, wrapped in a wild-cat coat, and covered with a huge cap of fox-skin. The form was bent and the face was that of an old man, but the eyes flashed like stars. The man stood on snow-shoes, and he carried a long staff in his hand.

Pauline shrank behind Zulma as she saw the apparition, and murmured:

"It is Batoche!"

"Yes, child, that is my name," said the old man, "and I am come to fetch you."

"To fetch her?" asked Zulma with a tone of authority.

"Yes, at her father's request."

"Come in and explain what you mean."

"No. It is unnecessary. Besides, the night is too far advanced. We must return together at once."

A few hurried words revealed Batoche's mission. The Bastonnais were on the forward march again. Quebec would be invested within a few hours. Large reinforcements would enable the Americans to make the blockade complete. Pauline's father was extremely anxious about the return of his daughter. Batoche, who was within Quebec, escaped from it, promising his friend to carry out his wishes. If Pauline tarried she would not be allowed within the gates. Father and child would be separated. There was no time to lose. A resolution had to be made. Would Pauline come?

Lamentations and condolences were out of the question. It needed only a few words of consultation to decide upon following the old man's instructions. Cary avowed that the information given concerning military movements was correct, and offered to escort Pauline securely through the American lines. A further hardship was the parting of Sieur Sarpy and Zulma from Eugene, under the circumstances, but they made the sacrifice bravely, and the youth, it is only fair to say, acted his part with pluck. He had brought Pauline out; he would take her back. If Zulma had followed her own impulses, she would have accompanied her brother and friend till she had seen them safe within the walls, but she was obliged to renounce this pleasure in consideration of her aged father.

Batoche declined a seat in either sleigh. He returned on snow-shoes as he had gone; and so fleet was his march through the by-ways and short paths of the country which he knew so well, that he reached the appointed destination ahead of the party.

It was after six o'clock, and the dawn was just breaking when the sleighs came within sight of the gates. Cary Singleton approached as near as he durst, when he stopped to take leave of his fair charge. Batoche walked directly up to the sentry, where, after a brief parley, he returned, accompanied by a single man.

"Pauline!" exclaimed the new comer, as he stood beside her, "I have been anxiously waiting for you. Come in to the town at once."

She bent down to him and whispered something in his ear. He turned and, smiling, bowed profoundly to the American officer, who returned the salute.

Cary Singleton and Roderick Hardinge had met a second time.

A moment after, the whole party had disappeared and the snow covered their tracks.

BOOK III
THE BURSTING OF THE TEMPEST

I
QUEBEC IN 1775-76

Quebec is the most picturesque city in America. Its scenery is unrivalled. Rock, forest and water combine to make its position an unfailing charm to the student of landscape art. As it is to-day, so was it one hundred years ago, or if there is a difference, it is in favor of the latter date, for the pick and the axe had then made fewer inroads upon the sublime work of nature.

Quebec is the most historical city in America. One of the very oldest in date, it is by far the most notable in stirring annals. From its earliest origin, it was the theatre of important events whose results stretched far beyond its walls, and swayed the destinies of the whole continent. Its records are religious, diplomatic, military, and naval. Its great men were missionaries, statesmen, soldiers, and sailors. The heroic explorers of the Far West were its sons, or went forth from its gates. Jogues looms up beside Brebœuf. Champlain and Frontenac open the luminous way along which have trod Dorchester and Dufferin. The blended glory of Wolfe and Montcalm is immortal, and the renown is hardly less of the young, ill-fated Montgomery. Where was there ever a greater sailor than Iberville? The history of the Mississippi Valley is linked for all time with the names of Marquette, Hennepin, Joliet, and Lasalle.

It follows that in this era of centennial reminiscences, no city in America is more interesting than Quebec, and an additional charm is that we have comparative ease in placing it before the eye as it was a century ago.

In the winter of 1775-76, the population was about 5,000 souls. Of these 3,200 were women and children. All the men were made to bear arms. Those who refused were ordered out of the walls. There were probably not one hundred English families in the town. The English language was spoken only by the military. The times were hard. Provisions at first were abundant, but fire-wood was scarce. Fortunately the winter on the whole was mild. The houses during the day were partially deserted. The men were on guard. The women were on the streets gadding. They found plenty of occupation, for the air was thick with rumors. A besieged city must perforce be a nest of gossip, a hive of cock-and-bull stories. The regulars looked smart in their regimental uniforms. The militia wore such toggery as they could get—grey homespun coat with red sash, cowskin boots, and the traditional *tuque bleue*. The trappers not being allowed into the town, furs were rare, and women of the lower classes were obliged to go without them altogether. The centres of attraction were the guard-rooms and sentry-boxes. There the episodes of the siege were recounted. There all manner of serious and comic incidents occurred to relieve the monotony of the long winter months. The principal barracks were in Cathedral Square, in that venerable Jesuit College which is to be pulled down during the present year. The three chief outposts were St. Louis, St. John, and Palace Gates. These were the three original French Gates, improved and strengthened by the great engineer, de Lery. Through them, sixteen years before, the army of Montcalm passed after its defeat on the Plains of Abraham, and then passed out again, crossing by a bridge of boats to the camp at Beauport. Through them one year later, the broken army of Murray rushed back in flight from the disastrous field of St. Foye. But for those strong gates built by the Frenchmen, the victorious army, under Levis, might have recovered Quebec, on that memorable day, and regained possession of New France. Bitter irony of fate! Along the avenue where Prescott Gate was afterwards erected, palisades were raised by James Thompson, Overseer of Works, to bar the advance of the Americans from that quarter, and his name, as we shall see later on, was intimately associated with the siege. All these defences were in Upper Town, or within the walled portion. In Lower Town and under the Cape, the eastern extremity was defended by batteries in Dog Lane or Little Sault-au-Matelot, and the western end at Près-de-Ville, by a masked battery. Going from one to the other of these constituted the round of military service. The Lower Town was chiefly guarded by militia. They went and came singing their French songs, the very best of military bands.

Vive la Canadienne
Et ses jolis yeux doux,

then received its consecration, and the light-hearted fellows kept step to *c' était un p'tit bonhomme* and *à la claire fontaine*. Along with the singing there was much good-natured conversation. War has its grim humors. One party standing in the Cul de Sac on the site of the chapel built by Camplain, made mirth at the expense of Jerry Duggan, late hair-dresser, in the town, who had gone over to the enemy and was "stiled" Major amongst them. Jerry was said to be in command of five hundred Canadians, and had disarmed the inhabitants of St. Roch, a suburb of Quebec, without opposition. Another party, grouped in front of the Chien d'Or, laughed heartily at the *Canadiens Bastonnais*, Canadians who had joined the rebels, because they were stationed on the ice of the river to keep patrol. "A cold reward for treason," they said. Mysterious visitors went in and out of George Allsopp's house in Sous-le-Fort street. Allsopp was chief of opposition in Cramahé's Council. The outposts were enlivened every night by the arrival of deserters. Some of these were spies. The information they gave of the enemy was very puzzling. Every morning at headquarters, when the roll was called, some one was found missing, having escaped to the Americans. About one third of every army cannot be depended upon. The length of the siege produced dearness of provisions, which had not been carefully husbanded from the start. So early as January, beef rated at nine pence, fresh pork at one and three, and a small quarter of mutton at thirteen shillings. Notwithstanding repeated refusals, the besiegers periodically approached the walls with flags of truce. A needless and unaccountable courting of humiliation. Every now and again the enemy succeeded in setting fire to houses within the walls. The consequent excitement relieved the monotony of the blockade, and was an event to talk about. The garrison made frequent partial sorties in quest of fire-wood, sometimes successfully, sometimes unsuccessfully. Fatigue parties dug trenches in the snow, without the walls, by way of exercise or bravado. Sentinels at the Block House and other exposed points were frequently frostbitten. A kind of sentry-box was fixed on a pole thirty feet high, at Cape Diamond. Thence could be seen the tin spire of St. Foye Church, but not the Plains of Abraham, beyond Gallow's Hill, where the besiegers lay in force. Over the American camp the red-flag waved. Some thought it was the bloody flag, by way of threat. But it was no more than a signal to the prisoners within the town. About one hundred men were picked up and formed into an Invalid Company to guard these prisoners. Among this guard were some "picqued who did not formerly perceive the meanness of their behaviour," as the old chronicle tells. On dark nights rockets were sent up and large fires made on the ramparts and the high streets to confound the enemy's signals. There was much generous rivalry between the French militiamen and the British regulars. The former were greatly encouraged by the priests, who went among them familiarly in their long black robes. The Seminary, in Cathedral-square, where the Bishop resided, was as much frequented by the soldiery as the headquarters of MacLean in the Jesuit barracks, on the other side of the square. Monseigneur Briand was as truly the defender of Quebec as General Carleton. The most curious signals of the Americans were fire-balls which burned from one in the morning till three. Whenever these were seen, the garrison prepared more actively for an attack. Spite of precautions on both sides, communication to and from the beleaguered town was carried on to a considerable extent. A bold, active man could always go in or out from the side of the river under the Cape, or along the valley of the St. Charles. The Continentals had not men enough to effect a complete blockade, and the garrison was not sufficiently numerous to guard every obscure outlet. But spite of these deficiencies, for eight long months—from November 1775 till May 1776—Quebec was virtually cut off from the rest of the world and the theatre of one of the most important military events in the history of America.

II
CARY'S MESSAGE

As soon as Pauline had entered the gates of the town, Cary Singleton leaped into his sleigh and turned his horse's head towards the camp. But before he could proceed, Batoche was at his side. The young officer had not had occasion to exchange a single word with the singular being, but his thoughts had been much occupied with him during the long night ride, and it was with some satisfaction that he now had an opportunity of addressing him.

"I must thank you, sir," said he, "for your service to the young lady."

"I did it for her sake, as she is my granddaughter's godmother. And for her father's sake, who is an old friend," replied Batoche, quietly. And he added immediately:

"I am prepared to do you a service, sir."

Cary looked at him in surprise. Was he in the presence of an enemy? Had he fallen into an ambush from which this man was willing to rescue him? Or if a friend, what service could he refer to? Might it be a message to Pauline? Strange as it may seem—and perhaps it will not appear so strange after all—the very thought, as it flashed upon him, created a throbbing sensation in his heart. Had this little timid girl, after only a few hours' interview, so ingratiated herself into his affections, that the unexpected opportunity of communicating with her once more excited a flutter of pleasurable surprise. Rapidly as these surmises passed through his mind he had not time to resolve them, before Batoche resumed in these simple words:

"I am returning at once to Sieur Sarpy's."

For a moment Cary was unable to make a syllable of reply. He looked hard at the old man as if to fathom his inmost thoughts. But the latter did not flinch. His countenance wore that expression of utter blankness and conscious unconsciousness which is an attribute of resolute men, and which only kindred spirits are gifted to understand.

Cary was as much impressed by his quiet manner as he had been by his singular offer. He asked himself the following questions sharply one after the other. What did this man know of him that he should connect him in any way with the Sarpys? How should he be in possession of the secret which had been hidden from all his comrades? Zulma did not know him when he presented himself at her door last night. Sieur Sarpy exchanged only a few words with him, and certainly did not treat him as a familiar. And who was this Batoche? Was he a friend or an enemy of the cause of liberty? Perhaps he was a spy?

During the interval Batoche stood immovable, while the snow piled in inches on his round shoulders, but at length, divining the thoughts of Cary, he said in a low voice:

"You are returning to Sieur Sarpy's, did you say?"

"At once."

"But the roads will be all blockaded."

"I know all the by-paths."

"Our troops are advancing and might arrest you."

The old man only smiled.

"I will give you a pass."

Batoche took off his glove and produced from his pocket a folded paper.

Cary opened it, and recognizing the signature of Colonel Meigs, returned it with a smile.

"I thankfully accept your offer," said he. "Here is a little message which you will deliver to Mademoiselle Zulma."

Saying which, he wrote a few lines in pencil on a leaf of his pocket book.

"She will receive it at noon," said Batoche, taking the missive, and without the addition of another word, he stalked away on his snow-shoes.

Cary returned to camp just in time to take part in the forward movement of his corps. The main body did not break up its quarters till five days later, but on the 29th November, the day on which the event just narrated took place, Morgan's riflemen were ordered to lead the van towards Quebec. That same afternoon, therefore, Singleton found himself nearly on the same spot which he had occupied in the early morning.

III
THE UNREMEMBERED BRAVE

The snow-storm continued in unabated violence. The low lines of the sky seemed to lie upon the earth, the sounds of nature were deadened to mystical murmurs, the long streams of flakes lay like a white curtain drawn aslant across the face of heaven, and universal silence pervaded the land. Everybody was within doors, where the exterior calm had penetrated, and where the families nestled around the hearth as if conscious of the visible protection of God. It seemed like a desecration that this holy silence should be disturbed by the iron tread of armed men, and that the peace sent down from above with every grain of snow should be violated by designs of vengeance and the thirst of human blood. Unseen through the storm, the riflemen of Virginia advanced towards the grey walls of the devoted town. Unheard through the tempest, the garrison of the ancient capital moved to the gates and ramparts. Unseen and unheard, the armies of Arnold and Montgomery, which had now combined, were making their last preparations to depart from Pointe-aux-Trembles and march for the final catastrophe in this dread tragedy of war.

Sieur Sarpy sat in his arm-chair after dinner absorbed in the reading of a book, and apparently under the blessed influence of the peaceful, noiseless weather. From the staidness of his manner, it was evident that he had forgotten the events of the previous night, and was unconscious or oblivious of what was going on among the belligerents around Quebec.

He was interrupted in his occupation by the entrance of the maid, who announced the arrival of Batoche. The sound of the name surprised him a little, but without moving from his seat, he said quietly:

"Show him up."

The two old men had not been many minutes together before they understood each other well. They were both of an age, and had known one another in former and better days. After the usual preliminaries of recognition were gone through, Batoche said:

"I have been on my legs for fourteen hours, and must return whence I came before night. I am old now and have not the endurance of fifteen years ago. Hence I must be brief, although my business is of the greatest importance. Please give me all your attention for half an hour."

Sieur Sarpy closed his book and holding up his right hand, asked:

"Is the business political or personal."

"Both. There is a question of crime on the one hand, and of mercy on the other. I appeal to your humanity."

At that moment Zulma appeared at the door of the room, but was about to withdraw at once, when Batoche turned towards her, and with a sweetness of manner that one would never have suspected in him, said:

"I hope mademoiselle will enter. I have no secret for her. We all know that she is her father's trusted counsellor. And mademoiselle will be pleased to learn that her brother and her friend, little Pauline, have entered safely within the gates of Quebec, and that the young officer, having rejoined his command, is now somewhere near the walls of the town. Before parting from him this morning, he requested me to hand you this little note."

Zulma's hand trembled as she took the paper, but she did not open it. When she was seated, Batoche immediately resumed:

"You are aware that Governor Carleton has arrived in Quebec?"

"Yes, we heard the guns of the Citadel proclaiming the event," replied Sieur Sarpy.

"That happened just ten days ago. It was the most terrible blow yet struck against our cause."

"Your cause, Batoche?" said Sieur Sarpy, looking up.

"Aye, my cause, your cause, the cause of us all. See here, M. Sarpy, this is no time for mincing words. We must stand up and take a part in this war. We did not provoke it, but it has come and we must join it. You may prefer to remain neutral. I do not say you are wrong. Your health is poor, you have a young daughter, you have large estates. But for me and hundreds like me, there is only one course. I am an old French soldier, M. Sarpy. Remember that. I fought on those plains yonder under the noble Marquis. I fought at St. Foye under the great Chevalier. I have seen this beautiful country snatched from France. For sixteen long years I have seen the wolves at work tearing from us the last shreds of our patrimony. They killed my daughter. They have made an outcast of me. I have prayed that the day of vengeance might come. I knew it would come. I heard it coming like distant thunder in the voice of the waterfall. I heard it coming in the wild throbbings of my violin. And, thank God, it has come at last! These Americans advance to meet us. They stretch out the right hand of fraternity. They unfurl the flag of liberty.

They too suffer from the tyranny of England, and they ask us to join them in striking off the fetters of slavery. Shall we not act with them?"

Sieur Sarpy's head fell upon his breast and he answered not. Zulma sat forward in her chair, with dilated eyes fastened on the face of the speaker, and her own features aglow with the enthusiasm that shot from him like living electric tongues.

Batoche who had risen from his seat during this impassioned outburst, now resumed it, and proceeded in more subdued language:

"If Carleton had not returned to Quebec the war would perhaps be ended now. He was beaten everywhere in the upper country, at Isle-aux-Noix, at Chambly, at Longueuil, at St. Johns. He fled from Montreal without striking a blow. All his men surrendered there and at Sorel. All his ships were captured. All his stores were seized. And do you know how he escaped?"

"In an open boat, I am told."

"Yes, in an open boat. He passed at Sorel, where the Americans were watching for him, and the oars were muffled in their locks so that he could not be heard. The boat was even paddled with open hands in the most dangerous places."

Zulma listened eagerly to these details, which she had not heard before. Sieur Sarpy's single remark was:

"Wonderful!"

"And do you know who piloted him?"

"Captain Bouchette, I believe."

"Yes, Joseph Bouchette. And what is Joseph Bouchette?"

"A French Canadian!" exclaimed Zulma, unable to contain herself.

"Aye, mademoiselle, a French Canadian. But for this Joseph Bouchette, a French Canadian, Carleton would never have reached Quebec, and the war would now be ended."

"By this you mean that the Americans would have Quebec, the only place in all Canada that is not theirs already," said Sieur Sarpy, with considerable energy.

"Just so. Now, it is about this Joseph Bouchette that I have come to see you."

Both Zulma and her father involuntarily started.

Batoche continued:

"Bouchette has committed a great crime. He has been guilty of treason against his countrymen. He must perish. There are hundreds who think like me, but are afraid to strike. I am not afraid to strike. He will suffer by my hand. The only question is the mode of punishment. Murder is repugnant to my feelings. Besides it would not be polite. The man was perhaps sincere in his devotion to Carleton, though I believe that he rather looked to the reward. But if sincere, that ought to be considered in mitigation of his sentence. Furthermore, he is a friend of M. Belmont, and that too shall count in his favor. I had intended to seize him and deliver him as a prisoner of war to the Bastonnais."

Sieur Sarpy made a solemn gesture of deprecation.

"Are you serious, Batoche?" he asked.

"Serious?" said the old man with that wild strange look characteristic of his preternatural moods.

"Bouchette is safe."

"Not from me."

"He is well guarded."

"I will break through any guard."

"But you cannot enter the town."

"I can enter whenever I like."

"When inside, you will not be able to come out."

"The weasel makes an invisible hole, which is never filled up."

Zulma listened with riveted eye, set lip, and distended nostril. Sieur Sarpy smiled.

"You will kidnap Bouchette?"

"I will."

"And fetch him to the American camp?"

"Yes."

"Well, what of that? Bouchette is no friend of mine. I know him only by name. How does all this concern me?"

"Precisely. That is just what I have come for."

Sieur Sarpy looked at his curious interlocutor with renewed interest, not unblended with concern.

"I have come from, and in the name of, M. Belmont. He knows of my plan and has tried to dissuade me from it. But in vain. He might warn

Bouchette or betray me to the garrison, but he is too loyal to France for that. He respects my secret. This, however, does not prevent him from striving to help his friend. He said to me, 'Batoche, if you must make a prisoner of Joseph Bouchette, go first to Sieur Sarpy and ask him whether he would receive him in his house on parole. He would thus be relieved of much unnecessary suffering, at the same time that he would be out of the way of doing you further mischief.' After some hesitation, I accepted this proposal of my friend, and here I am to communicate it to you."

"I do not accept," said M. Sarpy curtly and decidedly. "I would be ashamed to have a countryman of mine a prisoner in my house. If I took part in this war, I should do so openly, but so long as I remain on neutral ground, I will not allow my premises to be violated by either party. If Bouchette deserves to suffer, let him suffer to the full."

"Then he will suffer to the full," said Batoche rising rapidly and seizing his cap.

"No, he will not," exclaimed Zulma also rising and facing the old soldier. "M. Bouchette did only his duty. He has his opinions as you and I have. He has been faithful to those opinions. He has done a brave deed. He has shed glory on his countrymen instead of disgrace. Who constituted you his judge? What right have you to punish him? M. Belmont keeps your secret? I am surprised. I will not keep it. I do not consider it a secret. Even if it were, I would violate it. Promise me that you will desist. In the name of France, in the name of honor, in the name of religion, I call upon you to abandon your project. If you do not, I will this moment leap into a sleigh, drive to Quebec, find my way within the walls, seek M. Bouchette and tell him all. What do you say?"

During this impassioned harangue, the face of Batoche was a study. First there was surprise, then amazement, then incredulity, then consternation, then perplexity, then utter collapse. It was evident that the old soldier had never encountered such an adversary before her. The animated beauty of the speaker no less than her stirring words magnetised him, and, for a few moments, he could not reply, but his native cunning gradually awoke and he said slyly:

"Very well, mademoiselle, but what would the young officer say?"

Without noticing the covert allusion, Zulma answered promptly:

"The American officers are all gentlemen. They admire bravery and devotion wherever they see it, and they would not take unfair advantage of any enemy. But that is neither here nor now. Answer me. Do you persevere in your intention or not?"

"Mademoiselle, Joseph Bouchette owes his liberty to you," said Batoche, and, bowing, he walked out of the room. Sieur Sarpy attempted to detain him, but without success. He went silently and swiftly as he had come.

An author has said that a wonderful book might be written on Forgotten Heroes. Joseph Bouchette was one of them. By piloting the Saviour of Canada in an open boat from Montreal to Quebec, he performed the most brilliant and momentous single service during the whole war of invasion. And yet his name is hardly known. No monument of any kind has been raised to his memory. Nay more, after the lapse of a hundred years, the material claims of the Bouchette family have been almost entirely ignored.

IV
PRACTICAL LOVE

When Zulma found herself alone in her room, she opened the note of Cary Singleton. She noticed that it was moist and crumpled in her hand. It had been a sore trial to wait so long before acquainting herself with its contents, but she felt, as some sort of compensation, that it had served to nerve her to the animated dialogue which she had held with Batoche.

"That paper," she said, "urged me to be brave. I knew that he who had written it would have expressed the same sentiments under the circumstance."

The note was very brief and simple. It read thus:

"Mademoiselle,—

"I desired to speak to you last night a parting word, but I could not. I am gone from you, but whither, I cannot tell. The future is a blank. May I ask this grace? Should I fall, will you cherish a slight remembrance of me? Your memory will be with me to the last. Your friendship has been the one ray of light in the darkness of this war. Should I survive, shall we not meet again?

"Your devoted servant,

"Cary Singleton."

When Zulma had read the letter once, she smoothed it out gently on her knee, threw her head back into her chair, and closed her eyes. After an interval of full five minutes, she roused herself and took up the paper again. This time the cheek was white, the eye quenched, and the broad forehead seemed visibly to droop under the weight of a gathering care.

"Five lines ... eighty-four words ... lead pencil ... paper torn front pocket book...."

These were the only words she said, the effect of a mental calculation so characteristic of her sex. But swifter than words could have spoken, she went through the whole contents of the letter, replying to its every expressed point, supplying its every insinuation, and supplementing the effect of it all by her own kindred thoughts and feelings.

He had desired to speak to her last night as they parted in the snow-storm at the door of the lower hall. She had expected that word of farewell. It was to have been the culmination of the evening, the crystallisation of all the undefined and unexpressed sentiment which had passed between them. If he had not spoken, either through emotion, timidity, or from whatever cause, she would have done so. The presence of Pauline would have been no obstacle. The presence of her father would have been no obstacle. The presence of her father would have been rather an incentive. But at the supreme moment, the shadow of Batoche fell upon the lighted door, like a blight of fate, the current of all their thoughts were turned elsewhere, and the exquisite opportunity was lost.

And now he was gone. Alas! It was only too true to say that neither he nor she knew what future lay in store for him. The soldier always carries his life in his hands, and the chances of death are tenfold in his case.

When he spoke of their friendship and asked a slight remembrance, her own heart was the lexicon which gave the true interpretation to words that appeared timid on paper. Zulma was too brave a girl to hide the real meaning of her feelings from herself, nor would she have feared to confess them to anybody else. Least of all, in her opinion, should Cary ignore them. In other circumstances she would have preferred the lingering indefiniteness and the gradual developments which are perhaps the sweetest of all phases of love, but in the midst of danger, in the presence of death, there could be no hesitation, and Zulma concluded her long meditation with two practical resolves—the first, an instant answer to the note, the second, the devising of means to meet Cary again during the progress of hostilities.

When these determinations were made, her features resumed their usual serenity, her beautiful head rose in its old pride of carriage, and something very like a saucy laugh fluttered over her lips.

"I am sorry I offended old Batoche," she murmured, folding the paper and hiding it in her bosom. "He would have been just my man."

She had scarcely uttered the words when her father entered and said:

"Batoche asks to see you, my dear."

V
ZULMA AND BATOCHE

The old soldier made his appearance at once. He held his cap in his hand, his head was bowed, and he appeared slightly disconcerted.

"You have returned, Batoche," said Zulma, rising and advancing towards him.

"I have returned, mademoiselle."

"You are not offended with me, then?"

"Mademoiselle!"

"Batoche, I am delighted to see you."

The old man looked up, and satisfied that the welcome was sincere, said:

"I had walked nearly two miles, thinking of all you had told me, and forgetting everything else. Suddenly I remembered something. I stopped. I reflected. I returned at once and here I am."

Zulma burst out laughing:

"What did you remember, Batoche?"

"That perhaps you might desire to send an answer to the note which I brought. Excuse me, mademoiselle, I was young once. I know what girls are."

And his little grey eyes twinkled.

Zulma laid her hand upon his shoulder, and with a half serious, half jesting caress, replied:

"They call you sorcerer, Batoche. How could you thus divine my thoughts? Listen. It is an hour since you left me. During that time I have been occupied reading the note and reflecting upon it. I ended by deciding to answer it at once. But where was my messenger? I thought of you, and was expressing regret at your departure, when you were announced."

Batoche's face beamed with pleasure. Not only was he satisfied with the result of his sagacity, but it afforded him the keenest joy to be able to render a service to Zulma after the semblance of altercation which had taken place between them. In the strife of generosity the old soldier was not to be outdone, and he was rather flattered to believe that, if anything, the balance was to be in his favour. He gave expression to none of these thoughts, however. He contented himself with observing that, as the afternoon was advancing, and he must reach Quebec by nightfall, it was desirable that Zulma should make as little delay as possible.

"Certainly, Batoche," she replied. "If you will sit down a moment, I will write a few lines."

He did as he was desired. Zulma went to her writing table, spread out her paper and with great deliberation proceeded to her task. She wrote with a firm, running hand, and as from an overflowing mind, without stopping to gather her thoughts. No emotion was perceptible on her features—no distension of the eye, no flush of the cheek. She looked like a copying clerk, inditing a mechanical business letter. This circumstance did not escape the observation of Batoche. His knowledge of human nature led him at once to the conclusion that such wonderful self-possession must be the key to other admirable qualities, which, joined to the spirit which she had displayed in her defence of Captain Bouchette, convinced him that he was in the presence of one who, when occasion required, would be likely to play the part of a heroine. And what added to his silent enthusiasm was her matchless beauty as she sat opposite him, her shapely bust rising grandly above the little table and curving gracefully to its task, while the head, poised just a trifle to one side, revealed a fair white face upon which the light of the window fell slantingly. For such wild solitary natures as that of Batoche the charms of female beauty are irresistible from their very novelty, and the old hunter's fascination was so great that he there and then resolved to cultivate Zulma's acquaintance thoroughly.

"Who can tell," he said to himself, "what role this splendid creature is destined to act in the drama that is opening out before us? I know she is a rebel at heart. That proud white neck will never submit to the yoke of English tyranny. She is born for freedom. There is no chain that can bind those beautiful limbs. I will have an eye over her. I will be her protector. Her friendship—is it only friendship?—with the young Bastonnais is another link that attaches her to me. I will follow her fortunes."

Zulma finished her letter with a flourish, folded it, addressed it, and, rising, handed it to Batoche.

"I did not keep you waiting, you see. Deliver this at your earliest opportunity and accept my thanks. Is there anything that I can do for you in return?"

Batoche drooped his eyes and hesitated.

"Do not fear to speak. We are perfect friends now."

"There is something I would like to ask, mademoiselle, but should never have dared if you had not suggested it."

"What is it, Batoche?"

"I have a granddaughter, little Blanche."

"Yes."

"She has been my inseparable companion from her infancy."

"Yes."

"Now that the war has broken out, she is much alone, and that troubles me."

"Where is she?"

"In our cabin at Montmorenci. Pauline Belmont desired to keep her in Quebec during the siege, but to this I would not consent, because I could not see her as often as I wished."

"Let me have the child, Batoche. I will replace her godmother as well as I can."

"I thank you from the bottom of my heart, mademoiselle, but that is not precisely what I meant. I could not part from her for good, neither would she leave me. All I ask is this. I may be absent from my hut for days at a time. You know what military service is."

"Military service?"

"Yes, mademoiselle, I am a soldier once more."

"You mean...?"

"I am enrolled among the Bastonnais."

"Bravo!" exclaimed Zulma. "Whenever you have to absent yourself from home fetch Blanche to me."

How little either Zulma or Batoche suspected what strange events would result from this incident.

VI
THE BALL AT THE CASTLE

On the evening of that same day, the 1st December, there was high festival within the walls of Quebec. A great ball was given at the Castle to celebrate the arrival of Governor Carleton. There was a twofold sentiment in the minds of all guests which enhanced the pleasure of the entertainment— gratification at the Governor's providential escape from all the perils of his voyage from Montreal to Quebec, and the assurance that his presence would procure a gallant and successful defence of the town against the besiegers. The attendance was both large and brilliant. Never had the old Chateau beheld a gayer scene. The French families vied with the English in doing honour to the occasion. Patriotism seemed to revive in the breasts of the most lukewarm, and many, whose standing had hitherto been dubious, came forward in the courtliest fashion to proclaim their loyalty to King George in the person of his representative.

But M. Belmont was not one of these. When he first heard of the preparations for the ball, he grew very serious.

"It is a snare," he said, "set to entrap us."

A day or two later, when he received a formal invitation, he was so truly distressed that he fell into a fever.

"Happy malady," he muttered, "I shall now have a valid excuse."

Pauline nursed him with her usual tenderness, but could not extract from him the cause of his illness. She had heard, of course, of the great event which was the talk of the whole town, but never suspected that her father had been invited, and it was, therefore, with no misgiving that she accepted, at his solicitation, Eugene's offer of a trip to the Sarpy mansion, the particulars of which have already been set before the reader. A few hours after her departure, Batoche suddenly made his appearance with the startling intelligence that the Bastonnais would return the next day to begin the regular siege of the town, and the anxious father commissioned him to set out and bring back his daughter at once. In the course of the same evening Roderick Hardinge called and was very much concerned to learn the absence of Pauline, but was partially reassured when M. Belmont informed him of her expected speedy return. Roderick's visit was short, owing to some undefined constraint which he observed in the conversation of M. Belmont, and it was perhaps on that account also that he omitted stating the reason why he particularly desired to speak to Pauline. We have seen that he was waiting at the outer gate when she drove up in the early morning accompanied by Batoche and Cary Singleton.

As soon as they found themselves alone and safe within the town, Roderick said abruptly:

"I would not have had you absent to-day for all the world."

Pauline noticed his agitation and naturally attributed it to his fears for her personal safety, but she was soon undeceived when he added:

"You must by all means come to the ball with me this evening, my dear."

"To the ball?" she asked with no feigned surprise, because the events of the preceding day and night had completely driven the recollection of it from her mind.

"Yes, the Governor's ball."

It was in vain that she pleaded the suddenness of the invitation, her want of preparation, and the great fatigue which she had just undergone. Roderick would admit no excuse. His manner was nervous, excited, and at times almost peremptory.

"And my father?" she urged as a last argument.

"I saw your father last night. He complained of being unwell and evidently cannot come."

The slight emphasis which Roderick, in his rapid utterance, placed on the word "cannot" was not lost on his sensitive companion. She looked up at him with a timorous air.

"And what if my father will not let me go?" she asked almost in a whisper.

"Oh, but he will. He *must*, Pauline."

Her eyes were raised to his again, and he met them frankly.

"Let me be plain with you, my dear. If you will not go to the ball for my sake, you must go for your father's sake. Do you understand?"

She *did* understand, though for a few moments she had no words to utter. After advancing a few steps, she took her hand out of her muff, laid it in that of Hardinge, and without raising her eyes, murmured:

"I will go, Roddy, for his sake and yours."

This preliminary being satisfactorily arranged, Hardinge accompanied her to the door of her home, and after advising her to spend the day in resting from her emotions and fatigue, promised to call for her early in the evening.

He did so. To his surprise he found her cheerful and without the least sign of weariness or reluctance in her manner. She was arrayed in a rich and most tasteful costume, which gave a splendid relief to her quiet, simple beauty. To his further surprise he found M. Belmont in an agreeable mood, though still ailing. He was pleased to say that he quite approved of his daughter attending the ball, and especially in the company of Roderick Hardinge.

"This is another instalment of the reparation which I owe you, Roddy," he said, with a smile. "I confide Pauline to you to-night, and I do not know that I would do the same for any other young fellow in Quebec."

Of course no more was needed to put Hardinge in the most exuberant good spirits, and when, he drove off with Pauline, he hardly knew what he was doing.

The ball was opened when they reached the Castle. The Governor who had led in the first dance, or dance of honour, took part in a third and fourth, mingling freely with all the guests, apparently disposed to secure as many friends for himself and cause as possible. During this interval, Pauline and Roderick glided into the hall almost unnoticed, but it was not long before they were called upon to take part in the dance, and at once they attracted general attention. Nor was there cause to wonder at this. The young Scotchman looked particularly handsome in his dazzling scarlet ' tunic, while Pauline, in her rich robes of crimson satin and sprigs of snowy jasmine twined in her simple headdress, revealed a warm, ripe, glowing beauty, which was a surprise even to her most intimate friends.

After a time, the Governor took up his position on the dais, at the extremity of the room, directly in front of the Chair of State and under the violet fringes of the canopy. The Royal Arms flashed triumphantly behind him, while on the panels of the walls, to the right and left, his own cipher was visible. Those of the guests who had not yet been presented to his Excellency, seized this opportunity to pay their respects. Roderick and Pauline were of the number. As they approached the foot of the throne, they were joined by de Cramahé, the Lieutenant-Governor. This courtly man bowed profoundly to both and said:

"Lieutenant, I have a duty to perform, and you will please allow me to perform it. I desire to present mademoiselle and yourself to his Excellency."

So saying, and without waiting for a reply, he urged them forward to the viceregal presence.

Carleton received Pauline with the most deferential politeness, and added to the compliment by a kindly inquiry concerning the health of her father. Pauline trembled like a leaf at this phase of the interview, and timidly looked up to assure herself that the Governor was really earnest in his question. But his open manner dispelled all doubt, and thus, to the infinite relief of the girl, the sole drawback to her thorough enjoyment of the evening was removed.

Then her companion's turn came.

"Lieutenant Hardinge," said de Cramahé.

"Hardinge?" replied the Governor, extending his hand and bending his head to one side, as if trying to recollect something in connection with the name.

"Yes," rejoined de Cramahé. "Your Excellency will remember. He is the young officer whose exploits I recounted to you."

"Aye, aye!" exclaimed Carleton. "I do remember very well. Hardinge is a familiar name to me. This gentleman's father was a brother officer of mine under Wolfe. Yes, yes, I remember everything."

And taking Roderick's right hand in both his, he added aloud, so that the promotion might be as public as possible:

"*Captain* Hardinge, I have the honour to congratulate you."

VII
THE ATTACK OF THE MASKS

The ball concluded, as was the invariable custom at the State balls of the time, with that most graceful and picturesque of all dances, the Menuet de la Cour, which, brought over from France during the reign of Louis XIII., had enjoyed great popularity throughout the Province until the Conquest, and was retained by the British Governors of Quebec until a comparative recent period. The *pas marché*, the *assemblé*, the *pas grave*, the *pas bourré*, and the *pirouette* were all executed with faultless precision and stately beauty by a double set of eight chosen from among the best dancers in the room. The rest of the company was ranged in groups around the walls, some watching the figures with eyes of critical inquiry, others observing the costumes of the dancers and their involved movements with a simple sense of enjoyment. The rhythmic swaying of handsome men and women in the mazes of a dance often produces on the bystanders a sensation of poetic dreaminess, quite independent of the accompanying music, and which may be traced directly to the magnetism of the human form.

It is only true to say that nobody in the Menuet elicited more sympathy and admiration than Pauline Belmont. The perfection of her dancing, the sweetness of her face, the modesty of her demeanour, and the childlike reliance which she seemed to place on the cooperation of her stalwart partner, Roderick Hardinge, were traits which could not pass unobserved, and more than once when she swung back into position after the culmination of a figure, she was greeted with murmurs of applause. Several gallant old Frenchmen, who looked on humming the music which they knew so well, signified their approval by words allied to their subdued chat. Finally, when the second strain was over, the peculiar nineteen bars had been played, the *Chaîne Anglaise* had been made, and the honours performed by profound salutations to the distinguished company and to the respective partners, the executants retired from the floor and were immediately set upon by a mob of congratulating friends. Among them, the portly form of Carleton, with his white shaven face, and large pleasant eyes, was prominent. He addressed his felicitations to several of the dancers, and thanked them for the splendid termination which they had given to the festival. Near them stood his friend

Bouchette, who had been one of the lions of the evening, and who improved these last moments with a few words of lively conversation with Pauline.

"This has been a magnificent ball," said he, "worthy of our Governor and worthy of old Quebec, but what is a particular source of pride to me is that the belle of the evening has been a countrywoman of mine. You have shed glory on your race, mademoiselle. I will not fail to report this to my old friend, M. Belmont, and I am sure the delight he will experience will be a compensation for his absence."

Pauline blushed as she heard these compliments, and clung more closely to the arm of Hardinge. She faltered a few words of thanks, but her confusion was not relieved till the interview closed by the pressure of the crowds breaking up and making their way to the cloakrooms.

Shortly afterwards, the gay company had entirely dispersed, the lights in the Castle were extinguished one by one, and silence reigned where, only half an hour before, light feet beat time to the soft music of viol and bassoon, and the echoes of merry voices resounded through the halls.

One of the guests, who had tarried longer than all the others, issued alone and proceeded in the direction of Cathedral Square. Three o'clock pealed from the turret as he passed. The night was dark and of that dull, lustreless aspect which not even the white snow on roof and footpath could relieve. Not another soul was in the streets. The long square houses were wrapped in sleep. The solitary walker was of middle size and apparently in the prime of life. A fur coat was loosely thrown over his evening dress. His step was free and elastic, and he swung an ivory-headed cane in his right hand. He was evidently in the best of spirits, as a man should be who has dined well, danced to his heart's content, and spent an agreeable evening in the society of his superiors, and the company of handsome women.

When he reached the large stockade erected where Prescott Gate was afterwards built, he paused a moment in front of the guard, who seemed to recognize him and opened the wicket without the exchange of a pass word. He then began the descent of the steep and tortuous Mountain Hill, walking briskly indeed, but with hardly a perceptible acceleration of the pace which he had held previously. It was not long before he attained the foot of the Hill, and he was about turning the very dark corner which led into Peter street, where he resided, when his step was suddenly arrested by a shrill whistle on his left. He looked around, and listened, tightening his great coat over his breast, and grasping his cane with a firmer hand. He stood thus for several seconds, but hearing nothing more except the flow of the St. Lawrence, a few yards ahead of him, he attributed the sound to some sailor's craft in the harbour, and confidently resumed his march. He had not proceeded more than a few feet, however, when five men, muffled and masked, issued from a lane in the rear, threw themselves upon him and dragged him to the ground. Resistance was vain. The kidnappers gagged him, wrenched his cane from his hand, and covered his face with a cloak. They were about to drag him away, when a sixth figure bounded upon the scene.

"Halt!" was his single cry in French.

The men stopped.

"Release your prisoner."

They obeyed instantly and without a remonstrance.

"Ungag him."

They ungagged him.

"Restore him his cane."

The cane was immediately returned.

As soon as the prisoner felt himself free, and in possession of a weapon, he leaped out into the middle of the street and faced his enemies like the brave man that he was. He chafed, and fumed, and brandished his cane.

"What does this mean?" he cried.

No answer.

"Who are you?"

Still no reply.

"Do you know who I am?"

"Yes," said the chief, in a low cold voice, "You are Joseph Bouchette. We know you well. But go. You are free. You owe your liberty to an intervention superior to the hatred and vengeance of all your enemies. Thank God for it."

Bouchette, for it was indeed he, was dumb-founded and did not stir.

The chief repeated his order of dismissal in a tone that could not admit of denial, and the doughty sailor, without uttering another word, turned on his heel and walked leisurely to his home.

The masked men stood in a group looking at each other and at their chief.

"You have astounded us," said Barbin to the latter.

"Possibly," was the quiet reply. "But this is no time for explanations. Hurry out of the town and seek your hiding places in the forest. The morning is far advanced and it will soon be day. As for me, I have had no rest these two days and nights. I will creep into some hole and sleep."

"Goodnight then," they all said as they slunk into the shadow.

"Goodnight."

In the dreams of the tired Batoche, that night, was blended the sweetest music of the waterfall, and it seemed to him that there hovered over his couch the white spirit of Clara thanking him for the deed of mercy which he had wrought.

VIII
UNCONSCIOUS GREATNESS

It was more than a deed of mercy. It was politic as well. After Bouchette returned home, he was so agitated that he could not sleep. His chief concern was to know why he had been attacked and who were the men who attacked him. It was clear that the assault was the result of a deliberate plot. There was the rallying whistle. There was the disguise of the men. There was the gag all ready to hand. And his rescuer? Who could he be? and especially what could mean the strange words which he had uttered?

Gradually, as he became calmer, he was enabled to grasp all the elements of the situation, and at length the truth dawned upon him. He had been singled out for revenge by some of his discontented countrymen because of the service he had rendered the Governor-General. When he had satisfied himself of this, his first impulse was to rush to the Castle, announce the outrage to Carleton himself, and head a terrible crusade against all the rebel French. But, with a moment's reflection, his better nature prevailed.

"Never," he exclaimed, as he paced his room. "Never, I am a Frenchman before all. Loyalty to England does not require treason to my own countrymen. The personal insult and injury I can forgive. Besides, was I not rescued by an act of chivalry? If I have enemies among my own people, is it not evident that I have friends as well? No. I will not allow a word concerning this affair to escape my lips. If it becomes public it shall be through no fault of mine."

Having relieved his mind by this act of magnanimity, he threw himself upon a lounge and soon fell asleep. The sun was already high in the heavens, and it streamed into the room, but did not disturb the slumbers of the mariner who reposed as calmly as if he had not passed through a struggle for his life and liberty. It was noon when he awoke. Sitting up on the edge of his bed, some seconds elapsed before recollection went back to this event, and when it did, he simply said:

"I will now go and see my friend Belmont."

Meantime, at M. Belmont's the matter had advanced a stage or two. Batoche had found his way there after dismissing his associates, and, without disturbing the inmates, had entered by means of a private key given by his friend. He had gone to sleep at once, and it was eleven o'clock in the forenoon before he arose. His first step was to seek the presence of M. Belmont. To him he recounted the conversation he had had with Sieur Sarpy, and the singular part which Zulma had taken in it. M. Belmont listened with mingled surprise and concern. When Batoche continued and described the adventure of the preceding night, he became quite alarmed.

"This is terrible, Batoche," said.

The old man did what was very unusual with him. He smiled.

"There is nothing terrible about it, sir. Even if Bouchette had been captured, there would have been nothing terrible. Bouchette is not such a very important personage, and our men have no fears of retribution. They are quite able to take care of themselves. But I had promised Zulma that the man would not be disturbed, and I simply kept my promise. I was near being too late. It was far past midnight when I reached the town, after a weary tramp from Pointe-aux-Trembles. I knew all about the ball and that, of course, Bouchette would be there. We had planned to seize him on his way home from the Castle. Everything turned out as had been anticipated. Our men did their work to perfection. They acted with bravery and intelligence. It was a pity to spoil their success."

"Did you not arrive upon the scene in advance?"

"Yes, a few moments before the assault."

"Then why did you not prevent it altogether?"

"I hadn't the heart to do it. I wanted to give my men and myself that much satisfaction. I wanted to see how my companions would do their duty. Besides, although I had promised not to kidnap Bouchette, I did not promise that I would not give him a good scare."

"Scare?" interrupted M. Belmont contemptuously, "Bouchette is as brave a man as lives."

"Right enough," said Batoche with a giggle. "He showed fight and brandished his cane like a man. So far as scaring went, the attack was a failure."

"The whole thing was a failure, Batoche. It will ruin us. It will drive me out of the town. I suppose the garrison is in an uproar about it by this time."

"The assailants are not known and cannot be discovered."

"Exactly, and therefore the innocent will be suspected. Your great mistake was in doing the thing by halves. A real abduction would not have been so bad, for then the victim would not have been there to tell his story. As it is, he has no doubt told it to everybody, and there is no foreseeing what the consequences will be."

Batoche did not reply, but there was something in his manner which showed that he felt very little repentance for what he had done.

At this point of the colloquy the servant came to the door and announced Captain Bouchette.

M. Belmont was thunderstruck. Batoche remained perfectly impassive.

"Show him up," at length faltered M. Belmont.

Batoche made a movement to rise, but his companion stopped him abruptly.

"Do not stir," he said. "Your presence may be useful."

Bouchette came striding in boisterously and in the fullest good humour. He embraced his old friend with effusion, and accepted the introduction to Batoche in a genial, off-hand fashion. Of course this conduct put a new aspect on affairs, and M. Belmont was set quite at ease. Bouchette opened at once with an account of the great ball. He said that he had come purposely for that. He described all its phases in his own unconventional way, and especially dilated on the share that Pauline had taken in it. He grew eloquent on this particular theme. He assured M. Belmont that he ought to be proud of his daughter, as she had made the most favourable impression on all the guests and particularly on the Governor.

There is no exaggeration in saying that this was positively delightful to the anxious father, and that, under the circumstances, it went far towards restoring his peace of mind. It was, therefore, no wonder that the conversation, thus initiated, flowed on in a continuous channel of gaiety, in which even Batoche joined at intervals, and after his own peculiar manner. He said very little, indeed, perhaps not over a dozen words, but he chuckled now and again, rolled about in his seat and gave other tokens of satisfaction at the turn which things were taking. This, however, did not prevent him, from the comparative obscurity of the corner which he occupied, closely watching the features of the visitor, and studying all his movements.

At length, at a convenient turn of the conversation, M. Belmont inquired of his friend what the news of the day might be.

"Oh, nothing that I know of," replied Bouchette promptly, and quite unconcernedly. "I have just got out of my bed and came here directly."

If a mountain had been taken from the shoulders of poor M. Belmont, he could not have felt more relief than he did on hearing these few words.

He simply could not contain his joy. Leaping up from his seat, he slapped his friend on the shoulder, and exclaimed:

"Well, Bouchette, we shall have a glass of wine, some of my best old Burgundy. Your visit has done me a world of good."

The little grey eyes of Batoche were fixed like gimlets on the wall opposite, at the line where it touched the ceiling. There was a glassy light in them. He had gone off suddenly into one of his absent moods. But it was only for a moment. Recovering himself, he too rose abruptly from his seat, bringing his right arm down with a bang upon his thigh, and muttering a few inarticulate words.

The wine was quaffed with pledges and *bons mots*. A second round of glasses was indulged in, and when the interview closed at length, Bouchette thundered out of the house as heartily as he had entered it.

"Well!" exclaimed M. Belmont, closing the door and confronting Batoche in the hall.

"Well!" replied the other quietly.

"What do you say?"

"What do I say? I say that this man will never speak a word of what has happened. So you may rest easy."

"And what do you think of himself?"

"He is a great man."

"And a good one."

"A true Knight of St. Louis."

"A friend of his countrymen."

"Yes. I admire his generosity and magnanimity, and I admire the wonderful instinct of Zulma Sarpy who gauged him so well that she wrung his liberation from me."

When Pauline descended from her private apartments after a long day's rest, and was made acquainted with so much of the sailor's visit as concerned herself, she was deeply moved, and the more that she observed her father's intense gratification. The whole episode imparted a happiness to that house such as it had not enjoyed for many days previous, and such as it was not destined to enjoy later.

IX
PAULINE'S DEVELOPMENT

Insensibly a change was coming over Pauline. The sharp, varied experiences of the past month had a decisive schooling influence upon her. It is often the case that simple untutored natures like her develop more rapidly in days of crisis than characters fashioned of sterner material. There is no preliminary work of undoing to be gone through. The ground is ready prepared for strong and lasting impressions. The process of creation is hampered by no obstacles. There is, on the contrary, a latent spontaneity which accelerates its action.

Pauline herself was hardly conscious of this change. At least she could not formulate it in words, or even enumerate its phases by any system of analysis, but there were moments when her mind surged with feelings which she knew that she had never felt before, and she caught herself framing visions whose very vagueness of outline swelled before her like the shadows of a portent. At times, too, through these mists there flashed illuminations which startled her, and made her innocent heart shrink as if they were presentiments of doom.

She had seen so much, she had heard so much, she had learned so much during these eventful weeks. The old peaceful life was gone, and it seemed ever so far away. She was certain that it would never return again. Amid her trouble, there was even a tinge of pleasure in this assurance. That was, at least, one thing of which she was positive. All else was so doubtful, the future appeared so capricious, her fate and the fate of those she loved was shrouded in such mystery.

On the evening of the day on which occurred the incidents related in the last chapter, she was sitting alone in her room. A circumstance which, of itself, should have excited in her emotions of pleasure, threw her into a train of painful rehearsals. Her father was singing snatches of his old French songs in the room below—a thing he had not done for weeks. This reminded her of the visit of Bouchette, and from that point her mind travelled backwards to all the scenes, and their concomitants, of which she had of late been the witness. There was the snow-storm in Cathedral Square, when her father was summoned to the presence of the Lieutenant-Governor; there was the burning of Roderick's letter; there was the dreadful altercation and the happy reconciliation between him and her father; there was the firing on the handsome young American from the walls; there was the visit to the Sarpys; there was the night ride back to the town; there was the dazzling magnificence of the Governor's ball. And through all this she saw the weird form of Batoche, flitting in and out, silent, mysterious, terrible. She saw the yearning, anxious, loving face of Roderick Hardinge. She saw Zulma leaning towards her, and, as it were, growing to her with a sister's fondness. The spell of Zulma's affection appeared to her like the embrace of a great spirit, overpowering, irresistible, and withal delicious in its strength. And in spite of her she saw—why should the vision be so vivid?—the beautiful, sad eyes of Cary Singleton, as he sat beside her at the Sarpy mansion, or parted from her at the St. Louis Gate. She remembered how noble he looked as he conferred with Roderick under the walls, when bearing the flag of truce; how proudly he walked back to the ranks of the army, nor even deigned to look back when a miscreant fired at him from the ramparts. She recalled every word that Zulma had spoken about him, so that she seemed to know him as well as Zulma herself.

When Pauline had gone over all these things several times, in that extraordinary jumbling yet keenly distinct way with which such reminiscences will troop to the memory, she felt positively fatigued, and a sense of oppression lay like a burden at her heart. She closed her eyes while a shudder passed through her frame. She feared that she might be ill, and it required all the tranquil courage of her nature not to yield outright to the collapse with which she was threatened.

At length she bethought her of a means to regain her serenity. She would write a long letter to Zulma, describing the Governor's ball. She at once set about the task. But when the paper was spread out, she encountered a difficulty at the very threshold. Would she write about herself? Would she speak of Roderick? Would she repeat the salutation of his Excellency? Would she narrate her interview with Captain Bouchette? If she did, she would relapse at once into the train of ideas of which it was the object of her letter to get rid. Already, two or three times, she had detected herself gliding into them, with pen poised in her hand.

"No," she murmured with a slight laugh. "I will do nothing of the kind. I will write like a milliner. I will give a detailed account of the dress worn by every lady in the château. This may amuse Zulma, or it may disgust her, according to her mood when she reads the letter. But no matter. It will answer my purpose. Zulma has often scolded me for not being selfish enough. I will be selfish for once."

With this plan well defined, the writing of the letter was an easy and a pleasant task. As the pen flew over the paper, Pauline showed that she enjoyed her work. At times she would smile, and her whole face would light up. At other times she would stop and reread a passage with evident approbation. Page after page was covered with the mystic language of the *modiste*, in which Pauline must have been an adept—as what young woman is not?—for she made no erasures, and inserted no corrections.

"Now that I have come to my own costume, shall I describe it?" she asked herself, and almost immediately added:

"It would be affectation if I did not."

She forthwith devoted a whole page to the description.

Were we not right in saying that a great change had come over Pauline? She, who only a few weeks ago, was the simplest and most unsophisticated of girls, now knew the meaning of that dreadful word—affectation. She not only knew what it was, but she knew that it must be avoided, and she took particular pains to avoid it.

A little later on she asked herself again:

"Shall I make any mention of Roddy?"

The query was apparently not so easily answered as the other. She passed her left hand wearily over the smooth hair that shaded her temple. Her eyes were fixed vacantly on the green baize of the table. There was just the slightest trace of hardness, if that were possible, on her features.

At length she whispered:

"Zulma would think it strange if I did not. Besides, I know she admires Roddy. Yes, I must tell her about the Lieutenant—oh, beg pardon, the Captain," and she smiled in her natural way. "Of course she must hear of his promotion. Poor Roddy! How proud he was of it. And he seemed to cling to me closer afterwards, as if he meant that I should share half of the honour."

After detailing that circumstance, she added a few words about Carleton and Bouchette, and wound up by expressing the regret, which was sincere with her, that Zulma had not been present at the festival. She wrote:

"Captain Bouchette was kind enough to name some one whom you know as the belle of the ball. That was flattery, of course. But had some one whom I know been there, not only M. Bouchette, but the Governor himself and all the company, not excepting Roderick, would have acclaimed her queen."

This was not an idle compliment from one girl to another. It was a courtly tribute from woman to woman. Clearly, Pauline was making rapid progress.

The letter was immediately folded and addressed. Holding it in her hand, as she rose from the table, Pauline felt wonderfully refreshed. She glanced through the window, on her way down stairs, and a new horizon spread before her. Her misgivings for the time had departed, her doubts were dispelled, and all that remained was a certain buoyant hopefulness, which she could not explain.

She met her father below and inquired after Batoche.

"He is not here, my dear, but may return to-night."

"I have a letter for him."

"A letter for Batoche?"

"That is, a letter which I would wish him to carry?"

"For whom?"

"For Zulma Sarpy."

"Oh, that is very well. Write to Zulma. Cultivate her friendship. She is a grand girl."

Batoche did call again at M. Belmont's that night, but it was only for a moment, as he was about to betake himself once more out of the town. He accepted Pauline's commission with alacrity.

"I will deliver the letter myself," he said. "I am glad of the chance to see that magnificent creature again."

X
ON THE CITADEL

The next day, instead of experiencing the usual reaction, Pauline continued in precisely the same state of mind as when she handed the letter to Batoche. She was not by any means gay. For instance, she could not have sung a comical song with zest. But she was more than merely calm. There was a quickening impulse of vague expectancy within her which led her to move about the house with a light step and a smiling face. Her father was much pleased, as he too had not outlived the effect produced upon him by the visit of Bouchette. Furthermore, the weather may have contributed to the pleasantness that reigned in the house. The sun was shining brightly, the wind had fallen, and the snow lay crisp upon the streets inviting to a promenade.

Hardinge called about noon for the purpose of asking Pauline to accompany him in a little walk.

"I have a couple of hours before me—a thing I may not have every day—and a ramble will do both of us good," he said.

Pauline was soon ready with the cordial consent of her father.

After wandering through the streets for some time, and stopping to speak to friends whom they met, the two wended their way towards Cape Diamond. On the top of that portion of the citadel they were quite alone, and they could commune together without interruption. They both appeared to be pleased with this, each probably feeling that they had something to say to the other, or rather that they might touch upon topics, untouched before, which might lead to better mutual understanding. Roderick was a trifle graver and more reserved than his companion. Pauline made nothing of that, attributing it to his military anxieties, a supposition which his conversation at first seemed to justify.

"This is an exposed point," said he, "which in a few days none of us will be able to occupy. When the whole rebel army moves up from Pointe-aux-Trembles, they can easily shell us out of this side of the citadel."

"But it is a good point of observation, is it not?" asked Pauline.

"Capital, though not so good as that one higher up which is well guarded and where double sentries will always be posted."

As he spoke, Roderick caught view of moving figures on the highway near the Plains of Abraham.

"Look Pauline," he said. "Do you know those fellows?"

"I do not. Are they soldiers?"

"They call themselves Virginia riflemen. They are the advance guard of the rebel army. They have been prowling around for the past two days."

"Virginia riflemen, Roddy?" said Pauline looking up with an expression of languid inquiry in her dark eyes.

"Yes. You ought to know something about them. Don't you remember the young officer who escorted you to the gates the day before yesterday?"

"Oh," replied Pauline, with no attempt to conceal her surprise or interest, "you don't mean to say that he is down there among those poor unsheltered men?"

"I do, certainly, and I am sure he enjoys it. I would in his place. He has plenty of room to rove about in. It is not like being cooped up, as we are, within these narrow walls."

"Well, he is strong and hearty and can stand a little hardship. That's some comfort," said Pauline wagging her little head sympathetically.

This evidently amused Roderick, who replied:

"Yes, he is a stout, tough fellow."

"And so brave," pursued Pauline with growing warmth while her eyes were fixed on the plain beyond.

"Every soldier ought to be brave, Pauline. But I must allow that this man is particularly brave. He has proved it before our eyes."

Pauline answered not, but her attention remained fixed on the distant sight before her. Roderick burst out into a hearty laugh and said:

"Surely this is not all you have got to say about him. He is strong, he is brave, and—isn't he something else, eh, Pauline?"

She turned suddenly and answered Hardinge's laugh with a smile, but there was the tell-tale blood in her cheek.

"Come now, dear, isn't he handsome?" continued Roderick, proud of his triumph and full of mischief.

"Well, yes, he is handsome," answered Pauline with a delicious pout and mock-show of aggressiveness.

"And what else?"

"Modest."

"What else?"

"Refined."

"What else?"

"Educated."

"What else?"

"Kind."

"Kind to you, dear?"

"Particularly kind to me."

"Thank him for that. He could choose no worthier object of his kindness. Excuse my teasing you, Pauline. It was only a bit of fun. I quite agree in your estimate of this American officer. He and I ought to be friends, instead of enemies."

"You will be friends yet," said Pauline with a tone of conviction.

"Alas!"

A pause ensued during which despondent thoughts flashed through the brain of Roderick Hardinge. All the horrors of war loomed up in a lump before him, and the terrible uncertainties of battle revealed themselves keenly. He had never felt his position so deeply before. This rebel was as good as himself, perhaps better. They might have met and enjoyed life together. Now their duty was to do each to death, or entail as much loss as possible upon one another. Losses! What if one of these losses should be that of the lovely creature at his side? That were indeed the loss of all losses.

But no, he would not entertain the thought. He tossed up his head and drank in the cold air with expanded lungs. He felt Pauline's small hand upon his arm. The touch thrilled his whole being.

"Look, Roddy," she said pointing to the plain.

XI
HORSEMAN AND AMAZON

What they both saw was this. A band of some twenty men, members of Morgan's corps, stood in groups on the extreme edge of the plain. At a given signal a horseman issued in a canter from their midst. The animal was almost pure white, with small, well-proportioned head, small clean hoofs, long haunches, abundant mane and sweeping tail. Every limb was instinct with speed, while the pricked ear, rolling eye and thin pink nostril denoted intelligence and fire. The rider was arrayed in the full uniform of a rifleman—grass-green coat and trousers, trimmed with black fur, through which ran a golden tape; crimson sash with white powder horn attached; a black turban-shaped hat of medium height, flanked over the left temple with a black aigrette of short dark feathers, which was held by a circular clasp of bright yellow metal. The rider trotted around leisurely in a long eclipse until the snow was sufficiently beaten for his purpose. He then indulged in a variety of extraordinary feats, each of which seemed to be demanded of him by one or the other of his companions. Among these the following may be worth enumerating. He launched his horse at full speed, when suddenly loosening his feet from the stirrups and his hand from the bridle, he sprang upwards and threw himself with both legs now on the left, then on the right of the saddle. He leaned far forward on the horse's neck so that the two heads were exactly parallel, and next fell back into the saddle facing the crupper and holding on to nothing. He stopped his horse suddenly and made him stand almost perpendicular on his hind legs. Then, without the assistance of bridle, stirrup, or pommel, he secured his position and made the animal plunge wildly forward as if he were clearing a high hurdle, while he no more swerved from his seat than if he had been pinioned to it. Setting his horse again at his topmost bent, he took his pistol, threw it into the air, caught it on the fly, and finally hurled it with all his might in front of him. Then slipping one foot from the stirrup, he bent his body over to the ground, seized the weapon as he passed, recovered his position and replaced the pistol in its place, before reaching the end of his round.

The friends of the rider were not more intent in their observation than were the two spectators on the slope of the Citadel.

"Marvellous horsemanship," exclaimed Hardinge with enthusiasm. "The animal must be an Arabian or some other thoroughbred. Whose can he be? There is no such horse in these parts or I should have known it. And yet it is hardly possible that he should have come along with Arnold's expedition."

"And the rider?" murmured Pauline, advancing several steps in the earnestness of her gaze.

"Yes, the rider," continued Roderick. "See he lives in the horse and the horse in him. They seem to form part and parcel of one another. A magnificent fellow."

"Impossible," said Pauline, shading her eyes with her hand to sharpen her vision. "It cannot be."

"What?" queried Roderick.

"I thought perhaps...."

"But it is, Pauline."

"You don't mean it?"

"It is no other."

"Cary Singleton!"

Forgetful of everything, in her transport, she applauded with her gloved hands. Roderick took off his cap and saluted.

"This is a brave sight, Pauline, and well worth our coming thus far to see."

The girl was silent, and when at length she diverted her eyes, it was not to encounter those of her companion. A slight trouble arose within her which might have increased into an embarrassment, had not another incident almost immediately occurred to give distraction.

The rider, having finished his gyrations, returned to his friends, who after a brief parley dispersed, leaving him alone with a small group of two or three, among whom appeared to be a lady on horseback. At least, so thought both Roderick and Pauline. They did not mind the circumstance, however, and were on the point of retracing their steps homeward, when they noticed that two riders detached themselves from the rest and took the direction of the plain. It was easy to recognize Cary Singleton, and, in a few moments, as easy to see that he was accompanied by a lady. The twain went along at a gentle walk directly towards the St. Lawrence. The sun was still shining brightly, and as they rode, they were sometimes in light and sometimes in shadow, according as they passed the leafless maples that skirted the path. When they reached the high bank overlooking the river, they stopped for a few moments in conversation, Singleton evidently describing something, as indicated by the movement of his arm along the line of the stream and again in the direction of the town.

While they were thus engaged, the couple on the Citadel watched them closely without uttering a word. The reader will readily guess that Pauline watched the man, and Roderick the woman. Of the two, the latter was far more intent in his observation, the former looking on in rather a dreamy way.

At length, the officer and the amazon turned their horses' heads on their backward journey. As they did so, they both happened to look directly toward the town. Whatever it was that drew their attention, it was sufficiently interesting to cause them to stop and confer together. Then the lady made a sudden movement as if to advance straight forward, but she was restrained by her attendant, who pointing to the guns on the ramparts, made her understand that she must keep out of range.

It was at this point that Hardinge abruptly broke silence.

"I thought so," was his brief remark, uttered almost sternly between his teeth.

Pauline did not appear to hear him.

"I knew I was not mistaken," he continued a little louder.

Pauline caught the word and looked up in wonder.

"I have a right to remember her."

"What do you mean, Roddy?"

"It is the very same riding habit?"

Pauline was now perfectly astonished. Hardinge's face was aglow.

"I would know that form in a thousand."

"What form?"

"And that carriage."

"Roddy, you don't intend to say?"

"I tell you it is Zulma Sarpy."

"You are jesting."

"Look, she is waving her handkerchief."

And so she was. She twisted and brandished it, and, in doing so, agitated her horse to that extent that he fell back on his haunches and pawed with his front feet. Roderick took off his cap and remained uncovered a moment. Pauline shouted for joy and fluttered her handkerchief in return. Singleton doffed his plumed hat, bowing low over his holsters. It was a moment of exquisite excitement. But only a moment. Swift as the wind the riders dashed away over the plain. Turning suddenly, Hardinge recognized the danger of his position.

"Let us go, Pauline," he said, "we may be seen by our men and it would be very awkward."

They hurried down the slope of the Citadel and entered into the town without almost exchanging a word. Pauline was radiant. Roderick was somewhat sullen. Gradually, however, they both resumed their composure and sauntered for another half-hour together very agreeably, but talking of quite indifferent subjects.

"That spectacle was more than we had bargained for," said Pauline, taking off her gloves and laying her furs on the little central table of her chamber. "I certainly never expected to see him again. That graceful salutation of his was intended for me, no doubt. And I recognized him at once, while Roddy did not. On the other hand, he recognized Zulma, and I did not. Wasn't that strange?"

Pauline paused in her disrobing and thought over this. And the more she thought over it, the more it appeared strange. It appeared so strange that her features assumed a look of sadness and anxiety.

"What could Zulma be doing away from home to-day?" thought Pauline further. "How was it that she met the officer? What if she came purposely to see him? That would be just like Zulma. She is a fearless girl. She cares for nobody. She can do what no other young woman could attempt, without exciting criticism, or if there is criticism it falls harmless at her feet."

For the first time in all these days, Pauline experienced something akin to an envy of her brilliant friend. That is, she envied her spirit of independence. She, of the drooping eyes and shrinking heart, felt that she too would like to dare just a little, as Zulma did. Another proof of the transformation which was being effected in her. But in this particular, it was impossible for her to go beyond velleities. Much as she might change, Pauline Belmont could never be Zulma Sarpy, and if the dear child only knew it, it was not desirable that she should be. She had her own claims to admiration and love. Zulma had hers. These were almost radically different, but precisely their contrast enhanced the value of each.

"I wonder if Zulma received my letter," added Pauline after finishing her toilet. "It is possible that Batoche may have met her and delivered it. I hope he did. In that case she must have been particularly glad to see us and salute Roddy after his promotion. I am convinced of one thing. Much as Zulma admires Cary Singleton, she thinks a great deal of Roderick Hardinge. And I am equally sure that Roddy thinks a great deal of Zulma."

And Pauline, sitting before her fire, crooned the old songs of youth, while her mind wandered away and away, till the shadows of evening lay deep on her window squares.

XII
WAS IT DESIGN OR ACCIDENT

Batoche delivered Pauline's letter to Zulma earlier than he expected. He had intended to go out to the Sarpy mansion on purpose to do so, but to his surprise and pleasure, he encountered her that very day in the environs of Quebec. She was on horseback, accompanied by a servant. As soon as she spied the old soldier, she rode up to him and greeted him in the warmest language. A few words of conversation sufficed to reveal the intention of her journey. She had taken advantage of the splendid weather for a jaunt across the country and had chosen the direction of Quebec in order to learn what was going on between the contending armies. Batoche confined himself to a few words about her friends within the town and excused himself from saying more by producing the letter of Pauline. Zulma seized it eagerly, broke the seal and ran her eye over the numerous sheets. She said nothing, but the expression of her countenance was that of intense amusement, except towards the end of the reading when it changed to a look of curious gravity.

"I shall read it more leisurely when I get home," she said to Batoche, folding the missive and secreting it in her bosom, "and Pauline will be sure to receive a long answer. For the present, please give her my thanks and tell her that the things that she writes me are full of interest. It is very kind of her thus to think of me. Tell her that she is ever present to my mind. I am in no danger, but she is. I can roam about at my pleasure, while she is restrained within the walls. Tell her that I am prepared to do anything I can for her. Whatever she needs she will have from me, and you will be our messenger, will you not, Batoche?"

The old man signified his ready assent.

"If there is a necessity for it, I will go to Pauline even through the barricades and barriers. Wherever you lead, Batoche, I will follow. Tell her this, and now, adieu."

"Adieu?" said Batoche inquiringly.

"Yes, I will return home. I have had an agreeable ride. I might perhaps have advanced a little further, but now that I have met you, and received this precious letter, I am satisfied."

"It is not yet late in the forenoon," replied Batoche. "Mademoiselle might tarry somewhat longer. I think she might render her journey still more agreeable."

Through these simple words, Zulma was not slow to discern the meaning of her old friend. Her cheek reddened and her eye got animated, spite of the exertions she made to hide her emotions.

"Some of your old tricks of divination again," she said laughing. "Pray, why should I tarry longer?"

Batoche met her ardent glance with a flash of intelligence. Pointing to a little clump of wood, about a quarter of a mile to the right, he said:

"I gave him your note, mademoiselle. He was deeply moved. He declared he would treasure it all his life. Perhaps he has answered you already."

Zulma shook her head slowly, but made no interruption.

"He is there, mademoiselle, with his command. Perhaps in a few days, he may be ordered further forward. If he knew that you were so near him and did not see you, I am certain that he would be deeply distressed. If he knew that you were here, he would ride out at once to meet you."

Zulma still maintained silence, but she could not conceal the agitation which these words produced within her.

"Mademoiselle," continued Batoche, "will you advance with me a little, or shall I go on and tell him that you are here?"

"I put myself in your hands," said Zulma in a low voice, bending over to the old soldier.

Batoche darted a last glance at her, which appeared to decide him. He set forth at once in the direction of the camp, and before ten minutes had elapsed, Cary Singleton was riding in hot haste to meet Zulma. He persuaded her to remain a few hours in the camp in the company of his fellow officers and it was in her honour that he performed the tournament which we have described in the preceding chapter. And it was thus that they both unexpectedly were seen by Pauline and Hardinge.

XIII
THE INTENDANT'S PALACE

On the 5th December the whole American army marched up to Quebec. Montgomery, who had come down from Montreal with his victorious army, joined Arnold at Pointe-aux-Trembles and took command of the expedition. Flushed with the success which had laid all Canada at his feet, in a campaign of barely three months, the youthful hero advanced against the last rampart of British power with the determination to carry it or die. His troops shared his enthusiasm. The despondency of the preceding fortnight had melted away and was replaced by an ardour that was proof against the rigours of the season and the undisguised difficulties of the gigantic task which confronted them. They knew that the eyes of all their countrymen were upon them. The Congress at Philadelphia paused in its work of legislation to listen to the news from Canada. Washington was almost forgotten in the anxiety about Montgomery. New England stood expectant of wonders from the gallantry of Arnold. In far-off Maryland and Virginia, the mothers, wives and daughters on the plantations had no thoughts but of the postboy who galloped down the lane with letters from the North, where their loved ones were serving under the chivalrous Morgan. It was generally felt then, as it is now well understood in the light of history, that on the fate of Quebec depended, in great measure, the fate of the continental revolution. If that stronghold were captured, the Americans would be rid of every enemy from the North; the French-Canadians and the Indians, friendly to France, would be encouraged to join the cause of independence; while the moral effect in Europe, where Wolfe's immortal achievement was still fresh in all minds, would doubtless hasten the boon of intervention.

Montgomery, who was altogether a superior man, was keenly alive to all these considerations, hence when he moved up from Pointe-aux-Trembles he carried with him the full weight of this enormous responsibility. How far he was equal to it these humble pages will briefly tell for the hundredth time, and the writer is proud that he is allowed the opportunity to tell it.

Montgomery took up his headquarters at Holland House, and Arnold occupied Langlois House, near Scott's Bridge. Around these two points revolved the fortunes of the Continental army during this momentous month of December prior to the attack on Quebec.

It was in the latter building, on the morning after the arrival of the army, that Morgan, who, as we have stated, had preceded the main body by five days, and occupied the principal roads leading to the beleaguered town, received from Arnold the command to occupy the suburb of St. Roch, near the Intendant's Palace. This historical pile was perhaps the most magnificent monument in the Province. It was built as early as 1684, by orders of the French King, under the administration of Intendant De Meulles. In 1712, it was consumed by fire, when occupied by Intendant Begon, but was reconstructed by orders from Versailles. During the last eleven years of French domination, from 1748 to 1759, it became famous through the orgies and bacchanalian scandals of Intendant Bigot, the Sardanapalus of New France, whose exploits of gallantry and conviviality would have formed a fitting theme for romance from the pen of the elder Dumas. After the Conquest, the British had almost entirely neglected it, as they held their official offices entirely with the town. At the time of the siege, therefore, the edifice was in a deserted and somewhat dilapidated condition, but its large dimensions afforded shelter to a considerable number of Americans, and its advantageous locality suggested to Montgomery the idea of making it the headquarters of his sharpshooters. Morgan was ordered in consequence to place there a picked detachment of riflemen. This he put under the command of Singleton, who moved thither a couple of days after his interview with Zulma. From the high cupola of the Intendant's Palace, he kept up a regular fire on the exposed points of the garrison. The sentries along the walls were picked off, one after another; whenever a reconnoitring party appeared above the stockades, they were at once driven under cover, and even the workers of the barbette guns were often frightened away from their pieces. Whenever, as frequently happened, a few mortars were pointed on the town from the environs of the Palace, the sharp fusillade which accompanied them from the embrasures of the cupola, produced the liveliest commotion within the walls, causing the alarm bells to sound and sending battalion upon battalion of militia to the rescue. The Americans were very much encouraged by this sign of success, imagining that they had discovered a strong strategic point. The British were proportionately vexed, and Carleton determined on getting rid of the annoyance. For that purpose he brought a battery of nine pounders to bear upon the building. When Cary Singleton saw it mounted, he smelt mischief.

"We will be knocked off our pins, boys," he said, "but before we drop let every man of you bring down his man."

The contest was keen and animated. The riflemen of Virginia poured volley after volley against the artillerists, while the latter hurled their solid balls against the massive masonry. At first they fired low, battering in doors, splintering wood-work, unhinging shutters, and ploughing the floors. The old walls of the town were shrouded in clouds of white smoke. The Palace appeared like a ring of fire from the red barrels of the riflemen. At length, one of the British militia officers stepped forward and pointed a nine-pounder direct on the cupola.

Cary spied the movement and exclaimed:

"This is our last chance. Fire!"

Loud and clear boomed the roar of that fatal cannon shot amid the rattle of musketry. There was a crash, a shivering of timbers, and then a heavy fall. When the smoke cleared away, the Intendant's Palace was a heap of ruins. The cupola had entirely disappeared. Wounded men crept out of the debris as well as they could, some limping, some holding a broken arm, others bandaging their damaged scalps, but all trailing their muskets. Cary Singleton was borne away by two of his men badly hurt in both legs. The British officer who had aimed the victorious shot stood towering on the walls surveying his achievement. It was Roderick Hardinge.

"Well done, Captain," said Caldwell, commander of the militia regiment to which Roderick belonged, and who had entrusted his young friend with the destruction of the Palace. "That is a good work. I have watched it from the bastion yonder and come to congratulate you. I shall recommend you for immediate promotion."

And so he did. Before that day had ended Roderick Hardinge was breveted a Major. He was overjoyed, and after receiving the congratulations of his friends, he hurried off to tell Pauline of his good fortune. Her father was out of the house and she was quite alone. When she opened the door to Hardinge, her eyes were red with weeping, and she held a bit of written paper in her hand. There is no need to describe the meeting. Suffice it to say that the note had informed her of Cary Singleton's fall.

XIV
LITTLE BLANCHE

Zulma had not forgotten her promise to Batoche concerning little Blanche. The last time she had met the old man, the subject was mooted and the answer she received was that possibly within a few days he would have occasion to demand her good services in favour of his granddaughter. An unforeseen circumstance hastened their meeting. Sieur Sarpy having learned that an intimate friend of his, living at the village of Charlesbourg, was very ill and particularly desired to see him, proposed to Zulma that she should accompany him on the visit. There was no risk attending the journey, as although Charlesbourg lay not very far from Quebec, to the north-east and in the environs of Montmorenci, it was out of the beat of the besieging forces, and could be reached by a circuitous route free from all interruptions. The promise of immunity had no effect upon Zulma, who knew that she had nothing whatever to fear, but she accepted the offer eagerly through the motive of being near her aged father, and because the excitement of travel was a positive relief in her then state of mind. The journey was accomplished successfully and without incident. The weather was favourable and the winter roads excellent. Sieur Sarpy finding his friend very ill indeed, decided upon remaining two or three days at his bedside. The first day Zulma kept him company, but the second, having learned upon inquiry that Batoche's cabin was not a great distance away, she felt an irresistible desire to drive over and visit little Blanche. Her father did not think it worth his while to interpose any objections, although he really did not fancy the project. Strange to say, his sick friend favoured it. Smiling languidly, he said in a whisper:—

"Let your daughter go. She may be able to do some good. Batoche is a wonderful man. We all like him, however little we can make him out. I am told that his granddaughter is a very singular child. Let Zulma go."

She went accompanied only by her own servant. She would accept no other escort. When she debouched from the Charlesbourg road into the broad highway leading from Quebec through Beauport to Montmorenci and onwards, she heard the sullen roar of cannon and the muffled roll of musketry in front of the town. She stopped a moment to listen, remarking to her companion that the firing was brisker than usual. But she was not further impressed, and soon drove on. The directions she had received were so precise that no difficulty was experienced in finding the route to the cabin. The little path leading to it from the main road was unbeaten either by trace of cariole or web of snow-shoe, but her horse broke through it easily enough, and pulled up in front of the hut almost before it was seen. It was nearly indistinguishable, being white as the element by which it was surrounded, and silent as the solitude amid which it stood. The faintest thread of white smoke rose from the chimney. Not a sound in the environs could be heard save the dull moan of the waterfall. Zulma stepped lightly out of the sleigh, tripped up to the door and rapped gently. No answer. She rapped a little louder. Still no answer. She applied her ear to the small aperture of the latch. Not a breath was audible. Getting just a little excited, not through fear, but through the mystery of adventure, she drew off her glove and knocked vigorously. The door opened wide and noiselessly on its hinges, and across it stood a mite of a girl, dressed in white woollen. For a moment Zulma did not stir. She could not. The strangeness of that child's face, its weird beauty, the singular light in the wide-open eyes arrested her footsteps and almost the beating of her heart. And near the child was a huge black cat, with stiff tail, bristling fur and glaring green eye, not hostile exactly, but sharply observant and expectant.

"Blanche," said Zulma at length in a voice whose musical softness was as that of a mother's appeal. "*Bon jour*, Blanche. You do not know me. My name is Zulma Sarpy."

There was no fear in the child's face from the first. Now all doubt and hesitation disappeared from it. She did not smile, but a beautiful serenity spread over it. She joined her two little thin hands together, open palm to palm, and instead of approaching, retreated a step or two as if to make way for her visitor. Zulma entered and closed the door.

"I have come to see you, Blanche. Your grandfather has spoken to me of you, and I want to do something for you."

The child answered brightly that her grandfather had indeed mentioned mademoiselle Sarpy's name and told her how good she had been to him and how she had promised to be her friend. Both Zulma and Blanche being now perfectly at ease, our old acquaintance Velours testified her satisfaction at this issue of affairs by curving her long back and rubbing herself against the hem of Zulma's cloak. Blanche gave her visitor a seat, helped her to take off her furs, and soon the two were engaged in earnest discourse. Zulma looked around the room and moved about to examine the many articles of its quaint furniture. This afforded her the opportunity of asking many questions, to all of which Blanche returned the most intelligent answers. Indeed, the child gave proofs of very remarkable intelligence. There was patent in her a wisdom far beyond her years. It was something different from the usual precocity, because the range of her information was limited enough, and there was sufficient simplicity in her discourse to eliminate that feeling of anxiety and pain which we always experience in the presence of abnormally developed children. Zulma made her tell all about her grandfather, and thus learned curious details concerning a character which she intensely admired, notwithstanding the mystery which was set like a seal upon it—a mystery which Blanche's unconscious revelations rendered only deeper and more provokingly interesting. She spoke to the child, too, of her godmother, Pauline, and it was a delight to learn from those truthful lips how much more loveable her dear friend was than she had ever suspected. Zulma felt that her visit was more than repaid by the insight she thus gained into the characters of Pauline and Batoche.

Then she broached higher things. She spoke of God and religion. The untutored child of the forest rose with the occasion. There was nothing conventional in her mind or words on these topics—as how could there be under the wayward teaching of Batoche? But her intuitions were crystal clear. There were no breaks, no obscurations in her spiritual vision. It was evident that she had studied and communed direct with nature, and that her soul had grown in literal contact with the winds and the flowers, the trees and the water courses, and the pure untrammelled elements of God.

She knelt before the lap of Zulma and recited all the prayers she knew—the formulas which the priest and Pauline had taught her, and the ejaculations which she had taught herself to say, in the bright morning, in the dark evening, in the silent days of peace, in the crash of the tempest, or when her little heart ached from whatever cause as she passed from infancy to adolescence. The contrast between the styles of these prayers impressed Zulma very strongly. The former were such as she herself knew, complete, appropriate and pathetic in their very phraseology. The latter were fragmentary, rude, and sometimes incongruous in syntax, but they spoke the poetry of the heart, and their yearning fervour and indubiety made Zulma understand, as she listened to them through her tears, how it is that wayside statues of stone, and wooden figures of the Madonna in lofty niches, are said to hear and answer by visible tokens the prayers of the illiterate, the unfortunate, and the poor.

"Are you not lonely here my dear?" asked Zulma raising the child from her knees and stroking back her hair as she stood leaning against her arm.

"I am used to be alone, mademoiselle," was the reply. "I have never had any company but my grandfather, who is often absent. He seeks food for both of us. He kills birds and animals in the woods. He catches fish in the river. Nobody ever came to see us except of late when my grandfather has been called away by strange men and has remained absent longer than usual. When he is here he speaks to me, he tells me stories, he teaches me to understand the pictures in some of his old books, he plays the violin for me. When he is gone I take more time to do my work, washing clothes, cleaning the dishes, sweeping the room, mending my dresses. When this is done, if the weather is fine, I gather flowers and fruits, I sit at the Falls making wreaths for our pictures and my grandfather's crucifix. If it is dark or stormy outside, I sing canticles, repeat my catechism, and when I am tired I play with Velours. She never leaves me."

Blanche did not say all these things consecutively, but in reply to repeated questions from Zulma, who led her on step by step. And not the answers themselves, but the manner in which they were made, the tone of voice, the expression of the eye and the ready gesture, all increased her interest in this strange charming little being.

"But of late," she said, "your grandfather has been away several nights together. Were you left all alone?"

"Yes, all alone, mademoiselle."

"And you were not afraid?"

Blanche smiled and there was a vacant look in her eye which reminded Zulma of Batoche.

"The night is the same as the day," she said.

"Oh, not the same, my darling. At night wicked things go abroad. The wild beasts prowl, bad men frighten the innocent, and the darkness prevents help from coming so easily as in the day."

Blanche listened attentively. What she heard was evidently something new, but it did not disconcert her. She explained to Zulma that when the hour for rest came, she said all her prayers, put on the night-dress which Pauline had given her—this was always white, in all seasons—covered the fire in winter, closed the door in summer, but never locked it, and then went to sleep.

"When my grandfather is in his alcove, I hardly ever awaken, but if he is absent I always awaken at midnight. Then I sit up and listen. Sometimes I hear the owl's cry or the bark of the wolf. At other times, I hear the great noise of the tempest. Sometimes again there is not a sound outside, except that of the waterfall. While I am awake I see at the foot, of my bed the image of my mother. She smiles on me and blesses me. Then I lie down and sleep till morning."

The above is a cold rehearsal of the words which the child uttered. There was a pathos in them beyond all words that caused Zulma to shed copious tears.

"Dear little thing," she exclaimed, clasping her to her bosom. "You shall be no longer alone. I will take care of you. You will come with me this very evening. Will your grandfather return to-night?"

"When he does not return, he tells me beforehand. When he returns, he says nothing. He said nothing this morning, therefore he will return to-night."

In the earnestness of her interview, Zulma had not noticed the flight of the hours. When she looked up at the clock it was past five and the darkness was gathering. Turning to the servant who, after attending to his horse, had entered the room and taken a seat in a corner, she ordered him to go out upon the main road and see whether any one was coming. He came back with the information that several men were going rapidly in the direction of Quebec, appearing very much excited, but that none seemed to be coming from the town.

"It may be late Blanche," said Zulma, "before your grandfather returns, but I will wait another hour. Then we shall decide what to do."

At six o'clock it was very dark and a slight snow-storm arose. Zulma was getting anxious. She could not make up her mind to leave the child all alone, and could not take her along without first seeing Batoche. On the other hand, she must return to Charlesbourg to avoid any needless anxiety on the part of her father. She was in the height of her perplexity when she heard the shuffling of feet at the door.

"It is he," exclaimed Blanche, springing to the latch.

XV
IN BATOCHE'S CABIN

Batoche entered, supporting Cary Singleton under the arms. The latter could stand upon his feet, but it was with effort, and he needed the assistance of his companion. Zulma was thunderstruck on seeing the wounded officer. He was no less astonished at seeing her. Batoche smiled as he glanced over the room. But not a syllable was uttered, until Cary had found a resting place in the easy chair before the fire. Then a few hasty words explained the whole situation. Zulma burst into tears and lamentations, as she took a seat at Cary's side, but he soon comforted her by the assurance that he was not dangerously hurt.

"The doctor told me there was nothing broken. All I need is a few days of rest. Batoche was at my side when I fell. He took care of me and prevailed upon me to come out here with him."

Batoche smiled again while Cary spoke, then said in his turn: —

"The Captain would have preferred to go elsewhere to rest, and he consented to come with me only when I assured him that you were away from home."

"How did you know that?" asked Zulma.

"Oh, I knew it."

"You know everything, Batoche."

"I did not know that we should meet you in my humble cabin, but I thought it was not impossible. When I saw your cariole at the door, I was not at all surprised, but I did not tell the Captain of it."

"I was never more surprised and delighted in my life," said Cary.

Zulma was comforted. She totally regained her equanimity, and conversed calmly with Cary. After a time, when little Blanche began to set the table, she rose to assist and cooked the frugal meal with her own hands. Later, she helped Batoche to prepare the liniments for the young officer's bruises. Batoche was as expert as any medicine man among the Indians, from whom indeed he had learned the virtues of the various seeds and herbs which hung in bunches from the rafters of his hut.

A couple of hours thus passed away almost unnoticed. As eight o'clock struck, Zulma arose from her seat and announced her intention of remaining with her friend till the next day, when the nature of his wounds would be better known. Cary remonstrated gently, renewing the assurance that within a very few days he would be in perfect possession of his limbs. On the other hand, Batoche encouraged Zulma in her resolution. He declared he would regard it as a great favor if she would accept the scant hospitality of his hut for one night. Little Blanche said nothing, but she clung to the skirt of Zulma and there was an appeal in her eye which the latter could not have resisted even if she had been so minded. In her usual decided way, she ordered the servant to drive back to Charlesbourg, inform her father why she had remained behind, and return to learn her wishes the next morning.

"If I thought," said Batoche, "that Sieur Sarpy would be too anxious, I would go with your servant, and explain everything."

"There is no need," replied Zulma. "My father is convinced that I would do nothing to pain him, and I know that his high regard for Captain Singleton, and his confidence in yourself, Batoche, will make him completely approve, the course which I take. The chief point is that my servant should return at once in order that my father may have no fear that I have encountered an accident on the road."

And without further delay, the servant took his departure.

Quietude then reigned in the cabin. Little Blanche recited her prayers to Zulma, and was put to bed by her, when she went to sleep directly. Her strange manners and remarkable discourse had been a source of great interest to Cary. Batoche retired to his alcove, whence he did not issue for a long time. In the interval, Zulma and the disabled officer, seated before the fire, indulged in a low-voiced conversation. Cary thanked his wounds for this unexpected opportunity of pleasant repose. Going over all the circumstances, he regarded this meeting with Zulma as something providential. He had almost a suspicion that Batoche had had a secret hand in bringing it about, so impressed had he become with the wonderful resources of that singular man. Zulma was actually calm, but her heart was full of gratitude and there was a fervour in her language which showed that her sensitive nature was in harmony with the time and place in which she found herself. Never had Cary seen her more beautiful. The humbleness and poverty of her surroundings brought out into relief the wealth and lordliness of her charms. She sat like an empress in her wicker chair. The predominant thought with Cary, as he glanced at her admiringly, was this—that it was an episode to be remembered through life, an episode which he could not have expected in his wildest dreams, and which would never recur again, to sit thus, a thousand miles away from home, in a lonely hut, in the snow-piled forests of Canada, with one of the loveliest and grandest women of God's planet. Over and over again, as he took in quietly the significance of this fact, he closed his eyes and delivered his soul to full and uninterrupted fruition. There are brief hours of enjoyment—few and far between—which are full compensation for years of dull, common-place existence, or even of positive suffering. Cary was very happy, and he might have sat there, before the fire, the live-long night, without ever thinking of his own or his companion's fatigue. Zulma, while no less absorbed in her own delight, was more considerate. When ten o'clock was reached, she called Batoche from his retreat, and proposed to him the arrangements for the night. After these were settled, she told her old friend that she had a favor to ask him. She wished him to play the violin. He hesitated a moment, then with a quaint smile fetched the instrument from the little room. Taking his stand in the centre of the hut, he opened with a few simple airs which only drew a smile from the lips of his listeners, but all at once, changing his mood, he plunged into a whirlpool of wild melody, now torturing then coaxing his violin, till he seemed transported beside himself, and both Zulma and Cary fancied themselves in the presence of a possessed spirit. They exchanged glances of wonder and almost of apprehension. Neither of them was at all prepared for this exhibition of wondrous mechanical skill, and preternatural expression. Batoche closed as abruptly as he had begun. After a final sweep over the strings that sounded like a shriek, he held his bow extended in his hand for a moment, while his contracted features and fixed eye assumed an expression of listening.

"There is trouble in the air," he said quietly, as he walked back to the alcove to lay by his fiddle. "The day which has been so eventful shall be followed by a night of distress. We have been happy. Our friends are not so happy."

XVI
A PAINFUL MEETING

Deep silence followed these words. It was broken, after an interval of about ten minutes, by a great commotion outside and the rushing of Batoche to the door. Cary and Zulma remained in their seats awaiting an explanation which was soon forthcoming. Batoche entered supporting on his arm the drooping form of Pauline. M. Belmont followed, the picture of anger and despair. When Zulma saw her friend, she uttered an exclamation of pain and sprang forward to meet her. Pauline having shot a burning glance at her and at the figure sitting beside her, placed her hand upon her heart, and fell backwards in a swoon. Cary, forgetting his wounds, hobbled to her assistance. The whole household was bustling around the beautiful victim, as she lay unconscious in Batoche's easy chair. But the attack was only transient. Pauline soon recovered consciousness and strength under the action of restoratives, and the company was enabled to understand what combination of strange circumstances had thus brought them so unexpectedly together. M. Belmont drew Batoche into the alcove, where they had a long and loud conversation, the substance of which was that both the friends were in imminent danger, the one of his life, the other of his liberty. M. Belmont had been warned that day, through the friendly offices of Captain Bouchette, that he must not receive Batoche into his house any further. Batoche had lately been tracked in his nocturnal excursions to and from the town, the authorities had been made aware of his doings, and strict orders had been issued for his capture dead or alive. The man who was on his heels was Donald, the servant of Roderick Hardinge, who had apprised his master of the facts. Roderick, through delicacy, had not ventured to mention the matter to M. Belmont, but had commissioned their mutual friend, Bouchette, to do so. The Belmont house was hereafter to be closely watched, and if Batoche or any of his companions were found there, not only would they be seized, but M. Belmont himself would be arrested and tried by court martial. This threat was bad enough, but there was worse. M. Belmont had that day received an anonymous letter in which he was told that a sentence of banishment from the town was hanging over his head. Colonel McLean, commander of the regulars, and the highest officer in the garrison after

Governor Carleton, had included his name in this punishment along with several others. He had powerful friends in Lieutenant-Governor Cramahé, Captain Bouchette, and Roderick Hardinge, but the force of circumstances might render their interposition unavailable. M. Belmont did not know how much truth there was in all this. But, according as the siege progressed, spirits within the town were getting terribly excited, and he really could not tell what might happen. At all events, the letter had completely roused him, and he had decided, at whatever risk, upon coming to consult Batoche. He had intended to come alone, but his daughter, Pauline, guessing his intention, would not be left behind. She declared she would follow her father through every contingency. They had both contrived to escape from the town by the happiest combination of circumstances. Now that he was out of the town, he would go further than he had at first intended. He would ask Batoche's opinion about staying away from it altogether, thus forestalling banishment. In the casket which his friend had hidden for him, there were sufficient valuables in coin to answer his purposes, and fully cover all his expenses for months to come. Hitherto he had struggled hard against his fate and his feelings for the sake of his daughter. Now that he was forced to act, he would resume his liberty, and he hoped Pauline would become reconciled to the change. He was not too old, and he had sufficient bodily strength to carry his principles into practice if need be.

M. Belmont poured out his story with rapid animation, being never once interrupted by Batoche. When he had concluded, he grew calmer and was in a proper state of mind to receive the advice of his friend.

Batoche's words were few and deliberate. As for himself, M. Belmont need not fear any further trouble from his goings and comings in the town. He had no dread of the wolves, only hate. He laughed at their threats. There was not an Englishman of them all cunning enough to entrap him. He would continue his visits as he pleased, but he would never come near M. Belmont's residence. As to M. Belmont's personal case, he would simply advise him to maintain his ground, and not compromise himself by flight. He knew that his friend was no coward, but flight was a cowardly act. Then, there was Pauline to consider—an all-powerful argument. All his life had been consecrated to her—let it be consecrated to the end. He had made many sacrifices in her behalf—he should not recoil before this greatest sacrifice. The dear child might acquiesce, but it would cause her many a secret tear, and such as she were too good to be made unhappy. Besides, M. Belmont should think of his compatriots. He was their foremost man. If he fled, they would all be put under the ban. If he deserted them, what would many of them do in the supreme hour of trial that was coming?

M. Belmont listened attentively, almost religiously to the words of the man whom he had of late so much learned to admire, and whose wisdom was never more apparent than on the present occasion. He thanked Batoche warmly, but failed to say that he would follow his advice. Instead of that, he took him by the hand and drew him into the apartment where the young people were seated.

They too had had an absorbing conversation. It was the sight of Cary which had so suddenly unbalanced Pauline when she first entered the cabin. From a hasty note which Batoche had smuggled into the town, she had learned of his misfortune at the Intendant's Palace. She had been feverishly anxious to hear more about his fate. This was one of the causes why she decided upon accompanying her father in his perilous journey that night. She knew she would meet Batoche and gather full particulars from him. But she had no suspicion that she would see Cary himself. And the presence of Zulma was another mystery. But after she recovered consciousness, as we have seen, and, seated between them, had heard the explanation of everything, not only did her spirits revive, but she forgot all the other sorrows which waited upon her. Cary, too, completely overlooked his own ailments in the joy of her presence. And Zulma, without misgiving, without afterthought, was perhaps the happiest of the three, because she partook of the pleasure which her two friends experienced in each other's society.

Thus a full hour of unalloyed enjoyment passed away, after which the conversation necessarily drifted into more serious courses. It could hardly be otherwise in view of the circumstances by which they were all surrounded. Youth and beauty and love cannot always feast upon themselves. They must perforce return to the stark realities of life. They spoke of the war and of all the miseries attendant upon it—the sufferings of the poor, the privations of the sick, the anxieties of parents, the pangs of absence, the rigours of the cold, and the terrible sacrifices which even the commonest soldier is obliged to make. The two girls listened with tears as Cary graphically recounted his experiences, which, though relieved at times by touches of humor, were profoundly sad. Then Zulma, in eloquent language and passionate gestures, gave her view of the situation. Pauline was mostly silent. Her role was to receive the confidences of others, rather than to communicate her own. At times, in the march of discourse, the veil of the future was timidly raised, but immediately dropped again, with an instinctive shrinking of the three young hearts. That far they durst not look. The present was more than sufficient for them to bear. A gentle, merciful Providence would provide for the rest.

Who can gauge the effect upon the participants of this interview, in such a place, at such an hour, and amid so many singular circumstances?

It was deep, searching, and ineffaceable, and the sequel of our history will show that most of its culminating events were directly traceable to this memorable evening.

When M. Belmont stepped forward with Batoche, he at once addressed himself to Cary Singleton, asking his advice on the subject of the conference just held in the alcove. The young officer, after blushing and faltering at the suddenness of the appeal, replied in a manly fashion that, although he was an apostle of liberty with pistol and sabre, and entirely devoted to the cause, even to the shedding of his heart's blood, he could not presume upon giving advice to such a man as M. Belmont. He was too young, for one thing, and, for another, he was not sufficiently acquainted with the circumstances of the case. He added, glancing with ardour at the two fair girls beside him, that they would be better able to determine the question, Mademoiselle Belmont taking counsel of her father's welfare, and Mademoiselle Sarpy speaking for the benefit of her dearest friend. Thus appealed to, Zulma declared promptly that she had no opinion on the advisability of M. Belmont remaining out of the town, but that if he resolved upon doing so, she offered him, in the name of her father and in her own, a welcome home in the Sarpy mansion. In fact, she insisted that she would allow her to live nowhere else. Cary smiled and thanked Zulma with an approving nod. Pauline had not a word to utter, but her answer was only too painfully significant when she buried her face in her hands and gave way to a tempest of grief. Perplexity was painted on every countenance. Batoche alone retained his equanimity, and calmly, but with a tone almost of authority, he said:

"M. Belmont, it is near midnight. There is a long road to travel. A decision must at once be made. What do you say?"

M. Belmont still hesitated.

"Then, Pauline will decide. Come, my dear, shall we go or stay?"

Pauline immediately rose, and with a look of pathetic imploring, murmured:

"Oh, father, let us go."

M. Belmont instantly complied. As Batoche signified his intention of going along, in order to see them safe within the walls, Zulma earnestly demanded permission to accompany him. M. Belmont, Pauline, and Cary tried their best to dissuade her, but the old soldier silenced their objections by at once according his consent. The wounded officer having received the last attention for the night, the party took their departure. They reached Quebec without incident, and Batoche readily found an opening for them into the town from a ravine in the valley of the St. Charles.

Zulma and Pauline embraced each other fervidly.

"Before we separate, I have a dreadful secret to tell you," said Pauline.

"What is it, my dear?"

"Do you know who pointed the gun that wounded the Captain?"

"I do not."

"Can't you guess?"

"No."

"It was Roderick Hardinge."

The eyes of the two friends exchanged sparks of fire.

On the return journey, Zulma inquired of Batoche:—

"Do you know who fired the fatal gun against you from the walls?"

"I do."

"Does Captain Singleton know it?"

"He does not."

"Why did you not tell him?"

"On account of little Pauline."

XVII
NISI DOMINUS

Quebec was the centre of missionary labor for years before our Atlantic coast was thoroughly settled. The church of San Domingo is older, having been founded in 1614. That of Mexico dates from 1524, and that of Havana was established at an earlier epoch still. But none of these can be said to have exercised the same influence which distinguished the city of Champlain. From Quebec came forth nearly all the missionaries who evangelized the west and north-west. The children of Asisi and Loyola, whose names are immortalized in the pages of Bancroft, all set forth on their perilous wanderings under instructions issued from the venerable college whose ruins are still seen beneath the shadow of Cape Diamond. In the list of priests who resided at Quebec on the 1st October, 1674, is found the name of Jacques Marquette. Little did that modest man then dream of the glory which was soon to be attached to his labors and explorations. By the discovery of the Mississippi not only did he add a vast territory to the realms of his King, but he opened an immense field to the zeal of his Bishop, and extended the boundaries of the diocese of Quebec by thousands upon thousands of miles. Thus it happens that Chicago, Milwaukee, St. Louis, New Orleans, Cincinnati, Louisville, and all our Western cities, though they did not then exist, now occupy ground which was under the jurisdiction of the great Bishop, Francois Laval de Montmorenci, who was first raised to the See of Quebec two hundred years ago. It is no stretch of fancy, but the literal truth—and the picture is a grand one—that when Laval stood on the steps of his high altar, in that venerable fane which has since been raised to the rank of a basilica, he could wave his crozier over a whole continent, from the Gulf of the St. Lawrence to the Gulf of Mexico, and from the Red River of the North to the waters of Chesapeake Bay. Time has passed since then, and religion has progressed in such astonishing rates that sixty-two dioceses are at present said to have sprung from the single old diocese of Quebec.

The sixth successor of Laval was Briand, the last French Bishop of Quebec under British domination. All those who succeeded him were Canadian born. It was to him that M. Belmont addressed himself for final counsel. He found the prelate alone in his study, calmly reading his breviary, while a pile of documents, letters and other papers lay on a table at his side. He wore a purple cassock, over which was a surplice of snow-white lace reaching to the knees. On his shoulders was attached a short violet cape. A pectoral cross hung from his neck by a massive chain of gold. The tonsured white head was covered by a small skull-cap of purple velvet. A large amethyst ring flashed on the second finger of the left hand. Monseigneur sat there the picture of serene force. While all around him was uproar, within his apartment the atmosphere of peace reigned with a visible, tangible presence. The seminary where he resided was within a stone's throw of the barracks in Cathedral Square, but whereas the one was the continual theatre of anxiety and excitement, the other wás the scene of perpetual confidence and repose. And yet, this lonely man was a principal actor in the events of 1775-76. His influence had been, and was still, omnipotent and all pervading. From his quiet retreat he had sent forth a pastoral, at the beginning of hostilities, commending loyalty to Britain, and exhorting all his followers to obey the teachings and example of their curates. And his voice had been heard. But for him, there is no telling how different the circumstances of the invasion of Canada would have been. If Guy Carleton was Knighted for his successful defence of Quebec, surely Monseigneur Briand should have received some token of favor from those whom he so faithfully served. Without the spiritual power, the material force could not have availed, and the sword of the commander would have been lifted in vain but for the Bishop's crook that scattered the initial obstacles of the contest.

The prelate received M. Belmont with the utmost kindness, for they were old friends. Placing his thumb within the closed leaves of his breviary, he asked his visitor to unfold to him freely the object of his coming, although there was an expression in his countenance which showed that he divined the object. M. Belmont, who was agitated at first, gradually acquired sufficient self-possession to give a full explanation of his case. He detailed his grievances, his apprehensions, and explained the radical change which he had undergone in his political opinions. He ended by pointedly asking the Bishop whether he was not justified in taking a decided stand.

Monseigneur had listened unmoved to the whole history, occasionally smiling languidly, occasionally looking very serious. His reply was given in the kindest tones, but there was the conscious authority of the chief pastor in every word which he uttered.

"I too am a Frenchman, my friend," he said. "I have my feelings, my prejudices, my aspirations, like every other man. If I consulted only my heart, I believe you can guess where it would have led me. But I consult my head. I remember that I have a conscience. I am reminded that I have stern duties, as Bishop, to fulfil. The responsibility of them is something terrible. The cardinal doctrine of our theology is obedience to legitimate authority. The whole logic of the church is there. This principle permeates every department of life, from the highest to the lowest. It shines out through all our history. In the present instance, its application is plain. The English are our masters. They are such by the right of conquest—a sad right, but one which is thoroughly recognized. They have been our masters for sixteen years. In that time, they have not always treated us well. But there was ignorance rather than ill-will. Of late they have guaranteed the rights of our people and of the church. The Quebec Act is a standing proof of a desire of justice on the part of the English Government. And how do these Boston people regard the Quebec Act? Judge for yourself."

The Bishop here produced from among the papers on the table a pictorial caricature of the Act.

"See," he continued. "This represents Boston in flames and Quebec triumphant, and the print explains that thus popery and tyranny will triumph over true religion, virtue and liberty. Among the other personages, look at the kneeling figure of a Catholic priest, with cross in one hand and gibbet in the other, assisting King George, as the print again says, in enforcing his tyrannical system of civil and religious liberty: What do you think of that? Does it look like the real fellowship for us which they profess in their proclamations? Liberty and independence are fine words, my friend. I love them. But they may be catch-words as well, and we have to beware. Who assures us that the revolted Colonies are sincere? After all, they are only Englishmen rebelling against their country. Even if they are justified in rebelling, does that fact justify us in joining them? And what good reason have we to believe that they can better our lot? Will they respect our religion, language, and laws more than do our present masters? Reflect on these things. Do nothing imprudent. Remember your family. Respect your reputation. You have a fortune but it is not yours to waste by useless confiscation. It belongs to little Pauline. I respect your sympathies, and believe that you will soon have occasion to display them without premature action. This town will soon be attacked. Either the besiegers will succeed or they will not. If they do not succeed, you will be able to ease your heart attending to the sick and wounded prisoners among them. If they do succeed, and Quebec is taken, then Canada is theirs, and they will become our masters instead of the English. Then the duty of us all will be clear, and you will have no difficulty in making your adhesion."

The Bishop smiled as he laid down this common-sense proposition, and so did M. Belmont who was thoroughly convinced by its logic. He thanked

Monseigneur for his strong advice, and promised in most fervent language that he would carry it out.

"Do so, my son," added the Bishop. "I am pleased with your submission. Before a fortnight has elapsed, you will have reason to thank me again for the counsel."

M. Belmont got down on his knees, and the prelate, rising, pronounced the episcopal benediction over his bent brow, giving him at the same time the pastoral ring to kiss.

"Pray," said the Bishop, advancing a few steps with M. Belmont towards the door, "pray and ask your pious daughter to double her supplications that the right may triumph, and peace be soon restored. The shock will be terrible."

"But the town is very strong," replied M. Belmont.

The Bishop smiled again, and raising his finger in sign of warning, he repeated solemnly and slowly the grand lesson:

"*Nisi Dominus custodierit civitatem.* Unless the Lord keep the city, in vain they watch who stand guard over it."

XVIII
LAST DAYS

Zulma spent the next morning in the exclusive company of Cary. Batoche bustled in and out of the cabin, while little Blanche was kept busy at household work. The wounded man had had a good night, and thanks to the lotions and poultices of his old friend, felt much easier. About noon, the whole circle was most agreeably surprised by the arrival of Sieur Sarpy who drove up with his servant. He had come expressly to see Cary, and, while condoling with him on his accident, testified to his joy that he was on a fair way of recovery. He speedily commended the conduct of his daughter under the circumstances, and, in a long conversation with Batoche, took occasion to declare his cordial approval of the course which he had thought fit to pursue in the war. This commendation was very precious to the aged solitary, and he stated that it would serve as an encouragement to persevere, doing all in his power to keep his countrymen in the sacred cause of liberation.

Towards evening Zulma returned to Charlesbourg with her father, but on the following morning they both came to Montmorenci again, and thus for several days, until Cary having been pronounced by Batoche quite able to travel, they prevailed upon him to pass the remainder of his convalescence at the Sarpy mansion. Batoche, who had been kept in idleness by the illness of his friend, favoured the removal, as it gave him the opportunity of once more resuming his self-imposed military duties. For the same reason, he readily allowed little Blanche to accompany Zulma.

Cary remained five days with the Sarpys, and it is needless to say that the time rolled by as if on wheels of gold. What added to his enjoyment was that, through the medium of Batoche, Zulma managed to communicate daily with Pauline, and to receive answers from her, in every one of which she tenderly inquired about the young officer.

He would willingly have tarried longer in this delicious retreat, but at the end of the five days, having learned that stirring events were being prepared in camp, he decided that he was sufficiently recovered to take part in them. Indeed, he declared that he would take part in them even if he had to go on crutches. Zulma did not attempt to detain him. There were tears in her eyes when she bade him farewell, but the beautiful smile on her lips was an incentive to go and do his duty.

"If I fear anything, it is on your account," he said.

"Fear nothing," she replied. "I feel certain that we shall meet again."

On reaching camp, where his return was acclaimed by all his comrades, Cary learned that the end was approaching. The great blow was at last to be struck. The whole month of December had been wasted in a fruitless siege, and Montgomery determined that, for a variety of imperious reasons, he must attempt to carry the beetling fortress by storm. It was a desperate alternative, but the single gleam of success which attended it was all sufficient to cause its adoption.

XIX
PRES-DE-VILLE

Everything was in readiness. The only condition to be waited for was a snow-storm. It came at length in the early morning of the 31st December. The army fell into lines at once, and by two o'clock, Montgomery's arrangements were all perfected. Ladders, spears, hatchets and hand grenades were in readiness. The plan of battle was this. Montgomery, at the head of one division, was to attack Lower Town from the west; Arnold, at the head of the second division, was to attack Lower Town from the east, and they were both to meet at the foot of Mountain Hill, which they would ascend together, force the stockades on the site of Prescott Gate, and pour victoriously into Upper Town. In the meantime, Livingston, with a regiment of Canadians, and Brown, with part of a Boston regiment, were to make false attacks on Cape Diamond Bastion, St. John and St. Louis Gates, which they were to fire, if possible, with combustible prepared for that purpose.

Let us first follow Montgomery. Advancing from his quarters at Holland House, he crossed the Plains of Abraham, descended to Wolfe's Cove, and thence marched up the narrow road between the river and the towering crag of Cape Diamond. The night was dark as ink, a blinding snow-storm raged, and the sharp wind heaped the way with banks of drift. Silently the heroic column moved on, in spite of the terrible weather, until it reached a spot called Près-de-Ville, the narrowest point at the entrance of Lower Town. There it was stopped by a barrier which consisted of a log house containing a battery of three pounders. The post was under the command of two Canadians, Chabot and Picard, with thirty militiamen of their own nationality, and a few British seamen acting as artillerists under Captain Barnsfare and Sergeant McQuarters. Montgomery did not hesitate. Ordering his carpenters to hew some posts that obstructed the way to the barrier, he pulled them down with his own hands, then drawing his sword, he put himself at the head of a handful of brave followers, leaped over heaps of ice and snow, and charged. Sharp eyes were glaring through the loop-holes of the block house, the match was lit, the word trembled on tight-pressed lips. When the Americans were within forty paces, Barnsfare shouted "Fire!" and a volley of grape swept down the open space. Only one volley, but certainly the most fateful that was ever belched from a cannon's mouth. No shot was ever more terribly decisive.

The air was heavy with the groans of the wounded and dying. Thirteen bodies lay stretched in a winding sheet of snow. Foremost among them was that of Montgomery. There was a moment of silence, then the guns and muskets of the block house poured forth a storm of missiles. But all to no purpose, as the assaulting column, stunned by this first disaster, fell back in confusion and retreated precipitately to Wolfe's Cove.

When daylight appeared, and news of the combat reached the authorities of the Upper Town, a party under James Thompson, the Overseer of Works, went out to view the field. As the snow had continued falling, the only part of a body that appeared above the surface was that of Montgomery himself, part of whose left arm and hand stood up erect, but the corpse was doubled up, the knees being drawn up to the face. Beside him lay his brave aids, McPherson and Cheeseman and one sergeant. The whole were frozen hard. Montgomery's sword was found near by. A drummer boy snatched it up, but Thompson secured it for himself and it is kept to this day as an heirloom in his family.

Meigs, who served with Montgomery, pays this affecting tribute. "He was tall and slender, well-limbed, of a genteel, easy, graceful, manly address, and had the voluntary love, esteem and confidence of the whole army. His death, though honourable, is lamented, not only as the death of an amiable, worthy friend, but as an experienced, brave general; the whole country suffers greatly by such a loss at this time. The native goodness and rectitude of his heart might easily be seen in his actions. His sentiments, which appeared on every occasion, were fraught with that unaffected goodness which plainly discovered the goodness of the heart from whence they flowed."

Montgomery had said: "We shall eat our Christmas dinner in Quebec."

Alas.

XX
SAULT-AU-MATELOT

Arnold moved his division from the General Hospital in the St. Roch's Suburb, but not so secretly as Montgomery had done. The roar of cannon, the ringing of bells, the rattle of drums aroused and alarmed the slumbering town. His men crept along the walls in single file, covering the locks of their guns with the lappets of their coats, and holding down their heads on account of the driving snow storm, until they reached the point of their attack in Sault-au-Matelot street. This is one of the legendary streets of Quebec. It lies directly under the Cape, and is supposed to derive its name from a sailor who leaped into it from above. Creuxius has a prosier explanation: "*Ad confluentem promontorium assurgit quod saltum nautæ vulgo vocant ab cane hujus nominis qui se alias ex eo loco praecipitum dedit.*" Of Arnold's followers the most notable were Morgan's brave riflemen, and the whole column consisted of five hundred men. He marched in advance of them, animating their courage by word and example. His impetuous bravery led him to needless exposure in the attack on the first barrier, in front of which he was at once struck down by a musket-wound in the knee, and carried off the field back to the General Hospital, where, to his intense chagrin, he soon learned the defeat and death of Montgomery. The command then devolved on Morgan, who, after a gallant charge, carried the first barrier, taking a number of prisoners, and pushed to the second and more important one further in the interior of Lower Town. On the way, his men scattered and disarmed a number of Seminary scholars, among whom was Eugene Sarpy. Many of these escaped to Upper Town and were the first to acquaint Carleton with the grave condition of affairs. He instantly despatched Caldwell with a strong force of his militiamen, including a body commanded by Roderick Hardinge. Thus reinforced, the defenders of the second barrier made so stout a resistance that Morgan was completely baffled. In the darkness and confusion occasioned both by a murderous enfilading fire and the fury of the snow-storm, he could scarcely keep his men together. In order to recognize each other the Continentals wore a band of paper around their caps, with the words *Mors aut Victoria*, or *Liberty for Ever*, conspicuously written. But even this was of scant avail. For the purpose of further concentration,

Morgan decided on abandoning the open street and occupying the houses on the south side, whence he could keep up a telling fire on the interior of the barricade. He thus obtained some shelter, but he could not prevent his ranks from rapidly thinning under the artillery and musketry fire of the enemy. His men fell on every side. Several of his best officers were killed or wounded under his very eye. The brave Virginian stormed and raged, but his most valiant efforts were futile. There was a propitious moment when he might have retreated in safety. He chafed against the idea, and his hesitation proved fatal. Carleton sent out from Palace Gate a detachment of two hundred men, under Captain Laws, to march up Sault-au-Matelot street and take the Continentals in the rear. The movement was completely successful. Morgan was forced to understand his desperate situation and yielded bravely to fate. He surrendered the remnant of his shattered army, a total of four hundred and twenty-six men.

This was the dread culmination. The great stroke had been made and it had disastrously failed. Quebec still remained towering on its granite pedestal. British power still stood defiant. The Continentals had broken their victorious campaign against this gigantic obstacle. Montgomery was dead. Arnold was wounded. One half of the army was captured. The broken remnant shrunk back to its quarters amid the snowbanks of the St Foye road. Had Carleton been a great general he could have annihilated it at one blow.

There never dawned a gloomier day over an army than the 1st of January, 1776, over the American forces before Quebec. All their chances were gone, and they had to confront a menacing future. Still gloomier was the fate of the four hundred brave fellows who were cooped up in the Seminary. These prisoners were well treated by the British, but the loss of liberty was a privation for which no kind offices could compensate. Among them, of course, was Cary Singleton, who was not only a prisoner but grievously wounded.

BOOK IV
AFTER THE STORM

I
THE CONFESSIONAL

It was the eve of the New Year. The snow-storm continued in unabated violence, and the weather was so gray that the lines of earth and sky were blended and utterly undistinguishable. A little after the hour of noon, Zulma Sarpy knelt in the little church of Pointe-aux-Trembles. Beside her there were only a few worshippers—some old men mumbling their rosaries, and some women crouched on their heels before the shrine. A solitary lamp hung from a silver chain in the sanctuary, casting a feeble ray amid the premature gloom. An awful silence reigned throughout the aisles. Opposite the place where Zulma was stationed stood a square box through the bars of which faintly gleamed the white surplice of the parish priest, who sat there awaiting the confessions of his flock. The New Year is the chief of festal days among the French, and it is always ushered in by exercises of devotion. After going through all the needful preparation, Zulma rose from her seat and approached the dread confessional. Her demeanour was full of gravity, a pallor overspread her beautiful features, her eyes were cast down, her hands joined upon her breast. The influence of prayer and of silent communion with God could never be more perceptible. She looked like a totally distinct being from the one whom we have known in the preceding pages. Zulma moved slowly, and when she reached the door of the confessional, she paused a moment. But it was not through hesitation. She was recollecting herself for a supreme act of religion. At length she disappeared behind the long green curtain, knelt on the narrow stool within, and through the lattice poured forth her soul into the bended and keenly listening ear of the pastor. What she said we may not know, for the secrets of this tribunal are inviolable, but it is allowed to believe that the lengthy whisperings consisted of something more than a mere accusation of faults. They conveyed demands of counsel for guidance in the trying circumstances amid which the girl found herself, and in response the grave voice of the priest was heard in an undertone, advising, warning, and exhorting. Finally, the rite was concluded. The fair penitent bent her white forehead, the pastor signed the sign of salvation in the air, the stool was pushed back, the green curtain arose, and Zulma stepped forth to resume the place which she had at first occupied. We are dispensed from further describing her appearance. Longfellow, in speaking of Evangeline, has put it forth in one pregnant line.

"Serenely she walked with God's benediction upon her."

An hour passed, during which Zulma knelt immoveable, absorbed in prayer, and most of the other persons in the church followed her example by visiting the confessional in turns. At the end of that time, the priest, assuring himself that there were no further ministrations to be made, rose from his seat, opened the little door that held him in, and walked forward into the aisle. As he passed Zulma, he tapped her gently upon the shoulder as a sign that she should follow him. She did so at once, and the two glided noiselessly into the vestry. There the priest, after divesting himself of his surplice, turned towards the girl, and in the gentlest manner inquired after her health and that of her father. He then signified his pleasure at her punctual discharge of her devotions, in spite of the extremely inclement weather.

"It is a great festival, but it will bring no joy this year," he said.

Zulma, whose countenance still preserved its paleness and expression of extreme gravity, replied that the times were indeed melancholy, but that she nevertheless hoped to enjoy a quiet *Jour de l'An* with her father and immediate neighbours, having made all the necessary preparations to that end.

"You have not heard then, my daughter?" said the priest.

"Heard what, sir?"

"Of the terrible events which took place this night while we were sleeping."

Zulma looked up with a movement of deep anxiety and asked:

"What has happened sir?"

"Two great battles have been fought."

"Is it possible?"

"Many killed, wounded, and prisoners."

"Who, where, how?" gasped Zulma in agony.

"Quebec was attacked in two places."

"And captured?" demanded Zulma, unable to restrain herself.

"No, my daughter. Both attacks were repulsed."

Zulma clasped her hands to her forehead and would have sunk to the floor had she not been sustained by the good priest.

"Courage, my dear," he said "Excuse me for telling you these things, but I saw from your deportment in the church that you knew nothing of them, and I thought it would be well that I should be the first to inform you."

"Pardon my weakness, Monsieur Le Curé," was the meek reply. "I had indeed expected this, but the news is terribly sudden all the same. I entreat you to give me all the particulars which you know. I feel stronger now and can hear anything."

"I know little that is definite. In the general excitement, all sorts of rumours are aggravated when they reach us at this distance. But I am assured that General Montgomery has been killed and Colonel Arnold wounded. I knew these gentlemen. They dined several times at my table. They were fine men and I liked them well. I am distressed to hear of their misfortune."

"Have you heard of the fate of any other officers?"

"Of none by name, except that it was a certain Morgan who replaced Arnold and surrendered his army."

"Morgan?" exclaimed Zulma, and this time she was so overcome that she fell exhausted in a chair.

The priest was considerably surprised. Notwithstanding that his periodical visits to the Sarpy mansion had been interrupted during the American occupation of Pointe-aux-Trembles, he knew in a general way that Zulma had become acquainted with one or the other of the officers, which was the main reason why he judged that the early communication of the war news from his lips would be particularly interesting to Sieur Sarpy and his daughter, but he had no suspicion that Zulma's feelings went further, and had thus no idea of the effect which his words produced upon her. It was only when he saw her extreme depression and sorrow that he surmised something of the truth, with that instinct which is characteristic of men, who, themselves separated from the world by the stern law of celibacy, devote all their attention to the spiritual and temporal concerns of their flocks.

"Do not be depressed," he said, approaching Zulma's chair, and bending towards her with the kindness of a father towards his child. "Perhaps the news is exaggerated. We shall hear more towards evening, and it may turn out that the losses are not so great as represented. At least there may be no loss personal to yourself, my dear, and I trust that such will prove to be the fact. Therefore take heart. It is getting late. The snow continues falling and the roads must be blocking up. Return home and endeavour to maintain your soul in peace. To-morrow, you will come to early mass, when I trust that we shall have better news to tell each other."

In spite of the cheering words of the pastor, Zulma drove homeward with a heavy heart. She spoke not a word to her servant. Instead of raising her face to the storm and allowing the flakes to beat upon it, as was her wont, when her spirits were high, she kept her veil down, and the handkerchief which she frequently drew from under it gave proof that she was silently weeping. It often happens, that the most boisterous, lofty women bear their grief in unostentatious quiet, giving it a more forcible relief from contrast. Thus was it in the present instance with Zulma. Revolving in her mind all that the priest had told her, and having full leisure during the journey to appreciate all its terrible contingencies, she was completely prostrated when she reached home. On descending from the sleigh she glided softly to her room, where she locked herself in so as to be absolutely alone. She remained thus until nearly the supper hour, and after the shadows of evening had enveloped her.

II
BLANCHE'S PROPHECY

When Sieur Sarpy met his daughter at the table, he divined at once that something was wrong. He himself had heard nothing. The prevalence of the snow-storm had prevented any one from calling at his mansion, except the few needy neighbours who had gone early in the morning to receive their regular alms. The day had passed in solitude, and as the old gentleman had had no misgivings whatever, he spent his time most agreeably in the perusal of his favourite books. He must have happened on light and cheerful literature, because, when he concluded his reading and came down to supper, he was in more than his usual enlivened mood. But the spectacle of Zulma's swollen eyes, pinched features and constrained manner, checked his flow of good humour and arrested the pleasant anecdote which his lips were about to utter. Naturally enough he did not suspect the real cause of his daughter's sorrow. He knew that she had driven down to the village church for her devotions, and of course presumed that something had happened to her there. He was once on the point of teasing her about the scolding which he supposed that the priest had administered to her, but he immediately checked himself. With the well-bred old French gentleman deep respect formed perhaps the chief ingredient of the ardent love which he bore his daughter. He carried his consideration so far that he would not even question her. It became therefore incumbent on Zulma to break the painful silence. She detailed the narrative which the priest had given her, supplementing it largely with the comments dictated by her fears. The effect upon Sieur Sarpy was hardly less than it had been upon his daughter. He listened in profound silence, but with an anxiety and surprise which he did not attempt to conceal. For a long time he ventured to make no reply, and when at length he did so, it was in such hesitating language as showed that he was haunted by the same apprehensions which besieged his daughter. He had therefore scant consolation to offer her, and the evening meal thus passed without any break in that mental gloom which was deeper than the darkness which rolled in the exterior heavens.

Little Blanche sat at Zulma's side listening to the discourse with wide distended eyes, and that expression of vacancy which was so frequent with this strange child. Not a word had escaped her, and it was evident that the effect was as great upon her acute mind as upon that of her two companions.

"If Batoche would only come," murmured Zulma, passing her hand over her weary brow. "He would tell us everything. I wonder he is not here already."

"His absence is an additional cause for fear," replied Sieur Sarpy in a low voice.

"Still, I do not despair. He may arrive before the night is over."

"If he is alive."

"What, papa? You do not suppose that Batoche took part in the attack?"

"I do. I am sure he never quitted the side of Cary Singleton."

"I did not think of that. Alas! I fear you are right. In that case, who knows?"

"Yes, the worst may have happened to our old friend, and he may never return."

Both Zulma and her father instinctively looked at little Blanche. An angelic smile played upon her lips and her eyes were far away.

"Blanche," said Zulma, laying her hand softly on the child's shoulder.

"Yes, Mademoiselle. Grandpapa when he left me, two days ago, said *au révoir*. That means, 'I will see you again.'"

"But perhaps those bad men have killed him."

"What bad men? The Wolves?"

Zulma did not understand, but Sieur Sarpy understood very well.

"Yes, the Wolves, my dear," he said with a sad smile.

"Oh, my grandfather does not fear the Wolves. The Wolves fear him. They cannot catch him, no matter what great dangers he may be in. He may suffer, he may be wounded, but he will not die except near our cabin at the Falls, under the eye of my mother and with a blessing for me. He has often told me this at night as he held me on his knee, and I believe all that my grandfather says. No, Mademoiselle, he is not dead and will soon arrive to console you."

Zulma could not restrain her tears as she heard the simple pathos of these childish words, and suddenly a confidence sprung up in her heart, which sacerdotal speech had been unable to infuse. She pushed her chair from the table, lifted Blanche from her seat and set her on her own knees, pillowing the little head on her bosom, and imprinting warm kisses of gratitude on the slight forehead. Sieur Sarpy looked on, and appeared pleased. No doubt a similar assurance awoke within him.

"If Batoche comes at all, he will come to-night. We know his punctuality and his readiness to do a service. The weather is bad and the roads must be in a wretched state, but this will be no obstacle to his reaching the mansion. We learn, however, that a great many prisoners have been taken. Batoche may possibly be among them. In that case, we shall, of course, resign ourselves not to see him to-night."

Raising her head from Zulma's shoulder, Blanche said rapidly and with some animation:

"No, M. Sarpy, grandpapa is not a prisoner. He has always said that the Wolves would never catch him and I believe all that he says."

Sieur Sarpy smiled, and made no reply, but he had a vague belief that perhaps the child might be right after all.

III
THE PROPHECY FULFILLED

She was right. The evening wore away slowly. The servant cleared the table and trimmed the fire. Sieur Sarpy, instead of retiring to his private chamber, wheeled his chair to the hearth, and resumed the reading which he had interrupted before supper. Zulma continued to hold Blanche on her knee and, sitting before the glowing fire, they both dropped off into sleep. With the child, it was genuine slumber mingled with pleasant dreams, as the smile upon her lips and the lines that played upon her brow and cheeks clearly testified. With Zulma it was not real sleep, but somnolence, or rather the torpor of dim meditations. Her eyes were closed, her head was thrown back upon the rocking chair, her limbs were somewhat extended, while an air of forced resignation or preparation for the worse was set upon her noble features. The blue and yellow flames of the chimney flickered wantonly upon her face; the moan of the wind around the gable drummed into her ear, while the slow flight of the hours which she heeded not, yet noted distinctly from the strokes of the old clock, lapsed her soul farther and farther away into the vague spaces of oblivion. Gradually Sieur Sarpy, yielding to the influence of heat and solitude, dropped his book upon his knee, and closed his eyes for a brief respite of repose. But for the outside sounds of nature and an occasional gust in the fire place, everything within that room was as silent as the grave. The respiration of its three living beings was barely audible, a proof that at least none of them suffered from physical pain. Everything betokened peace and security. If the rest of the country-side was wild with war or the rumours of war, the Sarpy mansion lay in the bliss of a profound unconsciousness.

Suddenly Zulma moved about in her seat, and rolled her head from side to side on the chair, as if a vision was flitting before her and the light of the hearthstone. She slowly opened her eyes, closed them again tightly in order to strengthen their force, and opened them a second time. Ten o'clock struck. She had been resting for two hours. It was time that she should rise and retire to her room. She sat up erect and, in doing so, looked directly forward again. She could not be mistaken. There was really a shadow between her and the fire. By a rapid effort of her strong will, she acquired full consciousness and recognized Batoche. Another glance of almost aching velocity revealed to her that his brow was placid, his eye soft, and that the traces of a smile lingered at the corners of his lips. This spectacle at once reassured her. She felt that all was not as bad as it might have been or as she had fancied it was.

"Batoche," she said holding out her right hand, "you have surprised me, but it is a delicious surprise. You cannot imagine how glad I am to see you. Sit down."

Then little Blanche awoke and sprang from Zulma's knee into the arms of her grandfather.

"I knew it," she sobbed. "I knew he would come."

"Yes," replied Zulma. "Blanche told us, when we feared evil had befallen you, that you would surely come. She is a dear girl, and a prophetess like her grandfather."

A moment later Zulma had aroused Sieur Sarpy, and after a few preliminary words of welcome, Batoche was installed in a chair before the fire, with Blanche upon his knees, and asked to recount his story in its minutest details. Zulma had not dared to put him the single predominant question which was present in her mind, partially trusting, as we have seen, to the serenity of the old man's countenance, but he, with his usual keen insight, answered it before entering upon the course of his narration.

"It is all wrong and yet all right," he said with a swift wave of his arm.

Zulma looked at him imploringly.

"We have been beaten," continued Batoche. "The Wolves have triumphed. Many of our bravest officers were killed, but Captain Singleton was only wounded."

"Wounded again!" exclaimed Zulma.

"But not very seriously. He fell, but I raised him from the snow and he was able to stand alone, and walk."

"Did he escape?"

"He could not. I tried to induce him to follow me. He ordered me to fly, but he declared that he must remain with his command."

"What then?"

"He was taken prisoner, but, be easy. He is in good hands."

"In good hands?"

"Yes. I saw Roderick Hardinge directly in front, and I am sure that he recognized him."

"Heaven be praised for that."

"He is now within the walls of Quebec, but he will be well cared for."

Batoche then took up the account from the beginning and detailed all its circumstances, both from what he had witnessed himself and from what he had afterwards heard at headquarters. The report was graphic and lucid, such as might be expected from so intelligent a soldier. It was midnight before he had closed the history, and his companions listened to it with the most absorbed attention.

"And now about yourself," said Sieur Sarpy. "How did you manage to escape?"

Both Batoche and little Blanche smiled, the child nestling more closely and lovingly in his arms.

"Have I not always told you that the Wolves could not capture me? At least they will never take me alive. Although I and my men had enlisted only as scouts, when the final attack on the town was determined upon, I resolved to be present. I wished to be associated in that great revenge if it was successful, and, if unsuccessful, I wished to share the dangers of those who fought for our liberty. Besides I could not abandon Cary Singleton, my dear friend and the friend of the kind lady who had taken my granddaughter under her care."

Zulma accepted the compliment with a bow and the tribute of grateful tears.

"At first everything appeared in our favour, but after Colonel Arnold was wounded, the men fell into disorder, and I knew that we should have trouble. What added to our discomfiture, was that we were confronted mainly by our own countrymen. Our own countrymen, Sieur Sarpy. There was Dumas who led them. There was Dambourges who performed prodigies of valour. There was a giant, named Charland, who sprang upon the barrier and pulled our ladders over it to his own side. The sight of these things enraged and paralyzed me. If we had had only the English to deal with, we should have succeeded, but when the French lent a hand it was too much. When at length we were completely surrounded and our men fell on every side, Captain Singleton, as I have said, ordered me to escape. 'You can do no good now,' he said. 'We are lost. Fly and tell our friends all that has happened. Tell M. Sarpy and Mademoiselle Zulma that I have not forgotten them in this most terrible of all my misfortunes.' I obeyed these orders. The flight was almost as desperate as the advance. Accompanied by my men and several Indians, we threw ourselves into a narrow path along the river, till we reached the frozen bed of the St. Charles, which we crossed with the greatest difficulty. We had to run two miles over shoal ice formed by the high tides, and encountering numerous air-holes hidden from us by the darkness and the falling snow. After countless hardships and dangers, we succeeded in reaching the opposite bank, whence we could hear the last sounds of battle in the distance. We stopped to listen until all was quiet and we knew that the fate of our unfortunate companions was sealed. Then we made our way to the headquarters at St. Foye, where we were the first to convey the terrible intelligence to Colonel Arnold. There too we learned full particulars of Montgomery's defeat. After taking the needful rest, I disbanded my men to their houses for a brief furlough, while I turned my steps directly to this mansion. Here I am and I have told my story. Was I not justified in saying that it is all wrong and yet all right?"

IV
DAYS OF SUSPENSE

Now that Zulma knew all, her anxiety was hardly less than when she was left to her own painful surmises. It was a relief, of course, to be certain that Cary's wound was not a dangerous one, and that, as he was doomed to be a prisoner, he would have the good offices of Roderick Hardinge. Of the latter's kindly disposition towards her friend she had not the least doubt. Indeed, it added to her satisfaction to believe that he would treat Cary well precisely for her own sake. Thinking over this subject she found herself more than once mentally expressing a deep admiration of the British officer. She pictured to herself with intense vividness the beauty of his person, the manliness of his carriage, and the hearty warmth, ease, and culture of his conversation. At times she almost fancied that Cary's lot was not such a hard one after all, free from further dangers, exempt from the winter hardships of his former quarters, and enjoying the society of so congenial a character as Roderick Hardinge. A sad smile glided across her face as she thought that she would be disposed to bear a little captivity herself for the sake of such companionship. But all these feelings lay only on the surface. In the recesses of her heart, she grieved over the utter failure of the Americans, over their blasted hopes, their ruined expectations, and over the terrible catastrophe which had overtaken so many of their principal officers. She particularly bewailed the unequal share of misfortune which had overtaken Cary Singleton. Twice wounded and now a prisoner—surely this was an unusually rude experience for a youth of one and twenty. And then she was deprived of his company as he of hers. She wondered—and the thought, in spite of her, was an additional pang—whether he would feel the isolation as much as she. She had no knowledge how long the captivity would last. Batoche had not been able to enlighten her on this head. If the remnant of the Continental army retreated, these unfortunate men would doubtless be left behind to pine in their prisons. If the siege was to continue during the remainder of the winter, they would be kept to prevent them from swelling the ranks of the invaders. In either case, the prospect was very dark.

Zulma remained in this state of doubt and depression for a week, during which she and her father received further particulars of the great battles, so that now they understood their nature fully, but they learned absolutely nothing concerning the prisoners, nor indeed concerning any one within the walls of the town. Batoche, who came out to them a couple of times during that interval, stated that he had tried every night to contrive an entrance, but found all the avenues so closely guarded that he had to abandon each attempt. He added, however, that he was sure this extraordinary vigilance would not be kept up a length of time. So soon as the garrison became satisfied that the besieging army did not meditate a renewal of the attack—at least a speedy renewal—they would relax their watchfulness, which must be a severe strain upon the comparatively small number of the troops. This assurance afforded Zulma only slender consolation. It pointed to a further delay, and delay, with all its uncertainties, was what she was then incapable of enduring. A further source of society was that she and her father had no tidings whatever of Eugene since the great event. Previously they heard of and from him frequently through the visits which Batoche paid the Belmonts.

At the end of a fortnight, Batoche arrived at the Sarpy mansion with a bit of more definite news. He had not himself succeeded in penetrating to the interior of the town, but he had unexpectedly met in the woods, near his hut, at Montmorenci, a poor broken down countryman of his who had deserted from the militia. From him he heard that the prisoners were confined in a portion of the Seminary, occupying comfortable quarters, and precisely one of the causes of his desertion was that he and his companions were deprived of their best rations for the benefit of these fellows. He further stated that, at the battle at Sault-au-Matelot, the young students of the Seminary found themselves engaged and behaved pretty well, but none of them suffered. This was a source of great pleasure to both Sieur Sarpy and Zulma and it dispelled their misgivings about Eugene. Another piece of news brought by this deserter was that, after firing the fatal shot at Près-de-ville, the little garrison of the block-house fell into a panic and fled in the utmost precipitation, and it was only when they found that they were not pursued that they ventured to return.

"Ah!" exclaimed Batoche, "if the officer, who took the command after the brave Montgomery, had only pressed on, the block-house would have been carried, Arnold would have been reinforced, the combined assault would have been a complete success, and Quebec would now be ours."

"What is the name of that officer?" inquired Zulma.

"I do not know him, but I believe they call him Campbell."

"Coward, if not a traitor," exclaimed the girl, rising from her seat and exhibiting her scorn by a strange contraction of features.

Whatever the cause, the conduct of Campbell was inexplicable. There appears no doubt that he could have continued the assault successfully after Montgomery's death, and it is more than probable that his triumph would have insured that of Arnold. But there is no use speculating on this. A great commander has said that war is largely made up of accidents, favourable and unfavourable.

V
THE INVALID

Batoche displayed his usual foresight when he predicted that the garrison of Quebec would soon slacken its vigilance. Arnold with the small remnant of his shattered forces gave up all attempt at a complete investment, but confined himself to an alert blockade. He burned the houses in the suburbs that interfered with his plan of operations. On his side, Carleton made a sortie or two to burn the rest of the houses in St. Roch's, with the double purpose of clearing the spaces before his guns and supplying the town with fire-wood, which was getting short. With his two thousand men he could easily have pounced upon the five or six hundred Americans and routed or captured them, thus effectually raising the siege, but for some reason or other, which has never been satisfactorily explained, he preferred to pursue the Fabian policy, and trust to the return of spring and the arrival of reinforcements from the sea for ultimate deliverance. He kept his troops well in hand, but it was natural with the weary length of the siege and the long inaction which followed the attack on New Year's eve, his men should get more or less demoralized. The desertion mentioned in the preceding chapter was followed by many others, especially of American soldiers whom he had unwisely enlisted in one of his corps, instead of keeping them rigidly as prisoners.

These men seized every opportunity to escape, and through them Arnold soon became acquainted with all that was going on within the town. Among these sources of information were long letters written by his captive officers, in one of which it was stated that Captain Singleton's wound having induced a serious inflamation of the lungs, he had been allowed to be transported to the house of a private family. When Batoche became possessed of this important intelligence he immediately repaired to the Sarpy mansion and acquainted Zulma with it.

"I wonder who are the kind friends that have taken him in," said Zulma, after lamenting this new danger that threatened her friend.

"Can't you guess?" asked Batoche, and his knowing smile went straight to the heart of his companion.

"I hope that *you* guess true."

"Be assured of it, but to clear away all doubts, I am resolved to find my way into Quebec to-night. I have a plan that will succeed. The deserter whom I met the other day has given me his uniform in exchange for other clothing which will enable him to move about the country in safety. I will disguise myself in this uniform. The Wolves will take me for one of themselves. I will carry musket, knapsack, and all. If you have any message or letters for your friends, prepare them at once. I will carry them about me in such a manner that they shall not be discovered, and I will safely deliver them. I have made up my mind to get into the town to-night, and I will do it. I have a definite purpose and it shall be accomplished. Captain Singleton is sick and I must see him in person."

As Batoche spoke these words, his face was marked by a calm determination which was proof against every obstacle, and there was an expression of sadness besides, indicative of the concern which he felt for the safety of Cary Singleton's life.

The old man was as good as his word. On returning to quarters, he donned the disguise of the deserter, and, when the proper hour of the night came, went off to reconnoitre under the walls. He travelled long and wearily. Several times he was espied, or fancied he was espied, by the sentinels on the rampart. Once he was fired upon. But at length by dint of skill, courage, and perseverance, he managed to scale a parapet and drop quietly into a dark street, just as the sentry, returning on his beat, remained above him with glistening weapon. He crouched in a corner to make sure that he had been unseen and unheard. Very provocatively, the guard stood a considerable time gazing at nothing, but he stepped forward finally, and Batoche slipped away. He went directly to the house of M. Belmont, where, as his time was short, he would be best able to get all the information that he wanted.

"I promised M. Belmont," he muttered to himself, "that I would not go near his house again, but that was because I was a rebel. Now I am a loyalist, a devoted servant of King George, and I wear his glorious livery. There can, therefore, be no possible objection to my visit."

And the old man chuckled as he neared his destination.

It was not later than eleven o'clock, but the house was still and dark. There were no lights on the front, and the snow was untrampled on the stairs and sidewalk. Batoche hesitated a moment, fearing that some misfortune might have happened to his friends within the four or five weeks since he had last seen them. But on moving cautiously to the rear, he saw a bright light in the kitchen and a fainter one in an upper room.

"All is well," thought he, as he ascended the steps and knocked at the kitchen door. His rap echoed loud within, and he heard the shuffling of flying female feet. He then tried the lock, but found the door double-barred.

"I have frightened the maid and the house is barricaded, but I hope the girl will have sense enough to announce that somebody is at the door."

Presently the muffled stamping of manly slippers became audible and Batoche recognized the tread of M. Belmont.

"Who is there?"

"A friend."

"Your name?"

Batoche durst not give his name even in a whisper, for the winds of suspicion might bear it to headquarters.

"What do you want at this hour?"

"Fear nothing. Open the door and I will tell you."

"I will not open."

M. Belmont was not a timid man, but evidently these precautions had become necessary in the present demoralized condition of the town.

Batoche was in a quandary, but his native sagacity soon came to his aid. Putting his mouth close to the key-hole, he sent through it the low bark of the wolf. M. Belmont opened his eyes wide as he heard it, and a sickly smile spread over his face, but he lost no time in turning the lock. Through a very small aperture the stranger glided into the room.

"Batoche!"

"M. Belmont!"

A few whispered words explained everything—the disguise, the motive of the visit and all the rest. M. Belmont recovered his equanimity and led his friend to a front room.

"I have no time to lose. I must see him," said Batoche.

"He is very ill and now sleeping."

"Who is with him?"

"Pauline. She never leaves him."

"Stay a moment. Roderick Hardinge may be here at any moment. He calls every evening about this hour. He must not meet you."

"Never fear. It will be easy to keep out of his sight."

The two friends then ascended to the sick room—Pauline's own chamber. On the little bed lay the fine form of the young American soldier, stretched out at full length under snow-white coverlets. The face was drawn down and narrowed, the eyes were sunken, while the fever played in lurid lines about the cheek-bones and ample forehead. The masses of curly hair lay moist upon the pillow. By the dim light of the shaded lamp on the table near by, Cary looked like a corpse, silent, immoveable—how different from the manly figure which Batoche had seen doing battle by his side in the terrible defile of Sault-au-Matelot.

Pauline sat in a low chair at the head of the bed, the loveliest picture of sad, suffering beauty. There were dark lines under her eyes that told of long watches, and a slight stoop in her shoulders indicative of weariness against which the generous, loving spirit was struggling. When the stranger entered the apartment with her father, she neither moved from her seat nor made any sign. Her idea was that it was probably a soldier whom Roderick, unable to come himself, had sent to inquire about the invalid. But when the man approached nearer, and M. Belmont, preceding him, whispered something in her ear, she rose with the pressure of both hands upon her throbbing heart.

"Batoche!" she exclaimed in a smothered voice. "You are an angel of Providence."

"I heard he was ill and I came to see him."

"Yes, you heard he was ill and you came, at the peril of your life. You are a noble man, a generous friend. Oh, how he will be delighted to see you. He sleeps; we cannot awake him, but when he awakes, your presence will give him strength and courage. And Zulma——"

Just then there was a low rap at the front door, and the girl, interrupting her speech, stepped out of the room and down stairs.

"It is Hardinge," said M. Belmont "Go into the adjoining room, Batoche. He will not remain long. Perhaps, as the sick man is now reposing, he may not come up stairs at all."

It was some moments before he ascended, being engaged in a colloquy with Pauline, and when he did come up, it was only to gaze upon the sleeping man for a few seconds. He contented himself with saying to M. Belmont that he had just seen the doctor, who declared that this was the height of the crisis, but that the chances were largely in favour of the patient. Anything—the merest trifle—that would tend to cheer up his moral nature at this time, without unduly exciting him, would most probably determine a salutary change for the better.

M. Belmont smiled faintly as he heard this. He thought of Batoche's visit.

"That will be just the thing," he murmured inwardly.

VI
THE SAVING STROKE

When Roderick took his departure, Pauline accompanied him to the outer door, but she was not long away, being desirous to assist at the interview between Cary and Batoche. The old man stood by the bedside of his friend keenly observant of the symptoms which presented themselves to his practised eye. He that had so often been exposed to the severities of the Canadian winter and the hardships of the hunter's life was well acquainted with a malady which had more than once threatened his own days.

"Both his lungs are terribly attacked and he is very, very feeble," said he to M. Belmont and Pauline, "but the clearness of his complexion shows that his constitution is sound, and the repose of his limbs is proof that he is endowed with remarkable strength. He was struck by a ball under the right shoulder and the upper lobe of the lung was probably grazed. He held up against the shock, thus wasting much of the vital force which absolute repose from the beginning would have spared him. He is a very sick man, but I believe with the doctor that he will pull through. Indeed," added Batoche in that quaint oracular way which was no longer new to those who heard him, "Cary Singleton cannot, must not die. Not only is his own young life precious, but there are dear lives depending upon his. What would Zulma Sarpy do without him, she that is fretting at the very thought of his illness? And, Pauline, you, I am sure, would not have him die?"

The answer was two large tears that quivered in the eyes of the poor girl.

Presently, the head of the sick man turned slightly on its pillow, the body contracted a little and Cary opened his eyes. There was no bewilderment in the look. He awoke knowing where he was—not in a strange place, but among those whom he loved and who lovingly cared for him. Pauline was the first to approach him. She asked him a question, and he answered in her own language, as naturally as if the French had been his mother tongue. Batoche was delighted to observe this, regarding it as a satisfactory normal symptom. Cary accepted a draught from the hands of his beautiful nurse, then lay back on his pillow as if quite refreshed. At that propitious moment, his eyes encountered those of Batoche, who stood up a little towards the foot of the bed. A calm smile played upon his lips, intelligence beamed softly in his look, and, withdrawing his long emaciated hand from under the sheet, he extended it to his old friend.

"Batoche!" he whispered

The latter took the proffered hand reverently and pressed it to his lips.

"You know me, Captain?"

"Perfectly."

"I have longed to see you."

"And I to see you."

"But it was impossible to come sooner."

"I know it and you had to use that uniform."

As Cary said this he pointed to Batoche's disguise with a subdued laugh. He immediately added:

"And my friends, how are they? Mademoiselle Zulma and Sieur Sarpy?"

"They grieve at your misfortune and pray for your recovery. Mademoiselle's chief regret is that she cannot be at your side."

A radiance passed over the sufferer's face, and he said:

"Does she know in whose kind hands I am?"

"She does and that is her only consolation."

It was Pauline's turn to betray her emotion, by averting her head and wiping the tears from her eyes.

"Here are a few lines from her pen," continued Batoche, "written not many hours ago."

Cary held out his hand for the paper, partially raising himself on the pillow in his eagerness as he did it. He would have asked that it be read to him, when Batoche interposed with that quiet authority so familiar to him.

"Not to-night, Captain. Keep it for your first joy on awakening to-morrow morning."

The sick man smilingly acquiesced, and handed it to Pauline, saying:

"We will read it together at breakfast."

After a pause, during which Cary appeared to be collecting his thoughts, calmly, however, and without effort, he said to Batoche:

"You return to-night?"

"Yes, at once. It is growing late."

"You will see Mademoiselle Sarpy and her father. You will thank them for their solicitude. Tell them that my thoughts are with them. If I live and secure my liberty, my first visit will be to them. If I die—"

"Die, Captain, die!" exclaimed Batoche in a ringing voice that startled Pauline and her father. "A soldier does not die thus. All is not lost. We shall fight side by side again. A young man does not die thus. Death is for old men like me. A glorious future is before you. Die? You will not die, Captain Singleton. You must live for the sake of your parents and relatives in the old home of the South, and you must not break the hearts of these two Canadian girls, whose happiness hangs upon yours."

This last sentence especially Batoche blurted out in a kind of reckless enthusiasm. But he knew well what he said.

Pauline was amazed at the audacity of his speech. M. Belmont looked on in silent wonder. As to Cary he gazed with great open eyes, as if he was listening to a summons, delivered in a trumpet blast, from an unseen power that was omnipotent to save him. A glow of sudden health mantled his cheeks; his brow was illuminated with an air of intelligence quite distinct from the torpor of mortal disease which had lain upon it, and, as he stretched himself out more fully on his couch, he appeared endowed with a vigour that could only be born of confidence. It was evident, too, that, at the moment, he was perfectly happy.

"It is well," murmured M. Belmont, laying his hand upon his daughter's shoulder. "This is the blessed revulsion of which the doctor spoke."

Batoche seemed quite satisfied with what he had done, and a moment after he bade his friend farewell. Down in the hall, when alone with M. Belmont, he delivered his other messages, a letter from Zulma to Pauline, and from Sieur Sarpy to his son Eugene, which his friend was to send to its destination in whatever way might seem best so as not to compromise himself. He observed also with satisfaction that Cary had not breathed a word about military matters. This he regarded as a sign that the young man's mind was quite at ease.

VII
DONALD'S FATE

Before he took his departure M. Belmont solemnly warned Batoche of all the dangers which he incurred, reminding him that it is often more difficult to return from such an expedition as he had undertaken that night, than to get through its initial stages. Batoche was by no means insensible to his perils and, thanking his host, promised to exercise the utmost prudence. M. Belmont particularly called his attention to a patrol headed by Roderick's old servant, Donald, who was a desperate man, animated by the most deadly feelings against every one whom he even suspected of disloyalty towards the King.

"I know that he owes you a special grudge, Batoche, for your midnight incursions, and if he catches you, he will treat you without mercy."

The night was as dark as death, without a single star in the sky, or a solitary lamp in the streets. On leaving the house, Batoche shot boldly into a narrow lane that led towards the ramparts facing the St. Charles, and then slackened his step, creeping along the walls of the houses. This lane opened on a little garden which the old hunter was obliged to skirt along its whole length. He heard nothing, saw nothing, except that he fancied the leafless trees looked down upon him with shadows of warning. Batoche often said that he understood the language of trees, and certainly to-night the sight of them impressed his usually imperturbable soul so that he accelerated his pace. When he reached about one-third the length of the garden, he distinctly felt that he was followed. He turned around and saw a dark figure at a distance behind him. He knew instinctively that there was mischief brewing. He stopped; the figure stopped. He advanced; it advanced. He crossed the road diagonally; it crossed. He returned; it returned. He might have rushed upon his pursuer, but that would probably have occasioned outcries and other noises, which were naturally to be avoided. He had a recourse to flight. Swift as a deer he glided along the garden palisade, turned, and hid himself behind a large tree that formed the corner of the street. His pursuer was equally fleet and came up to him immediately.

"Give me your musket," he growled in broken French.

"No."

"Follow me to the guard-room."

"No."

"Who are you?"

"Your enemy."

The strange man advanced a step and looked full into Batoche's face.

"Ah! it is you, at last, and disguised in his Majesty's uniform. I knew I would catch you yet. Take this."

He raised an enormous horse pistol which he pointed at the old man's forehead. With the left hand Batoche struck up the levelled arm, while with his right he whipped out a long hunter's knife from his belt. The struggle was brief. The pistol went off grazing the edge of Batoche's fox-skin cap, and the hunter's blade plunged deep into the patrolman's heart. The latter rolled into the snow without a groan, and Batoche fled with the sound of footsteps, attracted by the pistol's report, sounding in his ears. He encountered no further obstacle, crossing the wall at the same spot which he had chosen in the earlier part of the evening, and almost in sight of a sentinel who was half asleep on his carbine.

"That fellow will never trouble me or M. Belmont again," thought Batoche. "And what is better they will not know that I did it. I am only sorry for Monsieur Hardinge, who will have to provide himself with another servant."

The death of Donald created a great excitement in the town. Besides that he was well known and much esteemed as a faithful, active soldier, the mystery that attended his fate aroused the most painful feelings. Was it due simply to a moonlight brawl, were any of the disaffected men of the garrison concerned in it, or had some of the American prisoners, in attempting to effect their escape, committed the deed? A thorough investigation took place, but no clue to the tragedy could be found. Roderick Hardinge was particularly distressed. After exhausting all the means of inquiry, a suspicion of the truth flashed upon him, and roused the stormiest indignation in his mind. His vexation was the greater, that, if his conjecture were correct, it would place him in a difficult position towards the Belmonts. Once already; as he only too well remembered, his military duties had led him to a bitter misunderstanding with Pauline's father, and several times since, the operation of the same cause had rendered their mutual relations very precarious. Both of them had made concessions, and the young officer was generous enough to admit to himself that M. Belmont had borne a very trying part in the most noble spirit. But, in the present instance, the element of publicity in Donald's death was a particularly disturbing circumstance, and it preyed so much on Roderick's mind that for two or three days he avoided calling at the house of M. Belmont. Pauline and her father noticed the absence without being able to account for it. They had indeed heard of Donald's death, but it never entered into their remotest suspicions that Batoche had anything to do with it. At length, when his mind was calmer, Hardinge went to inquire after the health of Cary Singleton. He made that appear the main object of his visit. In spite of himself he was constrained in manner while addressing a few words to M. Belmont, and even towards Pauline he appeared cold and formal.

On conducting him to the door, the girl ventured to ask him whether he was ailing.

"I am ailing in mind, Pauline. I have tried my best to make things pleasant with my friends," and he looked sharply at her—"but this outrageous murder of my old servant has upset nearly all my calculations. I don't know what may come of it yet."

Pauline understood nothing of his speech, but when she repeated it to her father, he grew very excited and angry.

"It is the hardest thing in life to serve two masters, my dear. Roderick is a fine fellow, but perhaps if you or I had known less of him, our course would have been simpler, and we should not have to live in perpetual fear and trembling. I think I know what is on his mind, which would explain the coldness of his manner towards both of us. While I will stand strictly by the promise made to Monseigneur, I will not allow myself to be made the butt of any man's humour, and if Roderick holds the same conduct towards me to-morrow evening, I will attack him about it."

M. Belmont's aspect was very decided as he spoke these words. Pauline, still comprehending nothing, retreated to the sick room with a load of apprehension at her heart.

VIII
THE BURDENED HEART

Nor was this her only sorrow. The morning after Batoche's visit; Cary's first thought, upon awakening, was about Zulma's letter. He asked Pauline to read it to him, which she did without delay. The note was short and simple. It expressed the writer's amazement and regret at the awful misfortune which had befallen Cary and his companions, and contained such sentiments of comfort as might have been expected from her warm heart and generous nature. The only remarkable sentence was the last one, which read as follows: "Do you know that all these adversities are making me selfish? It seems to me that I am harshly treated. I know that you are in good hands, but it is my place to be beside you, and I am jealous of the chance which Pauline has of nursing you. Tell Pauline this. Tell her that I am dreadfully jealous, and that unless she brings you to health within a very few days, I shall myself lead a storming party which will succeed in wreaking its vengeance. Pardon this banter. Give my love to Pauline. I write to her more on this subject."

These phrases were innocent and common-place enough, and they caused Cary to smile. Not so with Pauline. She read them with a serious face, and faltering accents, and when she closed, her eyes fell on those of the sick officer in a queer spirit of interrogation.

"A very kind letter, such as I knew she would write. I hope to be able to thank her soon," he said. "And she has also written to you, mademoiselle?"

This was spoken in such a way as to show plainly that Cary would have desired this second letter to be read to him. Pauline thus understood it, but although the paper was secreted in her bosom, and she instinctively raised her hand to produce it, she checked the movement and contented herself with saying that, among other things, Zulma had recommended her to take the utmost care of her patient.

"Indeed!" said Cary smiling. "That was the excess of generosity, but she might have spared herself the trouble. Let me say it again, mademoiselle. Not my own mother, not my own sisters, not even Zulma Sarpy herself could do more for me than I receive at your hands, and if I recover, as I now believe I shall, I will always hold that I owe my life to Pauline Belmont."

This little speech thrilled the listener. It was spoken in a calm, pathetic tone, and the last sentence was accompanied by such a look as carried a meaning deeper than any words. Words, gesture, look—none of these things had escaped the girl, but what particularly struck her with unusual significance was that, for the first time, her patient had addressed her as "Pauline."

Later in the day, when Pauline was alone for a few moments, she produced Zulma's letter and read it once more attentively. She could not disguise from herself that it was a noble letter, full of generous feelings and instinct with that sympathy which one true friend should testify to another on occasions of such painful trials. Zulma wrote eloquently of the dangers and anxieties which Pauline must have experienced on that dreadful December morning, and renewed her invitation to abandon the ill-fated town and take up her abode in the peaceful mansion of Pointe-aux-Trembles. "You are not made for such terrible scenes, my dear"—these were her words—"I could bear them better, for they are in my nature. You should be in my place and I in yours. I would thus be in a position to bear the fatigue of nursing him who is the dearest friend of us both."

This was the phrase which had puzzled Pauline at the first reading, and which perplexed her still at the second. It was on account of this sentence that she did not read the letter to Cary. What could Zulma mean by it?

"She is much mistaken," thus Pauline soliloquized, "if she thinks I am unable to bear the burden which Providence has laid upon me. I am no longer what I was. These two months of almost constant agitation have nerved me to a courage which I never thought I could have had. They have completely changed me. When I might have remained out of the town and gone to Pointe-aux-Trembles, it was I who persuaded my father to return to this house, and I do not regret it. I would not leave it now if I could. Much as I should like Zulma's company, and the benefit of her advice and example, I would not consent to exchange places with her."

Pauline glanced at the letter again.

"How curiously she words the letter about my poor invalid! She does not speak of him as *her* dearest friend, an expression which I would have expected her to use," here an involuntary tremour passed through Pauline's frame, "but she speaks of him as the dearest friend of *us both*. What does this mean? Was it written spontaneously, or on deliberation? It is a trap to draw me into indiscretions? No. Zulma is too true a friend for that. Alas!

The dear girl does not know, cannot know, will never know the full bearing of the words."

Pauline herself did not then know the full bearing of the words written with no intention of conveying the meaning which she attached to them. Notwithstanding all the changes that had previously taken place in her character, her sweet simplicity remained intact, and it was this very ingenuousness which had prompted her to admit Cary Singleton into her fathers dwelling. When the young officer fell sick in the hospital at the Seminary, it was Roderick Hardinge who acquainted her with the fact, expressing regret that he could not be more properly provided for. She at once suggested that he be transported to her home, offering to be his nurse. Hardinge readily assented, and, after considerable difficulties, obtained the necessary permission from the authorities. In all this transaction the conduct of the British officer was manly, noble, and above board, without afterthought; or the slightest trace of selfishness. It is simple truth to say that, notwithstanding her sincere admiration of Cary Singleton, Pauline acted in the matter through motives of humanity alone and out of her friendship for Zulma. She looked not to future contingencies. Indeed she never stopped to inquire that any contingencies might arise. Had she done so, a sense of duty might have restrained her deed of charity. That duty was the love she bore Roderick Hardinge, a love which had never been confessed in words, the extent of which she had never been able to define to herself, but which existed nevertheless, and which it had been her happiness to believe was fully reciprocated. But the heart travels fast within nine days, and, at the end of that time, it is no wonder that Batoche's visit, Zulma's letters, and Roderick's moodiness should have disturbed the poor girl's soul. Man is not master of his affections, and there is a destiny in love as in the other events of this world.

IX
EBB AND FLOW

Zulma's anxieties were no less than Pauline's. They increased from day to day, and she fretted herself almost into illness by her impatience. She knew that Cary's malady was of its nature a protracted one, and that the convalescence must necessarily extend over many weeks. She could hear from him only occasionally, and never with that fullness of detail which her affection required. She had recourse to many expedients to ease her mind, but failure in every instance only sharpened the edge of her disappointment. Her chief attempt was to obtain admission into the town for the purpose of aiding Pauline in nursing the invalid. She quite appreciated all the delicacy of the step; but, having obtained her father's cordial consent, she pursued it with all the energy of her nature. She applied for the necessary leave to her brother Eugene, who, having done soldier's duty, was supposed to be entitled to some little consideration at the hands of the authorities. Eugene was flatly refused. Zulma then enlisted the services of Roderick Hardinge, who somehow entered into her views with the greatest alacrity.

"She would make a charming prisoner," he said gaily.

But Hardinge failed. So did Bouchette, who had been approached in the matter by his friend Belmont. The affair created quite a stir in this small circle of friends, relieving the monotony of the siege for the time being. Cary Singleton was very much amused as well as touched by it. But when it was at length ascertained that the Governor, usually so good-natured, was strangely inexorable in the present instance, Pauline and her coadjutors gave up all hope of seeing Zulma among them. But the latter was not so easily discouraged. These rebuffs only added fuel to her desire, and though the time passed rapidly, she did not resign her project. Very seriously, she inquired of Batoche whether he could not smuggle her within the walls. The proposition at first struck the fancy of the old man, making his eyes glitter; but, upon second thought, he laughed it away.

"The trouble would not be so much to smuggle you in, as to know what to do with you when once we got you in," he said slyly. "Women are awkward things to handle in a camp of soldiers. No disguise can hide them from prying eyes."

As a last resort, Zulma resolved on appealing directly to Monseigneur Briand, whom surely Carleton would not deny. There were numerous and very glaring objections to this bold measure, but the impetuous girl over-ruled them all, and, after writing a splendid diplomatic letter, she had concluded arrangements to have it safely delivered to the prelate, when an unforeseen event saved her from the consequences of her amiable rashness.

As we have said, time had passed briskly on since the terrible events of the New Year's Eve. January had glided into February, and March had come with the promise of an unusually early spring. No military events of any importance had occurred, at least, none that had any connection with our story, and beyond the circumstances attached to Cary's long illness, there happened nothing which need make us linger over those bleakest months of the winter.

Singleton had so far recovered as to be able to walk about, but he remained very feeble, without the opportunity of taking that free exercise necessary to his complete restoration. It was awkward for him to tarry much longer in the house of M. Belmont. The seclusion of prison life was interdicted by the humane physician, while there were clear military objections to his being allowed to circulate in the streets of Quebec. Fortunately the doubt was solved by a partial exchange of prisoners which took place about the middle of March, and in which by a special privilege, Cary was included.

The parting from Pauline was very trying. The young man could not explain to himself the regret which it caused him. It grew out of something distinct from and far above his gratitude for her nursing, and the sense of obligation for the saving of his life which he was conscious he could never discharge. In those long afternoons, within the curtained gloom of the sick chamber: during those longer sleepless nights, with their companionship of silence and the sole intercourse of the eyes; in those frequent conversations made up for the most part of commonplaces, but relieved at times by unbidden revelations of the heart; in those brief but not infrequent visions of Pauline's beauty brought about by sudden graceful movements of her body, or when she appeared under certain favourable effects of the window light; in those intuitive glimpses of her real character made doubly attractive by its constant element of sadness, and the suspicion of self-sacrifice, Cary had woven about his heart an unconscious chain, the power of which he could not understand until called upon to burst it.

Nor did he gather any comfort from Pauline's attitude. When he announced his final departure to her, she heard him calmly, but her quiet was that of mental and physical weakness. There was no energetic self-control in her words or manner; merely a passive resignation. As she extended her hand, and felt the warm kiss imprinted upon it, she was an object of extreme pity, which added to the bitterness of Cary's sorrow.

The last farewell had been spoken and the two stood on the steps, at the foot of which a cariole was waiting to convey the released prisoner to his destination among his friends. Cary turned once more to meet the eye of Pauline. As he did so, he paused, struck by a sudden thought, and, going back a step or two, said:

"Pauline—allow me to call you by this name for perhaps the last time— Pauline, promise me one thing. Take care of your health. I fear that, after I am gone, you will replace me on that sick-bed, worn out by wearing weeks of watching."

Two livid spots burned on Pauline's cheek, and there was a glassiness in her eye. She leaned on the frame of the door for support, but mustered strength enough to answer that she felt no illness and hoped that all would turn out for the best. It was poor comfort; Cary had, however, to be satisfied with it, and drove away with a very heavy heart.

He had not been two hours in the American camp, when he met Batoche. It goes without saying that the meeting was of the heartiest, and, between them, a visit to Pointe-aux-Trembles was planned for that same evening. Zulma having heard of the negotiations for the exchange of prisoners, the coming of Cary was not unexpected, and there was great rejoicing that evening at the Sarpy Mansion, as over one who had been lost and was found, who had died and had risen from the dead.

X
ON THE BRINK

Another month had passed. With the middle of April the balmy spring-time was at hand. The snow had disappeared from mountain and plain; the rivers flowed clear and abundant in their channels; the trees were faintly burgeoning, and the heavens palpitated with an atmosphere of genial warmth. The cattle, confined for so many months in the darkness of stalls, lay basking in the sunshine, or trooped to the southern slopes where the young grass was springing. The sheep skipped on the hill sides. The doors and windows of the farm-houses were thrown wide open for a vital freshening. The children played on the stoop. White steam rose from the cracks and fissure of the heated granaries. The barn-yard was vocal with awakening sounds. The dove-cots buzzed with wooings; the eaves grew populous with swallows, and the thatched roofs of the pens and stables were covered with poultry grubbing for the earliest worm.

It was the resurrection of nature, nowhere felt with such keen exhilarance as in arctic latitudes. From the far off mountains, the clouds of murky vapour that lifted and rolled away, leaving the purple summits towering up to receive the first kiss of the rosy dawn and the last embrace of the golden sunset, were emblems of the winter's gloom replaced by that spring-tide brightness which aroused new hopes and a revived interest in the souls of men. The crocus of the glen, the anemone of the prairie, the cress of the sheltered waters, the hum of the first insect, the twitter from the mossy nest, the murmur of forest streams, were all so many types of human rejuvenescence and animation.

There was besides a moral feature to the splendour of the season. The dreary Lenten time was over, with its vigils and fasts, its self-abasement and penitence. The dread Holy Week had gone, with its plaints and laments, its confession of sins and cries for mercy, its darkened windows and stripped altars, its quenched tapers and hushed bells, its fourteen stations of that *Via Crucis* which rehearses the ineffable history of the Man of Sorrows and the Lady of Pain. The glorious Easter morning was there. Bright vestments gleamed, a thousand lights flamed from the sanctuary, perfumed incense circled heavenward, bearing the thanksgiving of opening hearts. From hillside to valley echoed the music of bells in every turret and steeple, even the bells of the churches and convents in the old beleaguered town that had so often sounded the alarm of battle during the night, taking on a new voice to celebrate the "great day which the Lord hath made." And even as the heavy stone was suddenly flung aside from the sepulchre under the shadow of Golgotha, giving freedom to the Master of the world; so the pall of winter was torn from the face of nature, and from the hearts of men was removed the burden which, during four long months, had made their torpor somewhat akin to that of the great beasts of the wilderness.

It was Easter Monday, a calmer day, but perhaps more enjoyable from the palpable assurance it afforded that the promises of its predecessor were really being fulfilled. The weather was magnificent, and the whole country resounded with the voices of men and women preparing for their work. Zulma Sarpy and Cary Singleton walked alone on the bank of the St. Lawrence, directly in front of the mansion. They moved along slowly, frequently stopping to admire the scenery spread out before them, or to engage in earnest conversation. Cary had entirely recovered from his illness, appearing stouter and stronger than ever before. He was clothed in his uniform, a proof that he had resumed active military duty. Zulma was seemingly in her usual health, and as she stood with her grey felt Montespan hat and azure plume, and brilliant cashmere shawl tightly drawn across her shoulders, her beauty shone in its queenliest aspects. No fitter companion for a soldier could well be pictured. Cary evidently felt this, as his frequent glances of admiration testified, and there were moments when to the observer he would have appeared as making the most ardent declarations of love.

Such, however, was not the fact. The young people had not reached that limit. Well as they knew each other, often as they had met, exceptional as were the circumstances which had surrounded their intercourse, they had never gone beyond a certain point of mutual confidence. They had often hovered on the edge, but sudden or unforeseen incidents had intervened, and thrown them back instead of advancing their suits. Zulma was sure that Cary loved her, but she had never ascertained that fact by any word of his. Cary could not doubt of Zulma's love for him, as her deeds and writings had eloquently shown, but she had never given him the opportunity, or he fancied he had never had the opportunity, of obtaining a decisive answer from her lips. On this day, their conversation was earnest and active, but inconsequent. It is often thus in that game of love which is conducted not in concentric circles, but in eccentric orbits.

To Cary the situation was becoming pressing, and he told Zulma as much in words which deeply impressed her. He foresaw that the end was approaching, that, with the return of the open weather, military operations must take a decided turn one way or the other. He was sagacious enough to foresee that there could hardly be other than one fatal result—the retreat of the Americans. Arnold had been superseded. Wooster, an aged officer, who had commanded during the winter at Montreal, doing a great deal of harm to the American cause by his inefficiency, and his religious intolerance towards the French Canadians, had assumed the control. From him little or nothing was expected with the present army. Reinforcements, although often promised and ostentatiously announced to the garrison through deserters and prisoners, were altogether out of the question, while it was known that, now the St Lawrence was clear of ice, a fleet of British vessels might soon be expected for the relief of Quebec. In a fortnight at furthest, Cary foresaw that a crisis must come. All this he confided to Zulma, knowing well that he was violating no duty in entrusting her with the information. The girl was astounded with the intelligence. It broke all her dreams. Her confidence in the success of the Continental arms had been unlimited. Notwithstanding their terrible reverses she never allowed herself for one moment to doubt that the champions of liberty would capture the last stronghold of British tyranny, and restore the old reign of French domination in America. She even tried to argue her companion into a reversal of his judgment, but failing in this, her instinct brought her face to face with the further personal result which Cary had altogether eluded.

The retreat of the Americans then took a more serious aspect. It implied mutual separation. It came to this—that, after six months of the closest intercourse, hallowed and purified by a series of the most cruel vicissitudes, Cary should be sent flying back to whence he came, while she would be driven again to the solitude of Pointe-aux-Trembles. Could this be? Should Cary be thus left to his fate? Would she be able to endure this sudden and enforced loneliness?

Singleton was outspoken and diffuse in his expressions of regret. He repeated over and over again that his failure as a soldier wounded his pride and disappointed his hopes, but that his separation from Zulma would prove the most terrible of pangs. Had he foreseen this, he should have sought death at the Intendant's Palace or at Sault-au-Matelot. Death in the house of M. Belmont would have been a relief and a benediction.

It was in vain that Zulma attempted to comfort him. Her heart was not in it, and she could, therefore, not go beyond the range of commonplaces. Finally, a deep silence fell upon both. They doubtless felt that they ought to go one step further and face a dread corollary. But they did not. Perhaps they durst not. Why not? Time will tell.

The conference ended in these words:

"I must return to camp, Mademoiselle. Let us postpone this subject. I have more to say, but require to collect myself."

"I too have more to say, Captain."

Cary almost started on hearing these words, the tone of which struck him as singular. He looked at Zulma, and found that her face was ashy pale. Her eyes were gazing far away across the St. Lawrence. He fancied—was it only a fancy?—that she was a little piqued.

"Shall we walk back to the mansion?" he asked almost timidly.

"If you please," was the quiet reply.

They advanced slowly across the open field, and up the avenue of trees, speaking little, and that little only on such objects as caught their eye on the way. Unconsciously they were fighting shy of each other. When they reached the greensward in front of the mansion, they paused and suddenly Zulma broke out into a hearty laugh.

"We are both children, sir," said she. "I thought you a great soldier and I find you a child. I thought myself a strong-minded woman and I too am a child."

And she burst out laughing again. Cary was puzzled, but could not repress a smile. He did not ask her meaning, and smiled only because he saw that her old serenity had returned.

Just then the setting sun poured through the intervening trees, flooding the green with glory, and lifting the twain as it were in a kind of transfiguration. They were idealized—he appearing like a knight of legendary days, and she a queen of the fairy land. Both were beautiful and both were happy once more.

Zulma knocked at the door, and the maid who answered the summons handed her a letter. She opened it hurriedly, glanced over the page, and throwing out her arms, uttered a moan of terror, while her eyes were fixed wildly on the young officer.

"What is it, mademoiselle? What is it?"

"Pauline is dying!"

XI
IN THE VALE OF THE SHADOW OF DEATH

Cary's presentiment had come true. After his departure, Pauline struggled against her fate for eight or ten days, but had finally to succumb. One evening as she sat alone in her chamber, the forces of nature suddenly gave way, she fell heavily to the floor in a swoon, and was carried to her bed in the arms of her father. The physician treated her at first as for a case of mere physical debility, resultant on her long watches during the eight weeks of Singleton's illness, and the extreme anxiety she had experienced for the safety of her friend. But when the malady remained obstinate to his prescriptions, and other insidious symptoms set in, pointing to a gradual decay of the vital energies, he divined that the ill was a mental one which would baffle his art unless he could ascertain its cause from the patient herself. Her confession of it would be half the cure. But he did not succeed in extracting this confession. Pauline did not know what ailed her. Beyond a great prostration she did not know that she was sick. She was unconscious of any cause for her present condition. This was her language, but of course the experienced old doctor did not believe a word of it. At the same time, however, he was aware that it was quite useless to press his interrogatory further, his knowledge of women being that there is no measuring the length, breadth, and depth of woman's secretiveness. He therefore consulted M. Belmont. From him he learned that an observable change for the worse in Pauline's manner was coincident with the young American officer's departure from his house, and even dated back from the latter days of his convalescence, when his departure was understood to be only a question of time. But beyond this M. Belmont's perspicacity did not go. He averred that he had not noticed any particular attachment between his daughter and her patient. She was nearly always at his bedside, but this was no more than could be expected from a tender-hearted nurse towards a poor fellow who had fallen among enemies, and whose life depended upon unremitting care. The young man had throughout acted like a gentleman, was cautious, delicate, reserved, and quite above taking advantages of his position to toy with the feelings of Pauline. Furthermore, the girl had long been devoted to Major Hardinge, and the Major was devoted to her. Indeed, their relations might be said to be of the tenderest character. Finally, this American officer, unless he was much mistaken, had contracted a strong affection for the daughter of Sieur Sarpy, an affection which was reciprocated, and he had every reason to believe that Pauline was well acquainted with that circumstance.

"Stop there," said the old doctor, taking a pinch of snuff and smiling slyly. "Here is perhaps a clue. Your daughter may have fallen in love with this young rebel—girls cannot help such things, you know—and the knowledge that his heart is turned to another may be precisely the thing that has preyed upon her mind, bringing her to her present pass."

"But she and Zulma Sarpy are intimate friends."

"So much the worse. Her feelings would be the more acute and the struggle against herself all the keener on that account."

"But Major Hardinge?"

"La, la, la! your Major. She may have loved him till she saw the other man, and then, *ma foi* — —. From a Major to a Captain, from a loyalist to a rebel is rather a descent, *eh, mon ami?* But what will you have? These things cannot be controlled. They happen every day. Do you know that she is plighted in any way to this Major?"

"She is not."

"How do you know?"

"She told me so."

"Under what circumstances? Excuse this freedom, my friend, but with the confessions of women everything depends upon circumstances. If it is under persuasion, a woman may tell you the truth, for their hearts are good after all. But if it is under compulsion, or threat, or by strategy, they are a match in fencing with the best of us."

"It was under a sense of duty, and only a few weeks ago. I was annoyed at Hardinge's manner to me and even to her after the death of that servant of his who was killed, you remember. I told Pauline I would resent that conduct if it were repeated, and on the same occasion I asked her whether she had engaged herself to him in any shape or form. Her answer was a simple, straightforward negative, and the child is incapable of untruth."

"This is very well. It removes one difficulty. Her mind does not suffer from any broken pledge towards the Major."

"But her love for him must remain."

"Not heaven or earth can dominate a woman's love. It is strong as death, immense as the sea, deep as the abyss, yet a glance of the eye, a wave of the hand, a smile, a toss of the head may change it for ever. Listen, Belmont. Your daughter loves the American officer. She grieves for Hardinge, she grieves for Zulma Sarpy. The diagnosis is complete. She is wasting away in a silent, hidden combat between herself and her friends. And I fear the worse."

"You do not mean that Pauline is in danger?"

"It is the duty of friendship to be candid with you. If there is not a complete change, within ten days your daughter will be dead."

"Gracious heaven!" exclaimed the poor father, his wail of horror sounding through the house and frightening Pauline from her trance. She screamed in her turn. M. Belmont leaped to his feet and was about to rush to her room, when the doctor restrained him.

"Do not present yourself in that condition. It might kill her. I will go and pacify her."

He did so. After a few minutes, he returned and informed M. Belmont that he was positive of the correctness of his conjecture, and advised an immediate change of scene for the girl.

"A change of scene? Are you dreaming, doctor? We are penned up like sheep in this unfortunate town. I am under a ban. I can expect no favours. The whole country is deserted or overrun with soldiery. And I must accompany her. Nothing on this earth could separate me from my child. I have lived for her. I will die with her. But oh, doctor, she will not die. Tell me she *shall* not die."

"Then she must leave Quebec."

"But, doctor!"

"It must be done. It is a case of life and death."

A painful silence ensued. M. Belmont bowed his head in his hands and moaned. "What shall I do? Who will help me? Who will intercede for me?"

At this juncture, who should make his appearance but Captain Bouchette? His presence was a revelation.

As soon as he saw him, M. Belmont became calm, and in a few words unfolded his difficulty to him.

"Rest easy, my friend," said Bouchette in his hearty way. "There can be no possible obstacle. I will go and see the Governor at once, and he will not refuse. It is a matter of mercy. General Carleton is the most soft-hearted of men."

Within an hour, Bouchette returned with the necessary permits duly signed and sealed. M. Belmont and his daughter were allowed to leave the town, the reason of their departure being fully stated, and a recommendation was added to the good offices of both friends and foes.

When Pauline was apprised of this measure, she rallied a little and smiled her contentment, but soon after fell into her habitual lassitude. The doctor, who was there to watch the effect, was not overpleased. He had expected a more marked result, and he almost feared that the relief had come too late. He therefore prescribed that the change should be postponed for a few days, until he had applied some stimulants and restoratives to the debilitated frame. It was during this critical interval that Zulma received a letter from her brother Eugene repeating the current rumour that Pauline was actually dying. He added, however, that a supreme effort would be made to transport her out of the town.

XII
IN THE FIERY FURNACE

On the third day after these occurrences, Pauline had rallied to the extent of being able to rise from her bed and sit in an easy chair. She signified to her father and the family physician that she felt sufficient strength to undertake the journey on the following morning. But she set a condition. She must see Roderick Hardinge at once. The young officer had all along been most faithful in his attention, calling morning and evening to visit her, but within the preceding ten or twelve days neither he nor any other stranger had been admitted to her room. When Pauline stated her request, the doctor shook his head. M. Belmont, however, promptly interfered with his permission.

"You shall see him, my dear. I will send for him immediately."

Hardinge was on duty at the ramparts, but he obtained a respite without delay, and hurried on his errand. Why did his heart throb as he hurried along the streets? Why did his hand tremble as he raised the knocker at the well known door. Roderick's instincts were true as are ever those of single minded men. A shadow had been on him for weeks, and he knew that it was now thickening into darkness. Spite of himself, a presentiment possessed his soul that whereas his military prospect was brightening, his career advancing, and the success of his cause was being every day more assured, his personal fate was waning, and the dearest hopes of his heart were verging to the gulf of disappointment. He could not formulate in words what the matter was. Pauline was exteriorly always the same to him, and yet there was a change. Had her love cooled? Had it diverted? Had he done anything to bring about any alteration? Had his political sentiments in any way affected his conduct towards her? Had he taken sufficiently into account the anomalous position in which she was placed by her father's stand during the war? Or were the causes deeper than all this? And his mind reverted to Cary, to Zulma, to a hundred little incidents of the past eventful weeks which his excitement magnified into possible determining causes of the boding change. This and much more had passed through his mind before reaching M. Belmont's house. But as he mounted the stair leading to the presence of Pauline, a great hope rose above all, and when he reached her room, he was in much the same state of feeling as on ordinary visits. Blessed intervention of Providence which gives one last moment of bliss before the descending stroke of destiny.

There is no need to dwell upon this painful interview. The dissection of the heart serves no useful purpose when there is no gleam of consolation to come from it. Pauline was quite strong to go through the ordeal. She was tender, too, and natural—indeed her own self throughout. After speaking of many things relating to former days, omitting nothing that she thought Roderick would like to have recalled, she came at length to the object of the interview.

"Do you know, Roddy, why I called for you?"

He replied that he had heard of her contemplated departure and that, while he deeply regretted the cause, he could only rejoice at any step undertaken for the recovery of a health which was dearer to him than his own.

Pauline's heart failed her as she heard those words. They pierced like a dagger. Her head became dizzy and she had to fall back in her chair for relief. When she recovered, she held out her hand, murmuring:

"Yes, Roddy, I have called upon you to say farewell. I am going and we shall never see each other again."

"Pauline!"

"I am going away to die. I should have liked to close my eyes in the old house, but for my father's sake, I am willing to depart and make a show for my life. It is useless, however. I shall die."

"Dear Pauline, do not speak so. Your case is by no means hopeless. A change of air and scene will revive you. We shall both see better days again."

"You may, Roddy, and that shall be my dying prayer, but not I. Alas! not I."

Still holding her white thin hand in both his, Hardinge threw himself at her feet, weeping and beseeching that she would recall these words of doom.

Pauline sat upright in her seat and, in a strangely quavering voice, exclaimed:

"Rise, Roderick Hardinge. Do not kneel to me. It is I should be prostrate before you. I called you to say farewell, but there is more. I could not leave without asking your forgiveness."

"My forgiveness, Pauline? What wildness is this?"

"Yes, your forgiveness. I have been false to you."

And here the poor girl utterly broke down. She averted her face in her chair and burst into a paroxysm of tears.

Roderick rose from the floor. He was in a whirl. Had he heard aright, or was he raving? He was at length brought to his senses by a soft voice requesting him to be seated and hear all.

"I could not help it, Roddy. It was all unconsciously. Had I known what I know now, it would not have happened. It was not I brought the circumstances about. It was all meant for the best by you and me. But the fatality came. It was a terrible revelation to me. That is the blow that has blasted my health and life. But the fault is mine all the same. Your conduct was noble throughout and you did not deserve it. I repeat that the fault is all my own. I am willing to expiate it. I am content to die. My death will end everything. Farewell, Roddy. One parting kiss and your forgiveness."

Strange that through this speech, sounding like the music of a broken harp, Roderick remained perfectly cool and collected. With acutest perception he understood everything now. The black cloud was rent and light poured down upon him. It was a light from heaven, for it warmed his soul to heroism.

"Pauline," he said in gentlest accents, "the spasm is past and I can speak to you, as of old. My words shall be few, because I see that this effort has spent you. You have done an injustice to yourself and me. My forgiveness, dearest? You have none to ask. You have done me no wrong. I had no right over you. We have known each other for long years and have loved each other?"

"Ah! Roddy, ah! how well!" sweet and low, as waters murmuring over pebbles.

"Yes, how well, Pauline. But love is not our own. It is disposed of by a higher will. We had hoped that it might end in something else—at least such was my hope."

"And mine, Roddy."

"But if this may not be, we must bow to the almighty power. Man is not the arbiter of his destiny. False to me Pauline? No truer heart ever breathed the air of heaven. You could not be false to any one. Oh! dearest, withdraw all these bitter words. Remember me, remember your old friend. May the blessing of God attend you. Go forth into a broader atmosphere, and amid brighter scenes to recover your health and that beauty which I have adored. Farewell, Pauline, farewell."

She heard him not. The poor shattered spirit, overcome by exhaustion, had drifted away into a merciful oblivion. He kissed her on the forehead and glided out of the room. At the door he met M. Belmont, whose hand he silently clasped. Then he stepped out into the world, a new man, purified as if by fire.

XIII
RODERICK'S LAST BATTLE

The next morning dawned bright and balmy. At an early hour, a closed carriage slowly approached the massive arch of St. John's Gate, accompanied by four or five persons on foot, among whom were Captain Bouchette, the venerable physician of the Belmont family, and Lieutenant-Governor Cramahé. The presence of the latter personage was a high honour to his old friend Belmont. When the vehicle stopped, and while the papers were being perused by the officer on guard, a final interview took place between the members of this little circle. It was a moment of trying emotion to all, and there were tears in every eye as the last embrace was given.

On a high embankment, level with the wall, and commanding a view of the gate, rose the solitary figure of Roderick Hardinge. Leaning on his sword, he stood in the young grass, under the budding boughs of a walnut tree. He had waited there till the carriage came. He would wait till it rolled away through the valley. There was a terrible moment, as it lingered before the guard-house, when he would have rushed down to plead his great love once more at the feet of Pauline. Perhaps at that critical time he might win his suit. Perhaps she was waiting for him and wondering in pain why he did not come. But, spite of his anguish, Roderick retained mastery over his soul. He checked this intention, feeling with cruel vividness that a sacrifice, to be a sacrifice, must be carried out to the end. Their last farewell was on yesterday. She had distinctly wished it thus. He would not disturb the vision of their parting—the closed eyes, reversed form, pallid cheek, and appearance of helpless misery. She too had suffered. He would not make her suffer more. And there was that kiss on the burning forehead. He could never forget that, nor would he allow impressions to intervene and possibly efface it.

So the noble fellow stood in the young grass, leaning on his sword, immoveable, stern, holding his forehead up against fate, and silently fighting a battle with himself compared to which the clash of battalions and the thunder of ordnance were mere child's play. And he conquered. A shadow of a smile fluttered over his lips as he resigned his last hope, and closed the door for ever to the cherished prospect of the efflorescence of love into fruition.

At that moment the friends of M. Belmont stepped aside, and, as the door closed, Roderick caught a glimpse of Pauline's dress. His imagination at once constructed the picture. She lay recumbent upon pillows, with her father at her side. Her face was pale, and her lips drawn down, but her eyes were animated with a glow that was a mixture of inquiry and regret. Was she really expecting Roderick? Alas! who can doubt it? She knew him too well not to feel that he must be somewhere in her neighbourhood, and the unerring instinct had its magnetic influence upon her.

At length the carriage rolled away, passing under the great shadow of the gate, and turned into the valley, leaving the old town behind. As the portals came together with a crash, and the heavy chains rattled, the echo of doom simultaneously smote the heart of her that was going and of him that was left behind. The beautiful past was over—and what was to replace it? A moment later, at a sharp angle of the road, Pauline turned her head on the cushion, and she saw him standing under the walnut tree. The vision was brief, as the horses took a sudden bound forward, but the poor girl had time to raise herself on her elbow and faintly wave a white handkerchief. Roderick beheld the token, and forgetting everything in the enthusiasm of the moment, rushed forward to the brink of the parapet. He would have leaped down in the face of a thousand pointed bayonets and dashed through the serried ranks of foes, but, alas! as he gazed once more, the vehicle had disappeared forever in the windings of the vale.

"Too late, too late!" exclaimed the poor fellow, turning on his heel and plunging the point of his sword into the tufted grass. "She is gone, never to return. Farewell to all my dreams of happiness, to all my hopes and aspirations. What is glory to me now? Why should I live to gather fame? Who is there now that will reap my laurels and wear them on snowy forehead for my sake? Oh, fate, oh, fate!"

And he walked away through solitary lanes till he reached his quarters, utterly broken down in heart. The whole forenoon he lay on his iron bed, oblivious of all the world and steeped in his own tremendous sense of dereliction. It was in vain that the golden spring sun streamed through his windows rocking the room in waves of splendour. The glad sounds of voices, in the Square, of men and women enjoying the beautiful weather in promenades, were unheeded by him. The great voice of cannon from the Citadel, answering some hostile movement of the enemy, was powerless to arouse him from his torpor. There is nothing so terrible to encounter as the last phases of a moral crisis, nothing so painful as to realize that one has yet two or three points to gain of that fatal resignation which he thought he had mastered. The cup of poison may be dashed off in a gulp of rapid determination, but it is the slow drinking of the dregs that is revoltingly loathsome.

Thus Roderick had to go through the ultimate stages of the combat once more and force himself to face the dread reality so that he should never again beguile himself with a single hope. This was really the situation as he understood it. He finally wrought himself up to that supreme point, and leaping from his bed, exclaimed:

"Where all is comfortless, there is at least this comfort. I had her life in my hands. By acting as I did, I have saved that life. This reflection shall be the prop of my misery."

He then composed his dress hastily, and walked out headlong to his regiment.

XIV
AT VALCARTIER

The ubiquitous Batoche was at a point, out of range of the garrison's guns, to meet the carriage. Although not communicated with directly by anybody, he knew all the particulars of M. Belmont's coming, and stood at the door of the vehicle, as if it was a matter of course. After mutual greetings and inquiries, he advised M. Belmont to drive out to Montmorenci.

"My cabin is small, but I have made it comfortable," said he. "There our sick child will have solitude, pure air, and a beautiful scenery. It is just the place."

"No, Batoche, thank you," responded M. Belmont, decidedly.

The old man raised his brows in surprise, but evidently reading into the motive of the refusal, he did not insist.

"Then go to Pointe-aux-Trembles. It is Zulma's most pressing invitation. If she had known you were coming to-day, she would be here herself to make it."

It was now Pauline's turn to speak.

"No, no, not there," she said, shaking her head and colouring deeply. "I am most anxious to see Zulma. Indeed, I *must* see her, but not at her house."

Again, Batoche did not urge his suggestion.

"My destination was Valcartier," rejoined M. Belmont, "and I see no reason to change my mind. Pauline needs absolute rest. She must be away from the noise of the world. Valcartier is the place—fifteen miles from the town, in the heart of a splendid landscape. We will go there."

"I will go with you," said Batoche.

The long journey, so far from fatiguing the invalid, proved a source of revival. The roads were good, the weather grew warmer with the flight of the hours, and the conversation of the old solitary was sparkling with amusement. He played with the situation like a consummate artist. He ranged over all sorts of topics, not studiously avoiding the illness of Pauline, or the names of Zulma and Cary, lest that might create suspicion, but touching upon them only rarely and incidentally, and as if they were matters of the least importance. The consequence was that he put Pauline into something like good humour. He made her smile faintly at several of his stories, and when she would relapse in the listlessness either of debility or retrospective thoughts, he would recall the light to her eye and the colour to her cheeks by some anecdote of stirring adventure. When after easy stages, the party reached Valcartier, Pauline was sufficiently strong to step out of the carriage, with the support of her father and Batoche. A proper house was chosen at a little distance from the hamlet, and all the arrangements were made for the convenience of the sojourners. Batoche remained with them two days, endearing himself still more to both, if that were possible, by his kind, intelligent attentions. When he was on the point of departure, Pauline said to him:

"Do not tell anybody that I am here."

"But I thought you said you wanted to see Zulma?"

"Not now. A little later."

"Very well. I will not tell anybody. I did not intend to."

And he smiled in his peculiar way. Pauline could not help smiling a little too, seeing clearly that the old wizard knew all.

Batoche's pleasant manner deserted him, however, on the way, and he thus discoursed with himself, as he trudged along:

"I could not insist on Montmorenci or Pointe-aux-Trembles, but Valcartier is a mistake. Pauline will not find there what she seeks. I have promised silence and will keep it. Indeed, I did not mean to divulge her retreat, for it is no business of a rough old fellow like me to interfere in the affairs of young people. But all the same Pauline's solitude must be found out, and I have no doubt it will be found out. If it is not, the poor child will pine and perish there just as certainly as she would have done within the walls of Quebec."

These previsions almost at once entered upon their fulfilment. Scarcely had Batoche turned his back on Valcartier, than an overpowering feeling of loneliness fell upon Pauline. The improvement which the excitement of the journey and the company of the aged soldier had induced disappeared immediately. M. Belmont's hopefulness was replaced by a new alarm, which was increased when he discovered that there was no physician in the village. This contingency he had not foreseen, having been assured by his own family doctor that Pauline, with the exception of a few tonics and restoratives which he furnished, needed no other treatment than rest and a change of air. In his anxiety M. Belmont called in an Indian doctor from the neighbouring village of Lorette, equal, he was told, to any member of the profession in the Province. The Huron, after visiting the patient, took M. Belmont aside and said:—

"The pain is here," pointing to the heart. "The Great Spirit alone can cure it."

Was it fated then that the gentle Pauline must die?

XV
FRIENDSHIP STRONGER THAN LOVE

Ever since Zulma had received her brother's letter referring to the critical state of Pauline, she had been in constant solicitude, which was only partially relieved by the intelligence of the projected departure from the town. The concern of Cary Singleton was no less. Indeed, it was of another nature and far more profound. When, at the door of the Sarpy mansion, he heard the words from Zulma's lips, "Pauline is dying," he sprang into his saddle and rode at full speed to headquarters, where he met Batoche, whom he instructed to use every means to communicate directly with M. Belmont. Through the old man he heard daily of the phases of the disease. But he was considerably surprised, and not a little annoyed that the latter had not apprized him of the issue of Pauline from the gates, and had been away two days without telling him of it. Cary and Zulma had many conversations on the subject of their mutual friend. The young officer opened his heart without reserve, having no conscience that he had anything to conceal, and relying implicitly upon Zulma as the person, of all the world, in whom he ought to confide, and from whom he might expect sympathy. This simplicity for a while appeared quite natural to Zulma, because she too was simple, and had followed all along the promptings of her heart, without any alloy of selfishness, or any suspicion of painful consequences. Notwithstanding the singular conversation which had taken place between them on the banks of the St. Lawrence, as has been recorded, their trust in each other had not slackened in the least, and while Zulma never feared for a moment that Cary might be lost to her, he had never gone into such self analysis as could have shown that a separation from her was within the range of possibilities, without any fault on his part, or any means on her part to avert the stroke. This condition of mind in Cary is easily comprehensible of him as a man and a soldier. Women credit men with craft and cunning in the ways of love. Such is not always the case. Oftentimes they are single-minded, and that very selfishness which is imputed to them is the motive that drives them headlong to the possession of the coveted object, regardless of the obstacles, possible and positive, which the cooler instinct of the woman generally observes. Zulma's state was more singular and needs a word of explanation. If we have succeeded in painting this character, the reader must have an impression of nobility free from all trace of meanness, and of self-willed force capable of the loftiest generosity. Zulma was a spoiled child, but this defect never dwindled to silliness. None understood better than she the relative fitness of things. There was never a speck of hypocrisy in her composition, and not the slightest shade of suspicion. Her character was diaphanous. She could check her thoughts and hold her tongue as few of her sex at her age could do, and, in the tournament of conversation with men, could manage the foils of reticence or half meanings as the best, but the foundation of her nature was truth, simpleness, and honour free from all guile. Our female readers will understand us fully if we say in one word that Zulma was in no sense a coquette. She was always sincere, even in her by-play, which was the secret of her power and ascendancy. This being so, the reader will be prepared for the statement that she never really supposed the peculiar relations of Cary with Pauline could affect her. Jealousy she had not, because she was incapable of it, but even if she had not been above this most diabolical of female vices, she could not have felt it, because she did not realize that there was any occasion for it. Hence when Cary spoke to her with deepest concern of Pauline's illness, of his fears of the result, and of his desire to do all in his power to avert the blow which threatened her, she entered fully into his spirit, and intensified his grief by the warmth of her own sympathies. And when, on hearing of Pauline's departure from Quebec, he declared he would follow her for leagues upon leagues— anywhere—to minister to her salvation, it was with spontaneous cordiality that Zulma added she would go with him and do all that was possible to save the dearest of her friends.

It is, therefore, no wonder that she, as well as Cary, was vexed at Batoche for not revealing the place of the sick girl's retreat. During three whole days, the old man was inexorable. Neither the young woman's coaxing, nor the soldier's serious displeasure could move him. His sole answer was:—

"Pauline will see no one but Mademoiselle Sarpy, and that only later."

"But I will see her," Cary would say, emphasizing the resolve with hand and foot.

"Then, find her, Captain," was the taunting reply.

It was some comfort to their mutual anxiety, however, that Batoche assured them of their friend's improved health.

But this situation could not last. At the end of the third day, the old soldier ran out to Valcartier, and was so alarmed at the relapse which he witnessed, that he almost immediately returned to quarters. Cary at once divined the truth from his altered appearance.

"Batoche, I command you to tell me where she is."

"Patience, Captain," was the reply, delivered in accents of sorrow and pity. "Your command is just and shall be obeyed. You have a right to see Pauline, and you shall see her. But Mademoiselle Zulma must go first. You will follow. I hasten to Pointe-aux-Trembles."

Zulma required no lengthy summons. She ordered the calèche to be brought out at once, and with Batoche, drove rapidly to Valcartier. What a meeting! Never had Zulma so much need of her self-possession. If she had yielded to her impulse, she would have filled the house with screams. It was not Pauline that lay before her—only her shadow. It was not the living, laughing girl whom she had known—the stamp of death was set upon every fair lineament. She bent softly down, laid her head beside the marble brow upon the pillow, folded her arms around Pauline's neck, and clasped her in a long, yearning embrace. Then they communed together, almost mouth to mouth, with that miraculous sweetness which is God's divinest gift to women. Pauline revived for the occasion. She was so happy to see Zulma. She, that had wished to die alone and forgotten—it was almost the dawn of resurrection to have her dearest friend beside her now at length. All was gone over, quietly, gradually, amid pauses of tears, and the interruption of kisses, yet so rapidly that, before half an hour had elapsed, Zulma had completely made up her mind. Brushing back the moist brown hair from the throbbing temples of the sick girl, she rose serene, majestic, with the light of a great resolution in her eyes, and the placidity of heroism on her beautiful features. Stepping out of the room she called Batoche.

"Take my calèche. Drive to the camp, and bring back Captain Singleton, at once. Tell him he must see Pauline before the set of sun, and that I desire it."

The old man comprehended and did not require to be told twice.

"Good," he exclaimed. "That is a grand girl. She understood it all at a glance. What I could not do, she has done. Pauline will now be saved. Poor Pauline!"

For three hours the friends were together, hand clasped in hand. Words were spoken that were full of ineffable tenderness. There were intervals of silence no less replete with happiness. There was a mutual language of thorough understanding in the eyes as well as on the lips. Zulma's theme was of hope. She quickly reached that point where she dismissed the idea of death and insisted on life for the mutual enjoyment of the twain. Not for Pauline's sake, but for her own, now that she knew what she knew, she saw it was necessary that death should be robbed of its sting and the grave resign its victory. Did Pauline acquiesce? She said not so—how could she dare, she that was dying without hope?—but there was a lambent gleam in her sunken eye, as of a ray of the future's sunshine playing upon it.

The afternoon passed softly, gently. The sun was gliding behind the trees and the long shadows crept over the valley faintly dimming the window panes. The holy hour of twilight had come. The angelus bells from the turret of the distant village church echoed sweetly on the tranquil air, and Zulma knelt by the bedside to murmur the *Ave Maria*. When she rose, she stood and listened. There were carriage wheels at the door.

"Do you hear?" she said.

Pauline opened great bewildered eyes and her features became pinched. Then turning rapidly, she hid her face in the pillow, sobbing convulsively.

"Oh, Zulma, this is too much. Why did you do it? It must not be. Oh, let me die."

She essayed to say more but tears choked her utterance.

"It is God's will!" whispered Zulma in calm, clear accents, still standing above her with a look of inspiration.

The invalid turned back on her pillow, cast an agonizing glance of gratitude upon her friend, and holding out her hand murmured.

"Heaven bless you, dearest."

XVI
THE HOUR OF GLOOM

The interview with Cary Singleton was not delayed a moment. Both he and Pauline desired that Zulma should be present, but she imagined a pressing pretext and glided out of the chamber. As she did so, her face was irradiated. Meeting Batoche in the passage, near the entrance to the house, she threw herself upon his neck and burst into silent tears.

"Courage, mademoiselle," he said in a pathetic voice. "You have been magnificent, and shall have your reward. Courage."

"It is over, Batoche. A momentary weakness which I could not resist. I am happier now than I ever was in my life."

Batoche looked at her with admiration and whispered:—

"There was only one way of saving her life."

"Yes, and we have adopted it."

"You have adopted it, not I. Yours is all the merit and you shall be blessed for it."

The two then went into the room of M. Belmont to keep him company, while he awaited with resignation the result of the conference in the sick chamber.

We may not dwell upon the details of the conference. Suffice it to know that it was consoling in the extreme to the invalid and supremely painful to the young officer. At sight of the wasted figure before him, Cary lost all control over his feelings. He remembered only one thing—that this girl had saved his life. He saw but one duty—that he must save hers at whatever cost to himself and others. The long watches of those eight weeks at the Belmont house came back to him, the tireless attention, the gentle nursing, the sweet words of comfort. Her illness was the result of his. That was enough.

Pleased as Pauline was to hear his words of gratitude and declarations of devotion, she gave him no encouragement to believe that they would have the effect of restoring her either in body or mind. The poor girl shuddered at the alternative in which she was placed. Zulma was so near—only a wall separating them. Roderick was so far—the ramparts of Quebec seeming to have receded beyond an infinite horizon. Death was at hand. Why recoil from it? Why not hail its deliverance with a benison?

Not in words did Pauline communicate these thoughts to Cary. With all her resolution she would have been utterly unable to do so. But he gathered her meaning only too well, the acuteness of his own suffering making him read on the suffering face of the patient the recondite thoughts which, on ordinary occasions, he would never have been able to fathom. But, in spite of all this, Pauline was happy in the simple presence of Cary. There were moments when she scarcely heeded what he said, so intent was she in the enjoyment of the assurance that he was really once more at her side. If she could have had this boon indefinitely, without the need of pledges or protestations, without the necessity of recalling the past, or facing the future, she would have been content, nor asked for anything beyond. This dream of a tranquil passivity was a fatal symptom of completely broken energies and proximate decay. But even this dream had to be dispelled. An hour had gone by and darkness had filled the room, an admonition to Cary that he must forthwith return to camp. When he informed the invalid of this she moaned piteously, and it was minutes before he could soothe her. Indeed she was not reconciled until he promised that he would be with her again as soon and as often as he could tear himself away from his military duties. Before leaving he leaned over her, and, while pressing her hand, imprinted a reverent kiss upon her forehead. He did it naturally, and as if by duty. She received the token without surprise, as if she expected it. It was the seal of love.

The calèche was waiting at the door, and Cary mounted it, after the exchange of only a few words with M. Belmont and Zulma. He was preoccupied and almost sullen. Batoche took a seat beside him and they drove away into the darkness. For nearly two-thirds of the route not a syllable passed between the two. The stars came out one by one like laughing nymphs, the moon sailed up jauntily, the low sounds of the night were heard on every side. Batoche was too shrewd to speak, but his eyes glared as he conducted the horse. His companion was buried in his thoughts. Finally the freshening breeze showed that they were approaching the broad St. Lawrence, a faint illumination floated over Quebec from its hundred lights, and the camp-fires of the Continental army broke out here and there in the distance. They reached a rough part of the road where the horse was put on the walk.

"Batoche," said Cary hoarsely.

"Yes, Captain," was the calm reply.

"The end is at hand."

"Alas! sir."

"You see those fires yonder? They will soon be extinguished. The English fleet is coming with reinforcements, and we cannot withstand them. We shall have to flee. But before we go, I trust we shall fight, and if we fight, I hope I shall be killed. I am sick of disappointment and defeat. I want to die."

These words were spoken in such a harrowing way, that for once, Batoche was thrown off his guard, and could answer nothing—not a word of argument, not an expression of comfort. Whipping his horse to his utmost speed, he muttered grimly:—

"You will not die, but I——"

XVII
THE GREAT RETREAT

A few days passed and the month of May was ushered in. Cary Singleton was right in foretelling that stirring events were at hand. A crisis intervened in the siege of Quebec. Since the disappearance of the snow the Americans had given some symptoms of activity. There was more frequent firing upon the town, and feints were made with ladders and ropes for escalades at different points. An armed schooner, named the Gaspé, captured during the autumn, was prepared as a fire-ship to drift down and destroy the craft that was moored in the Cul-de-Sac, at the eastern extremity of Lower Town. Other vessels destined for a similar service were also made ready. At nine o'clock on the night of the 3rd of May, the attempt was actually made. One of the fire-ships turned out from Levis, and advanced near to the Quebec shore without molestation, the garrison imagining that it was a friend. Success seemed almost within reach, when on being hailed, and not answering, guns were fired at her from the Grand Battery over the Cape. At this signal that they were discovered, the crew at once set a match to the combustible material on board, and sent the vessel drifting directly for the Cul-de-Sac. A moment more and she would have reached that coveted spot, and the shipping, with the greater part of Lower Town, would have been consumed. But the tide having ebbed about an hour, the current drove her back, notwithstanding that the north-east wind was in her favour. This failure was a terrible disappointment to the Americans. It was their last stroke against Quebec. Had the attempt succeeded, the army intended to attack the town during the confusion which the conflagration would necessarily have created, and the onslaught would have been a terrible one, because they were goaded to despair by their continuous ill-success, at the same time that they knew it was their final chance prior to the arrival of the British fleet, which was every day expected.

That fleet did not long delay its appearance. At six o'clock, on the morning of the 6th May, a frigate hove in sight turning Point Levis. The whole American army witnessed her triumphant entrance. The ramparts of the town were lined with spectators to hail the welcome sight. Drums beat to arms, the church bells clanged, and an immense shout arose that was re-echoed from the Plains of Abraham across the river to the Isle of Orleans. It was the acclamation of deliverance for the besieged, the knell of final defeat for the besiegers. The frigate was well named the Surprise, and she carried on board two companies of the 29th regiment with some marines, the whole amounting to two hundred men, who were immediately landed.

She was speedily followed by other war vessels containing more abundant reinforcements.

At noon of the same memorable day, the garrison, supported by the new arrivals, formed in different divisions, issued through the gates, and moved slowly as far as the battle field of St. Foye, where Chevalier Levis won his brilliant, but barren victory over Murray, on the 28th April, 1760. Carleton, now that he was backed by a power from the sea, shook off his inaction, and determined to deliver combat to the Continentals. But beyond a few pickets who fired as they fell back, the latter were nowhere to be seen. They had begun a precipitate retreat, leaving all their provisions, artillery, ammunition, and baggage behind them. Their great campaign was over, ending in disastrous defeat. They endeavoured to make a stand at Sorel, being slightly reinforced, but the English troops which pressed on under Carleton and Burgoyne, the commander of the fresh arrivals, forced them to continue their flight. They were obliged to abandon their conquest at Montreal, Chambly, St. Johns, and Isle-aux-Noix, and did not deem themselves safe, till they reached the head of Lake Champlain. Then they paused and rallied, forming a strong army under Gates, and one year later, wreaked a terrible revenge upon this same Burgoyne, who had superseded Carleton, by capturing his whole army at Saratoga, thus gaining the first real step towards securing the independence of the Colonies. Arnold fought like a hero at that battle, giving proof of qualities which must have insured his success at Quebec if the fates had not been against him.

XVIII
CONSUMMATUM EST

The flight of the Continentals caused the utmost excitement, not only in Quebec, but throughout the surrounding country. They had so long occupied the ground, that their sudden departure created a great void. Those who were opposed to them broke out into acclamations, while the large number who sympathized with them were thrown into consternation. Bad news always travels fast. Long before sunset of that day, the event was known at Valcartier, and on the little cottage occupied by M. Belmont, the intelligence fell like a thunder clap. It was useless for Zulma to attempt mastering her feelings. She rushed out into the garden, and there delivered herself to her agony. She had not foreseen this catastrophe, had never deemed anything like it possible. Now he was gone, gone in headlong flight, without a word of warning, without a farewell. After what had been happening within the preceding few days, a single, final interview would have helped to seal her resignation and reconcile her to her fate. But now even this boon was denied her.

It need not be said that M. Belmont's grief was also extreme, as we know the many reasons—personal and political, on account of himself, his countrymen, and his daughter—which he had to desire the success of the American cause. It was in vain for him to attempt concealing his emotion in the presence of Pauline. She immediately divined that something extraordinary had happened. Cary's behaviour during the last of his several visits had been so peculiar as to leave the impression that he was under the shadow of impending calamity. Only the evening previous, as he bade her farewell, his manner was strange, almost wild. He was tender and yet abrupt. If she had not known that he was dominated by a terrible sorrow, she would have feared that he was yielding to anger. He protested his eternal gratitude. He poured out his love in glorious words. He stood beautiful in the grandeur of his passion. And yet there was an indefinite something which made his departure painfully impressive to Pauline. His last words were:—

"If you will not consent to live, Pauline, there is only one thing for me to do. You understand?"

She understood perfectly well. The words had been ringing in her ears ever since, and now from her father's appearance the suspicion flashed upon her that perhaps they were fulfilled. Was Cary dead? Had he thrown away his life in battle? The doubt could brook no delay, and, gathering all her strength, she abruptly interrogated M. Belmont.

"No, not dead, my child, but— —"

"But what, father? I beg you to tell me all."

"They are gone. The siege is raised. It was unforeseen, and done in the utmost precipitation."

"And he too is gone!"

"Alas! my dear."

"That is as bad as death."

And uttering a piercing shriek, Pauline fell back in a swoon upon her pillow. The cry was heard by Zulma in the garden, and she rushed back into the room. The alteration in the face of the patient was so terrible that Zulma was horror-stricken. Pauline lay absolutely as if dead. No breathing was audible, and her pulse had apparently ceased to beat. Restoratives were applied, but failed to act. Although they did not exchange a word together, both Zulma and M. Belmont thought that it was the end. With the setting sun, and the coming of darkness, an awful silence fell upon the house, through which alone, by the terrified listeners, was faintly heard the rustling of the wings of doom.

Then the tempest arose, fit accompaniment for such a scene. Thunder and lightning filled the sky. A hurricane swept the landscape, with a voice of dirge, while the rain poured down in torrents. For long hours Zulma knelt beside the inanimate form. M. Belmont sat at the head of the bed with the rigidity of a corpse. But for the ever Watchful Eye over that stricken house, who knows what ghastly scene the morning sun might witness?

Through the storm, the sound of hoofs was heard, followed soon after by a noise at the door. Zulma turned to M. Belmont with a sweet smile, while he awoke from his stupor with indications of fear.

"Heavens! are our enemies so soon upon us?" he exclaimed, rising.

"Never fear," said Zulma, rising also. "It is our friends."

She went to the door and admitted Cary Singleton and Batoche. They were both haggard and travel-stained. It required but a glance to reveal the situation to them. The young officer, after pressing the hand of Zulma and M. Belmont, stood for several minutes gazing at the insensible Pauline. The old man did the same at a little distance behind. Then the latter gently touched the former upon the shoulder. He turned and the four held a whispered conference for a few moments, the speakers being Cary and Zulma, both earnest and decided, especially Zulma. A conclusion was soon reached, for M. Belmont hurriedly quitted the room. During his brief absence, while the two men resumed their watches beside the couch, Zulma carried a little table near the head, covered it with a white cloth, set upon it two lighted candlesticks, and a little vessel of holy water in which rested a twig of cedar. She did this calmly, methodically, with mechanical dexterity, as if it had been an ordinary household duty. Never once did she raise her eyes from her work, but, from the increased light in the room, one might have noticed that there was a spot of fiery red upon either cheek. Cary, however absorbed in his meditations, could not help casting a look upon her as she moved about, while Batoche, although he never raised his head, did not lose a single one of her actions. Who can tell what passed in the bosoms of the three, or how much of their lives they lived during these moments?

Zulma's ministrations had scarcely been concluded, when M. Belmont returned with the parish priest of Valcartier, a venerable man, whose smile, as he bowed to all the members of the group, and took in the belongings of the room, was as inspiring as a spoken blessing. Its influence too must have extended to the entranced Pauline, for, as he approached her side, and sprinkled her with hyssop, breathing a prayer, she slowly opened her eyes and gazed at him. Then turning to the lighted tapers, and the snowy cloth, she smiled, saying:

"It is the extreme unction, Monsieur le Curé! I thank you."

The old priest, with that consummate knowledge of the world and the human heart, which his long pastorate had given him, approached nearer, and addressed her in a few earnest words, explaining everything. Then he stepped aside, and revealed the presence of Cary. The two lovers folded each other in a close embrace, and thus, heart against heart, they communed together for a few moments. At the close, Pauline called for Zulma, who was on her knees, at the foot of the bed and in shadow. The meeting was short, but passionate. Finally, one word which Zulma spoke had a magical effect, and the three turned their faces towards the assistants, smiling through their tears.

The ceremony was brief. There in that presence, at that solemn hour, the hands were joined, the benediction pronounced, and Cary and Pauline were man and wife. The priest producing the parish register, the names of the principals and witnesses were signed. Zulma wrote hers in a large steady hand, but a tear, which she could not restrain, fell upon the letters and blurred them.

"Rest now, my child," said the priest, as he took his departure.

Pauline, exhausted by fatigue and emotion, immediately relapsed into slumber, but every trace of pain was gone, and her regular breathing showed that she was enjoying a normal repose. Then Batoche, approaching Cary, silently pointed to the clock.

"Alas! yes," said the latter, turning to M. Belmont and Zulma, "it is now midnight, and the last act of this drama must be performed. Our camp is thirty miles away, and the night is terrible. I rode here to accomplish one duty. I must ride back to fulfil another. It is a blessing she sleeps. You will tell her all when she wakes."

He continued in fervid words recommending Pauline to both Zulma and M. Belmont. He protested that nothing short of his loyalty to his country could induce him to go away. Had his army been victorious, he might have resigned service and remained with Pauline and her friends. But now, especially that it was routed, he could not abandon his colours, and he knew that Pauline would despise him if he did. To-morrow they would resume their flight. In a few days they would be out of Canada.

When he had finished speaking, he threw his arms around the neck of Zulma, thanking her for her devotion, declaring that he would never forget her, and that he would always be at her service.

"I confide Pauline to you," he said. "To no other could I so well entrust her. She saved my life. Let us both be united in saving hers. She has promised me that she will now try to live. With your help, I am certain that she will do so. It is my only comfort on my departure, together with the assurance that you will always be her friend and mine."

Batoche, too, had a word with Zulma. He predicted the reward of Heaven upon her abnegation, sent remembrances to his friends, and, in most touching language, begged her to assume the care of little Blanche, to whom he bequeathed a tearful blessing. When this was accomplished, he told M. Belmont that Blanche knew the secret of his casket and would reveal it to him. Then the final separation took place. Cary and Batoche left the house together. The next morning the former had joined his companions on their retreat, while the latter lay prone on the wet grass, at the foot of the Montmorenci Falls—dead. The lion-like heart was broken. It could not survive the ruin of its hopes.

XIX
FINAL QUINTET

＇

Eight years had elapsed. It was the summer of 1784. The great war of the Revolution was over and peace had been signed. Cary Singleton, having laid down his arms, proposed to travel for rest and recuperation. His first visit was to Canada in the company of his wife, and of M. Belmont, who desired to return to Quebec, and there spend the evening of his days. Having accompanied Pauline to Maryland immediately after her recovery—which had been very protracted—he had a led a tranquil life there, but now that age was telling, and that he had no further solicitude about the safety of Cary, nostalgia came hard upon him. It is needless to say that the journey was a most agreeable one. All the old places were revisited, all the old faces that had survived were seen once more. But the chief attraction for both Cary and Pauline was Zulma and Roderick. What had become of them? The latter remained in the army for a year after the deliverance of Quebec. Carrying his great disappointment in his heart, he joined the expedition of Burgoyne, and, of course, shared its fate at Saratoga. But as Morgan was in that battle, where he caused the death of the brave English General Fraser, and Cary was with him, Roderick received at the hands of the latter the same treatment which he had extended to him, after the battle of Sault-au-Matelot. Whereas all Burgoyne's men were kept prisoners in the interior of the country, Hardinge procured his liberation through the influence of Singleton with Morgan, and returned home renouncing military pursuits forever. He retired first to his estate in the country, but the solitude became painful to him, and he took up his residence in the old capital, where one of the first persons he met was Zulma who had just returned from Paris, after an absence of a couple of years. She was an altered woman, the fire of whose spirits had died out, and who carried the burden of her loneliness as bravely as she could. But her wonderful beauty had not yet decayed. Rather was it expanded into full flower. Like Roderick, she was alone in the world, her father having died within a year after the siege of Quebec. It was only natural that these two should gradually come together, and no one will be surprised to learn that, after a full mutual explanation, and with much deliberation, they united their lives. Neither will it astonish any one to be further told that their union proved happy in the solid fruits of contentment. They deserved it all, and it was literally fulfilled that the blessings of their great sacrifice came to them a hundred-fold.

Sometimes, when he was in a jolly mood, Roderick would say:—

"You remember, dear, that I once predicted I would catch my beautiful rebel. I have caught her."

And he would laugh outright. Zulma would only smile faintly, as if the reminiscence had not lost all its bitterness, but she would return her husband's caress with effusion.

We shall not linger to describe the meeting of the four friends—after so many years. Our story is verging to its close, and we have space for only a last incident. One beautiful afternoon, they were all gathered together at the foot of the Montmorenci Falls, around the humble grave of Batoche. It was a little tufted mound with a black cross at the head. In their company appeared the picturesque costume of an Ursuline nun. This was little Blanche, whom Zulma had placed in the convent after the death of her father, and who had decided to consecrate her life to God. By special dispensation from a very severe rule, she was allowed to accompany the friends of her childhood to the grave of her old grandfather. Zulma and Pauline planted flowers over it, and Blanche threw herself across it sobbing and praying. All wept, even the two strong men, as they gazed upon a scene which reminded them of so much.

Poor Batoche! What was there in the music of the waterfall that seemed responsive to this tribute of his friends?

During my first visit to Canada a few years ago, I met on the Saguenay boat a young lady whose beauty and distinction impressed me. I inquired who she was. An old gentleman informed me that her name was Hardinge, and on tracing up her genealogy, as old men are fond of doing, he made it clear that her two grandmothers were the heroines, and her two grandfathers, the heroes of this history. A son of Roderick and Zulma had married a daughter of Cary and Pauline, and this was their offspring. Thus, at last, the blood of all the lovers had mingled together in one.